ALASKA WEDDINGS

THREE-IN-ONE COLLECTION

SUSAN PAGE DAVIS

BARBOUR
PUBLISHING

Always Ready © 2009 by Susan Page Davis
Fire and Ice © 2010 by Susan Page Davis
Polar Opposites © 2010 by Susan Page Davis

ISBN 978-1-61626-115-3

Cover design: Kirk DouPonce, DogEared Design

Published by Barbour Publishing, Inc., P.O. Box 719, Uhrichsville, Ohio 44683, www.barbourbooks.com

Our mission is to publish and distribute inspirational products offering exceptional value and biblical encouragement to the masses.

 Member of the
Evangelical Christian
Publishers Association

Printed in the United States of America.

Dear Readers,

Writing and researching these stories was one of the greatest adventures of my life. Going to Alaska, I spent time with old friends I'd made in another cold place—Maine—and met dozens of new people who helped me learn what I needed for my books. I've named some of them in my acknowledgments. Thanks to Alaska's hospitality, I absorbed and enjoyed and then I let my imagination run away with me.

I learned all sorts of things about this great state. For instance, Alaska contains the easternmost, westernmost, and northernmost points in the United States. In Barrow, Alaska, the sun rises May 10 and doesn't set for three months. In mid-November it goes down, and the people don't see it again for almost two months. Alaska's mainland is only 51 miles from Russia across the Bering Strait, and our Little Diomede Island is (*gulp*) two and a half miles from Russia's Big Diomede Island.

Alaska has fewer miles of paved roads than any other state—and more licensed pilots per capita. And yes, it's true—if you cut Alaska in half, Texas would be the third largest state.

I loved Alaska—loved the people, the wildlife, the scenery, the art, the vastness of it. I got to see a bear in the wild and touch a musk ox. I flew up a glacier and toured a coast guard ship. I visited the Iditarod Trail headquarters and marveled over the people who came to Alaska and stayed.

I came home (yes, I live "Outside") and researched the technical topics. How do you put a dozen huskies into a harness? How do you safely knock out a polar bear so that you can pull his teeth without becoming his lunch? Oh, yeah.

Alaskans, I'm eager to come see you again! Readers, I hope you enjoy the journey through this book, and that you'll visit my Web site at: www.susanpagedavis.com. I'm off on the next adventure.

Susan

ALWAYS READY

Dedication

To all our military men and women, especially Michael. Thank you for all you're doing and have done.

Acknowledgments

A great many people helped me research and write this book, including: LuAnn and Dana Nordine; Aven Leidigh; Henry Kurgan of Homer by the Sea; pilot Kelly Leseman; Captain David MacKenzie, USCG (ret.); CWO Scott MacAloon, USCG; CWO-3 Peter J. Davenport, USCG; CWO-3 Gilman C. Page, USCG (ret.); Darlene Franklin; Lynette Sowell; James S. Davis. Thank you all!

Chapter 1

Caddie Lyle stood on the bridge of the ship, watching out the windows ahead as the farthest Aleutian Islands came into view. The crew of her ship, the U.S. Coast Guard's buoy tender *Wintergreen*, was carrying out its early summer assignment to check their most remote navigational aids and deliver supplies to a few isolated Native Alaskan villages. Volcanic mountains formed an eerily beautiful backdrop to the frothing seascape that stretched before them into infinity. The 225-foot ship seemed a tiny bit of flotsam.

The Bering Sea writhed all around the ship, tossing it up and down in nauseating plunges. Caddie braced her feet as a particularly violent lurch hit the ship and focused on a large map hanging on the wall across the room. Seasickness rarely overtook her, but she'd struggled the past forty-eight hours in the inhospitable waters of the North.

The skipper paused beside her and looked forward out the big windows at the barely visible land in the distance. "In a few hours, we'll be at the western end of the USA."

Caddie nodded and pulled in a deep breath. Her stomach settled down as the deck found a more level plane. "Can't believe I'm really out here."

"You can believe it. We'll put in at Attu soon. When our errand there's completed, we'll head on home."

Home and family seemed worlds away. Of all the people Caddie loved, only her father had seen these waters. Like her, he had come years ago with supplies for the Coast Guard station at Attu, the last in the chain of Aleutian Islands.

She stared out the side windows, where nothing but waves and sky existed. This wild setting reduced the massive *Wintergreen* to a fragile bark. But God was still above, keeping them afloat. She smiled at the thought.

"Sir," Lindsey Rockwell, their operations specialist, called to the captain from her post at the radio desk, "I'm getting a distress signal."

The skipper hurried to her side. "What type of vessel?"

"It's a Russian trawler. We're the nearest ship, although they may be just outside our jurisdiction."

"Let's go. What's their position?"

Caddie dashed to the desk where she worked when plotting the ship's course. As the captain gave the orders for a change of direction, she entered the new course on her computer console then carefully wrote it in the log.

In less than an hour, during which Lindsey maintained contact with the Russian ship's crew, the trawler appeared on the horizon. As they drew closer, Caddie could see that the fishing boat sat very low in the choppy water, sluggishly riding each wave and turning willy-nilly with the elements. She wished she had her camera but couldn't leave the bridge to fetch it from the tiny cabin she shared with Lindsey.

"Crew of fourteen in a small boat," Lindsey called out. "The skipper is now leaving the trawler, and he's the last man off."

"Where are they?" The captain searched the heaving surface with his binoculars.

"I've lost contact, but I assume they're pulling away from the trawler."

"Well, that thing's going under before we can reach it." Captain Raven shook his head.

Every man on the bridge scurried for binoculars. All was silent for several seconds as they scanned the water around the trawler.

Caddie prayed the fishermen could get far enough from their doomed boat that they wouldn't be capsized by the waves it made when it sank.

A shout came from outside. "Lookout reports the vessel on the horizon, sir," Lindsey said. "Small boat at two-eight-zero."

"There!" The captain pointed. "Alter course."

As the crew rushed to obey, he whirled toward Caddie. "Get down on the main deck, Lyle. I'll give you half a dozen hands to help get those Russians on board. You oversee the operation."

"Aye, aye, sir." Caddie turned and ran for the ladder, hearing the captain's voice echo over the loudspeaker. When she hit the bottom stair, seamen were already streaming onto the buoy deck. She rattled off orders to prepare to lower a workboat over the side to assist the Russians.

The small boat was swung out and lowered until it was even with the rail. She and the men grabbed life jackets. The deck crew scurried to man the falls that would lower the workboat.

Caddie hastily fastened her bright yellow life vest. She tried not to think too hard about the job ahead. Nerves wouldn't help her now. The boatswain was surely watching her from the forecastle windows above, but she avoided looking up there. She kept her eyes on either the Russian trawler or the men assigned to her. Boatswain Tilley always set her adrenaline pumping with his critical frown. Even when she did well, she sensed that he didn't completely approve of her.

The *Wintergreen* drew nearer to the small boat in which the fishing crew had escaped. It was little more than a rowboat, tossing on the violent waves. A dozen men huddled inside it, while two more clung to the gunwales, their bodies in the icy water. They'd never make it without help.

Caddie and her crew boarded the workboat and she radioed the bridge. "Boat crew is ready."

"Affirmative."

The deck crew lowered the workboat with her and the crew inside. It hit the water perfectly, on the crest of a wave, and she gave a mental cheer for the men manning the apparatus. She nodded for Jackson to start the motor, and they cut across the mammoth waves toward the Russians. Leaving the side of the *Wintergreen*, they caught the full force of the wind and rolling seas. She grabbed the gunwale beside her as a huge sweep of water caught them and heaved them skyward.

Lord, get us through this!

As they rushed down into the trough between waves, the thought that she and her crew might end up needing rescue flitted through her mind, but soon they were close enough to the Russian boat that her helmsman cut the engine so they could approach with caution. Two of the fishermen were leaning over the side of their craft, trying to haul another man aboard. Their boat tipped precariously. Caddie prayed that she could reach the men in time.

She radioed back to the ship, "*Wintergreen*, this is *Wintergreen 1*. We're approaching small boat to give assistance."

One of her seaman apprentices yelled, and she looked where he pointed. The beleaguered trawler's prow had tilted upward, and with the next large wave, it sank from sight. The Russians who saw it paused in their labor for a moment, staring back toward the empty sea where their ship had been. The two trying to help the man in the water seemed oblivious.

As Caddie turned her attention back to their small boat, a giant wave caught the little craft broadside and tilted the hull, spilling several of the fishermen into the water on the other side.

She yelled into the wind, "Hurry!"

Jackson nodded and moved the throttle, sending them between two flailing Russians. One of them swam toward the Coast Guard boat and caught hold of the side. Two seamen hurried to assist him. On the other side of the boat, the fisherman in the water thrashed and sank below the surface. His head bobbed up again, and one of Caddie's men tossed out a life preserver tied to a line. The man lunged at it and hung on as the seaman pulled him in.

Caddie assessed the situation. The Russian lifeboat was still afloat, though it had taken on a lot of water. She counted seven men in it. Two in the water held to the sides, though she wasn't sure they were the same two who had clung to it earlier. Another man floated between her and the other boat, and beyond it, a nearly submerged fisherman waved frantically.

With two Russians now in her boat, Caddie gestured to Jackson, urging him to approach the nearest swimmer. In less than two minutes, they had another coughing, shivering man aboard. A seaman's apprentice distributed blankets and extra life vests to those who needed them.

They were close to the little boat now. It was only half the length of the Coast

Guard workboat. Caddie cupped her hands and screamed to one of the men in it, "Are you okay?"

He looked blankly at her and pointed to the man in the water on his side of the boat. Caddie looked beyond to the man fifty yards out on the other side. That man didn't stand a chance, whereas the two clinging to the boat might last a few minutes while the Coast Guard helped their comrade. It was a judgment call, and she couldn't waste time agonizing over it. She threw the Russian in the boat a life jacket—their last extra—and waved Jackson to head for the swimmer beyond.

When she looked back, the Russian was leaning over to help the man in the water pull the life jacket on. If they couldn't hoist him into their boat, at least he'd float until she returned. On the other side, more Russian fishermen succeeded in lifting the other man who had clung to the gunwales at the side into the boat and comparative safety.

Jackson skillfully judged the waves and brought the workboat close to the swimmer. Caddie stared in disbelief. The bearded Russian held another man's head barely above the surface of the water. Jackson turned the boat and edged in closer. Caddie and the three Russians they'd rescued balanced the weight of the seamen as they leaned over to grab the inert man first.

As soon as they pulled the body away from him, the swimmer sank, thrashing his arms.

"No!" Caddie screamed. Jackson puttered close to where he'd gone down and swung the boat sideways.

Afraid they'd run over him, Caddie leaned over to peer into the water. A wave lifted them and drenched her. She fell back into the boat. How would they ever find him again? Was he already drifting to the bottom?

When the boat stabilized once more, she grabbed a life preserver and stood amidships, testing her balance as she swung the life ring back and forth. A moment later she tossed it out over the waves. Not until it landed with a splash did she see the fisherman's head. The man reached, fell short, rallied, and tried again. Once more, he failed to catch the life ring.

Awkward movements to her left caught her eye. Seaman Gavin, in the bow of her boat, had clipped a line to his life vest and handed the coil to another man. Now he stooped and was removing his boots. Before Caddie could protest, he dove over the side and swam toward the Russian.

Her heart leaped into her throat as she watched his progress. Even though Gavin wore the life jacket, he wouldn't be able to survive in this rough, icy water for long.

As the Russian man began to sink again, Gavin reached him and yanked him to the surface by his hair. The man dove toward Gavin, overwhelming him in an embrace that carried both beneath the surface.

"Pull them in," Caddie yelled. Three seamen jumped to obey.

Already, Gavin had popped up again and managed to turn the weakened Russian to a towing position. In minutes the two were in the boat.

Again Caddie evaluated their situation. They now had five Russians aboard, and the fishermen's boat held eight. Had they lost one? She looked all around, searching the waves. The Russians had four oars in the water and attempted to row toward the towering side of the *Wintergreen*.

Caddie cupped her hands and yelled at them, but the wind caught her words. One of the Russians saw her and raised his hand. Caddie shouted, "Five!" She held her gloved hand high, fingers outspread and then pointed into the bottom of her boat. "Five men!"

The Russian frowned then nodded. He jostled the man next to him and spoke to him.

"Should we head in?" Jackson yelled.

She swung around and scanned the sea again. There had to be one more man. When she looked back toward the Russians, their boat had reached the lee of the *Wintergreen* and huddled against the ship. Coastguardsmen above yelled instructions down at them, and one of the Russians reached for the ladder he could climb to safety.

Caddie pulled out her radio. "*Wintergreen,* this is *Wintergreen 1.* I have five Russian fishermen in my boat. Request you get a count on the passengers in their boat. There should be fourteen total."

During the pause that followed, she looked over the drenched men shivering in her boat. They shook with cold, despite the blankets. One man lay on the deck with his eyes closed, his lips blue. Caddie watched his chest for a long moment, terrified until it rose with his gasp for breath. Gavin also trembled uncontrollably. Several of her other men were soaked through and hugging themselves for warmth. They all stared at her, waiting for her order.

"*Wintergreen 1,* we've got eight Russians. Over," came the captain's voice over her radio.

Caddie's heart sank. "Any sign of another man in the water? Over."

"Negative. We've been looking. We thought you'd got the last one."

She inhaled deeply. "Await your instructions, sir. Over."

"Come aboard, Lyle."

"Aye, aye, sir. We're en route to the *Wintergreen.* Our ETA is five minutes." She nodded to Jackson. "Return to the ship."

The last of the eight Russians from the rowboat was climbing the ladder as Caddie's boat approached the ship. The now-empty, fifteen-foot wooden boat was tied to the ladder and bounced as each wave hit it. It swung around and crashed into the ship's hull.

"Careful!" Caddie turned to tell Jackson to ease in and let one of the other men latch onto the empty boat. They would have to move it out of the way and position the workboat beneath the davits to be lifted.

Just beyond them a giant wave towered. "Hold on!" she screamed and groped for a firm grip on the gunwale.

The wave hit them with a shock that pulled loose her grasp and threw her against the thwart. Air rushed out of her lungs. Icy water engulfed her for a few seconds. Amid the yelling and thrashing of the men, cold and weakness overwhelmed her. Then came excruciating pain.

⚓

Boatswain's mate Aven Holland picked his way among a horde of huge salmon, across the slippery deck of the fishing boat *Molly K.* The skipper, Jason Andrews, who fished out of Seward, had crossed his path before. He operated his boat just within the boundaries of safety and commercial fishing regulations. Aven determined to check every detail today.

Two of his crew of four seamen climbed up the ladder from the fishing boat's hold and crossed the deck to where he stood near the boat's owner. Aven took a few steps to meet them.

Seaman Kusiak kept his voice low and glanced past Aven, then back into his eyes. "Sir, their weight is off."

"Don't call me sir."

"Sorry. But it is."

"You sure?" Aven asked.

"Yes, s—Yes."

"How much?"

"Five hundred pounds, give or take."

Aven whistled softly. "I'll come down. We don't want to make any mistakes." Kusiak's shoulders relaxed. "Right."

Aven said to the second man, "Wayne, you stay up here with the skipper. Don't take any guff from him."

As he headed for the ladder, Aven called his commanding officer on his handheld radio. The law enforcement cutter stood off a quarter mile, waiting while three teams conducted inspections on fishing vessels.

Aven wished he'd gone to check another boat. But no, he'd asked for this one. Did he want to cross swords with Andrews again? He didn't like to think he was spoiling for a fight. Last time he'd let Andrews by with a warning on a minor violation and regretted it. Did he secretly hope for a rematch and a chance to catch the fisherman breaking the law? Aven had nothing to prove. Maybe he should have let the other boatswain's mate take this boat and avoided the confrontation with a man who already disliked him.

When the operations officer on the bridge of the *Milroy* answered his call, Aven said, "We have a weight discrepancy and will be issuing a citation."

He climbed quickly but carefully down into the work area in the lower part of the fishing boat. The deck below lay ankle-deep in fish, mostly big salmon. Refrigerated lockers on both sides bulged with thousands of pounds of fish. The footing was slimy and treacherous, the stench overpowering. Aven gritted his teeth. At least he was in charge of the detail now, but it seemed he would still end up weighing, measuring, and counting fish, the same as his men had been doing all day. He might never want to eat salmon again.

Two more seamen, wearing jackets and gloves in the refrigerated area, continued the inspection process of weighing, measuring, and recording. They probed into all the recesses of the ship to be sure they'd seen everything. Sometimes fishermen pulled in a catch and threw overboard the lower-grade fish they'd snagged, keeping only the top grade. The only way to prove this illegal and wasteful practice was catching the fishermen in the act. Or they might accidentally catch protected species. Apparently this crew hadn't tried to keep any illegal bycatch.

Checking the amount of fish in the hold against the numbers in the fishermen's records was tedious but doable. Aven spent more time doing this than anything else during Alaska's fishing seasons. The crew of his law enforcement cutter made sure commercial fisheries didn't harvest more than the law allowed from Alaskan waters.

The *Milroy* had been out a week from Kodiak, plying the most popular fishing shoals. The cutter's appearance in a new location this morning had no doubt made a lot of fishermen uneasy.

As soon as today's work ended and all hands were back aboard the *Milroy*, the cutter would head back to Kodiak. The quick thought of his home base brought an eager longing. Aven had been at this for eight years now, the last four in his home state's frigid waters. He didn't mind a cruise on the roiling, icy sea, but the hassle he got from fishermen who broke the law made the job less attractive. Still, it was worth being close enough to home that he could get to Wasilla to see his family several times a year.

Right now the fatigue of fisheries law enforcement had worn him down. He'd be glad to get back to Kodiak Island and spend some time on land. Maybe he'd even make it to church this Sunday.

Church. Would the buoy tender *Wintergreen* be in port now? If so, the new boatswain's mate third class would probably be at church Sunday morning. He'd met her there a few weeks ago, before her ship put out for an extended deployment. Caddie Lyle. He could picture her serious blue eyes and pert nose. She wasn't beautiful, but she had a wholesome attractiveness and a quiet determination that appealed to him. The memory of her perked him up considerably as they weighed the slippery, smelly fish. Next time they were both in port, he would ask her out. That settled, he got on with the job.

An hour in the cold storage unit was unpleasant, but it gave him enough time to double-check the seamen's weigh-ins. Time to issue the citation to the boat's captain. Meanwhile, he assigned another man to run through the checklist of safety requirements.

He emerged smelly and sticky into the fresh air on deck again, convinced his men's assessment was accurate. He pulled in a deep breath. It was summer in Alaska, but the sea air still held an arctic edge, and the waters remained icy cold. If a man fell over the side, the frigid waves would sap his strength in seconds, and his heavy clothing would drag him down.

On the main deck, Wayne still stood a few feet from Andrews, who looked none too happy. The rest of the boat's crew had stopped working and milled aimlessly about the deck, waiting for Aven's verdict. Adjusting his gait to the rolling of the boat, he walked over and handed the skipper his clipboard and showed him where to sign the inspection form.

"I can't talk you out of this?" the bearded man growled.

"No, sir. You can appeal if you wish, but we've verified the discrepancies in weight twice. You're carrying way more salmon than your records claim."

"Your scales disagree with mine."

Aven shrugged. "Ours were calibrated three weeks ago, and they're the official instruments. If you were off by a few pounds, we wouldn't think much of it." He turned to Seaman Kusiak. "Did you check on mandatory safety equipment yet?"

Kusiak nodded. "Yes. They've got most of what's required." He held out a form.

Aven looked over the checklist and noted the lack of two personal flotation devices and a case of flares whose expiration date had come and gone. The captain would face a stiff fine for certain because of the bulging refrigeration lockers below. The safety violations would add more fines and red flag the boat for another inspection soon.

Aven beckoned Wayne a few steps away, down the deck, and asked quietly, "Anything else I should know?"

"Just that they're not happy."

"They never are. Did they threaten you while I was below?"

Wayne hesitated.

"Come on." Aven walked several paces away and turned around so that he faced the captain and crew but Wayne had his back to them.

"The big guy in the red hat."

Aven scanned the crewmen and nodded.

"He said something to the skipper about how easy it would be to get the jump on us."

"What did Andrews say?"

"Said he was nuts. The Guard would be all over them like a flock of seagulls on a garbage dump."

"He's right. Anything else?"

"No, just muttering and dirty looks."

"Okay. You and Kusiak be ready to get down into the boat. We'll board in a minute." Aven strode back to the captain and met his gaze for a long moment. "Make sure you've got all your PFDs next time." He tore off the carbon and handed Andrews the citation. "You'll be notified soon when and where to appear in court."

"Yeah, right." The captain squinted at the paper. The wind fluttered it, and he reached up with his other hand to hold it steady. Half a dozen of his crewmen closed in around him, glaring at Aven and his team. The hulking man in the red knit cap looked over the captain's shoulder at the paper and swore.

Aven did a quick mental assessment. When a man's livelihood and that of his whole crew was threatened, anything could happen. The Coastguardsmen were outnumbered. Although he had a pistol, his men were unarmed. No telling what weapons the fishermen carried. Prudence dictated that they make their exit.

"Thank you, gentlemen," he said.

"Just get off my boat." Andrews glared at him.

The big fisherman spat out a filthy insult, advancing a menacing step toward him.

Aven held his gaze. "I'd advise you to stay calm. I have the power to arrest you."

Three other men fell in beside the big man. One of them held a hooked fish gaff.

Aven reached for the button on his radio. The big man swung fast—faster than Aven could react. The blow to his midsection sent him sprawling backward toward the rail where his men waited.

Chapter 2

Caddie lay on the bunk in sick bay and focused on the lights overhead. The painkillers were already taking effect. The stabbing pangs in her arm had eased, but she still felt the deep, throbbing ache.

Edward Smail, the hospital corpsman who'd dressed her fractured arm, hovered over her. "All right, that should keep your arm immobilized until we get home and a real doctor can look at it. Let me look at that bump on your head now."

Caddie blinked in surprise, but when she'd absorbed his words, she realized that her head *did* ache, too. She put her right hand up to her hairline and carefully fingered the lump.

"I didn't even know I'd hit my head."

Smail shrugged. "That arm's going to give you something to think about for at least six weeks. But you've got a goose egg, too."

"Can I go to my quarters?"

"No, I think I'd better keep you here where I can observe you until we reach Kodiak." He smoothed her hair back and pulled in an overhead lamp on an expanding arm. "Yeah, that's a good one."

"Concussion?" she asked.

"Maybe. I'm not a doctor, but the men did say you were pretty groggy for a while. Didn't pass out completely, but disoriented for sure when I first laid eyes on you."

She scrunched up her face, but that hurt, so she forced herself to relax. "We lost a man."

"What?"

"One of the Russians. There were fourteen on board, and we only got thirteen out of the water."

"I don't know about that. But I do know you did a good job."

She wasn't so sure. One man had died. How could anyone perceive that as acceptable?

The boatswain hadn't. She remembered strong hands lifting her to the deck of the *Wintergreen*, where the seamen had crowded around her. Distinctly, she'd heard Tilley mutter, "This is why men should take the hazardous duty."

"Can I sleep?" she asked. "I feel really tired."

Smail hesitated. "Okay, but I'll wake you up now and then to take your vitals and make sure you're still coherent."

She smiled wryly at that. "Right. I'm sure you've got a manual six inches thick to tell you exactly what to watch for."

"I sure do. This bump's not bleeding, so I'm going to leave it alone." Smail turned to put away his supplies and tidy the counter.

Caddie sighed and nestled into the pillow. She wouldn't think about Tilley. The captain had trusted her enough to send her out with a detail of six men. She would forget about the boatswain's perpetual scowl and his antipathy to female petty officers.

Maybe after a while, when she wasn't so benumbed, she'd roll over on her side. She couldn't lie on her left side because of her broken arm and the lump on her temple. She'd have to try her right side. Later.

What would her mother say? Her eyelids flew open and she winced. Mom would have fits. Caddie's first long deployment in Alaskan waters, and she'd been injured. Smail seemed to think she'd get several weeks of medical leave. She'd like to go home for a visit, though Mom would fuss over her. Would that be so bad? And would the Coast Guard pay for her flight? Probably not. Of course, if she left Kodiak, she wouldn't see Aven Holland again.

That was a depressing thought. She'd only met the *Milroy*'s boatswain's mate once—at church a few weeks ago—but she'd hoped to see him again soon. Whenever they were both in port again. Which could be tricky when they served on different ships.

But that's good, she sleepily reminded herself. If they were on the same ship, they wouldn't be allowed to date. But since she was on the *Wintergreen* and Aven was on the *Milroy*, they might actually have a chance. . . .

She drifted off into blessed velvety darkness.

⚜

Strong hands grabbed Aven and held him up.

"You all right, sir?" Kusiak's strained voice was close to his ear.

Aven pressed the throbbing spot on his abdomen where the punch had landed. He gasped for breath. "Don't call me—"

Reality rushed back to him. Half a dozen fishermen advanced toward them, clenching their fists. One held a knife, and the one with the gaff seemed focused on Aven. He grabbed his radio and pushed the call button. "This is *Milroy 1*. Request immediate aid. We're arresting the crew and impounding this vessel. They're armed and hostile."

"Affirmative," his superior replied. "*Milroy* is en route to *Molly K*, ETA ten minutes."

The briefest glance showed Aven that the cutter was already headed their way and had a Zodiac in the davits so more men could join him on the fishing boat as quickly as possible. The other inspection crews had probably returned to the cutter.

Give me ten minutes, Lord. Let us keep a lid on things for ten minutes.

He held up a hand and spoke firmly. "Stand back. You're under arrest. You'll be taken to shore and turned over to the state police."

The big man swung again, but Aven dodged the blow this time and came up with his pistol in his hand. As he straightened, he heard the smack of bone on flesh beside him, and his four men flew into the fray. Aven alone stood his ground, with his pistol leveled at the big fisherman in the red hat.

Kusiak tumbled into Aven, a gash on the side of his head streaming blood. Aven tilted the pistol and fired a shot just over the big man's head.

"Get back! All of you!"

In the shocked silence, the crew of the *Molly K* hesitated and looked toward their captain. Andrews stood a little apart, near the hatch, and Aven didn't think he'd taken part in the melee. He looked at Aven for a moment then his shoulders wilted.

"Do as he says." The knowledge that he'd lost his boat showed in the tight lines of his face.

The fishermen shuffled toward the bow. Aven's men scrambled to stand beside him again, keeping watchful eyes on their adversaries. Captain Andrews dragged his feet across the deck and turned slowly, standing amid his crew.

"All right, all of you hit the deck, and I mean *now*." Aven swept the pistol in a slow arc in front of him, panning the cluster of glowering men.

His seamen stood around him panting, still coiled tight with unexpended energy. Kusiak swayed. The wound on his temple bled freely, and Aven wondered how the young seaman could stay upright on the rocking boat.

He turned his attention back to the boat's crew. They were waiting, watching the huge man who'd led the confrontation.

"Hit the deck, or I'll drop you," Aven growled. If he lost control now, it was all over. Would he be able to pull the trigger if the man charged him? Yes.

The fishermen stared at him, waiting. The fierce wind buffeted them, pulling at their beards and clothing.

Captain Andrews dropped to his knees. One by one, the other men followed. The big man was the last to go down.

Aven exhaled.

⁜

Caddie awoke and looked warily around. The room was too big for a ship's cabin. Slowly the events of the last two days came back to her. The docking in Kodiak and her transfer to the hospital ashore. Surgery.

She grimaced. Her compound fracture required an operation, so the doctor could insert a pin at the elbow. The surgeon had assured her she would heal and be able to resume her duties in six weeks. She'd asked what that would mean as far as her career went, but he hadn't been able to tell her.

She struggled to sit up, but pain lanced through her bandaged arm. Hadn't the doctor said something about putting it in a cast? Not for a few days, she recalled.

It would have to wait until the swelling had subsided.

She spotted a button on the bed's side rail and pushed it. The head end of the bed slowly elevated. Progress.

Just as she'd reached a more comfortable level, a nurse entered the room. "Well, good morning! Feeling better?"

"Not really. My arm hurts."

"I'll get your meds." The nurse seemed to have a perpetual smile. Her uniform smock with green and purple dinosaurs might go over better in the children's ward. "Feel like eating breakfast?"

"Uh. . .maybe. What time is it?"

The nurse cocked her head to one side, still smiling. "Just after nine o'clock. It's a little late for breakfast, but I asked them to hold a tray for you."

"Thank you," Caddie said. She put her hand up to her head. The bump was still there, still sore. "Is it Wednesday?"

"Thursday. They brought you in yesterday and you had your surgery. You've slept a good ten hours."

"Oh." At least they hadn't wakened her every hour, as Smail had done on the ship.

"I'll come right back with your painkillers and breakfast."

The nurse left the room, and Caddie lay back, remembering the arduous rescue of the Russian fishermen.

"I didn't get to see Attu," she said aloud. She had looked forward to seeing the memorial commemorating the only battle fought on American soil in World War II. Her father had described it to her. . .and his mixed feelings of dismay and patriotism when he'd viewed it. Another chance to see the landmark wouldn't come soon.

A soft knock at the door again drew her attention. Aven Holland came in hesitantly, eyeing her with uncertain dark eyes. He held a rolled-up magazine in one hand. "Hi. Remember me?"

She couldn't hold back a grin then realized she was wearing a johnny, in contrast to his neat shipboard work uniform. She grabbed the edge of the coverlet and yanked it up to her collarbone. "Of course. Come on in."

He came closer and stood awkwardly a couple of feet from her bed. "I brought one of the seamen from the *Milroy* in for stitches, and they told me downstairs you were here."

"What happened on the *Milroy*? An accident?"

"Not exactly. We had a little fracas with the crew of a fishing boat. Had to impound the boat and haul them in. Kusiak got cut up a little."

"Wow. Sounds like a bad week for our side." She gazed up at him and her heart fluttered. His concern was evident, as was his discomfort. Could this well-muscled boatswain's mate harbor a shy side? She'd noticed a hesitance about him when they'd first met a few weeks ago, after the adult Sunday school class.

She'd gone to church in town with her friend Jo-Lynn Phifer and her husband. The young couple, who lived a few doors down from Caddie in base housing, had been married a year. Mark Phifer held a slightly lower rank than Caddie, and he served with Aven on the law enforcement cutter *Milroy*.

Aven looked even better than she remembered. And he'd cared enough to come up and see her when he'd heard she was hurt.

"Who did you say told you I was here?"

"I ran into a medic from your ship. Smail."

Caddie nodded. The hospital corpsman must have come to check on her.

"He said you had a tough time on a rescue mission and got smashed up just as you were about to reboard the *Wintergreen*."

"That's about right. A Russian trawler was taking on water. I'm not sure what happened—if they hit something or what. The sea was rough. Anyway, it was about to sink when we got there, and the crew had abandoned ship."

Aven nodded, gazing attentively into her eyes.

Caddie recalled their timid first meeting at church. Small talk, blushing, eyeing each other with speculation—too much like high school. But after they'd parted, she couldn't stop thinking about Aven. Her ship was deployed the next day for more than a month, and she'd received a rapid initiation to life in the Gulf of Alaska, then on into the Bering Sea. She knew Aven and Mark had been out on shorter cruises during that time, inspecting fishing vessels. She'd only been able to hope and pray that they'd be in Kodiak at the same time again when her ship returned to port.

"I wonder where my camera is," she said.

Aven's eyes widened. "Your camera?"

"I had it in my locker on the ship with my clothes and things."

"It's probably still there. I expect one of the *Wintergreen*'s officers will come in today and bring you up to speed. If they have to deploy without you, they'll send your things ashore."

Caddie nodded, trying to follow. Her head throbbed. "So. . .how long are you here for?" she asked.

"I'm not sure. I've got to fly to the mainland tomorrow. The fishermen we arrested will be arraigned in Anchorage. The police want me on hand in case they need my testimony."

"Doesn't that usually happen at the trial?"

"Well yes, but this is a messy situation. We arrested seven men, and we need to make sure the charges stick for all of them. The police don't want to take a chance of any of them walking, so they want me to give a deposition to the district attorney."

"The fishermen resisted arrest?" Caddie asked.

"Big time. Not the captain. But we'd already charged him with exceeding his limits and safety violations, so he's in custody, too. I'm afraid he's lost his boat for good." He tapped the magazine against his thigh and suddenly seemed to realize he held it. "Oh hey, I picked this up at the gift shop downstairs. Don't know if you like crosswords. . ." He held it out tentatively.

Caddie smiled and reached for it with her good arm. Amazing how much better she felt after just a few minutes of conversation. "Thanks a lot. I don't know how long I'm stuck here for. This might save me from dying of boredom."

"Could have been worse," he said. "I mean, you're not left-handed, are you?"

She chuckled. "No, I'm not."

"Well, listen, I'll be back for the weekend. Unless my ship's called out for an emergency, that is. If you're out of the hospital. . ." He anxiously scanned her face.

"Oh, I think I will be. I hope I can leave today. The doctor should be in soon to tell me."

"Your arm must hurt."

"It does. They tell me it will for a while."

"I'm sorry about that. Do you think you'll be in church Sunday? Or does your ship go out again?"

She gritted her teeth. "I don't think they'll let me go back on active duty for a while, so I should be there."

"Oh, of course," he said quickly. "I didn't think about that."

"I might get to go home and see my family for a while."

"You should if you can." She looked up at him, and he shrugged. "It's hard sometimes to keep touch with your family."

"Yeah." She wondered how Mom and Jordan and Mira were getting along back in Washington. "I guess it depends on what the doctor and my CO say."

The nurse bustled into the room carrying a tray. "Here we go. Sorry I got held up with another patient for a few minutes." She nodded at Aven. "Hello."

"I guess I'd better get going," he said.

Caddie wished he could stay, but that was silly. He had work to do. "Thanks for coming. It. . .means a lot to me." Had she said too much? She barely knew him.

Aven sucked in a deep breath and glanced toward the nurse. "Well, I hope to see you Sunday."

"Yeah."

He nodded and walked out, his back and shoulders straight.

The nurse gazed after him and sighed. "Now that's a keeper."

Caddie felt a blush rising from the neck of her johnny to the throbbing bump on her head. "Oh, he's just a friend. An acquaintance, I should say."

The nurse handed her a small cup with her pain pills inside. "He's not your CO, is he?"

"No. No, he's on a different ship even." Why did she feel she needed to say that?

The nurse smiled. "Yup. A real keeper."

Chapter 3

Late Friday afternoon, Aven drove a rented SUV into his family's dooryard in Wasilla. The big log house sat against a backdrop of mountains in the distance. He sat for a moment, soaking up the view—his favorite after the open sea.

A dog began to bark, and soon two dozen more picked up the chorus. His sister Robyn came around the corner of the house as the front door opened and Mom came out onto the stoop.

"Aven!" His mother hurried down the steps.

Robyn broke into a run and reached him first, flinging her arms around him.

"Hey, Sis." Aven let her kiss him and then embraced his mother.

"I can't believe you're here. Are you on leave?" Mom pulled away and looked him up and down.

"I had an errand in Anchorage. I have to go back tomorrow and fly out to Kodiak, but I can stay the night."

"Great!" Robyn looped her arm through his. "Come see the pups."

"Whoa. Let him bring his things inside," Mom said with a laugh. "Those dogs aren't going anywhere."

Aven opened the back door of the vehicle and hauled out his bag. He slung it over his shoulder and walked between them toward the log home.

Robyn looked great, as usual, in casual clothes, with her dark hair pulled into a braid. She never wore makeup, but then she'd never needed it. At twenty-two, she'd left the tomboy persona behind, keeping the sturdiness that came from everyday hard work mingled with grace inherited from their mother.

"How's Grandpa doing?" he asked.

His mother wagged her head back and forth, frowning. "He has a lot of pain from his arthritis. Hard to get around. But he wants to help all he can, so we find jobs he can do without too much discomfort."

As Aven entered the house, he struggled once more with the conflict he always experienced when he came home. Should he be here in Wasilla, helping them? Or should he go on with his career? His mother and sister shouldn't have to work so hard.

Grandpa Steve looked up from his recliner in the living room and grinned. "Well, well, well! Look who's here." He leaned forward and pushed on the arms of the chair, then sank back into the cushion with a little moan.

"Don't get up, Grandpa." Aven bent to hug him. "How are you?" He lowered his bag to the floor and sat down on the sagging sofa nearby.

"Awful. Just awful."

"Oh, come on, Dad. Don't be so negative." Aven's mother smiled, but the worry lines on her forehead deepened.

"Do you want me to lie and say I'm doing great? It takes me half an hour to get dressed in the morning."

"At least you can still dress yourself," Robyn said.

"Ha. There is that." Grandpa waved a hand, dismissing their opinions. "If anyone had ever told me how hard it was to get old, I'd have laughed. But now I'm starting to appreciate the old folks."

"You're not old, Grandpa," Aven said.

"Says you." He pulled off his glasses and polished them on his shirttail. "This climate isn't kind to the old bones. I don't know how the pioneers did it."

"You want to move to California?" Mom asked. "Just say the word, Dad. We'll pack up and move."

"No, don't start that." Grandpa winked at Aven. "Robyn would never go. She won't leave her dogs. And there's not much call for sled dogs in Southern California."

"I'm going to start supper," Mom said. "Aven, put your things in your room."

"I'll be back in a few minutes. I need to finish feeding the dogs," Robyn said, heading for the door.

"I'll help you." Aven rose and reached for his seabag.

"Better change out of that uniform if you're going out to the kennels with me." Robyn paused with her hand on the doorknob. "I'll meet you by the barn. I was measuring out food when you drove in."

Ten minutes later, Aven met his sister outside wearing frayed jeans that he left at home for times when he had leave. The barn was really only a log shed sturdy enough to secure the dogs' food against marauding bears. Robyn was about to make a trip among the kennels, where the adult dogs were chained to their individual doghouses.

"How many mutts do you have right now?"

"Counting my sled team and alternates, the pups, and the boarders, forty-two."

Aven whistled. "That's a lot of dog food and meat."

"I'll say." Robyn handed him a bucket full of food and pointed to the left side of the kennel yard. "Give those six a scoop each. Boffo and Scooter will be glad to see you."

The dogs were yapping again, demanding their supper. The sun was still high—it would barely sink below the horizon tonight. The dogs didn't seem to mind. After their meal, they would settle down for a snooze.

Aven laughed when Scooter yipped and jumped to the end of his chain. He reached to pat the aging husky's head. "Hey, fella. Long time no see." He stooped down, and Scooter licked his face. The old dog had been Aven's leader when he used to mush during his teen years. Dreams of the Iditarod Trail had faded once Aven joined the Coast Guard, but it was possible his sister still thought about it. The race of more than a thousand miles was every musher's dream. The short race the family had established a decade ago had fed his own interest when he was a teenager. With Robyn, the dog business had become almost an obsession.

He gave Scooter his food and moved on to the next dog.

When all the adults were fed, Robyn grabbed his sleeve and dragged him over to the puppy pens. "Look! Aren't they great?"

"They look terrific. Sold any of this batch yet?"

"Two are reserved. And, Aven, did I tell you? Craig Liston bought one of our two-year-olds last week. JoJo will run in the Iditarod next February."

"Wow, I'm impressed." Aven reached out and tugged Robyn's dark, thick braid. "Selling dogs to champion mushers. How cool is that?"

She grinned, and he thought how pretty his sister was when she wasn't carrying a load of worry. "It's super cool. And Craig and his wife stayed to lunch and talked to us for about an hour about racing."

"That's great. Are you going to enter any races this year?"

Robyn grimaced. "Can't afford to."

"The entrance fees are pretty stiff," Aven agreed.

"Not just that. I need to concentrate on training. I really need some new harness for the clients' dogs, though." Robyn sighed. "I should have one, anyway. People come here when we host the Fire & Ice, and the sponsors are getting around with beat-up old equipment and harness held together with baling twine and bubble gum. That doesn't make people want to buy pups from us or hire us to train their dogs."

"It can't be that bad."

"Nearly." Robyn's eyes flickered. "The profit from last winter's race only lasted a couple of months. We barely had enough for the last load of dog food. And Dr. Baker let us pay the vet bill in installments."

Again Aven felt a stab of guilt. He'd joined the service over eight years ago expecting to stay in only four years. But he'd discovered that he loved the sea and the life of the Coast Guard. Now that he'd worked his way up to boatswain's mate, he was able to help the family out. Since his father's death, he'd sent almost half his pay home to his mother every month.

But on days like today, when he saw how they struggled, he wondered if he couldn't do more good for the family here at home.

Robyn turned toward the house. "Come on. I shouldn't be whining to you, of all people. You're a huge help to us."

"I'm glad I'm able."

She nodded soberly. "I don't think we'd have made it through last winter without you. Mom wanted to sell all the dogs."

"But then how would you support yourselves?"

Robyn shrugged. "I don't know. Move into Anchorage and find jobs, I guess.

But we didn't have to. That's the good news. We got two teams of dogs in to train, and we sold a couple of yearlings. Between that, the Permanent Fund, the money you sent us, and what Mom invested from Dad's insurance, we got by."

"You should have told me things were tight. Maybe I could have done more."

"Well, we're doing okay now. You shouldn't have to put every penny you earn into this place."

Aven followed her back to the shed, where she stowed the buckets and locked the door.

"I'll come back out after supper and refill their water dishes." Robyn took his arm again, as though she wanted to reassure herself that he was actually within reach.

Aven looked back at the now quiet kennels. The dogs had been a hobby when he lived at home. His father had worked for an oil company, and the dog business didn't have to support them while Dad was alive. But now the Holland family lived close to poverty.

"I really need to get home more often," he said. "Grandpa's lost weight."

Robyn nodded. "He had it rough this spring, but I think he's a little better now."

"He won't be able to cut wood this year."

"Well, we still have about three cord left that's nice and dry, but we figured we'd have to buy the rest for next winter—you're right about that."

Aven knew he couldn't get enough time off now to do the job, but maybe he could contribute more to the cost of the fuel. His own expenses were minimal. He was glad he had a pay envelope in his pocket to give his mother. "So, how much does a team harness cost?"

Robyn shrugged. "More than I've got saved so far. I'd like to have a good one when I get it. You know, one that will last and look good to the customers who come to look us over. But don't worry. I'll keep saving my pennies, and someday I'll have it."

⁜

On Sunday morning, Caddie dressed in civilian clothes. She was proud of her uniform, but she also enjoyed wearing her civvies while off duty. Going to church in a dress brought a renewed sense of femininity, something easily lost on a ship with fifty men and only a handful of other women. And when she met people at church, she didn't want the uniform to cloud their perceptions of her. A Coast Guard petty officer's uniform carried expectations.

Of course, the cast on her arm detracted somewhat from the look she'd hoped for. She studied her reflection in the mirror. Her face wasn't as pale as it had been two days ago, when she'd come home to the tiny one-bedroom apartment she rented in the base housing units. And the snowy white sling would go with any color in her wardrobe.

The memory of a certain boatswain's mate's impromptu visit to the hospital also influenced her choice of outfit and careful grooming that morning. Aven had said he hoped to be back on Kodiak in time for church this weekend. She hadn't expected to meet a charming and eligible man during her assignment in the North. Was meeting Aven one of God's blessings for her?

She closed the closet on the neat row of uniforms, glad that her captain had sent her clothing and camera bag to her apartment the day she left the hospital. Maybe soon she'd feel like taking pictures again.

She walked to the nightstand and picked up the small, pewter-framed photo of herself and her father. Both wore their dress uniforms. Her mother had taken the picture after Caddie's graduation from basic training, and it ranked high among her treasures. "I love you, Dad," she whispered. She brushed back a tear and squared her shoulders.

Mark and Jo-Lynn picked her up right on time, and she dove into the backseat of their decade-old sedan. She was getting used to the awkward cast and moving about without jarring her injured arm.

During the ten-minute drive, she and Mark compared notes on their recent experiences at sea. Though Caddie knew Mark served with Aven, she didn't mention his name.

Neither did Mark. He launched into a tale of woe about his assignment to inspect a crab fishing boat in rough weather. "One man was seasick all day, from the time we boarded that boat. And I thought I'd have frostbite by the time we got done weighing all the crabs."

"Didn't you wear gloves?" Caddie asked.

"Well, yeah, but the cold still gets to you. They did their processing on the deck, and the wind chill was intense."

"Oh, like Caddie doesn't know that. It gets cold at sea up here, even in summer." Jo-Lynn swiveled in her seat and looked at her. "You're lucky you came home at all, girl. You got a crack on the head and a broken arm. You could have drowned."

Caddie nodded. "God protected me."

"I'm glad you weren't hurt worse. Have you told your mother?" Jo-Lynn asked.

"I called her yesterday. She wants me to come home for a while, but I haven't decided yet."

Mark pulled into the parking lot, and they all entered the church together.

"Hey, there's Aven Holland," Jo-Lynn whispered as they walked down the aisle looking for a place to sit. "He's staring at you."

Caddie glanced over the pews to her left and spotted him. She smiled and raised her Bible a little as a substitute wave. She felt her face flush and wished she could have left the sling and cast back in her apartment.

Aven's face lit up, and he returned her wave.

She turned her attention back to Jo-Lynn, knowing her face was scarlet by now. "Do you want to sit here?" She didn't wait for her friend to answer, but scooted into a pew and sat down halfway along the row.

A moment later, Jo-Lynn bent toward her and said, "I think he likes you."

Caddie opened her mouth to respond, but thought better of it and swallowed. She fought the urge to glance across the aisle and back. The music director walked to the podium, and Caddie resolved to keep her attention on the service.

Afterward was a different story, however. As the people surged into the aisles, Mark made a beeline toward Aven.

In less than a minute, Caddie found herself standing a yard from him as Jo-Lynn and Mark asked him how his trip to Anchorage had gone and if he'd be joining the crew of the *Milroy* when the cutter headed out again Tuesday.

His dark eyes flickered Caddie's way now and then as they talked, and his smile drew her in, too.

"When the pastor was talking about how the Lord abhors dishonest scales, I was thinking of the boat my crew boarded last Wednesday," he said.

Mark chuckled. "Yeah, you got a fellow who abhorred the honest ones, didn't you?"

"That's about the size of it."

"I hear they gave you a lot of trouble," Jo-Lynn said.

"Nothing we couldn't handle."

Caddie shivered. Whose adventure had been worse—hers or Aven's? She was thankful God had brought them both safely to their home port.

Aven wore his uniform today—most of the men did. Probably it was easier for them, especially those who were single, than maintaining a Sunday civilian wardrobe. He was an inch or two taller than Mark, and his short, dark hair lay shiny and clean, parted casually on the left. His shoulders remained straight, even as he relaxed and talked to his friend.

Their conversation turned back to the sermon they'd just listened to. Caddie was mildly surprised but pleased that Aven commented on how the pastor's message about honesty encouraged him to do his job the best that he could, even when it was hard. He seemed like just the kind of man Caddie could go for, but she didn't want to make any assumptions. Personal relationships in the military could be tricky.

Over the past six years, she'd found it best to go by the book. Life was less complicated that way. Besides, at twenty-four years of age, she wasn't sure she wanted to add romantic complications to the frustrations of her career. It was hard enough trying to do everything right when she was on duty—especially when the boatswain watched her every move—and studying the manual and the charts of the waters her ship would sail. Did she have time to think about romance?

Aven looked her way again, and his smile melted the iceberg of doubt in her stomach. If she didn't have time, she would make time.

"Sounds to me like you guys take way too much flak from those fishermen," Jo-Lynn said.

"Oh, I don't know," Aven replied. "They feel intimidated when we board their boats."

"Yeah," Mark said. "Especially when they know they've broken the law. We have to expect a little belligerence."

Aven turned to Caddie. "How's the arm?"

"It still aches some, but the doctor says it will heal well. I'm off duty for at least a month, though."

"So, you said you might go home?" Jo-Lynn asked.

Caddie hesitated, hoping the annoying blush would stay at bay. She didn't want to admit she'd postponed making plans until she knew whether or not she'd have a chance to see Aven again. "I might. Later this week, maybe. Right now I'm taking it easy and getting used to pulling clothes on over a cast."

Aven smiled. "I hope this hasn't soured you on Alaska."

"Oh, no. I'm glad I was assigned here. Sometimes I feel a bit. . ." She struggled for the right word and shrugged. "Inadequate for the job, I guess. But. . .the Lord is always there."

He nodded solemnly. "That's right. He's there for us even when we're weak."

Caddie straightened her shoulders a little. She would keep doing her best and focus on God's promises when she needed help in pleasing her exacting superiors. She had chosen this life, and she needed to do it well.

An image of her father flashed through her mind. He had sailed these same waters and met the same challenges she faced now. Her service was a memorial to her dad. Had she inadvertently added another layer of expectation to her workload? Did wanting to honor Dad increase the stress of her job?

"There are times when I think I make the job harder than it really is." As soon as the words came out, she regretted voicing the thought.

But Aven's eyes glinted as he nodded. "That's easy to do. Especially when we forget who's really in charge. Remember to rely on His strength."

"Well, hey, why don't we go get something to eat?" Jo-Lynn asked.

"Yeah," Mark said, "if we can find a place that's not too full of tourists."

"I know a seafood place," Aven said. "We might have to wait a little while for a table, but the food is good and it's not too expensive."

"Let's go." Jo-Lynn herded them all into the parking lot and nudged Caddie toward Aven's truck. "Go ahead with Aven. We'll follow you."

Caddie felt her face warm again, but Aven smiled. "Sure, if you don't mind my pickup. It's practically old enough to vote." He opened the passenger door for her and offered his hand. "Can you manage with that cast? I don't want you to hurt your arm."

"Thanks." As she reached for his hand, her stomach fluttered. His strong, warm fingers clasped hers, and he gave her just enough leverage to make her climb into the cab quick and painless. She wondered if he felt as nervous as she did. If so, he didn't show it.

Chapter 4

The harborside restaurant was crowded when they arrived shortly before one o'clock, but Aven didn't mind. He used the wait for a table as a chance to learn more about Caddie. She looked terrific in a muted green dress, and her hair seemed shiny and a little poufier than usual. He wondered if it felt soft.

"You like seafood?" he asked.

"Yeah. Do you?"

He nodded. "I've seen a lot of salmon lately, though. I'm not sure I want to eat it today." He eyed her, wondering what to ask next. There were so many things he wanted to know about her.

Mark and Jo-Lynn were conveniently studying a menu on the wall.

"See, they have beef and chicken, too," Jo-Lynn said.

Aven looked at Caddie and took a deep breath. "So you're heading home to recuperate?"

"If the doctor says I can and if I can line up physical therapy there."

"Where's home?"

"Washington." She added quickly, "The state, not D.C."

"Beautiful place to live. Your folks live there?"

"Just my mom, my brother, and sister."

Did that mean her parents were divorced? Not the best time to ask. Aven nodded and passed his key ring from his right hand to his left. He realized he'd done that about twenty times in the two minutes they'd stood waiting. He wasn't sure he'd even be able to eat. He shoved the key ring into his pocket. "If you're going to be in town tomorrow. . ."

"I'm taking her to the Baranov Museum tomorrow," Jo-Lynn said.

"Oh."

Mark poked Jo-Lynn with his elbow.

"What?" she asked.

"Aven has tomorrow off."

"So?" Jo-Lynn looked at Aven and back at Mark. "Oh. Sorry."

Caddie said nothing, but her gaze never left Aven's face. Suddenly he wished he was elsewhere. Jo-Lynn could be a nuisance. Of course, he probably wouldn't have had the nerve to ask Caddie to lunch if Jo-Lynn hadn't instigated the outing.

"That's okay," he said to Jo-Lynn, flashing a glance Caddie's way. "I wasn't going to do anything special tomorrow. I just plan to run a couple of errands."

"Caddie and I could do the museum another time." Jo-Lynn raised her eyebrows at Caddie with an "up-to-you" expression.

Aven gulped and dared to look steadily at Caddie. "I was going to go look over a dog harness for my sister. She needs a new one and she really can't afford it, but she heard about someone not far from here who will put together a custom harness at a reasonable price. She called him for an estimate a few weeks ago and decided it was too spendy, but I said I'd check into it." He looked away. "I thought you might be interested in going along, but. . ."

"Hey, *you* could take Caddie to the museum," Mark said.

"Oh, no," Aven said quickly. "Then Jo-Lynn wouldn't get to go."

Jo-Lynn waved away his objections. "I've seen it three or four times, while you guys were out to sea. I just thought if the weather's nice, Caddie and I could ride into town and take a look. The Baranov has tons of exhibits from the times when the Russians were here, but I don't need to see it again."

"Well. . ." Aven swallowed and turned his attention back to Caddie. "What do you think? We could swing by the harness maker's shop and then see the museum. If you want to. I mean, it might be fun." He stopped talking. Why was it so easy to give orders to a dozen seamen—male or female—on the ship without tripping over his tongue, but a simple invitation to a woman came out all mangled? In his years in uniform, he'd had only a handful of bona fide dates. Was it any wonder, when he couldn't offer a pretty woman a simple sentence without bumbling?

The hostess approached them with a brilliant smile. "Phifer party?"

Mark sprang to attention. "Right here."

As they fell in to follow her to their table, Caddie tossed a smile Aven's way, eyeing him from beneath her lowered lashes. "I'd like that. Thanks."

He barely heard her, but it was enough to send his ego soaring through the roof of the restaurant.

When they reached the table, he pulled out a chair for Caddie. She again smiled at him as she slid into the seat, holding her left arm cautiously away from the edge of the table.

Aven's stomach settled down. Talking to women on land wasn't so hard. Why had he anticipated an afternoon of indigestion? He might even order a steak.

⌗

When they entered the harness shop the next day, Caddie stopped just inside the door and inhaled deeply. The leather and oil smells reminded her of a saddle shop she'd visited once. A man who appeared to be in his thirties, with his blond hair pulled back in a ponytail and about two weeks' growth of beard, worked at a raised counter. Aven approached him, and Caddie drifted to a side wall where tooled purses, soft briefcases, dog collars, and leather cuff bracelets hung on display racks.

"My sister, Robyn Holland, called you a couple of weeks ago about a harness," Aven said.

The owner laid down his tools and nodded. "Yeah, I remember." He stuck out his hand. "Brett Sellers."

Aven shook his hand and introduced himself.

"Let me see. . ." Brett thumbed through a card file on the desk. "I quoted her a price on a complete set for ten dogs."

"That's right. She gave you the sizes?"

Caddie surreptitiously studied Aven's profile. He was about four inches taller than she was—five-eleven, she guessed—and even now, trying to act casual about his sister's errand, he maintained the officer's posture. His dark hair reflected the overhead lighting. The contrast between his precise grooming and Sellers's scruffy aura made her smile. Aven's clean-shaven cheeks were smooth, and his firm jaw had just enough roundness to give the impression he was not too pliable, not too obstinate. He wore his jeans and Henley pullover as well as he did his uniform.

"Yes, I think I have all the information I'll need," the harness maker told Aven as he came from behind his counter. "Doesn't your family host one of the smaller races every year?"

"Yeah, the Fire and Ice. My folks have organized that race for the last ten years."

"Never been to it, but I've heard of it."

"It's a fun race. Only a hundred miles, but it's got interesting terrain. Some of the mushers like to use it as a warm-up."

"It's earlier than the Iditarod?"

"Yeah. Middle of January."

Brett lifted a bundle of nylon straps and hardware and placed it on the counter. "This is the style I recommended to her. She said she wanted good quality, but nothing fancy."

Aven smiled. "That's Robyn. She doesn't want to spend any more than she has to, but she wants good stuff. She's been getting by with old, patched equipment."

"Can't do that on the trail," Brett said.

Caddie stepped forward, eyeing the heap of harness in surprise. "I thought it would all be leather."

Brett grinned. "Things have changed a lot over the years. Dog harnesses are lighter and more durable now. Leather deteriorates faster than synthetics, it stretches more, and it takes longer to dry out. Besides, dogs like to chew it. I love doing leatherwork, but I put together dog harnesses as a sideline. I've done a few custom leather harnesses for show dogs, but for real work, you want nylon or cotton webbing and lots of padding around the collar."

They chatted for a few more minutes, and Caddie listened as Aven told the artisan a little more about his family and the annual race they sponsored.

"I used to get around to some of the races when I lived in Fairbanks," Brett said. He pointed out a few of the nicer points of the sturdy harness.

Aven fingered the straps and nodded. "Okay, I'll take it. Can you put together what she needs while I wait, or should I come back?"

Brett grinned. "I had a feeling when she called Saturday and said her big brother would come look it over, so I took a look at the inventory. I just need a couple more components. I can have the full set ready in a couple of days."

Aven laughed. "She called again? She didn't tell me."

"Yes, she did. I'll have everything ready to her specifications." Brett rang up the purchase, and Aven paid for it.

"Why did you move out here?" Aven asked. "Not many mushers live on the islands."

"My girlfriend's family lives out here. She didn't like Fairbanks, so I agreed to move down here with her. I kind of like it here." Brett nodded toward the display wall. "I don't sell as many harnesses as I used to when I lived up there. I sell more tooled bags and dog leashes now than I do harness. But I do a fair amount of business over the Internet, and sometimes people call me for special orders."

Aven and Caddie went out to the aging pickup. Aven opened the door for her and helped her up carefully. She held on to her cast as she scooted into the cab.

"How's the arm doing?"

"Not too bad." She checked her watch. Not time for her medication yet.

Aven headed the truck toward the center of Kodiak.

"That was nice of you to get the harness for Robyn," Caddie said.

He flexed his shoulders. "Well, she needs it. The sponsors shouldn't show up on race day with equipment tied together with twine. She's saved up about two-thirds of the price, and I can kick in the rest."

"It sounded as though she may have guessed you'd do that."

"I didn't think so, but maybe I'm more predictable than I thought." Aven shook his head, smiling. "She was disappointed because she thought she had enough money, but prices were higher than she expected. She told me when I was home last weekend that she'd shopped online, but she couldn't find a set as good as she wanted for anywhere near what she could afford. So I said I'd come look at what this guy had to offer and see if it was well made and worth waiting for."

Caddie smiled. "She'll be so happy when she gets it."

"Yeah. I think I'll ship it to her. I'd like to take it to her myself, but I doubt I'll get home again before the end of summer. It's rare to get two or three days off together this time of year."

Caddie nodded. No need for explanations when they both understood exactly what life was like for Coast Guard personnel during tourist and fishing seasons. Either of their ships could be called at a moment's notice for search and rescue details. The one constant in their lives was unpredictability.

"The mountains here are unbelievable," she said, peering out the window.

"Yes, this is easily one of the most beautiful places on earth." Aven grinned at her. "Too bad the weather's so nasty most of the year."

"I expect I'll get my fill of it next winter, but it's green and beautiful right now."

"The Coast Guard will probably send you to the Fisheries Law Enforcement School for a few weeks during the worst of the winter."

Caddie glanced down at her cast and scrunched up her face. "Too bad I can't do it now, while my arm is keeping me from active duty. Hey, did I hear you say you're from Wasilla?"

"A few miles outside of town. My folks bought the place when I was little, back when Dad worked for the oil company."

"So you grew up there."

Aven nodded. "Yeah. Robyn was born here in Alaska, at the hospital in Anchorage. I'm a transplant from Pennsylvania, but I don't remember anything about it back there. I think I was two when we moved."

"My family's been all over, but we were in Washington when Dad died, so we stayed there."

"What happened to your dad?"

She pulled in a deep breath, determined not to get teared up talking about it. "He was in the Coast Guard. Don't know if you knew that."

"No, I didn't."

"Yeah. He actually died while he was on duty." She didn't like to think about it. Remembering how he'd lost his life brought on the doubts she regularly battled. If Dad wasn't tough enough, why should she think she was? "He served in Alaska for two years. At Homer."

"Really?" Aven slowed for a turn. "When?"

"A long time ago. Right before I was born. He was transferred all over the map afterward, but he kept talking about it and saying he'd like to come back. He loved it here."

"I can understand that." Aven eyed her cautiously. "So. . .he didn't die while he served in Alaska?"

"No. He was posted at Seattle when it happened." She smiled, hoping she could keep the tears in submission. "He talked a lot about coming back here. My mom didn't really want to come, though. She didn't like Alaska. She said Washington was far enough north for her."

"Was she depressed? Seasonal affective disorder?"

"Is that the same as light deprivation sickness?"

"Yeah. The fancy name they use for it now."

"Maybe. She didn't like it and said she just wanted to hole up in winter and not go outside when it was dark."

"How do you like it so far?"

"Oh, I like it. Of course, I've only seen the days-in-overdrive part."

He laughed, and she felt encouraged to go on.

"I've always wanted to come here. Probably because of things Dad told us. I decided to get posted in Homer if I could. Kodiak was as close as I could get, but my ship was in Homer a few weeks ago. The *Wintergreen* stopped there to leave off some buoys, and I got to see a little of the town."

"It's beautiful there," Aven said.

"I'll say. The bay is absolutely gorgeous. All those volcanic mountains, and the spit running out into the water. . ." It was easier talking about the incredible terrain than Dad. If Aven would just drop the subject, she'd feel better.

"So, your dad was an officer."

There it was again. "Yeah. He served thirty years. His last command was as skipper of a cutter out of Seattle. He used to joke that he'd served in nearly every district the Coast Guard has."

Aven kept his eyes on the road. "So. . .you've signed on for a career?"

"Probably. It's what I've always wanted to do. Well, since I was ten or so. I wanted to be just like Dad. I knew I couldn't serve under him, but I figured when we had leave together, we could talk about our life at sea. I thought it would be so neat, wearing the uniform just like he did." She smiled at her naiveté. "Dad's death gave me second thoughts."

"How so?" He pulled up at a stop sign and looked over at her.

Caddie shrugged, trying to marshal her thoughts. How much did she want to reveal? Too much might drive Aven away.

Dad had been away a lot during her childhood. It was only lately that she'd thought her ambition might be misplaced. Had the little girl thought somehow that joining the Coast Guard would bring her father closer in a way that would make up for all the times he was away at sea? While she was serving out of Woods Hole, Massachusetts, and her father was posted in Seattle, he'd been killed in the line of duty. Her unplanned visit home for his funeral had broken her heart. She'd returned to duty more determined than ever to make him proud.

She shook her head over the memories and frowned. "Sometimes I want badly to advance and become an officer. To be a captain, even. But then other days, I know I could never live up to my dad's record, so why even try?"

Aven checked for traffic and pulled forward. "Do you like the Coast Guard?"

"Sailing is fantastic, and the job is challenging. What I'm doing now is the hardest thing I've ever done, but. . .yeah, I like it."

He smiled, and she found herself smiling, too.

"So, what's there to fret about?" he asked.

She lowered her chin and looked toward the green mountainsides and distant gray waves. "I'm always second-guessing myself. Did I really do that right? Can I perform to my CO's expectations? Would Dad be proud of me if he were here?"

"I think I can answer that last one."

She stared at him, weighing whether or not he was serious. "Okay, how?"

"I'm sure he'd be very proud of you now."

"You can't know that."

"I think I can. A father who sees his child trying to emulate him, especially in an area where he excelled and was respected. . .yeah, that's something to be proud of."

"Thanks. I'll remember that next time I wonder if I'm doing this for the wrong reason." She blinked back the rogue tears that filled her eyes. "So, what about your dad? Is he still with the oil company?"

Aven shook his head. "He was flying on business a few years ago. His plane crashed."

Caddie caught her breath. "I'm so sorry." If they could only have one thing in common, that would have been the last thing she'd chosen. Yet his words took on deeper value because of it.

"How's your mom doing?" she asked after a long silence.

"All right. It's been hard. She and Robyn are getting along, though. I help them when I can."

"Does your mother work?"

"Yes, at home. The dog kennels were a hobby when Dad was alive, but it started turning a profit. Robyn's a very good trainer. She and Mom have kept things going. My grandfather lives there, too. He helps a little, but he can't do much now. Mom got Dad's insurance, and she has a small income from his retirement fund. Like I said, they get by. Just."

"That's a heavy load to carry."

"It can be. Sometimes I think I should leave the Coast Guard and go home to help them. Or get a better paying job somewhere. But so far, I don't feel God's leading me to do those things. So I keep on." He huffed out a breath and smiled. "So. . . do you still want to take in the Baranov Museum? We're almost there."

"I'd like that. I've heard so much about the Russian occupation and heritage, I'd like to learn more."

"You got it." He put on his turn signal and turned in at the museum's parking area.

He was out of the truck and around to her door while Caddie still fumbled with the seat belt release.

He opened the door and leaned on it, grinning at her. "Let's not get too weepy about our families, okay? This is going to be a fun day."

"I won't if you won't." She was glad her tears had cleared up without spilling over. "I am sorry about your dad, though. I'll pray for your mother and Robyn."

"Thanks. I'll pray for your family, too. Now, let's go see what made old Alexander Baranov such a big shot around here."

Chapter 5

Aven carefully taped up the box with the dog harness for shipping and prepared a label. When he'd finished, he sat down to write a note to Robyn.

Hey Sis,

I went to Brett Sellers's shop and took a look at his work. I like him, and I think a set of his harness is just what you need. He put one together, and I picked it up today. I'll ship it to you tomorrow morning, so watch for a big box.

He paused and read over what he'd written. He wasn't given to long reports on his activities. He called home now and then and e-mailed when he had a chance. Should he mention that Caddie had gone with him to the harness shop? When he'd gone home last Friday, Caddie was just a breath of hope. Now her presence in his life was a reality.

But if he said anything about her, he'd have to explain who she was and why she rode along and what they'd done for the rest of the day. And a gazillion other things. If he didn't lay it all out there, Robyn would call five minutes after she received the letter, breathless and eager to know all about the "new girlfriend." Which was sort of a joke. No one knew better than Robyn how rarely Aven dated.

Best not to mention Caddie yet, he decided. If things didn't work out, it would be too embarrassing to explain why. Yet, after today. . . His pulse jumped as he remembered how much fun they'd had, lingering in the museum until they'd thoroughly viewed every exhibit. He'd talked her into lunch. She'd insisted she wasn't tired but had taken some painkillers at the restaurant.

Afterward they'd gone to a bookstore where they spent another hour browsing and talking nineteen to the dozen about books they'd read and whatever else came to mind. Inconsequential things somehow had become fascinating when he discussed them with Caddie. She'd admitted at last that she was tired, and he'd reluctantly driven her back to the base.

Aven wished he could see her again, but he had to be on the bridge of the *Milroy* at 0500. And she would fly to Seattle in a couple of days to visit her family for several weeks.

He would miss her. He'd never felt this way about a girl before. Okay, woman. Boatswain's mate third class. His laugh echoed in his empty apartment. Most of the women he'd met since joining the military were either off-limits or nonbelievers.

Caddie was not only single and close enough to his rank so they could socialize, but she was a Christian. And she'd promised to drop him a postcard from Washington. He drew in a deep breath, thinking about that. He could look forward to that postcard waiting for him when he came in from his deployment next week.

How long would she be gone from Alaska? She'd said the doctor recommended six weeks off duty, but her captain had suggested she go back to light duty after four, if the surgeon okayed it then. Time would tell.

The letter lay unfinished on the desk. He wouldn't mention Caddie until after she came back to Kodiak. A lot could happen in a month, and he didn't want to get Robyn and his mother all excited about possibilities and have to disappoint them later.

Any time he'd had serious thoughts about a girl before, it hadn't worked out. Caddie was different, and he felt different—more alive and optimistic because of knowing her. Caddie intrigued him more now than she had when he first met her. Even so, he wasn't ready to believe it would last. It was too soon to hope too much. He picked up the pen.

It was great seeing you all last weekend. Wish I could come home for a longer visit. Maybe next month. This fall for sure. How's Grandpa doing? Sold any more pups lately?

He scrawled a couple more lines on his letter and signed it. He would hug the day with Caddie to himself for a while. If things progressed, he'd let Robyn in on it later.

⊰⊱

Caddie enjoyed her visit at home and treated her physical therapy sessions as a new challenge. Soon she was out walking daily around the small town outside Seattle, with her camera slung around her neck. She'd picked up photography as a child and loved finding just the right angle for a nature shot. Aspects of light and shade intrigued her. Birds and animals comprised her favorite subjects, and she wished she'd had more time to take photos in Alaska. Every day at home, she walked to the river half a mile away to capture the moods of the water on film. She looked forward to returning to Alaska and photographing its wild waters in all their fury and beauty.

By the end of the second week, when her younger sister, Mira, and brother, Jordan, left for camp, she wandered aimlessly about the house. She did as much housework as her healing arm would allow, while her mother was gone to work during the day, and walked longer distances to stay in shape. She missed her teenage siblings, but she was glad they had the chance for an adventure.

"We should have cancelled the kids' camp reservations," her mother said at supper one evening. "You don't have anyone to talk to while I'm at work. If we'd known you would be home—"

"No, I'm fine. I've found people to chat with when I go walking. And anyway, the kids have looked forward to camp for months. You couldn't change that." Caddie resolved to try to keep her impatience better camouflaged.

She'd sent Aven the promised postcard, depicting the Seattle skyline, and written her home address at the bottom. For nearly two weeks, nothing happened, but at last a return postcard came from him. A Kodiak bear nudged her cub up a verdant hillside. Caddie stared at it for a long time. She wished she had taken that picture. Even more, she wished she was back on the island.

That night she at last told her mother about Aven and showed her the postcard.

"Ah, now I see," was her mother's response.

"See what?" Caddie turned the card over and read his innocuous message again:

> We're in port for 2 days, then out again. The usual mayhem. Hope the arm's better.
>
> *Aven*

No revelations there.

Her mother smiled. "Tell me more about him."

To her own surprise, Caddie talked nonstop for ten minutes about Aven—what he looked like, his manners, his family, his faith, and his love of the sea.

"If you went back early, would you be able to see him?" Mom asked.

"I don't know. His ship could be out for weeks."

"But there's a chance."

"I suppose." Caddie nodded with a rueful smile. "You're right. If I go back, I'll be close by if his ship docks again."

"You should go."

She eyed her mother's placid features. "It's not like we've dated a lot, Mom. Only that one time."

"But it won't happen again if you stay here."

"Well. . .you wouldn't mind?"

Her mother shook her head. "I'll miss you, of course. I always do when you're gone. But it seems to me it's important to you. You need to do this."

⁜

When Caddie stood again on the dock at the base in Kodiak the following Monday, she knew she'd taken the right course. Her own ship's vacant berth gaped along one side of the pier. The *Milroy* was also at sea, but she needed no more than five minutes at the PX chatting with the wives of some of the seamen on board to tell her they expected the cutter to return by the weekend.

She spent the afternoon unpacking and setting up more physical therapy sessions and a checkup with her surgeon. She took out her camera and the new telephoto lens she'd bought in Seattle. Maybe this would be a good time to get some wildlife close-ups.

Jo-Lynn drove her to the doctor's office the next morning.

Caddie studied the surgeon's face as carefully as he examined her arm. Would he pronounce her fit for duty? What if her arm had been permanently weakened by the injury?

"Does that hurt?"

"No."

"How about now?"

She winced. "A little."

"When does your ship deploy next?" he asked, flexing her elbow gently while he fingered the joint.

"Not for eight days. It's scheduled to dock Saturday and go out again next Wednesday."

"Hmm."

What was that supposed to mean? She watched his eyes keenly.

The doctor's dark brows contracted as he extended her arm again. "I want to leave the cast on another week. You're not ready to lift or tug on ropes yet."

She smiled. He obviously hadn't much sailing experience. "But after a week? Can I go back to sea then?"

"I can't say for sure." He turned on his stool and consulted his computer screen. "The trouble with active duty is that they expect you to be active. They want you to do everything you did before your medical leave. But we want to avoid reinjuring that arm at all costs. Better to take a longer leave than to go back too soon."

"So...when will we know?"

He swiveled to face her again. "Come in Monday. I'll want another X-ray then. I'll send a copy of my report to your CO today, but I'm recommending at least another week of sick leave. We'll see how things look then. You may be able to resume light duty. And don't worry about it. Relax. See some sights. This is the best time of year to see Alaska. Enjoy it."

⚜

"This is the U.S. Coast Guard. Heave to." Lieutenant Greer, the skipper of the *Milroy*, spoke into the public address system, hailing the crew of a small cabin cruiser that danced over the waves in front of them. Beside him, Aven watched the small, quick boat dash for shallow water.

Greer brought his fist down on the wooden rail. It was plain to all that the vessel's crew defied him. The boat the *Milroy* pursued wasn't going to slow down, let alone heave to and let them board.

"You want us to fire a warning shot?" Aven asked.

Greer, who enjoyed the courtesy title of "captain" on the law enforcement cutter, shook his head. "Too close to shore. We don't want any accidents."

Aven stood beside his skipper on the bridge, watching helplessly as the runaway boat churned for a strait between two islands. "We can't follow them through there, sir. The tide's not high enough."

"Are you sure?" His skipper looked over his shoulder at him.

"Not unless the tide's high."

Greer frowned. "It's close."

The truth was the tide had turned an hour ago and the channel they raced toward would only let the 110-foot cutter escape without scars under ideal conditions. "Too risky." Aven's stomach clenched when he pictured what could happen if they tried it.

The skipper swore. "How long to go around to the east?"

Aven did some rapid calculations. "Too long."

The shores of the hilly, tree-covered islands drew closer. Aven's pulse thudded. If he were Officer of the Deck, he would never risk taking the cutter in so far an hour past high tide. He started to speak again but thought better of it. Couldn't contradict the captain.

As the smaller boat disappeared around a point of land, Greer called, "Change course."

Aven exhaled. They would survive to settle things with the boat's owners another day.

The cutter swung around, but the usually agile ship seemed to catch itself and stall. A loud crunch drew everyone's gaze to Greer. A shudder ran through the hull. The captain swore again. "Holland, get below and find out what's going on."

Aven ran for the ladder. As he scrambled down to the engine room three decks below, he could tell the *Milroy* had freed itself and was not hung up on anything below the waves. That was a relief. But there was bound to be some damage.

The chief engineer met him in the doorway to the engine room and assured him they weren't taking on water. "May have some trouble with the prop, though."

Twenty minutes later, Aven climbed more slowly up the ladders. He'd already reported to the bridge by radio. The boatswain had joined Greer. It was nearly time for the shift to change, and he would replace the captain as Officer of the Deck. The cutter moved sluggishly through the sea, and Aven didn't have to ask to know they were headed for Kodiak and repairs.

"You got that boat's call numbers, right?" Greer called as Aven entered.

"Aye, aye, sir." He'd given the information to the operations specialist before they'd scraped bottom, but he didn't say so. Greer's expression was sour enough. Aven walked over to the ops specialist's computer console.

The man rapidly keyed information into the computer and scanned the results. "Got it, sir. They're out of Larsen Bay."

"Larsen Bay?"

"Affirmative."

The town of about a hundred residents lay on the west side of Kodiak Island and catered to sport fishermen. Bears and salmon canning, that's what the village was best known for. Several commercial fishing boats operated out of there.

"Should we contact the state police?" Aven asked. Something about the Larsen Bay connection teased at his memory. When Greer hesitated, he shrugged. "We don't have proof they were smuggling. It was an anonymous tip."

The skipper turned toward the hatch. "Wouldn't hurt to let them go rattle the owner's cage. I'll be in my quarters."

Aven recorded the afternoon's events in the log, including the short-lived pursuit of the cabin cruiser. Occasionally citizens called in tips about illegal activities on the water, and the Coast Guard was expected to follow up on them. The fact that this boat's crew hadn't wanted to stick around and answer questions lent some credulity to the informant's call.

He hated adding that the *Milroy*'s propeller was damaged in the pursuit. That wouldn't look well for Greer. Overeager. Aven hoped the skipper wouldn't get into trouble over it. And it meant their deployment would be cut short. No telling how long repairs would take. If Caddie had been within a thousand miles, he'd have looked forward to docking in Kodiak, but she was probably still in Washington with her family.

⚓

Chicken noodle soup and a sandwich. Caddie decided to save money and eat in her apartment Thursday evening. Maybe tomorrow she'd ask around to see how much it would cost to fly to one of the best bear-watching spots on the island. She'd probably never have a better chance. She'd regret it if she left Alaska without at least trying to get some good Kodiak bear pictures.

The doorbell rang.

She turned off the burner, hurried to the door, and looked through the peephole. For a moment she doubted her eyesight. Quickly, she threw the deadbolt. "Aven! You're not supposed to get in until Saturday."

He clenched his teeth as he smiled. "We're back early. The *Milroy* needs repairs."

Caddie arched her eyebrows and held the door wider. "What happened? Nothing serious, I hope."

"Not really, but it will take a few days to fix." He stepped inside. "We got a little close to shore, and the propeller hung up on a rock."

"That's too bad."

"Yeah. So anyway, Mark called me a few minutes ago and said Jo-Lynn told him you were back. I hope you don't mind."

"Not a bit."

Aven took off his hat and looked around. "I'd say, 'Nice place you've got here,' but it looks just like my place."

She laughed. "Thanks. I think the one-bedroom units are all alike."

"That's a nice picture, though." He stepped closer to the framed photograph she'd hung between the two living room windows when she moved in.

"Thanks. That's my brother, Jordan, and his dog. I took it a couple of years ago when I went home on leave. They're both a lot bigger now."

"You took that? It's great."

Caddie looked at it critically. She liked it, too. Jordan at twelve, hugging the half-grown border collie pup. She'd caught both their expressions just right.

Aven swung around, his dark eyes gleaming. "It's terrific. Hey, I wondered if you'd like to go get something to eat."

Caddie thought fleetingly of the soup she'd started to fix. She couldn't ask him to share that and a peanut butter sandwich. The flush that zipped into her cheeks told her she wasn't ready to offer to cook for him in her apartment anyway.

"Well, sure. But. . ." She hesitated. Aven lived frugally to help his family. "If you'll let me pay my share."

He shuddered, his eyes twinkling. "Let's not do that I'll-pay-no-I'll-pay thing."

"Exactly. We'll both pay."

He held out a moment longer, making a comical face.

"Burgers." She tried to put enticement into the one word, and he fell for it.

"Okay, let's go."

She laughed and grabbed her purse and a sweater.

When they reached the restaurant, the tables were jammed with tourists.

"We could eat in the truck." Aven's plaintive tone caught at her heartstrings.

"Okay. That way, we'll be able to hear each other without yelling."

His face cleared and he smiled at her as they waited in line to order their food. The buzz of conversation around them made talking pointless, so she waited silently, but standing beside him sheared away the tedium. Ten minutes later they climbed back into his truck. He pulled out a cup holder rack, and Caddie fumbled with her good hand to situate the drinks.

Aven asked a brief blessing and handed her a wrapped sandwich. "Need help getting that open?"

"I think I can do it." Over the past three weeks, she'd developed an amazing one-handed agility, using the cast as a prop. "Do I dare ask how your ship came to grief?"

He gave a short laugh and shook his head. "It wasn't my fault, for which I'm extremely thankful."

"Oh, yeah. I know the exact feeling."

"We got a tip that a boat carrying drugs would be heading into a certain harbor this morning. It was a long shot that we'd find the right boat, since it was a small one, and you know what it's like looking for a little boat in the Gulf of Alaska, but we found her. Trouble was she was already pretty close to shore when we spotted her and hugging the coast. When we hailed her, she scooted for a channel we couldn't navigate."

"Terrific."

"Yeah." Aven took a bite of his cheeseburger and chewed thoughtfully. A moment later he reached for his cup and looked over at her. "There's something about that boat that bothers me a lot."

"Oh?"

"We traced the registration number. It belongs to a fellow who lives in Larsen Bay. I was assigned to call the state police when we docked, so they can check it out. And guess what?"

"No idea." She waited, knowing he would give her the rest of the story when he was ready.

Aven shifted in his seat and inhaled deeply. "The guy who owns the boat has the same last name as the fisherman who tried to deck me a month ago on the *Molly K.*"

"Same man?"

"His brother."

Caddie gave a soft whistle. "Is the fisherman in jail?"

"No. He should be. Most of them were fined. The big guy—his name's Spruce Waller—did ten whole days in the slammer. The guy who roughed up Seaman Kusiak is still in there—he'll serve 45 days and then a year's probation. The captain lost his boat and got a stiff fine."

"Sounds like he's suffering more than the rest, and you told me he didn't take part in the fight."

"That's right. The laws we have do that sometimes. It's too bad in a way. But this Waller character didn't have a record—which I find incredible, given his temper—and they let him off easy."

Caddie sighed. "And now his brother shows up in your sights."

"Right. It's got me wondering if Spruce, being out of work in the fishing biz, has started something new with his brother. I didn't see him on the boat we were after, but that doesn't mean anything. I didn't know when we were chasing them that his brother owned the boat, so I wasn't looking for him. He's a big guy, though. Six-two or so, and he must weigh around two-fifty."

"His brother may be hefty, too. Maybe they'd look similar from a distance."

"True. And there's another thing. I was thinking that when I went to his indictment, they said Spruce Waller had a cabin in Larsen Bay. But it turns out his place is in *Anton* Larsen Bay, which isn't far from here."

"But his brother lives in Larsen Bay, on the other end of the island?"

"Yeah, pretty much. You can't drive there from here."

"Still, it would be easy to go back and forth in a boat."

"No, too difficult. But it makes it less likely that the brothers are working together. Spruce's main residence is here in Kodiak, and his cabin is fifteen miles away." Aven popped the last bite of his burger into his mouth and crumpled the wrapper. After swallowing, he said, "That was good. Now how about dessert?"

Caddie chuckled. "Not for me, but go ahead. I'll wait here while you get it."

Aven left, and she settled back in the seat, looking out at the ocean view. The sun was still high in the sky. Most of the fishing boats were out, but pleasure craft dotted the harbor. A gull landed on the trash bin a few yards away, and once again she wished she'd brought her camera.

Aven returned a few minutes later, and the bird flew off with a scrap of a bun in its mouth. He held out a steaming cup to her. "Here. I remembered you like hot tea from that time at the restaurant."

"Thank you! That's very thoughtful."

He settled in beside her and put his own coffee in the rack while he opened a pastry package. "Sure you don't want some?"

"No, but thanks."

"You know, this whole thing with the Waller brothers is working on me. I'm trying not to obsess over it."

"Taking it personally?"

"Maybe." Aven frowned. "I shouldn't have let things get out of control on the fishing boat. I wasn't alert enough, and I let him get too close."

"It happens."

"Yeah. I was trying to radio in, and he took advantage of that second's distraction. Kusiak got cut up because of that."

"Is he okay now?"

"Yeah. He'll have an intriguing scar. The rest of us got bruised up a little, but. . ."

"But you're still mad about it?"

"Not mad exactly." He gazed at her then shrugged in defeat. "I've been praying about it. I don't want to go out there having it in for someone. Anger leads to mistakes. But I admit it bothers me that it happened on my watch."

"You could be right about what Waller's doing now, though. His brother may have talked him into running drugs with him. Maybe he can't get another job fishing because of his arrest."

"Naw, I doubt that. There are so many fishing outfits around. And we don't have proof they were carrying drugs. Just an anonymous tip."

"That boat ran from you, and it was definitely the brother's boat, right?" She watched his pensive eyes. He'd already considered that, she could see, and he didn't like the implications.

"Yeah, there was something going on that they didn't want us to know about, that's for sure. If I have anything to say about it, we'll catch up with them one of these days." He looked up and smiled. "Hey, let's forget about them for now. There's still hours of daylight left. It'll hardly even get dark tonight. What do you say we drive over to Fort Abercrombie?"

"I'd love to! I haven't seen it yet."

"Great. The stuff that's left from the World War II era is interesting." He stuffed his trash into the empty bag.

"I'm game, as long as you don't want to go kayaking or anything like that."

"When does the cast come off?" He glanced at her arm as he reached for the ignition.

"Maybe Monday. Maybe not. The doctor sounded like it was iffy. Pray for me. I don't want to be sidelined longer than necessary."

"No, but you don't want to go back to work too soon, either." As he threw the transmission into gear, his phone rang. He shoved the gearshift back into park and answered it. "Yeah? Okay." His dark eyes flitted to meet her gaze and he frowned. "Yeah, I'll be there as quick as I can." He clicked the phone off.

"Emergency?" Caddie asked.

"Afraid so. A charter boat needs help off Raspberry Island. I'm supposed to report to our sister ship, the *Shatney*. Half her crew's on leave, so any of the *Milroy's* men who can get there fast will go out on the *Shatney*. I'm sorry."

Caddie lifted her right hand and raised her brows. "You can't help it."

"They've sent out a smaller boat already, but they may need us. I'll drop you at your apartment. It's almost on my way." Aven's shoulders drooped as he backed out of the parking space.

"We can go to the old fort some other day," she said.

"I'll take you up on that. Tomorrow, if we're back in time."

"Sure. Or the next day. Whatever works."

"I'll call you as soon as we're in, if it's not too late."

When he pulled up before her housing unit, Caddie reached for the door latch. "Don't get out. I can fend for myself."

"You sure? Your arm. . ."

On impulse, she leaned over and kissed him on the cheek. "I'm sure. I'll be praying for you and the people on the charter boat."

"Thanks."

His reaction was a little slow, but the last thing she saw as she slid down from the truck cab was his smile.

Chapter 6

Aven arrived back at his apartment early the next morning. *Too early to call Caddie*, he reflected after consulting his watch. Robyn and Mom were probably up, fixing the dogs' rations, but he wouldn't hazard a guess as to whether Caddie would be awake at 0530 when she didn't have to report for duty. And if she was sleeping, he didn't want to wake her. She needed rest to help that arm heal.

After a quick snack, he called his sister instead.

Robyn answered and assured him that the family was getting along all right. "Grandpa's losing steam physically, but you knew that."

"Is his arthritis worse?"

"No, about the same as when you were here last. But he isn't able to do much of anything outside now. Mom's taken over all the chores he used to do and is taking care of him. I've had to pretty much run the business by myself the last few weeks."

"I'm sorry." Aven leaned on the card table he used as a kitchen table. He ought to be home, helping Mom and Robyn.

"It's not your fault. And, hey, I hitched my team up in the new harness yesterday. It was the first chance I'd had. I wanted to make sure it fit them right, and we did a ten-mile training run."

"Everything go okay?"

"They did great. I have a super team this year, Ave. I hope I can afford to take them in at least one race this winter."

"Too bad you can't run in ours."

"You know I can't run them in the Fire and Ice. We're the hosts. Duh! Besides, I'll be too busy. But I sure would like to do a short race, say in December. Or right after ours."

"Maybe you can. Wait and see how things go."

"I haven't given up on it."

"Are you and Mom going to be able to handle all the race preparations if Grandpa can't help you?" he asked. "That's a big job."

"It'll be tough, but I think it's worth it. We usually do a little better than break even, and it's our best advertisement. People come for the race and look over our kennels. I show my team off a little. Word of mouth is crucial in this business."

Aven wished he could take Caddie home to meet his family. It would be terrific if they could both get leave the week of the Fire and Ice and spend it in Wasilla, helping set up for the race.

"Hey, Rob, what would you think of me bringing a girl home sometime?"

"What?" Her shriek nearly pierced his eardrum. He held the phone away from his ear and cringed. "Did you say girl, as in female, young woman, dare I add love interest?"

She seemed to have come to a standstill, so he gingerly put the phone back to his ear. "Uh. . .yeah, I guess you could say any one of the above."

"Who is she? Is she Coast Guard? Or a townie? Tell me she's not someone you arrested."

Aven chuckled. "No way. She's a BM3. Stationed here. Serves on another ship."

"Oh, wow. That's perfect. She's a pay grade behind you. You can socialize, but she doesn't outrank you. Ave, that's fantastic. I want to meet her. When can you bring her? Can I tell Mom and Grandpa?"

"Slow down!" Aven couldn't stop grinning. "Yeah, I guess you can tell them. Don't make too big a deal of it yet, though, okay? We've only gone out a couple of times. I like her a lot, but things are still in the early stages."

"So tell me everything."

"Naw, I don't think so."

"Is she pretty?"

"Yes. And smart."

"Ha! I figured that. You wouldn't like her if she weren't. Is she a Christian?"

"Definitely."

Robyn sighed. "I'm so happy that you've found someone."

"Well, like I said, it's not officially. . .anything. . .yet. I wanted to tell you so you wouldn't be shocked later on, if it works out. But if it doesn't. . ."

"You always amaze me."

That didn't seem to fit the conversation, or at least not the direction he'd been steering it, and Aven scowled. "How do you mean?"

"You're so sure of yourself when you're working. You're comfortable with yourself physically. Spiritually, too, I think. But when the emotions enter the picture, you hem and haw and won't commit to a ray of hope, let alone a long-term relationship."

"What do you know about it? You're no closer to finding a husband than I am a wife. Further away by a long shot, I'd say."

"And I'm four years younger than you are." Robyn chuckled. "Besides, I don't tell you everything."

Aven picked up on her teasing tone. "Oh? Something I should know?"

"Not really, but when there is I'll tell you."

"Okay. And if things progress with Caddie, I'll keep you posted."

"Caddie? Her name is Caddie? Like a golf minion?"

Aven choked on a laugh. "Her real name is Clarissa, but that's her nickname, okay? I've never seen her carrying a golf bag."

"Got it. Sounds to me like you'd better latch on to her fast. Nice girls are hard to come by in Alaska, you know."

"Watch it!"

"What's her last name?" Robyn asked with a chuckle.

"You want a lot, don't you? It's Lyle."

"Lyle?"

"That's right."

"Why is that name familiar?"

"I don't know."

After a couple of seconds' silence, Robyn said, "Oh, that captain."

"Huh?"

"You know. The man who tried to save Daddy and Jim Haskell."

Aven's stomach dropped.

"That was the man's name, remember?" Robyn persisted. "The one who died in Puget Sound when Daddy's plane crashed."

Aven found it hard to breathe past the huge lump in his throat. "You're right. That was his name." How could he not have realized? Caddie had told him that her father was stationed in Seattle at the time of his death. He could only conclude that he'd been so distracted by his feelings for her that he'd allowed his brain to take an unscheduled furlough.

"Aven?"

"Yeah?"

"We love you. Come home again soon."

"I will if I can."

"And bring the Caddie girl."

He hung up with a smile, imagining Caddie, in uniform, holding a golf club out to her captain. Nope. He liked the mental image of her in the green dress she'd worn to church last month far better.

He sobered as he mulled over his conversation with Robyn about Caddie's father. It had to be the same man. But did that matter? Caddie obviously didn't know. Would it disturb her if she found out? He tried to imagine how he would feel if their roles were reversed. Not good.

He checked the time. Still too early to call her. He ought to catch a nap, but he doubted he could sleep now. He still wanted to see Caddie if at all possible. Maybe they could explore Fort Abercrombie together. But should he reopen the subject of her father? His chest ached as he sat staring at the phone.

This was a matter for serious prayer.

⁂

Caddie adjusted the focus on her camera and held her breath. She never would have dared get so close to bears in the wild on her own. But Aven had known where to find them and had driven close enough for her to get some great shots with her telephoto lens.

A mother brown bear scooped fish from the stream below them and tossed them to her cub on the bank, not seeming to notice the humans watching her. The youngster batted at the twitching fish. When the mother had supplied enough to satisfy her, the huge animals began to feed, ignoring the distant audience.

The stream gushed down a steep, green hillside toward the bay below. Caddie had never been to this part of Kodiak Island before. They had driven through rugged mountains but were only fifteen miles from the base. They'd passed Lake Buskin and navigated forest-covered slopes to come out on the northeast end of the island. The brilliant colors of spruce trees, grass, sky, and water thrilled her. In the distance, she glimpsed Whale Island and mountains all around the bay.

Aven had brought binoculars and continually swept the vista before them while Caddie concentrated on the bears. She'd be glad when the nuisance cast came off her arm. Two more days, maybe. Monday couldn't come soon enough for her. But she wouldn't let that affect her outing today. Even with the unwieldy plaster accessory, she was able to handle the camera and zoom in on the bears. Mira and Jordan would love them. After the animals enjoyed their feast, they lumbered into the brush.

She sighed and turned back toward the pickup. "What are you looking for?" she asked Aven.

He lowered his binoculars. "Remember the man I told you about—Spruce Waller?"

"The one who hit you."

Aven winced.

"Sorry." Caddie put her camera carefully into its case. "What about him?"

"That's Anton Larsen Bay down there. We're not far from his place."

"Here? There's no town."

"No, there's not." Aven swept the air with his arm, indicating the hillsides and the inlet below. "There are some cabins. You can't see most of them from up here. But I thought I might be able to spot a boat in the harbor."

"And?"

"Nothing."

No, not nothing. He had hoped to find evidence relating to the cases his ship's crew had recently worked on. She went to stand beside him. "Can you drive all the way down to the shore on this side?"

"I think so."

They stood in silence for a long time. Caddie knew the meager roads on the island led to only a few of the nearest villages. Those farther away—like Larsen Bay, Old Harbor, and Akhiok—could only be reached by boat or by air.

"You brought me here in hopes of seeing Spruce Waller, didn't you?" she asked softly.

He cocked his head to one side. "Okay, I admit I went by his apartment in Kodiak. He wasn't around. I figured he might be out here."

"Or off on his brother's boat," Caddie hazarded.

"Well. . .the state police tried to contact his brother, but he wasn't home and his wife said she hadn't seen him in three days. Not that I believe that, but he could be over here with Spruce, lying low until the cops ease up on him."

"You hope you can link Spruce to the smuggling his brother is involved in, don't you?"

Aven shrugged. "So far, that's just a rumor. But I have to admit, that might ease the pain of seeing our ship get staved up."

"And getting jumped by half a dozen fishermen?"

He bit his bottom lip. After a long moment of silence, he turned toward her. "I guess I should have told you what was on my mind before I drove out here."

"I don't mind being here. In fact, I'd love it if we could find the guy who owns the boat."

"Clay Waller."

"Whoever. But I don't want to mix things up with a couple of tough guys. My arm's still in the cast. I wouldn't be any help in a fight."

"I'm sorry, Caddie. You're absolutely right. Coming out here was foolish of me, and not asking you was selfish."

She reached up and touched his cheek. "I'm not trying to lay guilt on you. I'm just saying we should be careful." She looked down toward the bay. "Want to see how close we can drive to the shore?"

He hesitated. "It would probably be smarter to just forget it."

She watched his face until he raised the binoculars again. "We could hike on down there," she said.

"No. Too many bears around. All I brought for insurance is my pistol. We don't want to get too far from the truck."

"Then let's drive on a ways."

"You sure?"

"Yes. But if we find Waller, we don't approach him."

After half a minute of staring through the binoculars, he lowered them and faced her. "Deal. I'll be careful."

They got into the truck, and he drove another half mile. Aven's broody silence dragged Caddie's spirits down. Were the Waller brothers affecting him this badly? Or was there something else he hadn't told her?

When they came to a wide spot almost to the bay, he pulled over. "I don't want to get where they can see us. I'll turn around so we're headed out, and then we'll take a look-see." Aven maneuvered the truck into a better position, grabbed his binoculars from the seat, and climbed out of the cab.

Caddie opened her door and followed him, once more carrying her camera.

He stood off the edge of the road, scanning the terrain and water below them. "There's a boat docked down there."

"Where?" Caddie strained to see where he was looking. "Is that a roofline?"

"Yes. The cabin's above the water fifty yards or so, and the boat's moored down below. Come on." He plunged into the brush beside the road.

What about bears? Caddie glanced uneasily around and hurried to catch up with him.

Aven stopped inside the tree line beside a log cabin. He parted the branches of a clump of alders and again peered through his field glasses.

The sun glittered on the placid water of a cove below. Movement drew Caddie's attention, and she sucked in a breath. "Is that the boat you chased?"

Aven let out a sigh. "Hard to be sure. They had a canopy on when we saw it, and it had a dark stripe just below the gunwales, but. . ."

"But they're painting it." Caddie squinted and focused on the two men below them. "Do you think they would change the registration number?"

Aven rubbed the back of his neck and adjusted the strap on his binoculars. "People do it all the time with cars. Put on false license plates. Why not with a boat if they don't want it identified easily? They've painted over the name for sure."

"So they rename the boat, maybe change a couple of the numbers, and alter the appearance the best they can—maybe add something on deck to change the silhouette or put a different color canopy on top."

"Right, so that we can't be sure it's the same boat at a glance." Aven frowned. "I'd like to get closer."

"Do you think that's wise?" Caddie's pulse accelerated. Facing lawbreakers while in uniform may be part of her job, but out here, with only the waves for witnesses?

"Probably not," Aven said. "Wish I could see their faces." Again he studied the scene below.

"Would you recognize Spruce Waller?"

"Absolutely, if I could get within five yards of him. But I've never seen his brother that I know of." He pulled the binoculars from his face with a frustrated sigh. "The guy on the left has the same build as Spruce, but I can't be sure from here that it's him. It could be his brother or someone else entirely." He eyed the nearby cabin and looked again toward the small dock and the moored boat.

"Think what could happen if they saw us. I mean. . .that guy tried to kill you." Caddie clamped her lips shut, determined to say no more. Her heart thudded.

Aven said nothing but peered toward the boat again.

Caddie lifted her camera and focused on the man wielding the paintbrush. At that moment he straightened, and even from her distant vantage point, she could see that he was a large, muscular man.

"He's growing his beard out," Aven said.

As the man turned to speak to his companion, Caddie clicked a photo.

"I think I got a decent shot," she whispered. "We can enlarge it on the computer."

"Great." Suddenly Aven let his binoculars drop on their strap and grabbed her wrist, tugging her downward. "He's looking up here."

She turned her face away and whipped her silver-toned camera behind her then crouched still behind the shrubs. After a long moment, she hissed, "Think he saw us?"

"No. But it's a good thing we stayed behind the bushes."

She exhaled. "Maybe we'd better leave before he looks again."

Aven moved stealthily through the trees, and Caddie followed. They halted out of sight of the boat but farther from the pickup.

"There's a vehicle parked on the other side of the cabin," Aven said softly. "I'd like to get the plate number so we can be sure we've got the right man."

Caddie shivered. "Take my camera and get a picture."

"Good idea."

She handed it to him.

"Wait here," he said.

"Okay, but don't take any chances."

He darted in a crouch to the back corner of the building. For a minute and a half, he was out of sight. Caddie held her breath, listening and watching the spot where he'd disappeared.

At last he returned, racing almost silently toward her. "Got it." He seized Caddie's hand. "Let's get out of here."

Chapter 7

Playing Scrabble with the Phifers Monday evening kept Caddie calm, so long as she didn't think about Aven and their Saturday expedition to Anton Larsen Bay.

They'd spent a quiet Sunday on the base, but Aven had fidgeted all day, biding his time until he could contact his commanding officer.

"You'll hear from Aven soon," Jo-Lynn said, and Caddie realized she'd checked her watch again.

"Sorry. I didn't expect him to be gone all day."

Mark reached across the kitchen table for game tiles to replace his stock of letters. "They probably went to talk to the state police. Sometimes things like that take way longer than they should."

Caddie nodded. She hoped Aven hadn't involved himself in another confrontation with the bullheaded Spruce Waller.

Her cell phone trilled at five minutes after seven o'clock, and adrenaline sent her pulse rocketing.

"Hi. I wondered if I could bring your camera back to you," Aven said.

Caddie relaxed and smiled across the kitchen table at Jo-Lynn. "Sure, but I'm not home. I'm over at Mark and Jo-Lynn's."

"Okay, I'll come there."

"Is that Aven?" Jo-Lynn jumped up. "Ask him if he ate supper."

"Have you eaten?" Caddie asked. "Jo-Lynn has leftover lasagna."

"Sounds good. Tell her I'll be there in five."

Caddie clicked her phone off. "Thanks, Jo-Lynn. He's on his way."

"Aw, come on," Mark whined. "I've got a really good word. You're not going to quit the game, are you?"

With a laugh, Caddie looked to Jo-Lynn. "How about it?"

"Let me put a plate in the microwave for Aven and I'll come back."

A short time later, Aven ravenously attacked the food while the others finished their game.

"There," Mark crowed. "I used all my letters." He set out tiles to spell *brown* and prodded them into place with a fingertip. "I win."

"No, you don't." Jo-Lynn half rose, grabbing letter tiles from her own rack. "Caddie and I get one more turn, and I get double word score on *maw*, using your W."

"That's not a word."

"Yes, it is."

Mark scowled at her. "You're making that up. Do we have a dictionary?"

"It's a word," Aven said.

"I thought it was *Ma*, M-A."

Caddie laughed. "Maw is a different word. It means stomach, I think."

"Yeah." Jo-Lynn's eyes gleamed. "Like Aven is filling his maw with lasagna."

"Okay, I give up." Mark shook his head, glowering at the board.

Caddie said, "Cheer up, Mark. I still can't make any words, and I think you won after all." They'd given her the scorekeeper's job, and she quickly totted up the points. "Yup. Sorry, Jo-Lynn. He's got you by two points."

Jo-Lynn let out a sharp breath and stamped her foot. A moment later, however, she joined them all in laughter. "Okay, but I was close."

"You were, babe. Good match." Mark leaned over to kiss her.

Caddie shot a glance at Aven, and he winked at her. "Got any coffee, Jo-Lynn?"

Their hostess stood. "Sure. You want some, Caddie?"

"Yes, please."

"Mark?"

"Natch."

Jo-Lynn headed for the counter to measure the coffee.

"So, what did you find out?" Mark asked Aven. "Caddie told us you took her camera to the state police with pictures of some SUV you found out in the woods."

"That's not what I said." Caddie had learned by now that Mark was expert at teasing.

"Seriously, what happened?" Mark asked.

Aven laid down his fork and wiped his mouth on his napkin. "The skipper went with me, and we talked to the same state trooper I called after our cruise the other day. They sent two men out to Waller's cabin. Spruce Waller was there, but his brother wasn't. And the boat had disappeared."

"They moved it," Mark said.

"Yeah. I wish we could have gotten them to go out there Saturday night. Clay probably took the boat back to his place at the other end of the island. But the trooper wasn't in a hurry to rush out there again. He said he's got bigger fish to fry."

Caddie sighed. "I can understand that, since you didn't have any proof to begin with that they'd committed a crime. Other than not responding when your skipper hailed the boat, I mean."

"And you weren't even sure the second man working on the boat Saturday was the brother, were you?" Mark asked.

"Caddie's pictures say it was. The trooper ID'd Clay Waller from the photos."

"Even from so far away?" Caddie asked.

Aven nodded. "He said you did a great job with your telephoto."

Jo-Lynn brought them all mugs of coffee. "Well, quit looking so glum, all of you. The boys came home for an extra three days, and I'm not complaining."

"I'm not either," Mark told her, "but we have to report back to the ship tomorrow morning. What about you, Caddie?"

She pulled out a smile that she didn't feel. "I've been assigned to light duty on shore starting tomorrow."

Aven gazed at her over his coffee mug. "For how long?"

"I'm not sure. I saw the doctor again this afternoon. He thinks a couple of weeks. Then, if the cast is off the next time the *Wintergreen* goes out, I'll be aboard."

"Don't worry, Aven. I'll keep an eye on her." Jo-Lynn resumed her seat and smiled over at him. "Caddie and I can hang out while you guys are at sea."

"All right," Aven said, watching Caddie keenly. "I guess that's better than sitting around doing nothing."

"Watch it!" Jo-Lynn grabbed her spoon and drew her arm back as though about to attack him. "I may not be in uniform, but I do *not* 'do nothing' all day."

Aven laughed and turned to Caddie. "Let me drive you home?"

Caddie felt her face warm. "Thanks."

Mark's face clouded up in mock disgust. "She only lives two hundred feet away, for crying out loud."

"Yeah, and the sun will stay out until midnight," Jo-Lynn added.

"A lot can happen on a two-hundred-foot walk," Aven said sternly. "You just never know. I think she needs an escort." Under the table, his hand found Caddie's and he squeezed her fingers.

"Now that you mention it," she said, smiling at Jo-Lynn, "we should probably head out. The *Milroy*'s crew has to report early."

"Eh, we're used to it," Mark said.

"I think Caddie's right. We'd better skedaddle." Aven shoved back his chair. "Thanks for the lasagna."

The evening shone as bright as midday, and Caddie felt conspicuous as Aven walked her from his truck to her door a few minutes later. "Thanks for bringing my camera back."

He held the case out, and she took it with her good hand. "You're welcome. Thanks for getting those pictures. We saw your bear pictures, too. Couldn't help it, going through to retrieve the ones of the Wallers."

"That's okay."

Aven nodded. "Your shots of the bears are really good."

"Thanks."

"What are you going to do with them?"

"I don't know. Send copies to my brother and sister. Maybe make a Christmas card. I just like photographing wildlife." She held the camera against her side with her cast while fumbling in her pocket with her other hand for her door key.

"Well, I think you should sell them."

"What?" She jerked her chin up and stared into his eyes. "They can't be *that* good."

"Sure they can. They're every bit as good as the pictures they have in the tourist brochures."

"You think so?"

"Yeah. A lot of people would think so. It's a gift. My sister Robyn took about a thousand pictures of her dogs before she got any good enough to put on a brochure advertising the kennel and the sled race my family sponsors every year."

Caddie studied his face. The dark shadows under his eyes reinforced his serious tone. "Thanks. A lot."

Aven reached for the key ring she held. "Let me open this for you."

She surrendered the ring, and he slid her door key into the lock. "There." He stooped toward her and brushed her lips with his.

A sense of joy and loss swept over Caddie. Aven would be out two weeks this time. What if she'd been deployed again when he returned? They could go on missing each other in port for months.

She wanted to put her arms around him and cling to him, but even if she dared, the stupid cast would prevent that. She looked up at him and tried to think of the appropriate words for this uncertain parting.

"Caddie. . ."

"Yes?"

His jaw muscles tightened. He looked away for a moment, inhaling deeply. When his gaze returned to hers, she sensed that he'd reached a decision.

"There's something I need to talk to you about."

"Besides the Waller brothers?"

"Yes."

"Okay." She tried to divine from his sober expression what it could be. Nothing good or he wouldn't carry that air of dread and reluctance. "Do you want to come in?"

He exhaled. "Thanks. I promise I won't stay long."

She opened the door and led him inside. "Have a seat." She settled on the sofa she'd inherited from the last tenants.

He sat beside her and leaned forward, clasping his hands between his knees. She waited.

After a moment, he took a deep breath, but still said nothing.

"Aven, what is it?"

He jumped up and walked to the window, where he stood looking out at the parking area. "Look, there's something. . .it's nothing bad, really, but I figured I should tell you. If you found out from someone else. . ." He ran a hand through his dark hair. "Caddie, I wasn't trying to keep it from you."

Her stomach lurched. A dozen possibilities raced through her mind. He couldn't be married. Could he? Maybe he was being transferred out soon. Or perhaps he merely struggled with a way to let her down. But if that was the case, then why had he kissed her—sort of?

She stood and walked over to stand near him. "Please tell me what's wrong."

He turned and pulled his shoulders back. "It's about my father. I didn't realize it at first, but when I talked to Robyn, she made the connection. If it bothers you, I'm very sorry. I don't want to upset you. But I don't want to take this relationship any further until you know."

Know what? She blinked and pulled in a breath but couldn't say a word. Was his father a criminal?

Aven took her elbow gently and steered her back toward the couch. "Let's sit down."

She complied, shooting off a quick plea to heaven for serenity, no matter what. "Okay," she said when they were seated again. "There's something about your dad. You can tell me. Please."

He licked his lips and nodded. "Okay. See, when you told me your father was in the Coast Guard, I should have realized he was Captain Gregory Lyle. Wasn't he?"

"Yes, but. . ." She waited. There was more coming, of course.

"And he was stationed in Seattle three years ago, when he died."

"That's right. It's no secret."

"No, it's not. And he died in the line of duty."

She lowered her head. "Yes."

"Trying to rescue my father."

She jerked her head up and stared at him. As the pieces fit together in her mind, breathing became a chore. "Oh Aven, I'm so sorry. It was bad enough that we both. . ." She stopped and sniffed, thinking about their simultaneous grief, back before they knew each other. "You said the plane crashed. I didn't think about it being the same one. I figured you meant a commercial jet."

"No. It was a small private plane the oil company owned." Aven looked across the room at nothing. "Their pilot, Jim Haskell, was taking Dad to Seattle to catch a commercial flight to Houston. A storm warning was posted, but Jim figured they'd beat the weather. But when they got to Puget Sound, it came on suddenly and they went down in the storm. Jim managed to call for help before the plane sank, and the Coast Guard responded."

Caddie nodded. "My dad was on call. He and three other men went out in a rescue boat. They found a few pieces of the wreckage and were looking for survivors." She faltered and looked up at him, tears flooding her eyes and constricting her throat.

"It must have been awful weather," Aven said. "Your father was standing on the deck, and he got hit by lightning. That's what we were told."

"Yes. A freak accident."

"But if my dad wasn't out there. . . I mean, if he and Jim had listened to the weather predictions. . ."

Caddie eased back into the couch cushions, but they offered little comfort. Her chest hurt as she forced herself to look beyond the surface, to plunge past the natural reaction. She would not blame Aven, nor his father, though her natural inclination was to think—to say—that he had caused the death of another man by his foolishness.

"It's not your fault." She shuddered and closed her eyes for a moment, seeking strength she didn't feel. At last she was able to look at him again. "It's probably not even their fault. Weather patterns change quickly."

Aven sighed, and she could tell from the agitation in his dark eyes that he'd seen her struggle. "I thought about not saying anything, but I couldn't let you hear something and put two and two together. Caddie, I wish it had happened differently."

"Me, too." *Or not at all.* How many times had she cried out to God for understanding? Why her father? Why lightning? After all his years in the Coast Guard, with all his experience on stormy seas, why was Gregory Lyle the one to die that way? And now, to learn that Aven's father had—

She caught herself. She wouldn't even think that Aven's father was to blame. It would be too easy to let something like that fester and spread into a chronic bitterness. Her tears overflowed and a sob erupted from her chest.

Aven folded her in his arms and drew her close. "I'm sorry. I'm so sorry."

She heard the tears in his thick voice. They sat together for what seemed like a long time. She couldn't reconcile the warmth of his embrace with the sharp pain inside her. He began rubbing slow circles on her back with his sturdy palm, and she wilted against his chest, gulping to control her weeping.

After a long time, she sat up and wiped her eyes. "I'm sorry. I didn't mean to lose it like that."

"It's my fault," he said. "There must have been a better way to tell you."

"No. I'm glad you let me know now. You're right about that. It would have been harder later. But. . .I'm not upset with you. You hear me?" She leaned back and looked up into his glistening eyes, willing herself to believe it, too.

He nodded. "Yeah. I still feel bad about not catching on sooner and having to dump it on you, so to speak."

"Quit that." She tried to scowl, but the tears were too recent, so she sniffed and patted his chest softly. "It's going to be okay."

"If you're sure. . ." He studied her for a long moment. "I should probably leave now."

She supposed he had been there long enough, but she hated to see him go. "I'll see you. . ." *When?*

He reached up and caught one of her straggling tears and let his fingers linger gently on her cheek. "Yeah. Soon, I hope. I'll be praying for you."

"Watch yourself." She straightened and inhaled, determined to end this without crying again, even if they wouldn't see each other again for who knew how long. Knowing she would miss him tangled inextricably with her apprehension about resuming her duties and her turmoil over her own feelings for her father. She determined not to drift into another emotional maelstrom.

She reached over to touch his sleeve. "If you meet up with the Waller brothers, be careful. Not that you wouldn't be anyway, but. . .oh, you know what I mean."

"I think I do. *Semper paratus*."

She nodded. *Always ready,* the Coast Guard's motto. She'd been far from ready for his revelation. Would she be ready when the time came for her to serve again on the *Wintergreen*? "You'll do great," she said. "I'll pray for you, too."

Aven slid his arm around her, drawing her closer, and bent to kiss her with more confidence than he'd shown at the door.

She leaned against him for one more warm moment, relishing his strength and solidity. Then she pulled away with a sigh. Prolonging the farewell would have her in tears again. "Come on," she said.

When she stood, he rose and followed her to the door. He hesitated there. She smiled up at him.

"No bad feelings? About our dads, that is?" he asked.

She managed a smile. "I can't see any room for guilt in our generation."

He sighed and stroked her hair. "Thanks." He opened the door and went out into the too-bright evening.

Chapter 8

Three weeks later, Aven's ship docked in Seward to pick up an officer and leave supplies. He'd hoped the *Milroy* would return to Kodiak before Caddie's ship embarked again, but it looked like he'd just miss her. She was due to deploy at high tide the next morning, several hours before he would arrive in port.

He'd found the past few weeks frustrating, though he'd kept too busy to be bored. The days blurred into a haze until he felt that July had skipped over him somehow and August had arrived without fanfare. Five days into the month, the long Arctic days had noticeably shortened. The wind had a nip of autumn. Summer was a fleeting patch of sea smoke, already dissipating.

Tomorrow Caddie would at last go back on active duty. Aven had seen her only twice since the evening when he'd kissed her, and both events left him longing for more time with her. He'd managed to make a church service with her the first time, and on the second occasion, he and Caddie met for a quick cup of coffee on the base during her break from office work. It was unsatisfactory, though he'd received a few erratic e-mails when he was able to check his account. Each time, he'd replied with assurances that her notes encouraged him. But real time—face time—with Caddie was hard to come by.

He called her cell phone from Seward, where his skipper had logged them in for the night. At least he could get phone service here, which he couldn't for the most part on the sea.

"I'm so glad you called." Her voice held an air of confession. He'd learned her moods well enough to read doubts, dread, and lack of confidence in her choppy breathing.

"Tomorrow's the big day, huh?"

"Yes. I don't know what's wrong with me. The cast is off, my arm feels fine, and I'm going back to active duty. Yay."

Aven grimaced. "What's up really?"

She hesitated. "Nerves, I think. I don't know when this happened, but I'm scared to go back."

"Scared you won't do well?"

"Yes. And that I won't be able to pull my weight. I'm still not back to full strength. And then there's always Boatswain Tilley."

"I know him. He can be tough on petty officers."

"I can take tough. But if he goes on to humiliation, I'm not so sure. I guess the thought of going back has worried me more than I realized. Add to that the fact that I'll see you even less when we're both in and out of port, and I'm afraid I've let myself wallow in self-pity."

"I've been thinking about you all day."

"Thanks." Her voice held genuine warmth this time.

He smiled, glad he'd had the power to cheer her even a little bit. "Praying for you, too."

"I really need it. Aven, I can't imagine not having you there to give me a boost when I'm down."

"It works both ways. You pick me up just by letting me care about you." He glanced around to make sure no one stood close enough to hear him sweet-talking her. His shipmates would razz him for sure if they knew he was getting serious about a woman. But he meant every word.

"Thanks so much," she said.

"I wish I could see you tonight, but I can't. So just know that I'm thinking of you. I miss you, but I know sooner or later we'll get some time together, if it's in God's plan for us."

"I like that thought. I'm going to hold on to it." She definitely sounded more upbeat now.

His heart seemed about to melt, and he wished more than ever that he could see her. Squeeze her hand. Give her a hug.

"I'll miss you," she said. "But I feel a lot better because you called."

"I'm glad. And we will see each other again. Soon."

⚜

One short week later, Caddie stood between two seamen, watching as the ship's crane lowered a huge buoy to rest on the deck. She gave it a quick visual inspection and found it in good enough repair to stay out another year. Her team of five men would go over it thoroughly to be sure. They scurried to secure it in place, before the rollicking waves could shift the buoy and endanger the crew. She tried not to think of her last sea voyage and the injured arm that still ached in damp weather.

When the buoy was safely chained down, Caddie signaled the crane operator and instructed two of her men to check the mooring chain. Others prepared to change the lamp bulbs and repaint the buoy with special, quick-drying paint. In less than an hour, they should have it back in the water.

"What's that?" Seaman Morales asked.

She walked around to stand beside him. A yellow plastic streamer fluttered from the steel lifting eye at the top of the buoy. "You got me."

"Maybe someone used the buoy as a marker in a regatta," Morales suggested.

If so, it had been a very low-profile regatta. The Coast Guard was usually notified of boat races and other sporting events on the water. Frowning, Caddie gave the streamer a yank and broke it off. She handed it to Morales. "Trash."

He nodded and carried it away.

She circled the buoy, observing the seamen's labor. All worked with concentration that told her they were determined to make the paint job perfect.

As she watched them, her thoughts drifted to Aven. She'd received only one message from him since their last phone call—a brief e-mail. Even though he'd kept the tone general, his words had lifted her spirits.

> *Caddie, I'm in port. Going out again tomorrow. Hope things are going well for you. Psalm 93. BM2 A. Holland.*

She'd printed out the message on the bridge yesterday and tucked it in her pocket to savor later. In the tiny cabin she shared with Lindsey, she'd looked up the Psalm and read it slowly several times. Even though the Hebrew poem had been translated into English, it rang with splendor.

> *"The Lord reigns, he is robed in majesty; the Lord is robed in majesty and is armed with strength. . . . The seas have lifted up, O Lord, the seas have lifted up their voice; the seas have lifted up their pounding waves. Mightier than the thunder of the great waters, mightier than the breakers of the sea— the Lord on high is mighty."*

The verses fit her life so exactly that she closed her eyes and whispered, "Thank You for showing me this, Lord."

Now, as she stood on deck, the words came back to her. She felt like shouting them aloud for all the sailors to hear, but she kept quiet. Wouldn't Boatswain Tilley love it if she lost her head and started spouting scripture while her crew halted their work to stare at her?

She focused her attention on the job at hand. Refitting this buoy was the crew's last official task on this trip, and when it was over, they would head for Kodiak. The remote possibility that she would see Aven within the next few days considerably lightened her mood.

When the men had finished their work, she handed one of them her clipboard. "Perform the checklist and make sure this buoy is in top condition, Daley."

"Aye, aye, Petty Officer Lyle."

She held back a smile as the earnest young man began the new task. Daley was close to testing for a pay grade increase, and she'd been advised to give him more responsibility.

When he'd finished running down the checklist, he handed the clipboard back to her. "All set, ma'am."

"Don't call me ma'am," she said softly. He nodded. "All right then, Daley. I'll check our position." As buoy deck supervisor, she calculated their position herself, ensuring that the navigational aid would be returned to the right place in the water so sailors could trust it to keep them from straying into the shallows. "Men, take your positions to release the chain stoppers. Daley, signal the crane operator."

Daley gave the command, and the crane lifted the buoy again and swung it toward the side of the ship.

Caddie held her breath as she watched. That thing weighed as much as a small car, and the crew exercised great respect for airborne objects of that magnitude, standing well back in case anything went wrong and the buoy unexpectedly crashed to the deck.

It was nearly to the rail when a rogue wave caught the ship, interrupting its regular pitch and roll, tilting them sideways. Everyone grabbed the nearest stable object.

Caddie was near the lifeboat rack and braced herself against it. When the ship rolled back, the mammoth buoy swayed like a pendulum toward the rising rail.

"Watch it," Caddie called to her men. She turned and looked up at the crane operator. "Come on," she said under her breath. "Higher. Get that thing over the side."

Wind whipped her hair, and the deck slanted drastically beneath her feet. Behind her, a shout preceded a loud *thunk*. The deck shuddered. Caddie whirled. Men were scrambling as the buoy shivered in midair then swung out over the waves.

The ship shifted with the next swell. To her relief, the deck came back to near level. The huge buoy had cleared the rail and hung well over the side. The crane operator quickly extended the cable and lowered the buoy to the water.

She exhaled as her men rushed to the rail to watch.

"What's the damage?"

Caddie jumped. Boatswain Tilley, via radio, had spoken rather curtly in her ear. She swallowed hard and turned to look up at the forecastle. "I'll make an inspection, sir."

"No one hurt?"

"Negative." She did a quick mental count of her team, realizing she hadn't actually had time to find out but had spoken quickly to protect them and herself from Tilley's wrath. She strode to the rail trying not to appear in too big a hurry and addressed Daley. "Everyone okay?"

"Yes, ma'am. Petty Officer."

Caddie peered down at the buoy, which bobbed in the foaming water. She said into her radio, "Buoy in place. Over."

"The boatswain has left the fo'cas'l," a seaman replied. "He'll be on deck in a second."

Caddie gulped. If she hadn't guessed anyone else was listening, she'd have thanked him for the warning.

She ordered the men to clean up the deck.

They dashed about collecting scattered tools.

"Lyle."

Caddie managed not to flinch and turned to greet the boatswain. "Boatswain Tilley?"

"Was there any damage when that buoy hit the bulwark?"

"I don't believe so. There's a small dent in the rail. Some paint chipped off. Barely visible."

"Show me."

She straightened her shoulders and marched beside him to where the collision had occurred. "Right there."

Tilley scowled. "Have your men repaint this section of the rail. And when you dismiss your detail, you'll stand an extra watch, Lyle."

Anger boiled up inside her, but she quickly shoved it down and lowered her gaze. "Aye, aye."

"And the crane operator and the man directing him will report to the galley."

She glanced up at him then away. It wouldn't do any good to protest, though the men were not at fault. At least the buoy hadn't hit anyone or anything fragile. "Aye, aye."

Tilley turned on his heel and left the deck.

Caddie stood still for several seconds, calming herself and praying silently before she faced the tasks of dismissing the men and sending Daley and Ricker to KP duty. It wasn't fair. She hated taking the men's recreation time away from them. They'd done nothing to deserve it.

She didn't mind the extra duty for herself, though Tilley shouldn't have given her such an assignment. He wasn't her commanding officer. She wouldn't protest, though. Even if she had the chance to have the order rescinded, she didn't want to deepen Tilley's dislike of her. Another four hours on duty wouldn't hurt her, and accepting his disrespect might even help her to learn patience and submission. Still, she was tired and her arm had begun to ache.

She called her team to attention and gave orders for the small repair job. "Daley. Ricker. When you are dismissed, you will report to the chef in the galley and do whatever he instructs you to do." She didn't meet the men's eyes. If she smiled, grimaced, she would betray the emotion swirling through her. She mustn't give Tilley ammunition. He would accuse her of being soft or disrespectful—or any one of a number of adjectives she'd never considered. "You are dismissed."

She felt very alone as she watched the men leave the deck.

Chapter 9

I can't believe we both have this afternoon free." Aven set their golf bags down near the first tee of Bear Valley, the nine-hole golf course near the base.

Caddie's blue eyes shone as she gathered her things. "Me either. Thanks so much for thinking of this."

"Are you sure your arm can take it?"

"Pretty sure, but if it starts aching, I'll let you know."

"Good." Aven handed her a golf ball.

When he'd learned Caddie's ship would dock in time to allow them half a day together, he'd considered a kayaking venture. That probably would be bad for her arm, though. He wouldn't want to do anything to set her recovery back. He'd held back from asking her at first, for fear she might carry some nebulous resentment for his father's role in her own dad's death. But she'd gotten past that, and he appreciated that proof of her maturity.

"I'm really lousy at golf, in spite of my name," she said with a laugh.

He chuckled, recalling Robyn's comments about Caddie's name. "Me, too." He hesitated and decided to come clean. "Okay, I've only played on a golf course once, and that was here. I did so horribly I never came back."

"Sounds like we'll be evenly matched. And we'd better let anyone behind us play through."

Caddie set up her first ball and teed off.

Aven shielded his eyes and followed the ball's path. "Not bad. I guess." He grinned at her. "Actually, I'm not sure if that's good or not."

"Could have been worse, I guess." She flexed her left arm and smiled at him. "My arm feels fine so far. If I'm sore tomorrow, it'll be because I used my muscles more than usual, not because of the injury. That's pretty well healed now."

"I'm glad." He stooped to set his ball on the tee. "Now that the sun's getting lower, the breeze off the bay feels chilly for August."

"Yes, I'm glad I wore my vest today." Caddie stood back a little and waited for him to swing.

Just knowing she was watching made him nervous, and he completely missed the ball on his first try. "Oops." He took a deep breath and concentrated. The second swing was a little better, sending the ball flying up the fairway nearly as far as Caddie's had gone. Aven exhaled in relief. Maybe he should have chosen something he knew more about.

They blundered their way through the nine holes. Caddie kept him laughing, and in the end their scores were fairly even.

After they returned their equipment to the clubhouse, Aven tried to think of a way to prolong the interlude together. "How about a soda in the snack bar?"

Caddie glanced into the crowded shop. "There are a lot of people in there. What if we got drinks and took them outside?"

Aven bought two bottled soft drinks, and they hurried outside. They found a bench in the sun, and she seemed content to sit there with him, around the corner of the clubhouse where they couldn't be seen from the parking lot.

Aven slid close to her and rested his arm on the back of the bench behind her. "Warm enough?" he asked.

"Yes."

The breeze ruffled her hair and shot golden highlights through it.

"So, how did your cruise go? Everything all right?"

"Pretty much," she said. "How about you? You didn't say much about your last deployment. Any arrests this time?"

"No." He sipped his soda and inched closer to her, bringing his arm down around her shoulders.

She smiled without looking at him.

He felt comfortable, not awkward, with her now and was thankful for the milestones they'd passed. "We gave quite a few citations, but we didn't have to impound any boats or haul anyone in."

"Good. Hey, I didn't tell you about my grandmother's newspaper."

"No, I can't say that you have. Your grandmother has a newspaper?"

She chuckled. "No, she subscribes to one. She lives in Oregon, and she wrote and told me that they run a travel feature every Sunday. She suggested I write an article about Kodiak Island and send it to her paper."

"Are you going to?"

"Thinking about it."

Aven nodded, picturing Caddie's photos splashed across the page and her name in the byline. "Be sure to send a few of your bear pictures."

"Definitely. And I thought maybe I'd call a few of the charter boat owners and the people who have tourist lodges."

"Yeah, that'd make a great layout." He looked out over the brilliant green before him. At last Caddie was right where he'd yearned to have her. For weeks he'd longed to be with her, to hold her in his arms, and to have the chance for another serious, in-person talk with her. This was more than he'd hoped for. He sent up a silent prayer of gratitude.

She leaned away from him a little, and he felt a cool breeze cut between them.

"I wasn't entirely honest a minute ago." She frowned and met his gaze. "It's true nothing major happened on my deployment, but even so, I don't feel good about it."

"Why not?"

She shrugged. "Maybe I was away from the job too long. It seemed as though some of my shipmates felt I'd let them down."

"It's not like you were slacking. You broke your arm."

"I know. But. . .we were just getting to work as a real team and I left for a month. And things that bothered me before seemed worse this time. Like Tilley. I've felt from the start as though he was watching me, looking for something to criticize. It was worse than ever this time. Maybe he thinks it was my fault that I got hurt. And what about this—maybe it was."

"It couldn't have been. You were out there doing everything you could to save those fishermen. You didn't do anything stupid or negligent. The sea got you. That's all." Aven drew her gently back into the circle of his arm.

Caddie let him, and she nestled in against his sweatshirt, resting her head just below his collarbone. "Thanks."

He gave her a little squeeze. "All right. Aside from Tilley and feeling inadequate, how did it go?"

She sighed, and he wondered what thoughts plagued her. He sat still, waiting without speaking, stroking her shoulder gently.

After a couple of minutes, she pulled in a deep breath. "When I joined the Coast Guard, I thought this would be my life. Twenty or thirty years anyway."

"And now?" he asked.

"Now I'm not so sure. Since Dad died, I've had these doubts as to whether I really belong here. Did I join because I wanted to sail and have adventures? To serve my country? Or to make Dad happy? I'm doing well at the job, I think—that is, I was until I broke my arm—but now I wonder if I was wrong. Did I make a mistake going into the service?"

"No."

"No? Just like that?" She pushed away from him and studied his face.

Aven smiled. "Everybody goes through this. It's natural. You start second-guessing yourself, wondering if you've overlooked something major. It usually happens right before a test or a transfer."

"Think so?"

"Know so."

"I am studying for my next test."

"See? That'll do it."

She settled back in, and he rested his cheek against the top of her head. She snuggled closer against his side, and Aven closed his eyes for a few seconds. For that moment, he wished they were both far away from Kodiak, free from their military obligations. But only for a moment.

"You know how you mentioned the motto a few weeks back?" she asked.

"Semper paratus."

"Yes. Always ready. Well, I don't feel ready."

"For the physical strain?"

"No. It's more mental and emotional." She raised her head and looked fiercely at him. "We had a minor incident. The seas were rough and a buoy we were hoisting hit the ship's rail, but nobody was injured and none of the equipment was hurt. Tilley punished me and two others."

Aven frowned. "Some people do that. Was he hard on you?"

"No, not really, but it made me angry. With Tilley. He's a bully."

"He's a boatswain. It's part of his job to keep things running smoothly."

She shook her head. "This wouldn't help things run better. Those men did nothing wrong, and he had to know it. That wave that rocked us was a fluke."

"What did he do to you?"

She shrugged. "An extra shift. It wasn't that bad, and I managed to control my reaction. But it made me furious inside, and then it made me sad and depressed."

"Did you pray about it?"

"I tried. It didn't seem to help mend my attitude."

They sat still for a long time, until Aven stirred. "I don't have all the answers, but sometimes things happen in the service that we don't think are right."

"Oh, I know. This wasn't all that important. That's part of what worries me. Why am I making it such a big deal? Because Tilley made a big deal out of a small incident?"

"Maybe. But you need to keep your focus where it belongs. No matter what happens—no matter if your CO is a nutcase, or if you lose a man overboard, or if your paycheck gets lost on its way to your bank account—you have to remember that God's in charge. As far as God is concerned, I figure I'm still in recruit training."

Caddie tilted her head to one side. "I suppose so. I know I have a long way to go."

"We all do. But when I think of our motto, I don't just think of being ready to fulfill my duties or being ready to help people in trouble. I think about being ready for whatever God brings my way."

She let her shoulders slump and shook her head a little. "You make it sound easy."

"Sorry. It's not. It's easy to say but hard to do on a consistent basis."

"So, you don't think I made a mistake when I enlisted?"

"No. That's what you felt God called you to do at the time."

Her blue eyes glistened, and he wondered if she was on the verge of tears. Her voice cracked when she spoke again. "Does God change His mind?"

"No, but He might change yours."

She swung her half-empty bottle of cola through the air in a gesture of frustration. "But I was so sure!"

Aven shifted on the bench to face her squarely. "With me it's the opposite. I joined the Coast Guard mostly as a way to finance my education. After I got in, I found out I loved it. This is my education and career rolled into one. I just didn't know it eight years ago."

Caddie leaned back against the bench, and Aven ran his fingers over the back of her vest, between her shoulder blades. She nodded slowly. "I'm not making any rash decisions. I'll keep in mind what you said and try to take it as it comes."

"Good. One day at a time, and remember God knows all about it."

"Right. But I can't help wondering sometimes if I really belong in this uniform. Maybe I don't have what it takes."

"Don't say that. You've saved lives. Every day you're serving your country. Even if you don't stay in for the long haul, you've contributed a great deal." He turned her gently toward him. "And, Caddie, we wouldn't have met if you hadn't enlisted. This wasn't a mistake. It may be a step on the path to something different, but don't ever think it was a mistake."

⚓

When the *Wintergreen* docked on September 6 after a three-week deployment, Caddie could feel autumn in the air. All hands were instructed to bring their cold weather gear on the next cruise.

With ten days in port, she had a reasonable hope of seeing Aven before she sailed again, though his cutter was not at its mooring when she arrived home.

The next day, she was due on deck to help with the refitting of the ship, after which she could enjoy a three-day furlough. Before she left her apartment for the day, she took an unexpected phone call from Oregon.

"Miss Lyle?"

"Yes." She didn't recognize the voice, and anyone connected to her life in the Coast Guard would address her as "Boatswain's Mate Lyle" or "Petty Officer Lyle."

"This is Marshall Herting of the *Oregonian*."

Caddie caught her breath. "Oh, hello."

"I've been looking at your story on Kodiak. I like it very much."

It was a good thing he couldn't see her, with the silly smile she wore. "Thank you very much."

"We'd like to feature it in our next weekend edition. We'll be mailing you a check."

"That's wonderful. Thank you."

"Do you have any more travel stories?"

"Well, I. . .no, not really. I haven't prepared any, that is. I'm sure I could. Do you want more stories on Alaska?"

"We'd rather see some other destinations. Do you live in Alaska?"

"No. Yes. Well, for now." She swallowed hard. "See, I'm in the military."

"Oh?"

"Yes, sir. I'm in the Coast Guard. I'm stationed at Kodiak for now."

"Ah. That explains your choice of subject." After a pause, he said, "You did an excellent job on the story. You must have spent a lot of time preparing it."

"Quite a bit, but I enjoyed it. I was able to talk to several hunting and fishing lodge operators while I was off duty."

"Well, your photos are fantastic. Made me want to run out and buy a ticket to Kodiak."

Caddie laughed. "Come next summer. It's starting to get chilly here now."

"I may do that. Contact me if you come up with any more ideas."

"Thank you, sir. I will."

She clicked off her phone, smiling. The money from the article wasn't a huge amount, but the satisfaction she felt made up for that.

Quickly she keyed in her grandmother's number. "Hi, Gram? It's Caddie. I'm sorry to call so early, but I'm due at work in a few minutes."

"Hello, dear," came her grandmother's warm voice. "What are you up to?"

"I wanted to tell you that your paper is buying my story. They'll run it next weekend."

Gram's crowing could surely be heard throughout her senior citizens' complex. "Sweetie, that's terrific! I knew you could do it! You always used to write cute stories, and those pictures you sent home last spring were amazing. Now, what are you going to do next?"

"Next?" Caddie blinked. Apparently Gram wasn't satisfied with one article. "Well, Mr. Herting did ask if I had any more travel stories in mind. But I can't travel now."

"Hogwash. You travel all the time."

"Well, yeah, but he didn't want a whole series on Alaska."

"Can't you do research on the computer for other places?" Gram asked.

"Well, maybe, but it wouldn't be the same as going to the destination."

"I know. You'll have to sell Alaska articles to other newspapers. Magazines, too."

"Oh, Gram, I don't know. I don't have enough free time to figure all that out."

"But, sweetie, you're a natural. I've kept that letter you wrote me when you'd been to Homer. It made me cry. And the pictures you took of the mountains and the ship your daddy sailed on and that funny little lighthouse."

Caddie frowned. "You mean the Salty Dog?"

"That's it."

She stifled a laugh. The Salty Dog was a bar frequented by tourists on Homer Spit. Caddie had snapped the photo because of the odd architecture of the historic building-turned-tavern.

"Oh, Gram, I don't know."

"A lot of magazines have travel stories, not just travel magazines. My women's magazines each have one every month."

"Hmm." Caddie recalled a decorating magazine she'd seen in the doctor's office with an article about a New England farmhouse. Maybe they would take an article about decorating with Native Alaskan art. She was sure Jo-Lynn could help her find some local artists and collectors. "I'll think about that when I have time. Thanks, Gram! I love you."

Chapter 10

In late September, the *Milroy* plied the waters of Prince William Sound and Cook Inlet, checking salmon, cod, and scallop catches. Aven's sporadic communication with Caddie kept him eager for the next e-mail or phone call.

When his ship put in at Seward for half a day, he tried her cell phone but couldn't get through. Her ship was scheduled to take supplies to scientists doing research in the Walrus Islands State Game Sanctuary in Bristol Bay. But her latest e-mail came through just fine.

> *Hey, I've been thinking a lot about what you and my Gram said about my pictures and writing. That article for the newspaper got my ambition bubbling, and I've gotten guidelines for several magazines by e-mail. I had a chance this morning to get some fantastic shots of walrus in the wild, and now I'm looking for magazines that might be open to a photo essay. There's one that's looking for stories about women in unusual jobs, and I thought immediately of your sister, Robyn. Do you suppose she'd let me photograph her sometime? Gotta go! I miss you.*

Aven smiled as he reread the message. He clicked on "Reply" and typed:

> *I think that's a great idea, but you realize that to photograph Robyn and her dogs, you'd have to be within a thousand miles of her, right? Not that I think you can't do it. You've got the ingenuity to make it happen. Let's pray for a chance to go to Wasilla together.*

He hesitated for a moment. Taking Caddie home to meet the family would be a huge step. He'd never brought a woman home before. His mother and Robyn—even Grandpa—would assume things were sailing full steam toward permanence. Did he want them to think that?

In spite of the slightly scary factor, the idea sat well with him, and he clicked "Send." Too late to take back the invitation. Now for the prayer. It would be next to impossible to get a long enough leave for both of them at the same time. But then, God specialized in the impossible.

⚜

Caddie ducked into the crowded cabin she shared with Operations Specialist Lindsey Rockwell. Bunks, lockers, a shared desk—those took up most of the space.

But Caddie was used to tight quarters on a ship.

She was thankful to have other women aboard, even though Lindsey seemed a bit standoffish. The other two females—who bore the rank designation "seaman" despite their gender—had quarters nearby. Those two talked more than Lindsey, and in Dee Morrison's case sometimes to the point of annoyance. Because of the nature of her duties, Caddie didn't spend much time with Dee or her roommate, Vera Hotchkiss.

Lindsey was stretched on her bunk, the bottom one, which she'd occupied long before Caddie was transferred to the *Wintergreen*.

"Hi," Caddie said. "Whatcha reading?" She smiled and watched Lindsey's face to gauge her mood.

"Just a magazine."

Her listless voice set Caddie's internal mood gauge at "bored, a little tired, but not hostile." Did Lindsey resent her? Caddie had been away from the ship for more than a month. Had Lindsey wished she wouldn't return and reclaim her space in the cabin?

Caddie stooped and caught a glimpse of the cover. "That looks interesting. Do they have travel stories?"

"Travel? I guess so. Why? Are you taking a vacation?"

Caddie laughed. "No. I'm earning extra money by writing travel stories."

"For real?" Lindsey sat up and swung her legs over the edge of the bunk. "Is that what you've been working on with the laptop?"

"Yeah. I'm trying to sell articles and pictures."

"You take good pictures."

"Thanks." Caddie peeled off her jacket and hung it in her locker. "I heard we may go as far as Nome on our next deployment."

Lindsey shrugged. "Maybe."

"It'll be the farthest north I've ever been. I'd kind of like to see Nome."

"There's not much there. And it's kind of late in the season to head toward the Arctic Circle."

Lindsey flopped back on her bunk, and Caddie wondered if keeping the conversation going was worth the effort. A sudden idea jogged her, but she cast it aside. "So, do you know what we're having for supper?" Even to her, it sounded lame.

"No."

The idea wouldn't go away. Caddie took her hairbrush from her locker and snapped on the clip-on light so she could see what she was doing in the mirror inside the locker door.

Lord, is this thought from You, or is it a crazy whim of mine? I don't want to say something just to get Lindsey to talk. It could turn out all wrong, and I'd regret mentioning it.

She waited but felt nothing. Her hair was disheveled from the wind, and she began coaxing it into place with her brush.

"Did you get some good pictures when you went out to look at the walrus yesterday?" Lindsey asked.

"Yeah, I did. I'm hoping to sell some, but I'm not sure where yet." Caddie inhaled slowly. Her stomach fluttered, but she decided it was now or never. She turned and smiled at her roommate. "You know what I'd really like to photograph?"

Lindsey looked up from her magazine. "What?"

"You."

"You're not serious."

"Yes, I am."

Lindsey lowered the magazine and stared at her. "Why?"

Caddie smiled. *Hooked. Thank You, Lord. Help me to make good on this.* "I've found a magazine that's interested in profiles of women in unusual jobs. I'd love to do an article on you. Take some pictures of you on the bridge, maybe a few on deck. Then, for a change of pace, take some on shore when we get leave. Give the readers an idea of what our life is like. Four of us women, living on a ship with fifty men."

Lindsey's eyes crinkled. "I don't know. You think they'd buy something like that?"

"Yes, I do." Caddie sat down on the stool they used when sitting at the desk. "I thought about asking Dee or Vera, but let's face it, Dee's not very photogenic. Vera might be okay, but I think what you do is much more impressive. Not only do you live in a man's world, you've begun to climb the ladder of rank. I think it'd be a great story, Lindsey. And your eyes. . ."

"What about my eyes?" Lindsey scowled.

"They're gorgeous. I never know whether they're green or blue."

"Me either. It depends on what color the water is that day."

Caddie laughed and pointed a commanding finger at her. "See, that's part of your uniqueness. Any other woman would have said it depended on what color she wore that day."

Lindsey shrugged. "We've always got the ocean at our backs, or at least it seems that way."

"You're right. And that's what I want to get across. It's lonely out here, even though we're packed in like sardines."

The blue-green eyes flickered, and the ghost of a smile trembled on Lindsey's lips.

Caddie thought how seldom she'd seen Lindsey smile, and how pretty she was in that moment. "It'd make your momma proud," she teased.

At last Lindsey let loose with a genuine laugh. "Do you really think you could sell my story?"

"I'm not sure. But we could have fun trying."

⁜

"So what do you want. . .thirty days?" Lieutenant Greer asked.

"No, nothing like that," Aven said quickly. "A week, maybe?"

"Well, you've got time coming. But if I give it to you this month, you'll miss a deployment, and it will wind up being more than a week. If we're not in port when you've finished your business, you'll have to wait until we get back." Greer sat on the edge of his desk, studying the work schedule. "I might be able to give you ten days, starting two weeks from today."

"That's fine, but I don't want you to put the paperwork in yet. I need to get my ducks in a row."

"Oh?"

"Yeah, well. . ." Aven felt his face redden. "I need to coordinate with someone else."

The skipper tilted his head toward his shoulder. "What aren't you telling me, Holland?"

"Nothing you need to know, sir."

Greer's eyes narrowed. "You're not violating regulations, are you?"

"No. Absolutely not."

"Good. So what *are* you doing?"

Aven gritted his teeth. No way to get out of this. "She's on another ship." There. He'd said it.

Greer stared at him for a moment then laughed. "Is that all? Why so secretive?"

"I just. . .I didn't want all the men to know. I'd never hear the end of it."

"I see. All right. It'll be our little secret. Let me know when you want to begin your leave."

"Thank you, sir." Aven left the ward room to the sound of Greer's laughter.

He wasn't at all sure that Caddie could get time off, since she'd just finished a medical leave, but if the timing was right, he might be able to whisk her away for a few days during his ten days off duty. If it didn't work out, he'd just have to wait awhile.

He went in search of Mark and found him in the engine room, where the men had a weight bench and a stationary bicycle—the closest they could come to a gym on board. "Mark, I need your opinion on a private matter." It was a signal they'd worked out between cruises, when Jo-Lynn broke the news that she was pregnant. If Mark wanted Aven to find a quiet spot on the ship and pray with him, he asked for Aven's "opinion."

Now the tables were turned, but Mark picked up the signal, grabbed his towel, and followed Aven into the companionway. "What's up?"

"Didn't mean to interrupt your workout."

"It's okay."

Aven looked over his shoulder. So far, so good. A few seconds might be all they got alone. "Would you pray for Caddie and me? I want to take her home to meet my family, but we'd need at least three or four days. That's if we fly. She'll make a fuss if I try to pay for plane tickets, but I doubt she can take more time off, since she just had all that medical leave."

"Yeah, that could be tough to pull off."

At that moment, the ship's bell rang. Aven checked his watch. "I've got to run. I'm taking a detail to inspect another boat this afternoon."

"Have fun. I'm off until tonight."

Aven hurried up the ladder to the main deck. Just as he came into the open, his radio burbled. "Boatswain's Mate Holland, please report to the bridge."

Seaman Kusiak and another man had come on deck, and Aven called, "I'll be right with you." He hurried up to the bridge.

Greer waited. "The U.S. Marshal's office just informed us that the fishing boat we impounded in June is being auctioned in Anchorage."

"The *Molly K*?"

"That's the one."

Aven wondered why this was important to him. Impounded boats were sold at auction, and the money was put toward law enforcement equipment. The crews who made the arrests and impoundments weren't usually involved in that end of the case. "Is there a problem?"

"They're not sure. Seems Captain Andrews placed a bid on his boat."

"He's allowed to do that."

"Yes." Greer frowned and looked down at the printout in his hand. "But Andrews filed for bankruptcy after we took the boat. Now he shows up with a large chunk of cash to bid on it."

"And they want to know where he got it."

"That's right."

Aven followed his skipper to the big windows that looked out on the sea ahead. His team waited down on the main deck. In the distance, several fishing boats bobbed on the shallow waves.

"Is the marshal's office looking into it?"

"They may hand it to the state police," Greer said. "I told him we didn't have any information about Andrews's income, other than his fishing business, but we'll share anything we turn up."

Aven nodded. "It's unlikely that we will come across anything. Now, we might run into some of his former crew members in other places."

"Yeah." Greer sighed. "Well, I just wanted to let you know and to tell you to watch your back, Holland. You never know when one of those fishermen who attacked you will show up on another boat you're inspecting. And they carry grudges, believe me."

⚜

Caddie used her morning free time to photograph Lindsey at work on the bridge. With Captain Raven's permission, she took her camera to Lindsey's communications center while the ship sailed steadily toward civilization, on its way to refit buoys within Cook Inlet. She hoped they would get to go ashore in Anchorage, as she'd never seen the city, and perhaps Homer. She wouldn't have much chance to build her portfolio of wildlife photos, but she'd have breathtaking backdrops for her photos of Lindsey. The inactive volcanoes around Kachemak Bay would be perfect if they did stop at Homer. And while they sailed, with only ocean on every side, she found Lindsey a more accessible subject.

"I feel silly with you hanging around with that camera," Lindsey said with a scowl.

"Just do what you normally do," Caddie told her. "I'll snap a few candid pictures while you're working."

"It's too weird. The guys are all distracted, wondering what we're up to."

Caddie had wondered if the occasional stares the officer of the deck and two other petty officers at work threw their way would rattle her model, but she'd secured the go-ahead from Captain Raven in advance, and she wasn't going to throw away her chance.

"Ignore me," she said. "Ignore those guys, too."

She found that Lindsey was most relaxed when she stood back several paces and used her zoom lens to get the close-ups she wanted.

When Lindsey's shift was over, they went below to the mess hall and got a cup of coffee.

Sitting in a corner with her notebook on the knee of her blue uniform pants, Caddie smiled at her roommate. "Let's talk a little bit about your background. I don't think you've ever told me why you joined the Coast Guard."

Lindsey hesitated. "You want the truth?"

"Of course." Caddie smiled, but her interviewee wasn't smiling.

"I wanted to get away from home." Lindsey inhaled deeply, not meeting her gaze. "Things weren't good between me and my folks. I wanted out of there as soon as I graduated."

"Wow. That surprises me." Caddie couldn't help the mental contrast between her own years of longing to enlist in the branch of service that her father was a part of and Lindsey's apparently random choice. "Why the Coast Guard, though? Why not the army or the navy?"

Lindsey shrugged. "Their recruiter came to my school first."

Caddie forced herself to look down at her notebook and scribbled a doodle on her paper, pretending to take notes.

When she glanced up, Lindsey's nerves again showed in her sober face, and she twisted her mug back and forth in her hands. "I'm not sure I'd want you to print that in a magazine."

Caddie leaned toward her and lowered her voice. "I'm sorry. I didn't mean to barge right in on a sensitive topic. And I'd never put something you're uncomfortable about in the article."

Lindsey licked her lips. "Okay. Well, maybe we can talk about something else and come back to that later."

"Sure." Caddie sat back and checked her list of questions. "What do you like best about your job?"

"Hmm. I have to think about that. I suppose knowing I've done a good job. At least in the military, you know when you're doing okay and when you're not."

"How do you mean?"

Lindsey sipped her coffee and paused for a moment, looking off into space. "It's just that before. . .well, at home mostly. . .I never knew if I was going to get yelled at or what. I liked school better, because if I worked hard there and stayed out of trouble, I could do well. For the most part, the teachers were fair. And that's what I found in the Coast Guard. Basic training was tough, but I knew when I passed each part that I'd succeeded."

"You must have done well in your advanced training, too."

"Pretty well, I guess." Lindsey straightened her shoulders. "I was determined to make it. Because I wasn't going back. I had nothing to go back to."

Caddie studied her pinched face. Although sorrow shadowed her heart, Lindsey didn't want pity; she could see that. "You've done a good job."

Lindsey's features relaxed. She closed her eyes for a moment then opened them, still determined but less wary. "Thank you."

"It was different for me. I didn't want to get away from home so much as I wanted to get into the Coast Guard. My father was—"

"I know. Your father was an illustrious officer."

Caddie felt stung. Was this what had caused the underlying animosity she'd felt emanating from Lindsey since she'd transferred to the *Wintergreen*?

"Yes," she said softly. "I wanted to be like him. Now I wonder if my ambition was misdirected."

"Oh? He *was* a good officer. I've heard people talk about him."

"Yes, but. . .I'm not so sure he was a good father." Caddie squirmed a bit in her chair.

Okay, Lord, I'm supposed to be doing the interviewing here. Do You really want me to talk about this?

"Then why did you want to please him so badly?"

"That's just it. I didn't think that was my motive. At least, I never used to look at it that way, but. . .well, a lot of the time, Dad wasn't there. He was always off at sea. Mom stayed home with us kids, and she never got bitter about it. She built him up as a hero for us."

"What's wrong with that?"

"I don't think we ever really knew Dad for the man he was. Only the man we *thought* he was. Because we could only snatch time with him here and there. I'm not saying he wasn't a good person. Only that I didn't really know. And I think that might be why, as a kid, I fixated on joining the service. To be like him. To have that in common with him. To have something special with him that I'd never had before."

Lindsey sighed. "Well, trust me, a dream kind of father is way better than the kind of father I had. At least you didn't have to run away from him."

They sat in silence. A couple of sailors came from the galley and began restocking the supplies for the next meal.

Caddie thought about Lindsey's words. *Dear Lord, I don't think I've ever really appreciated the father You gave me. Please show me how to relate to Lindsey in a way that will help her.*

Her pulse picked up as she wondered what to say. Why was it so hard? Maybe because she'd always figured Lindsey would sneer if she tried to talk to her about spiritual things.

"You know," she said at last, "you're absolutely right. Even though my dad had some faults, and even though he never spent as much time at home as we all would have liked, he wasn't bad as fathers go. And I miss him a lot." Tears welled in her eyes. "These past few years, I've had to rely on my heavenly Father for security."

Lindsey's eyebrows shot up and that "Here it comes" expression crept over her face.

Caddie plunged on. "I've never said much to you about my faith. . ."

"I've seen your Bible on the desk in the cabin once or twice."

Caddie started to speak but caught herself. Her impulse was to apologize. But should she? She'd tried hard not to make an issue of her faith on the assumption that Lindsey would be offended. Had she instead erred in keeping quiet?

"We never went to church or anything when I was a kid," Lindsey said.

"We always did."

"Is that why you read the Bible? Because you were brought up that way?"

"I suppose it was at first. But now I read it because I want to. It tells me what God expects and how I should live. Best of all, it tells about Jesus Christ, and how He died for my sins."

Lindsey shook her head. "I never understood any of that—how people think that one person somehow took care of all the evil in the world. You only have to look around to see that it's still there. How did Jesus's dying help?"

Caddie inhaled slowly. She tended to sort all that she knew into mental pigeonholes. Which one should she reach into? "Okay, first of all, Jesus didn't die to clean up the world."

"He didn't? I thought everybody's sins were supposed to be wiped out somehow when He died."

"Well, in a way. . ." Caddie glanced at her watch. "You know, I have to report for duty in about twenty minutes. I'm not trying to get out of this conversation. I really want to discuss it with you. But I need to be where my Bible is when we talk about it. That way I can show you what God says in the Bible about sin and forgiveness."

"I don't know." Lindsey shook her head. "It doesn't make sense to me."

"But you've never read the Bible, have you?"

"No. I saw the Charlton Heston movie."

Caddie smiled. "There's a lot more to it than that. Look, tomorrow morning we're both free. Let's talk then, okay?"

"I guess so. What about the article?"

"Oh, I'm going to finish it. I'll work on it some tonight, and I'll need to ask you some more questions, but this is really important. About God, I mean."

Lindsey nodded slowly. "All right." She stood and reached for Caddie's coffee mug. "Just, please, if I tell you to stop, you won't keep on and on about it, will you?"

"No. I'll quit talking about it if you want me to."

"Great. See you." Lindsey walked away toward the window where they left the dirty dishes.

Caddie let out a breath. *Lord, help me to do better tomorrow. Let me get it right the first time so she doesn't tell me to shut up. Please?*

Chapter 11

Aven stared at the computer screen and scowled. No matter how he worked it out, Caddie couldn't get enough time off to go to Wasilla with him for at least two months. The *Wintergreen* would dock next week while he was at sea, but only for a few days, and then the ship would head out on a six-week cruise. Caddie would have to be back in Kodiak in time to join her ship for that cruise. No excuses.

He had so much leave stacked up that he really should take some anyway. He ran a hand through his hair, unable to decide what to do.

His cell phone rang, and he pulled it out. "Yeah, Holland."

"This is Lieutenant Greer. A gentleman is here from the U.S. Marshal's office, wanting to speak to you."

"Me?" Aven cast about the recesses of his mind for a reason.

"Affirmative."

A few minutes later, Aven boarded the *Milroy* and entered the wardroom.

Greer stood and gestured toward a lean, middle-aged man wearing a suit. "Holland, this is Deputy U.S. Marshal Ralph Eliot."

Aven shook his hand.

"You remember I told you about the *Molly K* being auctioned?" Greer asked as they all sat down.

"Sure," Aven said. "And the former owner bid on her."

"That's right. Have a seat. Eliot, here, has more news about that." Greer nodded to the deputy marshal.

"Jason Andrews bought his boat back," Eliot said. "Paid cash for it. Forty-seven grand."

Aven gave a low whistle. "I thought he filed for bankruptcy. How could he have that much socked away?"

"That's the question." Eliot reached into his inside jacket pocket and took out a small notebook. "This summer, Andrews was practically going bust. You know how all the fishermen have complained that the catch is poor this year."

"Yeah," Aven said. "They have to go farther to fill their quotas."

"Uh-huh. Well, Andrews was falling behind on his house payments. He told his bank in June he couldn't make the regular payment. They cut him some slack and let him refinance. Then he loses the boat. Financial disaster, right? But then he comes up with all this money for the boat on a couple of months' notice."

"He didn't sell the house, did he?" Aven asked.

"Nope. He and his wife are still living in it, along with three daughters and one grandkid."

"Okay, I give up. Where did the money come from?"

"That's what we'd like to know. The scuttlebutt is that the men of his crew scraped it up for him."

Aven pulled back and frowned. "That doesn't make a lot of sense. His men were worse off than he was. How could the six of them come up with that much money?"

"That's a good question. And did they just do it out of the goodness of their hearts?"

Aven thought about it, but it still didn't add up. "Six men pass the hat because they feel bad for their boss and come up with forty-seven thousand dollars in cash? I don't think so."

Greer tapped a pen on his desk. "Maybe some of them had some assets. Or some connections. I wonder if they all felt guilty. After all, from what Holland tells me, it was their fault he lost his boat."

"That's right," Aven said. "I gave Andrews a citation, but then the men started a brawl. That's what clinched it. If they hadn't assaulted us, we never would have impounded the boat."

"That's what I thought." Eliot studied his notebook for a moment then slid it back inside his jacket. "I wanted to check the details of the confrontation with you before I talked to Andrews's crew."

"You're going out and talk to them all?"

"Going to try. Most of them live in the Seward area. That's where Andrews lives. But two of them live out here on Kodiak."

"Spruce Waller being one," Aven said.

Eliot's eyes narrowed. "Yeah. Do you know something about him?"

"Not really. Just that his brother, Clay, has a boat and someone gave us a tip a few weeks ago that he was running drugs." He looked toward Greer. "Our cutter chased him, but he outran us and ducked into a channel we couldn't navigate."

The lieutenant nodded in acknowledgment. "That's right. The tip came in as an anonymous call to our communications center. I learned later that a woman made the call."

Aven continued, "A few days after we tried to run that boat down, I saw Spruce Waller and his brother repainting a boat over at Anton Larsen Bay. I think it was Clay Waller's boat, tied up in front of Spruce's cabin. But I wasn't a hundred percent sure."

"Did you do anything about it?"

"I told the state police, but they didn't seem to give it high priority. They did enlarge the pictures I gave them and confirmed the two men doing the painting were Spruce and Clay Waller."

Greer scratched his jaw. "We speculated that after we impounded the *Molly K*, Spruce Waller may have started working with his brother, but we don't have any hard evidence."

Aven nodded. "So what if the Waller brothers are running drugs, and some of that drug money went to buy Captain Andrews's boat back?"

Eliot drew in a deep breath. "That would be hard to prove."

"But if you *could* prove it, you'd put the drug runners away," Aven said.

"Yes, and we'd get to auction the *Molly K* again." Eliot smiled. "Any ideas on how we might do that?"

Aven's adrenaline surged. Finally, he could *do* something. "I'd be happy to go with you when you interview the two crewmen who live near here."

"Great." Eliot brought out the notebook again. "Spruce Waller and Terry Herman. Both live in Kodiak."

"I'm free this afternoon. Let's try Herman first," Aven suggested. "He may be easier to catch up with than Waller."

Half an hour later, Aven stood back and let Eliot knock on the door of a weathered duplex.

A baby was crying inside. The door swung open, and the wailing increased in pitch.

A young woman gazed at them. "Yes?" Her plain features hovered between curiosity and fear. Aven took in the ragged flannel shirt she wore over a tank top and faded jeans. No makeup. Her only jewelry consisted of a wedding ring and a cheap digital watch.

"I'm Deputy U.S. Marshal Ralph Eliot, and this is Petty Officer Aven Holland with the Coast Guard. We'd like to speak to Terry Herman."

The young woman looked them up and down, eyeing Eliot's suit and Aven's uniform. Aven wondered if he should be watching the back door. The baby's wails became screams.

"Come on in." She swung the door wide open and turned to scoop the baby out of a mesh playpen. "Terry, you got company." She and the baby disappeared through a doorway, and the crying stopped.

A lanky young man in jeans and a faded black T-shirt unfolded himself off the sofa and stood eyeing them. Eliot again made the introductions.

Herman nodded at Aven. "I recognize you. Am I in trouble again? Because I paid my fine."

"We just want to ask you some questions," Aven said.

Herman hesitated then shrugged. "As long as I'm not in trouble." He plopped back down on the sofa and nodded toward a ragged armchair. "Have a seat."

Eliot crossed to the sofa and sat on the end farthest from Herman. Aven took the chair.

"Mr. Herman," Eliot said, "what are you doing for work now?"

Herman huffed out a breath. "Nothing at the moment. I've got a lead on a job. Got to do something when you have a family."

"How have you been living for the last couple of months?"

"Off our savings. It's gone now, though. Crystal's folks helped us some, but I'm probably going to start at the cannery soon." He wouldn't meet Eliot's eyes.

"You're not going to work for Jason Andrews again?" Aven asked.

"Not hardly. He lost the boat."

Eliot said, "You didn't hear? He bought it back at auction a few days ago."

"Huh. No, I didn't know."

"I heard a rumor that his crew had got up the money so Captain Andrews could bid on the boat."

"Maybe so."

"Did you help raise the money?" Eliot asked. "Is that where your savings went?"

Herman rose and walked over to the window. He stood with his hands on his hips, his back to them. "No. I didn't have anything to do with that. We didn't have much put away, and we've spent it mostly on food and rent."

"Do you know who did get the money for Andrews?"

Herman turned and shook his head, staring at Eliot. "Look, I paid my fine. They said if we hadn't gotten into that fight, nobody would have been arrested and the skipper would have kept the boat. Well, it wasn't my fault." He looked over at Aven, his dark eyes anxious. "I'm sorry about what happened. It wasn't my idea to jump you and your men. If it was up to me, we wouldn't have done it. But Spruce was riled, and all the others said they'd back him up. I felt like I had to take part. I got a few licks in, I admit it, but I paid my fine, and I've got a record now. And no, I don't want to go back to working with them again. I want to stay out of jail. Like I said, I've got a kid now. I need to be working a steady job, not mixing it up with the Coast Guard."

Aven caught his gaze and held it for a long moment. "Apology accepted."

Eliot took out his pocket notebook and jotted in it. "Are you saying you think you'd get into trouble again if you went back to work for Captain Andrews?"

"I dunno."

"How long had you worked for him?"

"Just since spring."

"And before that?"

The young man walked back to the sofa and plunked down on it. "I used to go out with Ned Carson's crew. But he died, and his widow sold his boat to someone off the island. So when I heard this Andrews fella needed men last spring, I jumped at it. Needed a berth on a boat, and I didn't ask questions."

Aven leaned forward and asked, "Who told you about the job?"

"One of the men working on the *Molly K.*"

"Spruce Waller?" Eliot asked.

Herman swiveled and stared at him. "Yeah. How. . ."

Eliot shrugged. "He's the only other one of Andrews's crew who lives in Kodiak. How did he connect with Andrews, do you know?"

"No. I think he'd been with him awhile, though. I was hard up for work, and I heard Spruce at a bar one night, talking about leaving to go salmon fishing, so I asked him if they needed help. He said his boss might be hiring and to go with him the next morning. That was that."

"Okay," Eliot said, scribbling in the notebook. "And what's Spruce doing now?"

"I don't know. Haven't seen him since the hearing." Herman's eyelashes lowered and screened his dark eyes.

"Are you sure?" Aven asked.

The young man jerked his head around to look at him. "He went to jail. I was glad I didn't, except for that one night. Since I heard Spruce was out, I've stayed away from places I thought he might be."

"Bad blood between you and Waller?" Eliot stopped writing and arched his eyebrows.

"Not really. But I don't want there to be. Waller's trouble."

"In what way?"

Herman clamped his lips together and shook his head.

Aven bent toward him and clasped his hands together loosely. "Terry, if you know anything it would be in your best interests to tell us."

"Is that a threat?"

"Not at all. But we're going to talk to every man who was on the *Molly K* the day of the fight. We know Captain Andrews didn't have the money to buy the boat back. But he came up with it, and we *will* find out where he got the cash."

"And if we find out you knew," Eliot growled, "you can kiss your wife and baby good-bye, because you'll be doing time for obstructing justice." He rose and stood over Herman, his notebook dangling from his hand. "If you know anything at all, now's the time to speak."

"Terry, tell them about Spruce." The young woman stood in the doorway behind Eliot. She held the baby up against her shoulder and patted his back as she spoke. "If you don't tell, you could get in worse trouble from them than you will from the Wallers."

"Hey, that's great. Hold it!" Caddie snapped the shutter. "Fantastic." She bounded the few steps to Lindsey and showed her the last few shots on the digital camera's small screen.

Lindsey nodded grudgingly. "Not bad. You're a good photographer."

"Thanks. And that necklace is perfect for you." Caddie smiled through gritted teeth and whispered, "Too bad it's only four hundred dollars."

Lindsey chuckled and took the silver and carved wood necklace off. "Yeah, it's really sweet." She went to the counter and handed the necklace back to the shop owner. "Thank you very much."

"I'll be sure to mention your shop in the article," Caddie said, tucking the woman's business card into her pocket.

As they walked outside into the cool sunshine, Lindsey zipped her jacket. "It would be easy to spend a lot of money in a hurry here."

They ambled down the sidewalk in Homer. Most of the tourists had left a month ago, and many of the shops had closed for the season.

"I'm glad we got a chance to have some time ashore together," Caddie said. "If we get enough pictures today, I may be able to finish putting the article together while we're docked in Kodiak next week. Maybe I can send it off before we put out for the long cruise."

"That'd be great." Lindsey paused to study a window display of embroidered sweaters.

"Just don't get your hopes too high," Caddie reminded her. "There's no guarantee the magazine will buy it."

Lindsey shrugged. "It's been fun doing it anyway. And I'm glad we got to know each other better."

"Me, too." Caddie smiled at her.

Getting to know Lindsey had turned out to be the best part of this deployment. For the past three days, they had studied the Bible together during their off-duty hours. Caddie had shown her friend several scripture passages about sin, forgiveness, and salvation through faith in Christ. Her curiosity whetted, Lindsey had asked if she could borrow Caddie's compact Bible and started reading through the Gospels on her own.

"Hey, look," Caddie said, nudging her. "Cups Café. Isn't that the one Dee and Vera were going to have lunch at?"

"Yes. It's darling." Lindsey tilted her head back to look at the wildly painted teacups and saucers on the roof of the little building. "We've got to eat here. Let me snap your picture under the sign first."

After she took the photo, they went inside and paused just inside the door to exclaim over the stained glass panels and handcrafted objets d'art throughout the crowded room.

"There they are!" Caddie had spotted Dee and Vera at a table in a far corner, waving frantically. "Let's join them. I don't see any other free tables." She and Lindsey squeezed between the diners and reached the other two young women.

"Imagine, the entire female contingent of the *Wintergreen* here at the same time," Dee said with a laugh. She gestured to the ornately decorated dining room. "Like it?"

"Love it," Caddie said.

"We're about finished," Vera told her, "but you two can have our table."

"Thanks." Lindsey picked up a glass-beaded napkin ring. "I think I want to live here."

"Order the Cobb salad. It's great." Dee slid out of her chair. "We've got to head back now. See you later."

As the lunch traffic in the café thinned, the chatter quieted, and Caddie and Lindsey picked up the conversation they'd begun that morning on the way into town.

"I read the last two chapters of Matthew this morning," Lindsey said. "I couldn't stop reading. It was so. . .powerful."

"The Crucifixion and Resurrection?"

"Yes. I wish I knew as much about the Bible as you do. I can't believe I've lived this long assuming I knew what it was about but never read any of it. When do I get to the part about the Ten Commandments?"

Caddie chuckled. "That's in the Old Testament, way back near the beginning. You're reading about the time when Jesus lived, which was much later than Moses."

"Oh." Lindsey's brow puckered in a frown. "Why did you have me start reading near the end?"

"Because I wanted you to read about Jesus. You had so many questions about why He came to earth and how His death could help us."

"Mmm. I get it. And what I read this morning. . .I mean, if the part we talked about before is true, about Jesus being God, then"—Lindsey's eyes shone with unshed tears—"it makes sense to me now. He *had* to be the one to pay for our sins."

Caddie reached over and squeezed her hand. "Just wait until you read John. There's so much there about Jesus's nature and His ministry. Oh, I'm going to ask the waitress if there's a bookstore near here. I want to get you a Bible of your own and see if I can find a good, basic study book. That will help answer your questions."

"You're teaching me a lot. I appreciate it."

"Thanks, but I seem to be going at it in a haphazard fashion. I keep wondering if I've skipped over something important. Maybe we should start reading Genesis at the same time. Begin with creation. A chapter each of the Old and New Testaments every day."

Lindsey's laugh burbled out. "I was sure you were a fanatic of the worst kind. Do you know, I avoided being alone with you in our cabin because I was afraid you'd try to preach to me?"

"Really." Caddie swallowed hard. *Thank You, Lord, for helping me not to have that impulse.*

"Yes. But now I can't wait to have an hour free to talk about the Bible with you. It's crazy."

"Not crazy. It's God's doing."

Lindsey nodded, her eyes glinting. "I believe that now, but a week ago I'd have used that statement as proof that you were off your rocker."

The waitress came to take their orders, and for a minute the friends turned their attention to the menus. When they'd made their decisions and learned where to find a bookstore, Lindsey looked across the small table at Caddie. "I never thought I'd say this, but would you ask the blessing, please? And. . .I've decided to call my folks when we get back to Kodiak. Would you please pray for me, that I'll know how to talk to them and what to say?"

"Of course. And when you think of it, maybe you can pray for me. I've started a new correspondence course for the next rating."

"Still figuring to follow in your dad's footsteps?"

"Unless I feel God's leading me otherwise. So I need to keep with the program—you know, keep studying and learning."

"How will you know if God wants you to do something else?"

Caddie pursed her lips. "Well, I know He wants me to stay with the Coast Guard for at least another year and a half, because that's the obligation I have left. But after that. . .who knows? I've decided to keep on as though this is my career for the next fourteen years or so. I want to be ready if it is. And if He has something else for me, He'll show me how to prepare for that."

"Like going to work for a magazine, maybe?"

"I doubt it, but. . .you just never know, do you?" Caddie wondered if Lindsey longed for a family and a real home. The question was on her list for the article, but she hadn't quite had the nerve to ask it yet. Voicing the question would force her to face her own yearnings, and they seemed to be stronger since she'd met Aven.

A woman bustled into the restaurant and joined a young man at a table near Caddie and Lindsey. Her smart black jacket and pants, paired with a lavender silk shirt, pegged her in Caddie's mind as a businesswoman, not a tourist.

"Sorry I'm late," she said to the man.

He jumped up to hold her chair. "You're not late. I got here a few minutes early. I was going to stop at the Hailey Gallery down the street, but they're closed. I thought they were staying open this fall."

"Didn't you hear?" the woman asked. "They've been robbed."

Caddie raised her eyebrows at Lindsey to see if she had overheard. Lindsey pulled a sympathetic face.

"That's awful," the man said. "What happened?"

"It was in the paper. Someone hauled over twenty thousand dollars' worth of scrimshaw and carvings out of there sometime Sunday night."

Lindsey leaned toward Caddie and whispered, "That's fifty of those necklaces I modeled for you."

Caddie nodded. It wouldn't take long for thieves to snatch up a valuable inventory in this neighborhood.

"Hey," said Lindsey, and Caddie snapped back to attention.

"You said something?"

Lindsey grinned. "Yes. Dessert is on me."

⁂

Terry Herman's face clouded and he scowled at his wife. "Shut up, Crystal."

Aven wished he were elsewhere.

"No." She stepped forward. "This is what got you arrested in the first place."

"How do you figure?" Terry asked.

"You knew stuff was going on, but you kept quiet. So instead of getting arrested for drugs, you got pinched for assaulting fisheries cops."

"I couldn't rat on guys I worked with."

Crystal scrunched up her face and shook her head. "You could have just quit and tried to get on a better boat. One where they did things legal."

"I told you to shut up."

Eliot held out one hand in supplication. "All right, folks. Let's stay calm." He sent Terry a meaningful look. "Mr. Herman, as I said before, if you have information that could help our investigation, now is the time to speak. Because withholding stuff like that is a crime."

Terry lowered his head into his hands. "Man, oh, man. Why can't you shut up, Crystal?" He looked up at Eliot. "If I talk to you, Spruce Waller and his brother will find out. No telling what they'll do."

"They won't do much if they're in jail," Eliot said.

Aven glanced over at Crystal. "Mrs. Herman, would you have any coffee?"

She stared at him as if he'd asked for champagne, but after a moment her tight features relaxed. "Sure." She crossed the room and laid the baby on a blanket in the playpen. He stirred and whimpered, then lay still. Crystal went into the kitchen, and Aven heard water running.

Eliot arched his eyebrows at Aven, as though inquiring if he wanted to speak.

Aven nodded and said quietly, "Terry, your wife is right. Talking to us is the best thing you can do right now."

"What if I say no? Are you going to arrest me again?"

Eliot sat down again and let out a breath. "Not today. But I can make it difficult for you to find work, and I'd really like to see you working again. You've got a nice family. You should be bringing home a paycheck, not bouncing in and out of the court system."

Terry stared at the threadbare carpet for a long moment, his lips twitching. At last he looked to Aven. "Listen, you gotta believe me. I don't really know anything, just things I heard the other guys say on the boat, you know?"

"Tell us what you heard," Aven said.

"Spruce Waller's not the main one you want. It's his brother, Clay."

"He's running drugs into Alaska on his boat," Aven said.

Terry's eyes widened. "Yeah. I mean, that's what I heard. He goes out to sea and meets a boat coming in."

"Where from?"

"I don't know. Hawaii? Mexico? All I know is they don't want to touch land, so Clay goes to meet them and gets the stuff."

"He pays them in cash and passes the stuff on to street dealers?"

Terry frowned and flicked a glance at Eliot but continued to address Aven. "I really don't know what he does with it. And if I'd known he was mixed up in drugs, I never would have gone with him to try to get a job. But I did go with him, and. . . well, I heard that sometimes he sends things out of Alaska when he picks up the drugs."

Aven studied his face. "What kind of things?"

Terry looked over his shoulder toward the kitchen. "Look, Crystal doesn't know this. I didn't tell her. She's got friends. . .her brother's married to a Native Alaskan, you know what I'm saying?"

"No." Aven glanced at Eliot, but the deputy marshal shook his head. "What *are* you saying, Terry?"

Herman lowered his voice and leaned toward him. "They're sending out Alaskan art. Bootleg art. Trading it for cocaine. That's what I heard. Don't know if it's true. But I did see Spruce grab a piece of plastic tape off a buoy one time. Another guy— Rowe, I think it was—said it was a signal that someone on the mainland had some stuff for him."

"What kind of stuff?" Aven asked.

Terry shrugged. "Stuff to trade, I guess. Spruce would tell his brother, and they'd go get it. Captain Andrews found out, and he told Spruce that if he didn't get his boat back for him he'd turn in his brother." He jumped up and walked to the kitchen doorway. "That coffee ready, Crystal?"

Eliot said softly, "There've been several big heists on the Kenai Peninsula. Some high-end art galleries and shops have been hit." He started to rise.

"We have to drink the coffee," Aven hissed.

"Okay, but the quicker the better."

Crystal came into the room carrying two steaming mugs. Terry followed with a plastic half-gallon milk jug and a sugar bowl with a spoon sticking out of it.

"Just milk," Aven said. He accepted a mug from Crystal and poured as much milk into it as he could to cool it down.

Crystal walked over to Eliot and handed him the other mug. "Did he tell you?"

"He's been very cooperative," Eliot said. "We'll try not to let anyone know, though."

"Good." She went to the playpen and leaned over it for a moment, watching the baby. She straightened, glanced at her husband, and walked out of the room.

"Look, that's it," Terry said. "I really don't know anything solid. It's just rumors."

"That's right," Aven said with a smile.

"And you didn't tell us anything," Eliot added.

Aven gulped down half his coffee and held the mug out. "Thanks. Keep your head down. Hey, I think my CO knows someone at the cannery. I'll ask him if he can put in a word for you."

He and Eliot hurried out to the deputy marshal's rental car.

"Waller's house first?" Eliot asked.

"Yes." Aven gave him directions to the apartment building. They arrived a few minutes later, but no one answered the door at Spruce Waller's place.

"Now what?"

Aven said, "Last time I went looking for him, he was at his cabin at Anton Larsen Bay."

"How far is it?"

"You can drive it in twenty or thirty minutes."

Eliot checked his watch. "You up for it? It's almost four o'clock."

"Let's do it."

Aven navigated Eliot over the same roads he'd taken Caddie on earlier. His thoughts flew to the *Wintergreen*, and he prayed for her as they passed the riverside where they'd watched the bears. Another thought occurred to him as he recalled the tip his commanding officer had received about the boat they'd pursued. "You know what?"

"What?" Eliot asked.

"Greer said it was a woman who called in reporting that the boat—which we now know was Clay Waller's—was picking up a drug shipment. It wouldn't surprise me if the one who made that call was Crystal."

At Waller's cabin, they drove into the yard and got out, looking around. Aven looked first for Clay's cabin cruiser, but the slip in the cove was empty. A small aluminum boat lay upside down on shore a few yards from the dock. Spruce Waller's SUV was parked beside the cabin.

As Eliot approached the door, Aven slipped around the side of the building. A back door opened into a lean-to woodshed. Eliot knocked on the front door, but the sound reverberated through the cabin with no response.

After fifteen seconds, Eliot pounded on the door again. Nothing.

Aven stepped into the woodshed and lifted the latch on the back door. It swung wide, and a musty smell of dust and old ashes greeted him. He drew his sidearm. "Eliot?"

"Yeah?"

"I'm going in the back."

Eliot yelled something, but Aven didn't hear it. He was already inside, peering past the muzzle of his pistol into the dim interior of the cabin. He looked all around the back room, which seemed to be Waller's bedroom, then walked through the larger front room. He opened the front door.

Eliot stood on the step outside, a pistol in his hand.

"He's not here," Aven said.

Eliot exhaled and pushed his hair back. "Don't do that again. He could have blown your head off."

"He didn't."

"Yeah, well, there's also the little technicality about search warrants."

Aven blinked as he considered that. "Yeah, true."

Eliot peered past him, looking beyond Aven into the dim interior. "You sure he's not hiding someplace?"

"Pretty sure." Aven turned back into the cabin.

Eliot hesitated, looked over his shoulder, and followed. He did a more thorough search than Aven had with no more results.

"So now what do we do?"

Eliot threw him a resigned glance. "Lock the front door and leave."

"He could be anywhere out here."

"Yes, and he could be watching right now through the scope of a rifle."

Aven squeezed his mouth shut tight and waited for further instructions.

"On the other hand," Eliot said, "he could be out in the boat with his brother. Come on. We might as well go back to Kodiak and have dinner."

They got into the car, and Eliot drove in silence. Several times, Aven started to speak, but thought better of it. He'd definitely broken some rules. Had he come down a notch in Eliot's opinion?

As they neared the shopping district in Kodiak, Aven's phone rang. "Hello."

"Mr. Holland? That is. . .Aven Holland?"

"Yes?"

"This is Brett Sellers. I don't know if you remember me, but I made the dog harness for your sister."

"Of course I remember you."

Eliot looked over with raised eyebrows.

Aven shrugged in apology.

"Yeah, well, I hope she likes it," Sellers said.

"She does. She's very happy with it." Was this going to be a sales pitch for more equipment?

Eliot parked in front of a seafood restaurant, and Aven reached to unbuckle his seat belt.

"Well, I saw something that could be related to a crime. I didn't want to call the police, but it's been bothering me all day. Then I remembered you and how you have some sort of law enforcement job. I thought maybe I could run it by you, and you could decide whether the police ought to know."

Aven hesitated with his hand on the door latch. "Okay. What is it?"

"There's a shop next to mine that sells souvenirs. You know, plastic totem poles. Plush polar bears."

"Yeah, okay. What about it?"

"I stopped in there this morning before opening time to see if I could borrow a coffee filter. The owner was packing up some merchandise, but it was way better quality than what he usually carries."

Aven frowned. "So? Maybe he's upgrading his inventory."

"No, listen. He wasn't unpacking it. He was wrapping it and putting it in crates. I saw carved walrus tusks and whale baleen."

Aven's heart skipped. "Is the owner a Native Alaskan?"

"No way. His hair's blonder than mine. He claims he has Russian blood, but I'm skeptical."

"Okay. It's possible he bought the things legally. Tell you what." Aven shot Eliot a glance. The deputy marshal was watching him keenly. "There's a man from the U.S. Marshal's office in Anchorage here in Kodiak right now. Can I bring him to your shop in about twenty minutes?"

"Uh, well. . .it might be better if you just went straight to his. I wouldn't want him to know I ratted on him." Sellers sighed. "He'll know anyway, I suppose."

"It could be perfectly innocent," Aven said.

"Could be. Doubt it. He tried to cover it all up quick when I walked in."

Aven took the name of the souvenir shop and signed off.

Eliot leaned against his car door, waiting. "Well? What was that?" he asked.

"Maybe a wild-goose chase. Head down the street. We've got a tip on allegedly stolen artwork."

Chapter 12

When the *Wintergreen* docked in Kodiak three days later, Caddie went straight to her apartment. She would have only one day off before she was expected back on duty to help ready the ship for their long deployment. The wind held the bite of autumn, and the bitter winter of Alaska would come hard on its heels.

Her dreams of a relationship with Aven seemed to slip away with the summer. Would they ever seize enough time together to get to know each other better? Even though his ship was in port, he might not be able to see her. His last e-mail had told how busy he'd been helping the U.S. Marshal's office track down some smugglers.

She didn't even know how long Aven would be posted in Kodiak. What if he were transferred away? Although his family lived in Alaska, he might be transferred thousands of miles away. She would have to ask him about that.

She dropped her seabag on the rug and wearily sorted the mail she'd picked up. Her spirits lifted when she opened an envelope from the *Oregonian*. The check for her travel story was a nice bonus and would cover most of the Christmas gifts she wanted to buy this year. Already she'd looked over mukluks for Mira and snowshoes for Jordan.

When she came out of the shower half an hour later, the phone was ringing. She ran to answer it, hoping Aven might be on the other end of the connection.

"Hey, you're back!" Jo-Lynn's cheery voice floated to her.

"Yes. How are you doing?"

"Fine, after eleven every morning. Not so good before that. I'm eating like a horse once the morning sickness passes, though. I've got to be careful. Want to come for supper tonight?"

"I think I'd better stay in and get to bed early. How about if I come see you tomorrow?"

"Sure," Jo-Lynn said.

"So. . .I guess Mark's home, too. I saw the *Milroy* at the docks."

"Yeah, they've got a few more days."

I will not ask about Aven, Caddie resolved.

Jo-Lynn saved her the trouble. "Hey, Aven's been tearing into this smuggling case. Did he tell you about it?"

"Not much. Just that he's been busy. I've hardly heard from him in the last week."

"You'll have to get the details from him, but it has something to do with an art theft."

✢

Caddie caught her breath. "When I was in Homer a few days ago, people were talking about an art gallery being robbed. That probably has nothing to do with what you're talking about, though."

"I don't know," Jo-Lynn said. "But I gather there have been a lot of these thefts, and the stolen artwork is being smuggled out of Alaska and sold in Japan and. . . well, like I said, I'm not up on the details, but Mark and Aven were talking about it yesterday."

Caddie slept late the next morning and awoke grumpy and discouraged. Would her relationship with Aven go anywhere or not? She sat on the bed in her flannel pajamas and opened her Bible. Her schedule of reading took her to the last chapter of I Timothy. "But godliness with contentment is great gain," she read. The simple words convicted her.

She had so much—a good job, a loving family, godly friends in Jo-Lynn and Mark, and a new friend in Lindsey. She was thankful for all of them, she realized, and for Aven, too. But was she content?

Lord, thank You for all You've given me, she prayed. *If Aven and I never move beyond friendship, he is still a wonderful gift from You. Help me to treasure each moment we've had together without demanding more. If You want us to grow closer, I'll cherish the time You give us. If not, then help me not to poison my heart with discontent.*

She rose and dressed in jeans and a wool sweater. If Jo-Lynn didn't feel like going out, maybe Caddie could run some errands for her. She stuffed her cell phone into a deep pocket and grabbed her wallet.

Walking down the street toward the Phifers' duplex, she found that her land legs were wobbly. She'd grown so accustomed to the rolling deck that the pavement seemed unpredictably stagnant.

She found Jo-Lynn eager to get out of the house.

"Mark's got to work all day on the ship. I don't suppose you'd drive me to the grocery store?"

"I'd love to," Caddie replied, snatching the car keys from Jo-Lynn's hand. "My cupboards are bare, and I'm craving fresh fruit."

Jo-Lynn laughed as she reached for her windbreaker. "Hey, I'm the one who's supposed to have cravings."

They spent the day together, and Caddie declined another dinner invitation.

Back in her apartment, she faced an evening alone, determined to continue giving thanks to God. She settled down at the table with her laptop to work on the final draft of her magazine article about Lindsey's career. After a half-hour's work, she phoned Lindsey to check one last detail.

"Hey," Lindsey said. "Remember I told you that I was going to call home this week?"

"Yes. Did you?"

"Uh-huh."

"How did it go?" Caddie asked.

"Well. . .sort of up and down. You know, I hadn't spoken to my parents for more than three years. Mom told me today that. . .that my dad left her. He's been gone over a year."

"Lindsey, I'm sorry."

"Yeah. Well, Mom seemed. . .not happy about it, but almost relieved. It was so weird. I was speechless. And you know what? She wants me to come home at Christmas."

"Are you going?"

"I don't know yet," Lindsey said. "But we talked for quite awhile. I think we'll keep on talking. And maybe. . . Well, we'll see. Keep praying for me, okay?"

"Absolutely."

Caddie got the information she needed for the article and went back to work, thanking God for Lindsey's breakthrough with her mother. A knock on the door at eight thirty startled her. She rose and walked toward it, her heart racing. No one called this late.

"Caddie?"

Relief flooded her as she hastened to throw the dead bolt.

"Aven! I'd about decided I wouldn't see you this trip."

"I'm sorry. My original plan was to spend every possible second with you when your ship docked. God had other plans."

They stood eyeing each other awkwardly for a long moment. Caddie at last stepped aside. "Would you like to come in for a few minutes?"

"If you don't mind. I've missed you, and I'd like to tell you what I've been up to."

"I'd like to hear it. Excuse me a minute, and I'll put some coffee on. . .or would you rather have hot chocolate?"

"Chocolate sounds great." Aven's fatigue showed in a shopworn smile. "Seems like I've been running all week and haven't had time to relax."

"Jo-Lynn and Mark said you've been busy."

He followed her into the tiny kitchen and leaned against the counter while she filled two mugs with water and heated them in the microwave.

"I don't know how much you've heard, but a fellow from the U.S. Marshal's office has been here on the island for several days. He came looking for Spruce Waller and Terry Herman."

"Who's Terry Herman?"

Aven rubbed the muscles on the back of his neck. "That's right, you didn't know about him. Let's see, where should I start? Terry is one of the fishermen from the *Molly K.*"

"The boat you impounded back in June?"

"That's right. See, the *Molly K* was auctioned by the marshal's office a week or two ago."

"Standard procedure." Caddie opened a cupboard and took out the bag of marshmallows she'd bought that morning. Her hands shook slightly as she ripped it open. Mentally she berated herself. After telling herself for days that a permanent relationship with Aven, or the lack of one, would not shake her new serenity, she was trembling at his nearness.

"Yes, but the odd thing about the auction was Captain Andrews, the former owner, not only showed up for the sale. . .he bought the boat back."

Aven apparently didn't notice her jitters, for which Caddie was thankful. "Good for him."

"Well, yes, I suppose so. Except the marshal's office wants to know where he got the money. Forty-seven thousand in cash."

"Cash?" That sounded odd, she had to admit.

"Yes, and they'd heard that the crew raised the money."

"And this is bad?" She handed him his mug and a spoon.

"Well, yes. Because none of these guys has that kind of money. Or if they do, they shouldn't. So when the deputy marshal—Ralph Eliot, his name is—came out here to talk to the crew who live in Kodiak, I went with him. The first man, Terry Herman, told us he had no proof, but he understood while he worked on the boat that Spruce Waller's brother was running drugs in his boat."

"Just like we thought." Caddie smiled. "Now I'm getting the picture. That's why you've been tied up the last few days. You've been out chasing the Waller brothers again."

"That's right."

She led him into the living room and sat down on the sofa.

Aven sat in the chair across from her.

"So, did you catch them?"

Aven's face drooped. "No. We went to Spruce's apartment and his cabin. He wasn't around. We asked his friends and neighbors, but nobody could tell us where he was. Or if they knew, they wouldn't admit it. We took a small boat—borrowed one of the rescue boats—and went all the way to Larsen Bay to look up Clay Waller. And guess what?"

"He wasn't home either."

"Bingo. His wife said he was away. Again. Said he and his brother went out to scout some boats. They're thinking of buying a fishing boat together, she said. But she had no idea where they went to look at these hypothetical boats."

"Where do you think he is?"

"I don't know, but if I were a betting man, I'd put my money on him and Spruce being somewhere together."

Caddie sipped her cocoa. "They took Clay's boat?"

"Uh-huh."

"Jo-Lynn said something about stolen Alaskan art."

Aven nodded. "Yeah. Terry Herman mentioned it. He'd heard a rumor that Clay Waller was somehow getting scrimshaw and other artworks on the black market and trading for cocaine. And we actually arrested a man—that is, Ralph Eliot did—who had some stolen artworks in his possession."

Caddie listened avidly as Aven related to her how he'd gone with the deputy marshal to the souvenir shop. "The shop owner, Thomas Harper, refused to admit the stuff was stolen. But Eliot contacted the state police, and the goods Harper was packing to ship matched a list of things stolen from a shop that had just closed for the season."

Caddie inhaled sharply. "Not in Homer?"

"No, here in Kodiak."

"Oh. Well, a store in Homer was robbed just before we docked there last week. Or maybe it was an art gallery."

"That doesn't surprise me. This ring has apparently been hitting businesses in several towns. Most of them, as it happens, are near where men who worked on the *Molly K* live."

"Do you think the whole crew is involved in this art and drug smuggling ring?"

"Not the whole crew. Terry Herman wasn't, and he didn't want to be. He was on the fringe of it and heard bits and pieces. He wasn't going to tell us, but his wife bullied him into it. And I really don't think Jason Andrews was involved. He had some violations of fishing regs, but his business seemed legitimate, and he was out there working hard at catching salmon. I don't think he used the *Molly K* for smuggling. It's Clay Waller who seems to be in the thick of it. And I think he's gotten Spruce and some of his friends to do some work for him."

"You mean. . .drug dealing?"

"I don't think so. But possibly some of the thefts. Since we impounded Andrews's boat and they lost their jobs, some of them are hard up. Clay may have promised them some quick money. If he had a potential buyer for high quality art, he needed to come up with a good supply in a hurry."

"How will the state be able to get enough hard evidence to prosecute them?" she asked.

"They're going to lean on Captain Andrews and see if they can get any more information out of him. We suspect now that he knew what the Wallers were up to and held it over Spruce's head. He definitely has a grudge against Spruce for causing the trouble that lost him his boat."

"So, if he threatened to turn Spruce in unless he gave him the money for the auction. . ."

"That's my take." Aven shrugged. "But Andrews is smart. I doubt he'll spill it.

He knows he'll lose the boat again permanently if he does and maybe go to prison, too. If you ask me, the police will have to crack this case through the art theft angle. If they can catch the people stealing art and get them to give up their contacts, the whole ring may fall apart."

Caddie lifted her mug and took another sip. "I guess the police have a better chance than we do of catching the boat owners bringing in drugs."

His thoughtful brown eyes held her gaze. "Caddie?"

"Hmm?"

"I've missed you."

She smiled. "I've missed you, too, and I admit I was wondering if I'd ever see you again."

He raised his chin just a hair. "Mind if I come over there and sit with you?"

"Not a bit."

He brought his mug of chocolate with him but slid his free arm around her as he sat down. "This is more like it. I wish I could say I'd never go away again, but I can't do that."

"I know. I can't, either."

He nodded. "Just so's you know, if I don't come see you for a while, it's not because I don't want to."

She set her mug on the coffee table and snuggled into the warmth of his embrace.

⚛

The *Wintergreen* plunged over the sea amid freezing rain and howling wind. Though it was only mid-October, Caddie was chilled to the bone. She tugged at the hood of her parka and pulled it in tight around her face. The cruel face of the Gulf of Alaska sneered at her today. With the seas so choppy, it would be next to impossible to inspect the buoys they'd set out to examine.

Over the loudspeaker came Boatswain Tilley's grating voice. "All hands stand by for rescue duty. Repeat. . ."

Caddie's radio burbled, and she nestled it close to her ear inside her hood. "Lyle speaking. Over."

"We've spotted a small boat that appears to be in distress at oh-two-five degrees. Prepare your crew to man a workboat."

"Affirmative." She hurried across the deck to Jackson, knowing he wouldn't hear her over the wind unless she got within a yard of him. "Let's get ready to lower the workboat."

As the *Wintergreen* approached the scene, she tried not to think about her last rescue mission in a small boat. All on the buoy deck could see that a thirty-foot motorboat had been thrown up on a rocky island that was mostly underwater at high tide. Buoys they were scheduled to refit clearly marked the safe channel between this treacherous shoal and the mainland, and one on the shore shone brightly. Despite the warnings, the boat had apparently wrecked in the unusually rough seas.

Since the *Wintergreen* was far too large to get close to the damaged vessel, the smaller workboat was pressed into service.

Tilley strode onto the buoy deck as Caddie and several sailors prepared to launch it. "You stay here, Lyle," he shouted at her. "I'll handle this operation myself."

She opened her mouth and closed it again, but unvoiced questions teemed inside her. Did he think she couldn't handle the boat in this rough water? Was it because she'd been injured last summer in the last major rescue operation she'd conducted? Or was he just spoiling for some action?

She oversaw the launching of the boat with Tilley and three others in it. As soon as they were well under way, she hurried under cover, out of the driving rain and up to the bridge.

Captain Raven was Officer of the Deck, and he greeted her with a nod.

Using high-powered binoculars, Caddie could clearly see the beleaguered cabin cruiser. The stern rose and fell with the waves, while the bow appeared to be driven up on the rocks. The craft was not about to float loose unless an unusually large wave lifted it, since the tide had begun its gradual receding.

Two men clambered on the rocks near the bow of the boat, apparently inspecting the damage to the hull, while a third stayed in it, waving and shouting to them.

"What will we do?" Caddie asked the captain. "Tow them in?"

"I think the boat's too badly damaged for that. Looks to me like a big hole in the bow. Can't be sure, but it doesn't look seaworthy from here." He squinted again into his binoculars. "We'll be out of daylight in an hour. We'll probably help them secure their boat and then take the men off the island. They can go back when the sea is calmer and salvage their boat."

Caddie stood beside him as they watched the *Wintergreen*'s workboat approach the rocky islet through the turbulent waves. When Tilley's boat was within hailing range, she saw the boat stand to. The coastguardsmen were visible on deck, all wearing foul-weather gear. The men on the island waved to them.

"What on earth?" Raven lowered his binoculars for an instant and then looked back through the instrument.

Lindsey was at the radio desk when Tilley's voice came over the staticky airwaves. "*Wintergreen*, this is *Wintergreen 1*. Vessel in distress is declining assistance. Request orders from the OOD."

Raven strode to Lindsey's side and spoke into the radio. "It's too dangerous to leave them out there in this weather. Take them off the island."

"Sir, they've indicated they don't want our help. Request permission to return to the ship. Over."

"Negative. Get those fools out of there."

Lindsey flashed a glance at Caddie, cringing slightly as though she was glad she didn't have to take the orders Raven was giving. If civilians declined assistance, the

Coast Guard generally left them to their own devices—unless lives were in danger. Captain Raven must believe the men on the little heap of rock would likely not survive the long night there.

With the frigid rain and buffeting winds, Caddie had to agree. When the tide turned and rose again, that boat, staved up as it was, might float off and sink. Then what would happen to the men? They might be swept off the rocks if the wind and high seas didn't abate.

Captain Raven issued curt orders to the other men on the bridge to keep the buoy tender as steady as possible in its location. To Tilley he relayed a request for the registration number of the stranded boat.

Their momentum and the current had brought the buoy tender closer to the wreck. As the captain gave instructions to move it back, Caddie again studied the island with the aid of binoculars.

She caught her breath. The damaged vessel had the same lines and colors as the one she and Aven had seen the Waller brothers working on at Anton Larsen Bay. Not only that, one of the men on shore had the same hulking shape as Spruce Waller. "Sir?"

"Yes, Lyle?"

"That boat, sir. The one on the rocks."

"What about it?"

"I. . .think I've seen it before, sir."

Chapter 13

I can't be sure from this distance," Caddie said, staring through her binoculars at the boat on the rocks. "But when we get the number. . ."

"Where did you see it before?" Captain Raven asked.

"Moored in Anton Larsen Bay, getting a paint job." Quickly she told him about her expedition with Aven and the deputy U.S. marshal's quest for the Waller brothers.

Raven's eyes narrowed. To Lindsey, he snapped, "Get the registration number from Bo'sun Tilley *now*."

He resumed his vigil with his binoculars until Lindsey called to him a few minutes later. "Captain, the name on the hull is *Miss Faye IX*, and the registration number is not currently assigned to any registered boat."

"Check it against the boat registered to Clay Waller of Larsen Bay."

A few moments later, Lindsey said, "Only one digit is different, sir."

"I should have sent more men on this detail." Raven turned to Caddie. "If you were closer, could you swear it was the same boat?"

"I think so, sir."

"And the same men?"

She gulped. "Maybe. I only saw them from a distance and in pictures." Her concern lightened as she realized she had the deciding evidence in her possession. "Sir, I have the photos on my camera's digital card in my cabin."

"Get it."

Five minutes later, she puffed back up the final ladder to the bridge. Captain Raven was again consulting with Tilley via radio as rain sheeted off the windows.

Caddie approached him with the digital card, and he waved her toward the communications desk. She held it out to her friend, and Lindsey took the little square card and popped it into a slot on the computer console.

"We can't let him see the ones you took of me." The tension in Lindsey's voice prompted Caddie to swing around so that her body blocked Raven's view of the computer screen until Lindsey had located and enlarged the best photo of Spruce Waller standing beside his brother's boat with a paintbrush in his hand.

She turned to Raven. "This is the man I told you about, Captain. He's Spruce Waller, the one who started the fight on the *Molly K* last June that led to the boat's being impounded. This other man, I'm told, is his brother, Clay." She pointed to the second man in the photo.

"He's the one who owns that boat out there?"

"Yes, sir. If it's truly the same boat. There's a better picture of the boat they were working on that day." She asked Lindsey, "Could you please bring up the picture before this one? I didn't zoom in quite so much, and the lines of the boat are clearer. You can also see where they've primed over the boat's name."

Raven studied several of Caddie's digital photos then straightened and went back to the window, staring out and scowling.

"Sir, Boatswain Tilley is calling in again," Lindsey said.

The captain again went to her desk.

"I've told the crew of the craft in distress to prepare for boarding," Tilley said. "They're still objecting."

"Approach with caution," Raven replied. "We believe some of those aboard could be dangerous."

"Captain, there looks to be only three of them."

"Watch yourself, Bo'sun."

"Affirmative."

Tilley's workboat now hovered only yards from the beached cabin cruiser, bobbing on the waves.

"Will they be able to land and remove the crew?" one of the petty officers asked the captain.

Raven rubbed his forehead and gritted his teeth. "That remains to be seen."

The fading light obscured the details of Tilley's maneuvers, but a few minutes later a seaman called in.

"*Wintergreen,* this is *Wintergreen 1.* Request additional personnel and equipment."

Raven's gaze bored into Caddie's. "Lyle, I'm calling for a law enforcement cutter, but we can't wait for them to get here. Take six men in the Zodiac. We'll issue sidearms."

"Aye, aye, sir."

As she dashed for the hatch, she heard him say into the radio, "*Wintergreen 1,* we have *Wintergreen 2* en route to assist you. ETA fifteen minutes. What is your current status?"

⁑

Aven relayed to Mark Phifer and five other men the orders Lieutenant Greer had given him. "We'll get in close and get an assessment. Be prepared to launch our boat fast, depending on the situation."

The men all agreed.

"Greer will sweep the island with the ship's guns if needed, but we want to avoid casualties if at all possible. Unfortunately, the *Wintergreen* landed some men and got into a confrontation. Shots have been fired, and they couldn't get their men off the island. Our priority is to get those men off safely. If we can catch the Waller brothers, too, that's gravy." He didn't know which personnel were involved in the melee. He hoped Caddie was safe on her ship. Too bad it was raining and nearly full dark now. The conditions would make their mission more dangerous.

As they quickly worked to make sure their small surfboat was ready for their operation, a seaman ran onto the deck. "The skipper sent me down to tell you, so he doesn't have to say it on the radio, in case the smugglers can hear."

"What?" Aven stopped checking their equipment and peered at him. Rain ran off his hood onto the deck.

"The *Wintergreen* sent out a second boat. They have two landing parties ashore now. . .or will have soon. The captain felt those ashore needed relief immediately, so he didn't wait for us. Greer says use extreme caution. We don't want any friendly fire casualties."

Aven set his jaw and looked ahead, where he could make out distant lights in the storm. "Tell the skipper we're ready to launch anytime."

The seaman ran toward the hatch.

Mark clapped him on the shoulder. "Quit worrying, Aven."

"They should have stood off and waited for us."

"Like he said, they thought it was necessary to go in."

Aven sighed, wishing the *Milroy* could go faster. He put his radio close to his ear. He heard what he had dreaded to hear—Caddie's voice from the smaller boat that had deployed from her ship. "This is the *Wintergreen 2*. . ."

⚜

The Zodiac, with Caddie and six other crewmen in it, rushed toward the island and Tilley's boat in the twilight. Tilley would have left at least one man on his boat, she knew. The rain still poured down in torrents, and the wind whipped up the waves. Caddie hoped they were not too late to prevent violence. She recalled Aven's account of his past confrontation with Spruce Waller. Even though the burly fisherman knew backup was only minutes away last June, he'd attacked Aven and his men.

Where was Aven now? No doubt hundreds of miles away. She hoped his ship was docked somewhere in a safe haven for the night.

She kept their course as steady as possible, headed for the *Wintergreen 1*. As they approached, she heard Tilley radio the ship. He reported to the captain that his landing party had been fired on and were pinned down on the rocks. Captain Raven instructed the seaman in the workboat to stand offshore farther and told Tilley to keep his head down and wait for assistance.

Caddie didn't enter the radio chatter, not wanting to clutter the airwaves. She assumed the smugglers on the island could hear them. Raven's orders to the seaman on the workboat meant he would back off to avoid drawing fire. If the smugglers had thought of hijacking Tilley's boat, that would stymie them.

She instructed Gavin, who was at the helm of the Zodiac, to bring them in on the side of the workboat away from the shore. The seaman on the *Wintergreen 1* and

103

two of the men in the Zodiac secured the smaller inflatable to the workboat so they could talk without using the radio.

"I'm going to land around the other side if I can," Caddie told the seaman she recognized as Michaels. "Can you stand off a little farther so that you're behind us and turn on your spotlights when we're in position? Illuminate them for us. Shine those spots right in their eyes if you can."

"I'll do my best," Michaels said. "But make sure you leave a guard with your boat. They shot at us when we arrived and took out a big window. Tilley told me to back off. I think they've got a shotgun. They might try to rush the Zodiac and get away in it."

"That would be a foolish thing for them to do, but you're right," Caddie said. Desperate men took foolhardy action.

With the smaller Zodiac, Caddie and her party had the advantage of being able to land directly on the rocky island. She directed Gavin to take the craft around the islet to the side away from the damaged boat. Without running lights, they risked hitting an obstacle, but she felt it was critical to preserve as much surprise as possible. At the spot that appeared to have easiest access for a landing, Gavin nosed the Zodiac to shore.

In minutes, Caddie and five of her six seamen were ashore and climbing over the rocks toward the beached cabin cruiser. After some hesitation, she'd left Dee Morrison with the Zodiac and given her instructions to stand offshore until summoned in.

The islet was little more than a large pile of rocks in the bay, less than a hundred feet long at this stage of the tides, with a blinking buoy on the highest point. At high tide, it would appear to rest in the water. The jagged black rocks in the center hid the damaged boat from Caddie's view, but she could see the stern lights of the *Wintergreen*'s workboat clearly.

She sent one of the young seamen, McQuillan, scrambling to the top of the rocks ahead of her. He jumped back down beside her, panting. "They're holding the bo'sun and his men down behind the rocks on the left. Two-eight-oh degrees. I saw the bo'sun and at least one of his men. There are two of the civilians near their boat's bow and one on board."

Her heart thudded. "Did they see you?"

"I think so."

Caddie nodded and prayed silently for wisdom and safety. The renegades already knew she and her crew were coming.

"What now?" Seaman Torres asked.

"They may not realize how many of us there are," Caddie said. "Three of the *Wintergreen 1*'s crew are ashore. So far as we know, there are three hostile civilians. They may all have small arms."

"Okay," Torres said. "How are we going to do this?"

She crouched behind the boulders and motioned all the men in close. The rain still beat down on them, but the gale had declined to a stiff breeze. "I'm pretty sure these civilians are part of a smuggling ring. For some reason, they're determined not to let us approach them or their boat, even though its hull is caved in. McQuillan says one of them is still on their boat. He's probably monitoring our tactics on the boat's radio. We can't exactly ask Captain Raven or Bo'sun Tilley for instructions or they'd hear our plans."

They all nodded in understanding.

"We six are all armed," she continued. "I expect Tilley is the only one in his landing party with a gun." Standard procedure was for the petty officer to carry a sidearm, but the seamen would not be armed unless danger was anticipated. "We have to assume all three smugglers are armed, though."

"Right," said Torres.

Caddie pulled in a deep breath. "It's pretty dark now. I asked Seaman Michaels on the *Wintergreen 1* to shine his spotlights on the enemy's position on my signal. He's trying to hold his position behind Tilley and his men. If we rush out of the dark, we have a pretty good chance of overrunning the enemy position or at least of relieving Tilley and his men."

"Tilley will help as soon as we make our move," McQuillan said.

"Yes, if he still has ammo."

The men nodded soberly and checked their weapons.

"I'll give them one more chance to give it up," Caddie said. She pressed the call button on her radio.

"This is *Wintergreen 2* landing party. Request *Wintergreen 1* order hostiles to surrender, and if declined, go with our plan. Over."

"Affirmative," said Captain Raven. "Michaels, proceed."

Seconds later, the seaman's voice boomed out over the loudspeaker from the workboat, shouting down the wind. "This is the U.S. Coast Guard. Lay down your weapons and raise your hands over your head."

Caddie and her men inched up the rocks and peered down at the other side of the island.

"Repeat. Lay down your weapons and prepare to be approached by Coast Guard personnel."

A shot rang out from near the beached boat. A man popped up from behind the rocks that covered Tilley's party and squeezed two shots from a pistol, then ducked down again.

Caddie's blur of an impression told her that the man was not Tilley. Why was someone other than the boatswain shooting?

The men sheltering in and behind the *Miss Faye IX* let loose a barrage of fire directed toward Tilley's party. The workboat's floodlights came on, throwing the scene into bright relief.

"Now." Caddie swung around the boulder that had shielded her and hopped to the next rock, holding her pistol before her.

One of the smugglers, crouching between their boat's bow and a black rock, jerked around and stared toward them.

Caddie recognized the large, bearded figure of Spruce Waller. His long gun came up, pointing at her men, and Caddie let off a round in his general direction, not pausing long enough to get a good aim.

The man flattened himself behind the hull of the boat.

All around her, pistols discharged. She reached a fairly flat stretch of rocks and ran forward, brandishing her weapon. To her left, her peripheral vision caught the shadows of two men leaping up from Tilley's position and running forward.

The man in the smugglers' boat went down. Spruce Waller rose on his knees and fired, then jerked back onto the ground, his weapon flying to one side.

McQuillan tackled the third man on the jagged rocks, and two others ran to assist him.

Caddie hastily collected their adversaries' weapons while her men secured the prisoners. "How bad is the wounded man?" she asked Torres.

"Petty Officer Lyle!"

She whirled toward the voice.

One of Tilley's men waved frantically. "The bo'sun's hit!"

Chapter 14

Aven's stomach churned as he waited for his orders.

The *Milroy* passed the much larger *Wintergreen* and drove steadily toward the small workboat near the rocky island in the bay. The radio chatter had lessened and all but stopped during the last few minutes. The rain seemed to let up, but a drizzle still dampened everything, and the cold wind kept working conditions uncomfortable.

His men waited with him on the dark deck, staring toward their destination—a pile of black rocks with a constant warning buoy. The temporary addition of small boats looked innocent from this distance.

A sudden glare of floodlights illuminated the island, and with binoculars, Aven could see figures moving about. The *Milroy*'s engine and the wind drowned any sound from the tableau, but from this side, it looked like a miniature battle. Had the *Wintergreen*'s crew forced a confrontation with the drug smugglers?

At last his radio came to life again.

A man's voice drawled in an almost bored tone, "*Wintergreen*, this is *Wintergreen 2*. We have two casualties needing medical assistance. One of them is a prisoner. Total three prisoners requiring transport. Request permission to transfer prisoners and our wounded to the *Wintergreen*. Over."

Captain Raven of the *Wintergreen* replied, "Negative, *Wintergreen 2*. Law enforcement cutter *Milroy* approaching. Hand prisoners over to them unless critical medical care is needed. Transport our wounded personnel to *Wintergreen*."

Aven's adrenaline surged. One of the *Wintergreen*'s crew was wounded, as well as one of the prisoners. Was Caddie safe?

Caddie hurried with Seaman Jackson to the place where Tilley and his two men had crouched behind the rocks.

Tilley lay on his side, both hands clamped to his thigh.

"They hit him right away," Jackson said.

Caddie frowned at him. "Why didn't you report it?"

"He didn't want them to know they'd got him. They might have rushed us. And he knew you were on the way."

She climbed over a rounded rock and knelt at the boatswain's side. "Tilley, how you doing?"

Pain flickered across his taut features. "Not so good. It's bleeding a lot."

"We'll get you out of here. I've got one of my men calling it in. We'll transport you immediately to the *Wintergreen*." She noted the position of the wound. To her relief, the entrance wound was on the outside of his thigh. Probably it hadn't severed the femoral artery. "Do you think the bullet hit the bone?"

"Not sure. Maybe not. All I know is it hurts."

"Let me put some pressure on it, if you can stand it. We'll put you in the Zodiac and get you out to the ship."

Engine noises nearly drowned her words and obscured the now-busy radio traffic. She turned to look down the bay and saw a ship approaching. Not the *Wintergreen*, but a patrol boat half as big. Reinforcements. She grinned. A law enforcement cutter. No doubt the crew was ready to land, armed to the teeth. She squeezed Tilley's leg at the point of the wound. He groaned but didn't protest. *That's good,* she thought. Knowing him, if it were broken, he'd be cussing a blue streak.

Gavin came to her side. "McQuillan has gone to help Morrison beach the Zodiac."

Tilley said between his clenched teeth, "Did you search that boat yet?"

"Not yet." Caddie looked up at McQuillan. "Can you take over here? Pressure on the wound until we get him to the hospital corpsman."

She let the seaman take her place and rose. Three of her men had brought the prisoners together on the rocks facing the *Wintergreen 1*.

"Libby," she called. "Come with me."

She and the seaman approached the damaged boat.

Caddie climbed into the *Miss Faye IX* and quickly made sure no one else was aboard. The cabin seemed warm and quiet, since the wind no longer howled about her. When she saw the sophisticated radio equipment, she pursed her lips, but they were too chapped to whistle. Clay Waller knew where to put his money.

"Lyle."

She turned toward Libby's voice.

"Take a look in these lockers."

She walked to his side and peered into the cupboard he'd opened. A crate full of plastic bags lay inside. Each bag bulged with a white powder.

"I'm betting it's cocaine," Libby said.

They quickly opened more lockers. Caddie had never seen so much contraband. She put in a call on her radio.

"*Wintergreen,* this is *Wintergreen 2.* We have a cargo on the hostiles' vessel that appears to be narcotics."

"*Wintergreen 2,* I copy," came her captain's voice. "Turn all evidence over to the petty officer now landing from the *Milroy.*"

Caddie jerked her head up and stared toward the cutter now anchored just beyond the workboat Tilley had commanded. She smiled for the first time all evening. Aven had arrived with the cavalry.

Mark came directly to the *Miss Faye IX*. "Lyle!" He grinned at her. "Looks like you got the job done, hey?"

"I think so. Captain Raven says to turn this pile of contraband over to you." She shined her flashlight on a part of the drug stash.

"Happy to accept." Mark glanced around then leaned toward her. "Aven was worried sick about you. Better show your face outside."

She felt her face flush. When she left the cabin, Libby was waiting to give her a hand as she climbed over the gunwale and dropped to the rocks below. They scrambled over the boulders toward the *Milroy*'s landing party.

Aven had his back to her as he helped lift Tilley into the Zodiac manned by Seamen Morrison and McQuillan. As soon as he was settled, Tilley growled, "Let's move. Somebody radio the *Wintergreen* and tell them."

"Got it," Aven called and shoved the Zodiac off the rocks. He turned, reaching for his radio. As he spotted Caddie, his face broke into a huge smile. "This is *Milroy 1*," he said into the transmitter. "Inform *Wintergreen* her boatswain is being transported in *Wintergreen 2*, who requests permission to come alongside."

He took two long strides to reach Caddie. They stood for a moment in the cold mist, appraising each other.

What was he thinking? If the men weren't here, would he light into her for endangering herself? Would he take Tilley's tack and berate her for wanting to do "a man's job"?

Aven nodded slowly. "Looks to me as though you did a good job, Petty Officer."

Three weeks later, Caddie got her lunch tray in the mess hall and sat down with Lindsey.

"What's up?" Lindsey asked, lowering her voice so that it reached Caddie beneath the level of the chatter surrounding them. "You've been smiley-eyed all morning. Did you get a message from Holland?"

Caddie chuckled. "I don't know anyone in Holland."

"Very funny. You know who I mean."

"Did you realize that when we dock it will be less than a week until Thanksgiving?"

"No," Lindsey said, "I didn't know that. But I guess you don't want to talk about whatever it is that's—"

She stopped talking, and the lunchtime buzz dropped away as suddenly. Caddie looked toward the hatch. Captain Raven had just entered. He walked to the middle of the room.

"At ease, everyone. I have an announcement—the kind I like making in person." His gaze darted about the room, lingering for a moment on Caddie and Lindsey. "It's my pleasure to tell you that BM3 Lyle is now BM2 Lyle. Congratulations, Second Class Bo'sun's Mate."

Caddie nodded, blushing, as the twenty men present, along with Lindsey and Vera Hotchkiss, began clapping and cheering.

"Thanks!" Caddie waved and concentrated on her food.

"I'm also pleased to report that Bo'sun Tilley is doing well. However, he's got several weeks of rehab ahead, and he's decided to take retirement. He won't be returning to the *Wintergreen*."

A surprised murmur rippled over the room.

"Carry on," the captain said. He smiled at Caddie and left the compartment.

"That's great about your promotion!" Lindsey grinned at her, still clapping. "So that's what made you so happy."

"Thank you. I just. . ." Caddie picked up her knife and attacked the chicken leg on her plate.

"Have you sent a message to your mom? She'll be so proud of you."

Caddie shook her head. "Not yet."

"Why not?"

"No time. I just found out this morning." A tear popped over Caddie's eyelid and trickled down her cheek. She swiped it quickly away with her napkin.

"Oh, wait a minute," Lindsey said, tilting her head to one side. "You're thinking of your dad, aren't you?"

"Maybe. I don't know."

"Sure you are. Wishing he could share this moment with you."

Caddie wagged her head back and forth. "There have been a lot of moments he hasn't been there to share with me." *Some even before he died,* she thought.

"Yeah, but. . ." Lindsey raised her hands, palms out. "Okay, I'll be quiet. Sorry. But it would be nice if you could get home for Thanksgiving."

"I'll settle for Christmas," Caddie said.

"Yeah, it's great that they've timed our next deployment so that most of us will be able to take leave at Christmas. I've decided to spend it with my mom. Maybe not the whole time, but a few days anyway."

"That's wonderful."

Lindsey smiled brightly. "Hey, does Aven— Oops, sorry."

Caddie chuckled. "I don't know what his plans are yet or what his December schedule looks like. He got home for a week right after our run-in with the *Miss Faye IX*. I was glad he had the chance and went to Wasilla."

"If he's in Kodiak next week, maybe you can spend Thanksgiving together."

"Maybe, but I'm not planning on it."

Lindsey nodded. "Same as always, where men are concerned, huh? We can't count on them being there."

❖

Aven stood on the deck of the moored *Milroy*, watching the harbor.

"Hey, Holland," Mark shouted. "You ready to go home?"

"No, go along without me."

Mark laughed. "I heard the *Wintergreen* will be here within the hour. Guess we won't see you tonight."

Aven grinned. "If she needs to stay on board or is too tired to eat out, I'll drag myself over to your place."

"Hey, did you hear they're holding the Waller brothers in Anchorage until their trial?"

"No," Aven said. "I'm glad they didn't let them out on bail. Is Spruce still in the hospital?"

"I don't know. I just heard from the skipper that all three of the smugglers were denied bail." Mark swung down the metal stairway onto the dock and headed off whistling.

This was silly. Even when the ship came in, it would be awhile before she could leave. Maybe long enough to run to the florist? Or should he save the money toward a trip to Wasilla together, or even toward extra for his family this month?

In the end, he stuck it out and was on the dock waiting when the *Wintergreen* put in. At four o'clock the sun was nearly down, but seeing Caddie's face when she spotted him was worth the nearly three hours he had whiled away. When she came off the ship, he didn't care if all the sailors in the Seventeenth District saw. She flipped the hood of her parka back, dropped her seabag, and ran toward him. He pulled her into his arms and held her right there on the dock.

"Welcome back," he whispered near her ear. He tossed her bag into the back of his pickup and drove her home.

All the way, she smiled and told him about things she'd seen since their brief meeting on the rocky island where she'd caught the smugglers. He stopped at the post office, and she dashed inside, returning with a handful of mail.

When they reached her apartment, she jumped down from the truck. "Want to come in?"

"Uh...what do you think? Want some time to get settled? I can come back in a while. I thought maybe we'd eat out tonight?"

"Great. Give me an hour?"

He went away for the time stipulated and wound up hanging out with Mark and Jo-Lynn. He took their good-natured teasing but turned down Jo-Lynn's offer of a snack.

At last he was back on Caddie's doorstep. There had to be a way to spend more than an evening together every few weeks.

Her blue eyes lit up when she opened the door. She pulled him inside, and he hugged her again. Her draped green shirt was soft and very unmilitary, and her blond hair lay in shimmery waves about her shoulders.

"You look great."

"Thanks. Aven, I sold the article."

"Which one?" He slid his hand over her satiny hair.

"The one about Lindsey. Remember, I told you about it. And the magazine wants more profiles. So maybe I can do the one we talked about—on your sister."

"That'd be great." He let her slip out of his arms to get her coat and purse. "Say, have you got Christmas leave?"

"Yes. Thirty days. Have you?"

He nodded. "Are you going home?"

"I thought I would." She eyed him uncertainly.

"You should," he said, "but what about. . .I don't suppose you could come back for the last week? Fly into Anchorage?"

Her heart-stopping smile spread over her face. "I'd love to. And I can see Robyn work her dogs then."

"And take pictures," he added.

"If your family doesn't mind. . ."

"They're begging me to get you there."

"I'd love to."

She flowed back into his embrace, and he stooped to kiss her. Perfect.

Epilogue

Caddie and her uncle waited on the bridge of the *Milroy*. Watching out the window, they saw Jo-Lynn and Lindsey emerge onto the main deck below. Aven, who now served as boatswain of the cutter, stood on the main deck below, with their pastor, Mark Phifer, and Lieutenant Greer. The petty officer who had volunteered to run the sound system today started the wedding march, and Caddie smiled up at her father's younger brother.

"Come on, Uncle Jack. Looks like it's our turn."

"Okay, honey. Be careful."

She clung to his hand on the ladder as they went cautiously down to the deck. Once on stable footing, they walked slowly in time to the music, toward where the minister stood. Mark and Jo-Lynn's baby let out a whimper, and Dee Morrison, who had volunteered to hold him during the ceremony, bounced the infant gently and shushed him.

The brilliant early July sun smiled down on the moored cutter. A gentle breeze fluttered Caddie's veil and the long skirt of her gown. She picked out her mom, smiling at her through tears, and Mira and Jordan grinning from ear to ear. The only one missing from her family was Dad. She'd cried a little last night, when Uncle Jack had arrived looking so much like her father. Now she was able to smile at them without weeping.

"Isn't this kind of weird?" Jordan had asked her last night. "You and Aven being married and still being on different ships, I mean."

"It may be hard for a while, but we'll manage," Caddie had assured him.

Aven's mother, sister, and grandfather stood on the other side, smiling as well, but her focus came back to Aven.

He and his two groomsmen stood at attention in their dress uniforms, but Caddie had opted for traditional gowns for herself and her bridesmaids. Lindsey had threatened to throttle Caddie if she had to wear her uniform instead of a pretty dress, and Jo-Lynn had pointed out that she was a civilian, anyway, and they all ought to be dressed in similar styles.

Aven's dark eyes shone as Caddie and Uncle Jack approached.

When handing her over to Aven, Uncle Jack leaned over and kissed her on the cheek. "Bless you," he whispered, and pressed her hand before going to stand with Mom.

Mira popped off a flash picture with Caddie's camera.

Caddie looked up at Aven and read his lips as he mouthed, "Love you."

She couldn't speak, her heart was so full, but she gave his hand a squeeze as they turned to face the pastor.

After his welcome to their families and friends, the pastor said, "Folks, we're gathered here in a somewhat unusual venue to witness the union of two people who've chosen careers full of adventure, and yes, sometimes danger. These young people have pledged to serve the United States of America, and as the motto of the Coast Guard says, to be 'always ready' when they're needed. Well, I'm here to tell you all that I've spent several hours talking to Aven and Caddie, and I can assure you, they're ready for this."

The people chuckled, and Caddie sneaked another look at Aven. His energy flowed to her through their clasped hands, and her anticipation mounted.

She would be a petty officer for another year at least, but after that, who knew? Only the Lord. Whatever He brought her way, she would be ready. And today, she would begin her new life as Aven's wife.

FIRE AND ICE

Dedication

To Debbie,
We are so glad you are part of our family!

Acknowledgments:
Special thanks to Rhonda Gibson, Lisa Harris, and Dana and Luann Nordine,
who helped make this book possible.

Chapter 1

Robyn Holland stooped over the yearling pup and worked the harness gently over his legs.

Grandpa Steve brought out two more experienced dogs and hooked them to the towline. The veteran dogs would run in the wheeler position—at the back of the team, nearest the dogsled.

The yearlings, Muttster and his littermate Bobble, wriggled and danced, eager to run in the crisp new snow with the big dogs. Robyn hooked them to the towline farther forward, each one beside an older dog who had pulled sleds for several years.

At the very front, Grandpa positioned their pair of leaders, Tumble and Max. "Everybody set?" Grandpa asked.

"Yeah, but I think you'd better let me take them around the loop once before you take over." Robyn patted the youngest dog's head and stood. "It's the first good snow we've had in weeks, and the trail's going to be fast."

"Finally."

Robyn frowned. "It won't be like pulling the ATV, you know."

"I know."

She bit her lip. Her grandfather had grown frail last winter, his arthritis keeping him from doing much of the dog training that kept them solvent. But when summer arrived and his doctor started him on a new drug regimen, he'd perked up. One of the jobs he'd enjoyed through the fall months was driving teams of dogs hitched to the Hollands' ATV. In the old days, Grandpa had used a light cart for training on dirt trails, but the acquisition of the ATV three years ago had increased their training options. It gave the dogs more weight behind them, to hold them steady during fall training, building muscle and stamina.

There was plenty of snow now, the last week in December. Grandpa seemed as eager to get out with the sled as the dogs did. He'd suffered a bad cold and hadn't driven any of the teams since they'd put the cart away in early November. He felt better now, and with plenty of snow on the ground he couldn't wait to get out on the trail again. But could he control a team of eight dogs, two of which had only minimal training?

"I'm just saying, they were frisky Saturday. Today they're excited by the fresh snow *and* frisky. That sled weighs a lot less than the ATV."

"I can handle them," Grandpa insisted.

117

"Oh, I know. It's just that—"

"Hey, I was racing dogs before you were even thought of." Grandpa glared at her from his place at the back of the sled. "Are you going to get the snub line, or do I need to?"

"I'll get it."

Robyn walked to the line that anchored the team's leaders to one of the few trees in the dog lot. This year's crop of puppies pressed against the link fence of their enclosure, watching the big boys. The other mature dogs also stood, panting as they gazed at the fortunate ones who'd been chosen.

She looked toward Grandpa, and he nodded. No use arguing with him, even when he was wrong. But he *had* been running dogs decades longer than she had.

With misgivings, she unsnapped the line.

"Hike!" At Grandpa's quiet command, the dogs leaned into their collars and pulled. They made a quick start. The leaders lunged forward, hauling the youngsters with them. The other dogs in the team kept pace, and the sled zipped over the packed snow in the yard, toward one of the trails they used most.

Robyn wished she had hitched up a few dogs to their old sled so she could follow along. But then Grandpa would accuse her of babysitting him.

She watched them until they were out of sight and went to get her plastic toboggan from the barn. In winter she used it to haul water and food to the dogs. She gathered up a dozen water dishes. The water froze and the dishes had to be emptied and refilled several times a day or the dogs would dehydrate.

Her mother put on her coat as Robyn entered the back door of the kitchen carrying half the dog dishes.

"Hi, honey. I'm just about to leave for work. I see Grandpa got his way."

"I couldn't stop him. He'll be all right." Robyn met her gaze and felt another flash of doubt. "He wanted to go so badly."

"He's a good trainer. He knows what he's doing." Her mother picked up her keys and purse.

"Yeah. And it will be a short run today—just a couple of miles. He'll be back soon." Robyn put the water dishes in the sink and walked outside with her mom.

They both turned without speaking toward the dog lot. The dogs barked and wagged their tails.

Robyn couldn't help smiling. "They're all so happy that we've got plenty of snow."

"Yes, it was sparse for a while there." Her mother peered toward the trail Grandpa had taken.

Robyn walked over to the male dogs' enclosure, opened the gate, and went in. She stooped to pat Scooter, her brother's retired lead dog. He was more of a pet than a team dog now, but she sometimes harnessed him with yearlings to teach them trail etiquette. Scooter rubbed against her hand and woofed.

She stroked his ears and straightened. The mountains to the north were solid white against the clear blue sky, with shadows of purple, gray, and navy delineating ridges and cliffs. Who else on earth had such a beautiful place to live and work?

"Here they come." Her mother's voice held relief.

Robyn straightened and peered toward the trail. She could hear the dogs running and the faint jingle of the leaders' bells. As she left the enclosure and secured the gate, Tumble and Max burst into sight. "They're coming awfully fast."

She and her mother stepped back as the team tore into the yard. Robyn backed up against the fence, debating whether to interfere.

"Whoa." Grandpa was riding the brake, but the dogs were still pulling too hard.

A shot of adrenaline hit Robyn. They took the curve in the pathway too fast, and the sled swung around on one runner. Usually by this time of year, the snow was deeper and the sides of the trail banked, but now the sled weaved all over the place. Grandpa wasn't heavy enough to slow the breakneck pace.

The young dogs used the near wreck as an excuse to leap in excitement, and the older, steadier leaders seemed to catch their mood.

"Tumble!" Robyn stepped forward. "Whoa, Max!" They raced past her with the sled swaying so wildly Robyn had to jump out of the way.

Grandpa's mouth hung open, and he looked ahead, judging the stopping distance needed before they would crash into the shed that held dog food and tools.

"Dad!" her mother yelled.

Robyn took off in a sprint. If she could jump on the runner beside Grandpa, that might slow them down enough.

"Whoa, you numbskulls!" Grandpa clutched the handlebar and braced for the impact. The sled swung around before Robyn could reach it and hit the corner of the wall.

Max and Tumble swerved at the last second, dragging the young dogs with them. The wheelers took the weight of the sled as they tried to turn and avoid the shed, but Coco slammed into it with her right shoulder. She yelped in pain as the sled slid sideways and tipped over, dumping Grandpa to the ground.

Robyn ran forward. "Grandpa! Are you hurt?"

Grandpa Steve raised his head and looked after the team that still ran, pulling the damaged sled. "Get the dogs! The dogs, Robby! Don't let them run free."

He was right, of course. Robyn ran after the sled, calling to the leaders and reasoning to herself that if he were seriously hurt, he wouldn't have yelled at her like that. Her job was to make sure they stopped running before they got to the highway.

She called to the leaders again. At last Max turned them, just before they reached the road. They made a wide arc into the unbroken snow, and it slowed the dogs down. They came back toward her, panting and wagging their tails. The two youngsters still danced in their harness. The sled skidded along behind them on its side. Coco limped, and her harness mate, Rocky, seemed to have his outside hind leg tangled in the lines.

Robyn spoke sternly to the leaders, and they lay down, eyeing her sheepishly. The wheelers followed, and after a moment the dogs in the middle slunk down and put their chins on their paws.

Robyn took several deep breaths. They were dogs. They were trained to run and to love pulling the sled. It wasn't really their fault.

It was her fault.

She'd known deep down that Grandpa couldn't handle a team of fresh dogs anymore. He'd once been a strong man, but those days were over. Between the weight he'd lost in the last year and the muscle he'd lost through lack of exercise, he never should have attempted the stunt. And she should have stopped him.

She unhooked the sled and left it beside the driveway, gathering the end of the towline firmly. "Hike." Grimly, she walked behind the eight dogs. More subdued now, they obeyed and headed back toward the dog lot, where their individual doghouses sat.

To her surprise, Grandpa still lay on the ground near the shed. Her mother knelt beside him in the snow.

"Is he okay?" Robyn called.

"We're taking it slow and easy," Mom replied. The look she threw Robyn did nothing to allay her fears.

Robyn tied the team up with a snub line and hurried to Grandpa's side.

"They got away from me," he said ruefully. "I just couldn't hold 'em."

"Well, Dad, don't fret about it. We need to take you to the ER and make sure you didn't do any serious damage."

"Naw, I don't need to go to any hospital."

"I'll make the rest of the decisions today, thank you." Robyn's mother stood and arched her eyebrows. "Can you help me get him up?"

"Is it serious?" Robyn asked.

"I don't think anything's broken, but he bumped his head on the sled and landed pretty hard on his hip."

Robyn lowered her voice. "You're taking him in?"

Her mother hesitated. "If he can walk, we'll take him inside and let him rest. If not, we'll get him to the car and head for the hospital."

"Now, Cheryl," Grandpa protested through clenched teeth, "all I need is a heating pad."

"We'll see." She knelt again beside him.

Robyn got on his other side and slid her arm under his head, around his shoulders. "You ready, Grandpa?"

He strained to sit up but quickly lay back with a moan. After a moment, he said,

"Let me roll over on my side. It'll be easier that way."

Gently, she rolled him over. He seized her wrist. With both women lifting, he got to his feet with a groan. "Oh man, that hurts."

"Can you put weight on it?" Mom asked.

"I'm not sure."

"Robyn, honey, go bring my car around here."

"I'll drive," Robyn said.

"No, you stay and put the dogs away. And call the store. Tell them I won't be in this morning."

Robyn dashed around front and brought the car to the dog lot. By the time she got there, Grandpa sagged heavily against her mom, his face contorted in pain. They got him into the backseat, and her mother drove away, her mouth set in a grim line.

Robyn walked slowly to where she'd tied up the team. "Made a real mess, didn't you all? That will teach us to put two rookies in the team at once. Shouldn't have rushed it."

But she knew the accident hadn't happened because of the yearlings. She'd run half-grown pups with her team many times in training. That was how they learned. And each had been harnessed alongside an older, calmer dog. No, it was Grandpa's refusal to face the reality of his condition, and her reluctance to force him to admit it.

She felt Coco's leg. "You all right, girl?"

Coco licked her hand.

"I know it wasn't your fault." Robyn reached into her pocket for a treat and slipped it into Coco's mouth. Her hands shook as she unhooked the dogs one by one, led them to their kennels, and removed their harnesses. All the time she berated herself. They couldn't afford mistakes like that. How badly was Grandpa injured? Would Medicare pay for his treatment? The sled would need repair. She'd have to back up several steps in the new dogs' training. How many slow, steady runs would it take to undo what happened today? How long before they knew they were no longer in control?

She would have to proceed cautiously, to make sure she stayed in control and the dogs never tasted that freedom again. Her mind raced, thinking of ways to set things up so that today's fiasco never occurred again. Some extra weight on the sled next time would be a start. And she wouldn't run this particular group of dogs together again for a while. She'd take one or two of this batch at a time, mixing them with others who hadn't taken part in the episode.

She went into the house and filled two buckets of water. As the water ran, she remembered to call her mother's supervisor at the store. She cleaned out the dogs' dishes, surprised that the ice hadn't melted yet. It seemed like hours since she'd brought the dishes in. Most of them had thawed enough that the thick circles of ice fell out when she tipped the dishes up in the sink.

She carried the water to the dogs then dragged the sled up near the barn. She might be able to fix the wooden frame.

An hour later she still bent over it, almost finished, when her phone rang. She fumbled in her pocket for it. "Mom?"

"Yeah. They're doing a CT scan, but the doctor wants to keep Grandpa here overnight regardless of the results."

Robyn exhaled and fought back hot, painful tears. "Mom, I'm sorry."

"What for? It wasn't your fault."

Robyn swiped at her eyes with her free hand and sniffed. "I never should have let Grandpa drive. What was I thinking?"

"Oh, as if you could stop him."

"I know, but—"

"Honey, listen to me. We both know he's grown frailer over the last few years. He's done better this summer and fall, but he's still not strong. The trouble is, he's independent, too. He doesn't want to think he's too old to ever mush again. And neither one of us wanted to tell him the truth, because we love him."

Robyn pulled in a deep breath, knowing her mom talked sense. "If the dogs had a mind to, they could have been in Palmer in an hour. At least Max and Tumble turned the team around and came back."

"Yes, thank the Lord. They brought the team back safe. But it's time Dad stopped mushing, just like it was time he quit driving the truck."

Robyn swallowed hard. "I don't like to think of it. He's loved sledding all his life. And he's taught me so much!"

"I know, honey. But this is the way it's got to be. Now, if you're okay, I'm going to call the store and see if they can use me for a few hours. We can come in together and see Grandpa tonight."

"Okay." Robyn knew they needed the money. Mom couldn't afford to miss her part-time job if she didn't have to.

She put her phone away and went back to work on the sled. Grandpa made this sled, and it was a good one. He was never far from her thoughts as she worked. Without his mentoring, she'd never have learned as much about dogs as she did. She certainly wouldn't have had the opportunity to go into dog breeding and training as a business.

But today she felt like Alaska's biggest failure.

⁜

The next morning, Robyn rose at her usual time—five o'clock—and began preparing the dogs' breakfasts. Though Grandpa usually got up an hour later nowadays, she missed him, knowing he wouldn't be around today. The knowledge that he wouldn't eat breakfast with her after she'd fed the dogs saddened her.

"There've been a lot of changes in the last few years," Grandpa used to say, "and I've been against all of them."

Robyn pushed up the sleeves of her hoodie and sniffed. She could do without any more changes herself. First her older brother, Aven, had joined the Coast Guard. Then their father had died three years ago. Now she'd lost Grandpa, too, at least temporarily. Would it be just her and Mom from now on?

She opened the refrigerator for the meat she'd put in there to thaw overnight. Some people fed commercial food, but the dogs performed better if they ate mostly meat, so that's what the Hollands fed. Grandpa Steve had experimented over the years with several different feeding programs, and he'd worked out his own formula for a summer diet, changing to one with more fat and certain other nutrients as the racing season approached.

Since his arthritis had worsened, Robyn did most of the heavy work. Grandpa still played a big role in training teams for serious mushers and tending the dogs they raised to sell. He loved playing with the puppies, too.

"Hey, honey. Need any help?"

Robyn turned in surprise to see her mother, eyes puffy from sleep, standing in the doorway.

"No, I'm fine, Mom. Go back to bed."

"Figured I'd help you this morning and then run to the hospital to see Grandpa before work." On Wednesday afternoons, Cheryl put in four hours at the grocery store on the highway.

"I'll be okay." Robyn flashed a smile she didn't feel.

"Well, be careful if you do a training run."

"I will." She was always careful; but then, accidents had a way of catching you unaware. She hefted two buckets of dog feed and carried them toward the back door. "If Coco's still limping, I'll call Rick Baker to see if he can look at her. And maybe I'll call Darby later and see if she can come play with the puppies for a while."

Her mother sprang forward to open the door for her, so Robyn wouldn't have to set the buckets down. "She'd probably love to, and I'll feel better if I know you're not all alone here."

"Mom, don't let Grandpa's accident worry you too much. He's going to be okay."

"I don't like his head injury. That CT scan they did yesterday showed a little bleeding in his brain. That's not good. I'll feel better when the doctor says he's going to be all right."

⁜

Rick Baker was headed out the door with his medical bag when his phone rang. He paused in the kitchen and answered it.

"Hi, Dr. Baker? Rick? It's Robyn."

He smiled at her tentative greeting. "Yes, it's me, Robyn. Is anything wrong?" The pretty young woman next door rarely called him, and if she did, it usually meant her dogs needed his professional care. Sometimes he wished she wanted to see him because he was Rick, not because he was the vet who lived close by. He'd been too busy, though, to pursue the idea or the woman.

"One of my dogs had an accident yesterday. Actually, eight of them did, but Coco seems to be the only one who's hurt. She and Grandpa."

"Your grandfather was injured?"

"Yes." Her voice drooped like a slack towline. "He's at the hospital."

"What happened?"

She hesitated. "It's my fault. I let him take a team out. He thought he could handle them. I tried to tell him they were too much for him, but he wanted to do it so badly. I. . .I caved."

Rick could almost see her mournful dark eyes. He knew she was well past twenty years old, but today she sounded like a frightened kid.

"Is it serious?"

"We're not sure yet. They did some tests yesterday, and they're going to do a few more today. Mom's there now."

He glanced at his watch. If he stopped at the Hollands', he'd arrive at the clinic a few minutes late. But Robyn sounded like she needed a little reassurance. "Would you like me to take a look at Coco before I head for Anchorage?"

"Oh, today's your day at the clinic, isn't it?"

"Actually, I'm doing two days a week now. But I can take a quick look."

"I'd really appreciate it."

Ten minutes later he walked across the Hollands' dog lot with Robyn. She described the runaway sled and showed him where the team had collided with the shed wall. She took him into the female dogs' enclosure and led him to Coco's tether.

He stooped to greet the injured husky. "Hey there, Coco." He let the dog sniff his hands before touching her. "Where does it hurt, girl?"

"She hit her right front leg hardest." Robyn squatted beside him. "She's probably sore all over today."

Rick took his gloves off and ran his hand over the dog's shoulder and leg. "It's a little warm, and there seems to be some swelling. Not broken, though."

She nodded. "So, rest? What else?"

"Did she eat her breakfast?"

"Yeah."

He checked the dog's eyes and general appearance. Coco seemed alert and happy to see him. He felt her pulse and watched her respiration for a moment. "Okay. Give her a couple of days off, and make sure she keeps warm." He glanced toward the doghouse. The Hollands were good about providing shelter and bedding for their dogs in winter. "If she seems better then, start light exercise. Let her run free if you can, or put her on a leash and walk her around for ten or fifteen minutes. If she's no worse the next day, do a little more. . . . And I'll try to stop in again tomorrow and see how she's doing."

"Thanks."

He stood and pulled his gloves on. "No problem. And if she's worse, give me a call." They walked toward the gate. "I hope your grandfather's all right."

"Mom will probably come back for lunch before she goes to work. She'll tell me what the doctor said then."

Robyn looked young and vulnerable in her blue quilted jacket. Her dark hair hung in a thick braid over her shoulder, and her eyes held self-reproach.

"Hey." He reached out with his gloved hand and tilted her chin up. "You're not blaming yourself for your granddad's accident, are you?"

She shrugged. "I shouldn't have let him take the team out."

Rick considered that. Steve Holland was a stubborn old man. He'd forgotten more about dogs than most men ever learned, and he could dig in his heels when he wanted to.

"Who does your mother blame?" he asked.

Robyn hesitated a moment and looked down. "Grandpa."

"And who does Grandpa blame?"

"Himself."

Rick nodded. "So tell me, who's blaming Robyn?"

She smiled sheepishly but said nothing.

"Right. We all know you couldn't have stopped him, don't we?" Before she could protest, he turned her chin again, so that she looked up into his eyes. "This is not your fault."

"Okay." She held his gaze, and Rick took his time soaking in the view. He'd known Robyn a little over a year, and she intrigued him. She had a toughness the Alaska terrain and family hardships had taught her, but she had a tender side, too—the one that made her feel guilty when she didn't deserve it. She stirred a protectiveness in him, but he sensed she wouldn't accept that from a man unless she was desperate. Or in love.

"I'm going to call you tonight," he said on impulse.

Her eyebrows rose, forming delicate arches.

He nodded. "I want to check on Coco and your grandpa. So be ready with a report this evening."

She smiled. "That's nice of you. Thanks."

"No trouble." He left her and walked out toward his pickup. Fifteen minutes late, but fifteen minutes well spent. And tonight when he called, it would be as much to gauge Robyn's spirits as to check on the two patients. He looked forward to it, and he hadn't even left her driveway yet.

Chapter 2

At about eleven o'clock, Robyn heard her mother drive in. When she went into the house, her mom was just ending a phone conversation.

"Hi, honey. That was a potential customer. A man from California is interested in buying some dogs."

"That's great," Robyn said. "It would be good to sell a few yearlings. That would help our cash flow and give us more space for boarders."

"Yeah. He...wants to buy some breeding stock. He's coming next week to look over what you have."

Robyn stared at her. "I don't want to sell my breeding stock, Mom. You know that."

"Honey, we may not have a choice. Besides, you've got some adult dogs you planned on selling, haven't you?"

"A few." Robyn washed her hands at the sink. Since Dad died, they'd gotten by with the dog business and her mother's part-time job. But Mom worried a lot about their finances. She never seemed to believe they would have enough money to pay the bills each month. Sometimes Robyn thought Mom would rather get rid of all the dogs and live a "normal" life. But Robyn couldn't live without dogs.

She picked up the towel and dried her hands. "How's Grandpa?"

"Not so good. His bruises look terrible today." Mom shook her head and sighed. "It's his head injury that's got the doctor worried though. He's concerned enough that he wants to monitor Grandpa for another day or two."

"Well..." Robyn eyed her cautiously. "I guess that's best for him."

"Yes, I'm sure it is. It could get expensive, though."

"Won't Medicare pay for it?"

"For the hospital stay, yes, if it's not too long. But his muscles won't be used to working when he's ready to leave the hospital. The doctor said they'll probably transfer him to a skilled care nursing home for a couple of weeks of rehab."

Robyn let that sink in. No wonder her mother hadn't discouraged the dog buyer.

"I don't want to sell my breeding dogs, Mom. Or my leaders. I need them for training."

Her mother nodded but said nothing. They finished eating in silence.

❧

Darby Zale arrived at the Hollands' home soon after the school bus passed.

Robyn called to her and let her in to wait while she pulled on her jacket, boots, and gloves.

At sixteen, Darby hovered between exuberant kid and gorgeous woman. Her thick auburn hair and flawless skin frequently motivated Robyn to pray that she wouldn't be envious. It wasn't fair for a girl as young as Darby to look so good without even trying.

Darkness had already fallen, and Robyn put on her headlamp and handed Darby a flashlight before they went out the back door.

"They're getting so big!" Darby sidled through the gate with Robyn, into the puppy enclosure at one side of the dog yard.

"Yeah, they're getting pretty good at taking a few commands. It's time to start putting the puppy harness on them."

"Oh, I love it when we do that."

Robyn nodded. "Okay. I've got six dogs I want to take out for a training run. Why don't you play with the pups while I do that, and afterward, we'll do a short session with them."

"Great!" Darby gladly hung about the Hollands' kennels to help with the dogs and learn about sledding and training. Robyn got the team's harnesses ready and coached Darby through slipping one onto Rounder, an energetic three-year-old she hoped to sell soon. If the potential customer wanted fast, strong sled dogs and didn't care about breeding. . .she refused to think about it for the moment.

She handed Darby another harness. They hitched up the rest of the team she would exercise—several veterans and one yearling. Robyn hooked the towline to the repaired sled and waved to Darby, who stood near the puppy pen.

Getting out onto the trail always made Robyn feel more alive. She didn't mind sledding in the dark, though it hid the valley's magnificent scenery from her. You had to get used to it, or you wouldn't get much training time in Wasilla. This time of year, the area got only about four hours of daylight, and the air temperatures generally stayed below freezing. The dogs loved it.

She belonged out here, too. The crisp, fresh air and the firm snow perked her up and made her want to ride on and on. The dogs pulled eagerly beneath the moon. Her initial concerns about the sled she'd repaired seemed unfounded—it moved just as it should and held together.

She swung behind Rick Baker's house. The veterinarian had assured her that she could take the dogs over his property any time, and Robyn liked having some different scenery for the dogs. Rick's land also held a short section of the 100-mile trail for the Fire & Ice, the annual race the Holland Kennel sponsored in January. Several other landowners let them run over their property and turned out to help man checkpoints for the race.

As the dogs pulled her along, she prayed silently for Grandpa. If he went to the rehab place, would he be able to come home in time for this year's race? They'd received forty-eight entries—a record number for the Fire & Ice. Some of the names on the list impressed even Grandpa, who knew every musher in Alaska. A few well-known dog racers liked to use the Hollands' race as a warm-up for longer competitions or a training ground for young dogs. That suited Robyn just fine. It gave the Hollands an opportunity to display their kennel and dogs they had raised to potential customers.

The race fell on January twenty-third this year, which gave her only a few weeks to complete all the preparations. Without Grandpa's help, she would carry most of the load.

When she got back to the house half an hour later, Darby came smiling from the puppies' enclosure. "How'd they do?" she called.

"Perfect." Robyn stopped the team and started to set the snow hook. "Hey, do you know how to use one of these?"

"Not very well," Darby admitted, eyeing the metal hook uncertainly.

"Well, come on, girl. Now that we've got plenty of snow again, it's time you learned." Robyn beckoned her over and showed her how to push the hook into the snow near the sled, so that she could step on it and anchor it well while holding onto the sled's handlebar. She had the dogs move forward a little, putting tension on the anchor line.

"Now, if you want to release it, they have to back up." She pulled back on the sled, and the dogs inched backward. "As long as they're pulling on the line, if you've set it right, they can't go."

"That is so cool. Can I try it?"

Robyn grinned. "When you can do it right, I'll let you mush around the yard."

Darby was an apt pupil, and in less than ten minutes Robyn unhooked the two youngest dogs from the towline and rearranged the four older dogs.

"Okay. Don't forget to hold onto the sled when you take the snow hook off. If you can stand on the brake with one foot while you do it, that's even better." Robyn stood near the leaders, just in case. She didn't want another runaway team.

Darby pulled on the rope attached to the top of the hook and released it without trouble. The dogs twitched when they heard it come out of the snow.

"Brake," Robyn called.

Darby quickly put all her weight on the brake board.

"You're good," Robyn assured her. "Now wind up the rope and stow the hook. You don't want it dragging along behind the sled."

Darby fumbled with the line. "I'm nervous."

"Take your time. The dogs will know you're antsy, and they will be, too." Robyn was glad she'd cut the team down to four dogs. She'd considered letting Darby take them outside the enclosure today, but thought better of it. With a little more practice, Darby would gain the confidence she needed to control the team without the aid of a fence. For now, a trot around the path inside the yard would be enough.

After Darby's short ride, they put the dogs and the harness away and spent some time with the puppies, putting the small harness on each one for just a few minutes. Robyn was pleased that most of them obeyed her "sit" and "come" commands without error.

"Guess I'd better get home." Darby looked toward the sky. The moon still hung overhead.

"Thanks for the help," Robyn said. "Do you want me to drive you home in the truck?"

"No, I'll be okay if I leave now."

"Take the flashlight."

"Thanks. Can I come back tomorrow?"

"Yes. Oh—call first. I'm not sure if Grandpa's coming home or not."

"I hope he will. Bye." Darby dashed down the driveway.

Robyn went into the house and filled the woodstove. She liked to have a hot supper waiting when her mother got home from work. Afterward, she would feed the dogs with the aid of the lights in the dog lot and a powerful flashlight. Half the year at least she did her chores after dark or before the sun rose. She'd never lived anywhere else, so she expected it. But Aven had told her he'd had trouble sleeping when he went for his Coast Guard training in New Jersey. The sun never seemed to rise or set at the right time. After that, he'd served for a while in the Gulf of Mexico, and between the lack of snow and the comparatively long daylight hours in winter, he'd felt displaced at first.

"I kind of liked it after a while," he'd confessed to her. "It was too hot in summer, but the rest of the year was nice. I don't think people got as depressed as they do up here in the winter."

She puttered about the kitchen, thinking over what her mother had told her at noon. Grandpa's medical care could place a financial burden on them. He didn't have a large amount of savings. Most of what they all earned went for family expenses and maintaining the dogs and equipment. They'd each received a payment in the fall from Alaska's Permanent Fund, and right now they were solvent. But that would only go so far.

Robyn's biggest income came from selling puppies and older dogs she and Grandpa had trained. Sometimes she trained dogs for other people, but most serious mushers trained their own dogs. Right now she had a team of eight belonging to a sledder who had suffered appendicitis and undergone surgery. He'd asked her to take some of his dogs for six weeks and keep them in shape, so he wouldn't lose ground on training for the upcoming races. The other forty dogs out back were Holland dogs. Their upkeep was a spendy enterprise.

Mom came home about six o'clock with the trunk of her car full of groceries.

Robyn couldn't help noticing the fatigue lines at the corners of her eyes as she helped unload. "Are you going to the hospital tonight?" she asked.

"No, I don't think so. I called the nurses' station before I left work. Grandpa's doing all right and resting. I told her we'd come in the morning. I don't have to work tomorrow, and I thought you'd like to see him."

"Yes, I would."

Her mother nodded. "The doctor might know for sure by then what they plan to do to continue treatment."

"If they move him to a nursing home, will it be in Anchorage?" Robyn asked.

"I'm not sure yet. Guess we'll have to do some research."

"Maybe I can get online later."

Her mother smiled wearily. "That would be good. Would you like help feeding tonight?"

"I can do it," Robyn said, though she'd have been glad for an extra pair of hands. Her mother looked wrung out.

"Okay, then I'm going to pack a few things to take to Dad tomorrow. He wants his razor and his Bible. I'll take some clean clothes, too, in case they release him."

Robyn took out her cell phone and checked it before she went out to feed the dogs. They'd given up the landline to save money the year before and relied on their cells now. She hoped Rick would remember his promise to call her.

⁂

"Hey, Rick, any chance you can cover for me next Monday?" Bob Major, the principal partner of the Far North Veterinary Hospital in Anchorage, stopped him in the lobby before Rick could get out the door.

"Uh..." Rick quickly tabulated all the things on his agenda for Monday. "I don't think so, Bob. I've got a lot of patient visits lined up in the Palmer area and office hours in Wasilla. Besides, you already said you need me next Thursday."

Major shrugged. "It was worth a try. I'll have to rearrange my schedule is all. Or have Lucy rearrange it." He looked toward the receptionist's desk and winked at her.

Lucy, who had worked for Bob and his partner, Hap Shelley, for several years, rolled her eyes. "What else is new?"

Bob laughed. "I'll see you Friday."

"On call only, right? We're officially closed for New Year's, Hap told me."

"True, but we've got some inpatients you'll need to treat, and there are always a few emergency calls."

"Right. I'll be here." Rick nodded at Lucy and escaped. The drive home to Wasilla would take a good forty-five minutes. He disliked the commute, which would probably get harder as winter went on. Why had he ever agreed to do two days a week in Anchorage? He'd left full-time practice with Far North a year ago, but the other two doctors insisted they still needed him to man the clinic some of the time. Rick had agreed to continue working one day a week in Anchorage and opened his small veterinary practice in Wasilla. He'd reasoned that he might not have enough business to support him up there and should keep the ties to the larger practice strong in case his new venture didn't work out.

Talk about underestimation. Despite the fact that several other veterinarians worked in the area, he'd soon found that he couldn't handle all the business waiting for him in the Mat-Su Valley if he'd cloned himself. But Bob had pleaded with him a month ago to add a second day to his weekly commitment at the Anchorage clinic. Rick had reluctantly agreed. Now Bob wanted him to cover on extra days.

Rick slid behind the wheel of his pickup, thankful he'd had the courage to refuse. The way things were going, they'd soon try to draw him back into the Anchorage practice full time. Bob and Hap had already hinted that they'd started looking for a new partner to replace Bob when he retired. It would be a secure position for Rick, and a better income. He could move back to Anchorage and not have to drive so far. In the city, most of the patients came to him. In the valley, he made as many house calls as office visits. And he wouldn't be risking his life savings on a new venture.

But every time he drove to the city, Rick found himself a little more certain he didn't want to do that. He loved his log home on the outskirts of Wasilla. The building he rented in town for his practice wasn't ideal, but it was adequate. He hoped one day to build a spacious new facility, where he could provide complete services, within a few miles of Iditarod Headquarters. Maybe he'd be the one bringing in a partner. It was a big dream, but at thirty-three, Rick knew what he wanted. His own practice. His own home. Someday, his own family.

He used the first part of the drive to pray for his patients and his work situation then popped in a CD. By the time he reached his driveway, the tension was gone. A slight pang of regret nudged him as he unlocked the door to the empty house. It would be nice to have someone waiting for him. But with his long days on the road, he didn't feel he could have even a dog at home. He wouldn't like to neglect one, and he couldn't see taking one with him to the clinic. Too complicated.

The house was cold. He ran the heat low while he was away from home. A fire in the woodstove tonight might be enough to keep him warm. He'd heard temperatures would fall later in the week, though, to zero or below. He'd have to rely more on the furnace.

After he'd gotten the place warmed up and fixed dinner in the microwave, he remembered he'd promised to call Robyn.

She sounded a little breathless when she answered.

"Hi," Rick said. "Everything okay over there?"

"Yes, thanks. Coco seemed a little better tonight. I rubbed her shoulder for a few minutes when I fed her."

"Good. How's Mr. Holland?"

"Well. . .they're keeping him tonight and maybe tomorrow. But Mom says the doctor will probably recommend rehabilitation after that. Instead of sending him home, they may put him in a skilled care home for a little while."

"That may be what's best for him right now," Rick said. "I know it's hard to face, but if he needs therapy, let the professionals help him. Chances are he'll feel better and be able to do more when he finally comes home than he did before the accident."

"Maybe." She sighed. "I've been praying all day. I know Grandpa would hate having to go somewhere else. He doesn't like being away from home anyway, and being in the city would be a double blow for him. Mom thinks the rehab place would be in Anchorage."

"That's rough," Rick said. "I hate to think of you and your mom having to go back and forth a lot. If it's any help, I'd be happy to give either of you a ride when I'm going that way."

"Thanks a lot."

He wished he could put a smile in her voice. Robyn usually presented a sunny attitude. What would cheer her up? One thing came to mind. "Hey, I was asked today if I'd help oversee the 'dropped dog' station for the Iditarod in March."

"Oh, that is so cool. I'd love to get that assignment."

"You want to help? I can try to get your name on the list of volunteers."

"Really?" She hesitated. "We always do something during the Iditarod, usually here in the valley. But it would be great to help tend the dogs during the race."

"Yeah. I always feel bad for mushers who have to drop a dog, but they do get tired or injured sometimes. We'll give them the best care when they're flown to Anchorage, until their owners can pick them up again."

"Let me talk to Mom about it, okay? If she wants to help at one of the checkpoints up here, I should probably stay with her."

"Just let me know. Can't guarantee you a spot, but I'll use what influence I'll have as a team leader."

"Thanks."

She sounded happier now, and Rick hated to end the conversation. Tomorrow was New Year's Eve, and there'd be a celebration downtown. Should he ask her? People would be out watching the Northern Lights and generally raising a riot. He'd planned to avoid the noisy gathering. Besides, did he really want to stay up that late after a full day making his rounds? He decided not. "Well, I'll stop in tomorrow and take a look at Coco."

"Good. Oh, I plan to go with Mom around ten in the morning to see Grandpa."

"I'll come earlier. Eight all right?"

"Perfect."

"Robyn, if you need help with anything, let me know."

"Thanks, I will. I know you're busy."

"Hey, I mean it. And I plan to help out at your race this year, too."

"Oh, good. I was hoping you would. I tentatively put you down for prerace vet checks, and we'll have you evaluate the dogs when they finish, too, if you can do it."

"Fantastic. I love the way all the people in town help out on race day."

"Me, too," she said. "Only three weeks to go. My friend Anna is keeping track of the volunteers, and she said nearly all the spots are filled. It's always a blessing to see the people come out and help us."

Rick signed off and settled in his recliner with a book, but his thoughts kept drifting back to Robyn and their conversation. It reaffirmed his decision about Far North Veterinary. They could find another vet. His place was here in Wasilla now.

⁂

"Why can't I just go home?" Grandpa Steve folded his arms across his chest and glared up at his doctor.

"I don't think you're ready just yet," Dr. Mellin said with a smile. She shone her flashlight into Grandpa's eyes, observing with a frown. "A couple of weeks at rehab will do a lot for you. It'll give you a chance to regain your strength and balance. We don't want you to go home and have a fall and wind up back in here."

Robyn glanced at her mother. Leave it to Grandpa to kick up a fuss, but then, she'd expected that.

"Isn't there a place here in Wasilla?" Mom asked.

Dr. Mellin straightened and shook her head. "I'm afraid not. Will it be a hardship for you if he goes to Anchorage?"

Mom shrugged. "Some, but we'll do whatever we have to. Won't we, Dad?"

He snorted and refused to meet her gaze.

"Grandpa," Robyn said, "you've got to do what the doctor says. When you get better, then we'll bring you home."

"People go into nursing homes and don't come out."

Robyn almost laughed at his passionate scowl, but something in her stomach twisted. He mirrored her fear exactly, down to the childish expression.

"Mr. Holland, I'm only recommending this because I think it's the best course of treatment for you. We can't keep you here more than another day, given your condition."

"What does that mean?" His eyebrows pulled together as he looked up at her.

"It means you're getting better, but you're not completely well. Your head injury seems to be healing, and in a few days your bruises will go away. But your muscles need some attention. Let us get you the treatment you need and send you home in a couple of weeks in good shape."

"A couple of weeks? You hear that, Cheryl? I can't come home for two weeks."

"That's my estimate based on what I see today." Dr. Mellin consulted the chart. "If you behave yourself, that ought to do it. No guarantees though. So. . .I'll refer you, and if nothing's changed for the worse, we'll release you tomorrow."

Mom stood. "How will he get to the rehab place?"

"He doesn't really need an ambulance. If you are able to drive him to Anchorage, it would save the expense. I think he'll ride fine in a private car for that distance."

"Mom, I can take him," Robyn said. "You have to work tomorrow afternoon."

"I could take the day off. I think I'd like to take him myself, honey." Mom smiled at her. "No offense, and if you want to come along, that's fine. I just want to be there to help him get settled."

"Will I be able wear my own clothes?" Grandpa threw back the covers. "These johnnies are worthless. I want my pajamas."

Dr. Mellin smiled. "I think they'll let you wear pajamas, sir. And now you should rest. I'll pop in this evening to see what you're up to. Don't run the nurses ragged today, you hear?"

"Who. . .me?"

Mom peeled back the blanket and replaced the sheet over Grandpa's thin legs. "Dad, she's kidding."

"Ha."

Dr. Mellin laughed and headed for the door. "See you later, Mr. Holland."

"After awhile, crocodile." He frowned up at his daughter-in-law. "Cheryl, they don't know how to make apple crisp here."

"Relax. I brought you some cookies."

"What about my razor?"

"Yes. Do you want to shave?" Mom asked.

"Not now. What kind of cookies?"

Robyn pulled the plastic container from her tote bag and sat down on the edge of his bed. "Gingersnaps and peanut butter. Mom had a bake-fest last night. Which do you want first?"

"Ginger snaps." He looked around at the nightstand and spotted a glass of water with a straw in it. "Can you reach my drink?"

Robyn handed it to him.

After the first cookie, Grandpa switched to peanut butter. "How's Coco doing?" he asked.

"She's okay. Dr. Baker looked at her yesterday and again this morning. He thinks she'll be fine."

Grandpa's eyebrows shot up. "Rick made two house calls?"

"Well. . .yes, if you want to get technical."

"Are we paying him for it?"

"I. . ." Robyn looked around helplessly at her mother.

"I think Rick stopped in as a neighbor, Dad. Don't worry about it."

"But if he's doing vet stuff, we should pay him."

"I'll make a point of asking him to send us a bill," Mom said.

Grandpa sighed and lay back on his pillows. "I made a big mess, didn't I? I bet my vet bills are going to be a lot more than Coco's."

His eyelids drifted shut, and Robyn glanced at her mother. They'd stopped at the billing office on the way in. Most of this hospital stay would be covered, but they'd learned only seven days of Grandpa's rehab would be paid for. If he stayed in treatment longer than that, the family would be expected to pay for it.

Mom had leaned back in her chair and closed her eyes. She looked exhausted. Robyn determined to ask Darby to help her feed in the morning. She needed to be finished early—in time to go with Mom when she moved Grandpa to Anchorage.

Chapter 3

Darkness had fallen when they returned to the house the next afternoon. Robyn was surprised to see Rick's pickup in the yard when she drove in.

He ambled around the corner of the house from the direction of the dog lot as she parked. "Hi," he called. "Need any help?"

"No, thanks," Mom said. "We don't have much to carry."

"How's Steve?"

"All settled at the nursing home."

"That's good. I hope he does well there." Rick looked at Robyn. "Hope you don't mind, I went out back and looked at Coco. She seems to have recovered well."

"I think so, too. I asked Darby to take her out on the leash for a few minutes this morning. I'll be around tomorrow to work all these lazy dogs."

Rick smiled and walked with her as she followed Mom into the house. "It's a big job, getting them all in shape. Especially in this cold weather."

"Yes. And I have several I hope to sell. They need to be in top condition when the buyers start looking."

"When will that be?"

Robyn stopped in the living room and faced him. Mom was in the kitchen, out of earshot. "Actually, we have someone coming next week to look at a few of the dogs."

"You don't sound too happy about that."

She took a breath and looked away. "I'm not. He wants breeding stock, and those aren't the dogs I want to sell right now. But. . .I may not have a choice."

"Everything all right?" Quickly he added, "I don't mean to pry, but if there's anything I can help with. . ."

"Things are a little tight financially. But hey, they always are around here." She pulled out a smile for him.

"I've been praying for your family."

His simple statement comforted her. She'd picked up on a few things he'd said in the past, but he'd never come to the little church her family attended in Wasilla. Grandpa had a bolder nature than she did though. He'd pinned Rick down verbally once while he was examining a new litter of puppies. Robyn wished she'd been there. Grandpa had told her later that Rick shared their faith. Actually, Grandpa's exact words were, "Just what we need. A vet who knows his Bible *and* his medical books."

136

"Thank you. Pray that we'll have what's needed for Grandpa's care, and that he'll be ready to come home soon, so we don't have to pay too much."

"How long will he need physical therapy?"

"The doctor estimated two weeks—which is more than he's covered for."

Rick nodded. "Got it. I'll be praying about the race, too. It's not that far away, and I know your grandfather usually helps a lot with that."

"Three weeks." Robyn caught her lower lip between her teeth.

"Are you nervous about it?"

"Yeah. I'm not sure how we'll do. There's a meeting next Saturday for all the volunteers. If you're busy, it's okay."

"I'll be there. What time?"

"Ten o'clock, at Iditarod Headquarters. They're letting us use the meeting room."

"Nice."

She nodded. "Mom is helping a lot, but it's been tough since my dad died. Grandpa and I do most of the race preparation, and we get friends to help. My brother and his wife plan to come the week of the race. Aven's terrific. He'll do all the last-minute heavy work. Ormand Lesley is our race marshal. He does a lot of work, too. And we've got people organizing the mushers' drop bags and communications and—oh, a thousand other things."

"Even a race of this scale is a ton of work, isn't it?"

"It sure is. But we've done whatever we had to in order to keep it going these last few years. The success of the Fire & Ice is important to our business."

"I thought it might be. I'm happy to volunteer my services for the day."

"I'll give you the toughest duties."

He grinned. "That's what I want. Let me at it. And if the route will allow me to do the check-in exams and then go off to another spot farther down the line, I'll do it. I know the teams loop around and come back to the start, but I might be able to help someplace else for a few hours. Whatever you need."

"That's terrific. I'll take you up on it." She stood for a moment, looking up into his gleaming eyes. Rick Baker could surely give a girl ideas.

"Hey, let me help you feed the dogs tonight," he said.

"Really? You don't need to."

"I know. I want to. You've been gone all day, and I'll bet you're tired."

"Okay, you asked for it. I've got meat in the refrigerator. The rest of it's out in the barn."

She led him into the kitchen. Mom bent over a base cabinet and pulled out a frying pan. "Feel like a grilled cheese sandwich, Robyn?"

"Sure. Thanks. Dr. Baker's going to help me feed the mutts, so it won't take long."

"Rick, have you had supper?" Mom asked. "It's not fancy, but I can make a few extra sandwiches without any trouble."

"Well. . ." He eyed her with his eyebrows arched.

"Why not?" Robyn asked. "You'll be earning your keep."

He laughed. "All right. Thank you, Mrs. Holland."

"It's Cheryl. And thank *you*. I think Robyn and I are both frazzled tonight."

A note was tacked to the door of the shed they referred to as the "the barn."

Happy New Year! I cuddled the puppies for a bit and cleaned out their pen. See you tomorrow.

Darby

Rick read it over her shoulder. "She's a good kid," he said.

"Yes. She loves dogs, and she's a big help to me lately. I wish I could afford to pay her."

"She's getting paid in the knowledge you're giving her."

Robyn nodded. "I promised her I'd teach her to drive the sled this winter. She's had a couple of lessons. She'll be good at it."

In less than twenty minutes, Robyn had doled out the dog food and meat, while Rick filled the water dishes. Robyn took a few seconds to pat and speak to each dog. She never liked being away from them all day. Tomorrow Darby would probably spend most of the day here. Training runs and puppy lessons would fill the hours.

Rick walked with her back to the house. For a few seconds, everything felt in sync. If she could just forget about their finances, Grandpa's accident, and the buyer coming to look over her best dogs, life would be close to perfect right now.

⊰⊱

Robyn went about her chores in the dark Monday morning, trying not to think too hard about the day's schedule. The buyer was to arrive at nine a.m.

When she went inside after her morning feeding and cleanup, Mom was vacuuming the living room. She shut the vacuum off when Robyn came in. "Just slicking up a little. I'm glad we got the Christmas tree out of the house, but it left needles all over the rug."

Robyn didn't feel like doing anything special to get ready for the buyer, but that attitude would only show her immaturity. She raised her chin. "Do you want me to do anything to help?"

"No, just eat breakfast and try not to fret. Mr. Sterns will be here in an hour or so, and then we'll know one way or another if he wants to buy some dogs. Worrying about it won't change things."

"Mom—"

"Don't tell me you don't want to sell any dogs." Her mother put her hand to her temple and sighed. "I'm sorry, Robyn. The last few days have been. . ."

"I know. And I'm sorry." Robyn sat down on the arm of the couch. "I know it's been hard, going back and forth to see Grandpa. And I didn't like what the therapist said yesterday any better than you did."

Her mother came over and sat down in the chair opposite her. "Honey, we can't afford the skilled care for long. What little we had put away will be gone soon, but the physical therapist thinks Grandpa may need extended treatment."

Robyn nodded, mulling over what they'd heard the day before. "Six weeks, he said. Grandpa sure didn't like that."

"Neither do I," her mother admitted. "It's far longer than Dr. Mellin thought he'd need. But the therapist was right that Grandpa's still very weak. If he came home and took a bad fall, we'd be in a worse situation."

"So what can we do?"

"I hope they'll let us bring him home after a couple of weeks and drive him in for his appointments. Even using all that gas would be cheaper than keeping him in rehab."

"Mom, if we sell the breeding stock, our business will collapse." Robyn held her gaze and plunged on. "Selling good quality pups and trained sled dogs is our bread and butter. The race helps, but I don't see how we could continue running the Fire & Ice without a breeding kennel to support it. And your job isn't enough."

"I know all that." Mom pulled in a deep breath. "Sometimes I wonder if. . ."

"If what?"

"If we should sell the property and the business."

Robyn stared at her. "Everything? Sell the house and. . .no. We can't. What would we do? Where would we live?"

"I don't know, sweetie. I just think some days that we can't keep on the way we are."

"But. . .you don't want to move into Anchorage, do you? Get jobs there? Housing is really expensive in the city."

"That's true. And we own this place outright." Her mother ran a hand through her short, curly hair. "I don't know what to think. I just know things can't stay the same. I suppose we're better off in a house we own than paying rent. But with Grandpa's care. . ."

"Let's see what that social worker can tell us," Robyn said. "Dr. Mellin thought we might not be figuring right on the coverage. She said the government would use the patient's savings if insurance or Medicare won't pay for the treatment, but they can't take everything we have, too."

"You're right." Her mother stood and gave her a wan smile. "Hey, I'm going to do a little dusting in here. Why don't you eat something? And take off your jacket."

Robyn looked down at the grubby jacket she wore when she cleaned the dog pens. Usually when customers came, she changed her clothes and tried to look somewhat professional. Today she was so downhearted, she didn't really care if Mr.

Sterns thought she looked scruffy.

As she poured milk on her cereal a few minutes later, she heard her mother's phone ring. If that was Philip Sterns, she was glad he had Mom's number, not hers. She didn't want to talk to him until she had to.

A lilt in her mother's tone drew her to the door between the rooms. Mom smiled at her and mouthed, "Aven."

Her brother's name was the first thing to make her smile since Rick Baker's visit on Friday evening. Robyn did miss the traditional telephone, with extensions that allowed them all to share a conversation at once. She thought of asking Mom to use the speaker phone feature but instead concentrated on finishing her cereal. She'd get the details later.

Mom talked for a few minutes, giving Aven an update on Grandpa's condition. "That sounds great. Here, let me give the phone to Robyn. You can tell her yourself."

Robyn took it and put it to her ear. "Hey, how you doing?"

"Terrific. Caddie and I are planning to come up the Saturday before the race and stay all week. We want to spend some time with Grandpa and the rest of you."

"That's wonderful." Unexpected tears filled her eyes. "This is a good time for you to come."

"Oh? Better than usual?"

"We just need a little head-patting." Robyn wiped a tear away with her sleeve.

"Hey, kiddo, it's going to be okay. We'll talk everything over when I'm there."

She sniffed. "Good. Because Mom and I are kind of discouraged right now."

"I know. We're praying for you. We'll see you soon."

She signed off and handed the phone back to her mother. As she wiped away another tear, she smiled sheepishly. "Don't know why he makes me cry. I'm glad he's coming."

"Yes. Maybe he can help us make some decisions about your grandfather's care." Mom slid the phone into her pocket and held her arms out to Robyn. "Honey, I'm sorry that you're feeling so sad."

Robyn hugged her. "I don't mean to get upset. I just don't think this is a good time to think about selling our land and our dogs when they support us, even if we don't have much."

Her mother patted her back. "I know. Let's talk about this later. I think I hear someone driving in."

"Oh, great!" Robyn stepped back. "My face is all blotchy, isn't it?"

Mom chuckled. "Go clean up. I'll offer him coffee."

⁂

Philip Sterns stood when Robyn entered the room. That was a good sign, in her book. He looked to be about forty, with long, sturdy limbs. His hair receded off his forehead, and he wore glasses. Robyn tried not to form an opinion at first glance, but she didn't like him. His ears stuck out noticeably beyond the bows of his glasses, and his teeth looked overly white, like snow no one's walked on.

"Robyn is our head trainer now," her mother said as Robyn shook Sterns's hand. "My father-in-law helps her, but she's the boss."

"I'd be happy to show you the dogs I'm ready to sell," Robyn said. She put on her best jacket and led Sterns out the back door and to the dog lot.

"You have a gorgeous location." He looked appreciatively toward the mountain peaks.

"Thanks." She opened the gate to the enclosure for the adult male dogs. From puppies to retirees, all the dogs began barking as soon as they entered the yard. "Hush now," Robyn called softly, and the din subsided to an occasional yip.

"How do you make them do that?" Sterns asked.

She laughed. "One of the first things I teach my dogs is to be quiet unless there's something to bark about. Otherwise, our neighbors wouldn't be too happy."

"That's a pretty good trick."

"I understand you're new to dog sled racing," she said.

"Yes. A friend of mine took me to a couple of races in the Sierras last winter, and I fell in love with the sport. I've bought a couple of dogs, but I understand Alaskan huskies are the best."

"We like to think so, too."

He laughed. "I've done some research, and I'm thinking about doing some experimental breeding."

Robyn stopped with her hand on the latch of the gate. "How do you mean?"

"I'd like to try crossing huskies with some greyhound blood."

She nodded slowly. "Have you done any reading about that sort of crossbreeding?"

"A little. Oh, I know it's been tried before, but I have some ideas of my own."

"I see. Have you bred dogs before, Mr. Sterns? Or is this a new interest, since you became enamored of mushing?"

"I haven't actually raised any animals myself yet, but I want to. I've read that it's best to raise and train your own team. They know what you expect better that way."

"That can be true, but for someone new to the sport, it might be best to start with a team that's already mature and trained to mush. Get used to running the team, and make sure you like it. Then, if you want to get into breeding. . ."

"Oh, I know I like it." He grinned at her. "My friend let me drive his dogs a few times, and I'm hooked. What I'd really like to find is a team that's ready to go now, and I could do a few short races this spring. Then I can breed the dogs and start building my custom team. And next year. . .well, I'm thinking maybe I'll try to qualify for the big one."

"The. . .the Iditarod?"

"That's right. Oh, I know it takes years to master it, but I plan to be up there soon with Mackey and King and the rest."

Robyn swallowed hard. "That's quite a goal to work toward." She wanted to say more but decided to leave it alone. If he pursued the matter, he'd soon learn how tough it was to qualify for the Iditarod.

"This fellow is one of my best right now," she said, stooping to pat Max. She'd really miss him if she sold him, but the price she had in mind would pay for a lot of dog food. "He's a good lead dog, and he's strong."

"Is he. . .uh. . .can I breed him?"

"No, but—"

"I want to breed dogs and raise my own team," Sterns said, his face eager. "I'm serious about that."

"Mr. Sterns, I'm not really selling breeding stock right now. I raise dogs and train them to race. If I think they won't make good sled dogs, I sell them as pets. But I don't usually sell my breeding dogs."

"When I told your mother on the phone, she said you might need to sell a few."

Robyn's chest squeezed. "I'm sorry if there was a misunderstanding. That's not really my intent right now."

"Oh. Well. . .which one is your best sire? I did a little reading up on your kennel before I came. Isn't Tumble the one? Everyone wants pups with his bloodline, right?"

She hesitated then led him to Tumble's kennel. He greeted her with a quiet yip and licked her hand. "This is Tumble, and you're right. He's our primary sire right now. But he's not for sale."

She showed Sterns several other male dogs that did well in harness, but Rounder and the others didn't seem to impress him. Hero, a big black-and-white Siberian husky, bared his teeth and growled when the man approached him. The other dogs eyed Sterns with indifference. She took him over to the female dogs' enclosure. Coco ran to the end of her tether and strained eagerly toward them.

"Oh, I like this guy," Sterns said.

"She's four years old." Robyn determined to ignore his mistake. "She's a good team dog. I use her as a wheeler or anywhere else on the line except the lead. She's strong, and she has a lot of stamina. With a little more experience, she might work into lead, but right now I use her farther back."

"Has she had any litters?"

"Yes. One. I've got some of her pups I'm working with now." She thought about offering to sell him some of the female pups, but the idea of putting them into the hands of an inexperienced person for their sled training made her cringe.

After looking at half a dozen more females, Sterns nodded and shoved his hands in his pockets. "I like them all. What do you say I take those three"—he nodded toward Coco and the two others nearest her—"and Tumble."

Robyn sucked in a deep breath. "Tumble isn't for sale. I can give you one of his sons—a two-year-old showing a lot of promise." She supposed she could sell three adult females and be all right. But Tumble was out of the question.

"I'll tell you what." He smiled and peered at her through his glasses. "I'll meet your price on all the females without any dickering. And for Tumble, I'll give you triple what you're asking for the two-year-old."

Robyn's heart sank. How could she turn down that kind of money when they needed it so badly? If Mom were out here with them, she'd probably accept the offer. But it would set Robyn's breeding program back years. Tumble's offspring were becoming known in racing circles. Mushers noticed his pups wherever they ran, which would include the Yukon Quest and the Iditarod this year. She wanted to be ready when they won. She had no doubt more dog owners would bring their females to Holland Kennels for breeding.

She swallowed hard. "I'm sorry, Mr. Sterns. I stand by what I said. You can bring your females here to be bred, but Tumble isn't for sale."

He studied her for a long moment. "How about if I go back to Anchorage and give you a couple of days to think it over? Talk to your mother about it. I'll come back Wednesday."

"I won't change my mind."

"Are you sure about that?" He smiled again. "I'm not prepared to take the dogs I buy today, anyway. I've got a rental car. I'll have to come back with a truck."

"We can crate and ship the dogs for you, if you want. We've trucked dogs to the airport for our customers before. It's no problem. But I really think Max is a better dog for you. You said you'd like a lead dog you can race this spring."

He shook his head. "I still think we should let this sit for a couple of days. We'll talk again Wednesday."

Chapter 4

After supper Robyn hitched up six dogs for a two-mile run. The snow was eighteen inches deep on open areas, and the trail conditions were perfect. Mom had gone to Anchorage and would be back later, after Robyn got home.

Half a mile out, just after she crossed onto Rick's land, Tumble barked and surged forward. The other dogs caught his energy and pulled faster, too. Soon Robyn saw what inspired them. Someone with a flashlight was coming toward them on snowshoes.

She recognized Rick as they reached him. He stepped off the trail and waited for her to stop the team. Robyn set the snow hook and greeted him.

Rick pushed back his hood and grinned at her. "You're looking good. How's it going?"

"Well, Mom called a little while ago and said Grandpa did well on his therapy sessions today. But they're still giving him pain meds for aches and pains."

"It takes the old bones longer to heal than it does young ones."

"Yeah."

"Did the buyer come to look over your dogs?"

She nodded. "Philip Sterns. I don't like him. He doesn't know much about dogs, but he wants to race this year and he thinks that by next year he'll qualify for the Iditarod."

"Hmm. Does he have someone to mentor him?"

"I'm not sure. He did mention some friends who got him interested in sledding, but he's not ready to own good dogs, Rick. He'll ruin them."

"So you don't want to sell to him."

"Not really, but. . .the truth is, we need the cash, and Mom is pushing me to close the deal. He's coming back Wednesday."

"How many dogs does he want?"

"Four in all. I don't have much problem with selling him three females, although he'll probably mess up their training. But he wants to start his own designer breeding program, and he knows absolutely nothing about dogs."

"That's tough to accept."

"I'll say. And he wants to buy Tumble. I told him and Mom absolutely not, but. . . well, he's offering us a bundle for him." The team was restless and wriggled in their harnesses. "I shouldn't stop long. They want to run, and they deserve it. But thanks for letting me sound off."

"Sounds like you have a tough decision to make," Rick said. "I'll keep praying for you."

"Thanks. I admit I get riled when I think about selling off our breeding stock. The business would go under."

"And your mom wants to do that? Does she want to get out of the kennel business?"

Robyn sighed. "I don't know. But she pointed out today that we may end up having to sell everything anyway, and it would be better to sell the best dogs now at a good price than to wait and have to sell in a hurry at reduced figures when we're desperate."

"I'm sorry. I had no idea things were that bad."

"I'm not sure they are, but Mom seems to think that Grandpa's situation will break us. I don't know much about insurance and Medicare and all that, but it doesn't seem fair. Sometimes I wonder if she's just tired of this life and wants to move into town."

Rick's eyes widened. "You mean. . .sell your house and everything?"

"She's mentioned it. Please keep that between us. I don't think it's going to happen, but when Mom gets fretting about money, she says things like that."

"That's a lot to deal with." He cocked his head to one side. "Do you think maybe you don't like this Sterns fellow because making a deal with him could signal the end of your family's way of life, or do you have something specific not to like about him?"

"Besides the fact that he's green as grass?" She thought about it for a moment. "He came with a pocketful of cash, but that's not really unusual. People know they can't always use a credit card or write a check out here in the hinterlands. I guess the thing I like least is the way the dogs reacted to him. They didn't seem to take to him." She looked up and smiled ruefully. "That and the fact that he has fancy clothes and is staying at the swankiest hotel in Anchorage."

"Mmm. Real 'dog racing' people don't usually put on airs."

"Yeah. Is he a rich guy who fancies getting into a hobby that will make him look rugged to his friends?"

"People like that usually tire of it when they learn how much work is involved."

"Exactly," she said. "Then what will become of these beautiful dogs?"

⚜

Rick stepped closer to Robyn—as close as his unwieldy snowshoes would let him. He laid his gloved hand on the sleeve of her parka.

"Listen, I don't know if this would help you or not, but I'll be in Anchorage all day tomorrow. I have a friend with the state police, and I was thinking. . ."

Her eyes glistened with what might be hope, so he plunged on.

"He may not be able to do anything, but I could ask him to look into this guy's background and just make sure he's legit."

"Wow, that would make me feel better. Even if they didn't find anything—I mean, if he doesn't have a police record, that's good, right?"

She gave him Sterns's full name, the hotel where he was lodging, his cell phone number, and the town in California where he claimed he lived. Rick was glad to be able to do something to help her. His concern for the Hollands had grown over the last few days, and he wanted to take away some of Robyn's anxiety.

The dogs whined, and she reached for the snow hook. "We need to get going. Thanks for listening, Rick."

"Anytime. And be careful. I saw a moose not far from here yesterday."

"Okay, I'll stay alert. Don't want a moose tearing into my team."

He watched her and the sled team move down the trail into the trees. *She'll be okay,* he told himself. Though he'd heard of a few instances where a moose had savaged a dog team that couldn't escape its wrath, that was a rare happening. Usually the huge animals lumbered into the woods as soon as they saw someone coming. And Robyn knew what she was doing. He was more worried about her financial straits.

He was beginning to care for her beyond friendship, and he didn't like to think that her family might leave the area. His friend Joel Dawes might not be able to help him out. Maybe he should have broached the subject to Joel before mentioning it to Robyn, but her uneasiness about the potential sale to Sterns had overcome his caution. Assurance that the prospective buyer was honest should help Robyn feel easier about selling some of her treasured dogs to him.

Rick set out once more on his snowshoes, mulling over the Hollands' situation. If Cheryl seriously wanted to sell the property, he wouldn't mind adding to his own land. But he didn't suppose he had enough money for that. Opening his new practice in Wasilla last year had tied up all his savings. He wondered, too, who owned the Hollands' property. Robyn's father had died in an accident several years earlier. A plane crash, if he remembered correctly. Was the deed in Cheryl's name—or Grandpa Steve's?

An hour later he got home and built up his wood fire. Relaxing with a cup of cocoa and a handful of cookies from a store package, he found that he couldn't stop thinking of Robyn. When he considered his hours spent at Far North Veterinary, it now bore directly on the amount of time he had available to spend with her. The drive to the city on Sunday for church tired him out and took him away from his Wasilla patients—and Robyn. Definitely time to focus his efforts.

He looked at his watch. She'd have put the dogs away by now and buttoned down the kennel for the night. He pulled out his phone. "Hey, Robyn? It's Rick." He felt suddenly like he was back in high school, calling a girl from chem lab and wondering what to say next. "Just wanted to see how your ride went."

"Good. No moose that I saw. And I'm pleased with the way the dogs are progressing."

"Glad to hear it." He loved the way she talked about her dogs—businesslike, but with the pride of a mother.

"I'm thinking of entering a short race next month, after we're done with the craziness here," she said. "It's a great way to get the dogs used to competition and crowds."

"Sounds like fun."

"Hey, do you remember what I told you earlier, about. . . about our property?"

"Yes." He sensed that she didn't want to say too much over the phone.

"Well, my mom says Sterns is interested."

"In the whole place?"

"Yes. I'm having a hard time with this. It makes me furious that she told some-one like him—someone we know nothing about."

"Did she talk to him again since this morning?"

"Apparently he called her tonight, after she left the nursing home. She phoned me on her way home. She hasn't gotten here yet, but. . .well, you promised to pray for me. Would you pray that I don't have a rip-roaring, knock-down-drag-out with my mom?"

"Yes. I surely will. I'll do that right now. And I won't forget tomorrow. If I can find out anything about this guy for you, I'll call you."

He hung up still feeling her alarm. Would trying to help her put him in the middle of a bitter family dispute?

⁜

Robyn waited up for her mother, her anger simmering. She planned what she would say when Mom walked through the door. This wasn't fair. Robyn's name might not be on the deed to the property, but she ought to have a say in what became of her home and her business.

Even though her thoughts made sense to her, she knew her attitude was wrong. Mom had worked hard, even before Dad died. She'd helped in the kennel business, too, but had finally taken the job at the store to supplement their erratic income. When it came right down to it, Mom had probably suffered most of all the family.

She'd moved with her husband and two-year-old son from civilized Pennsylvania to the wilds of Alaska. She never complained about the cold or the light depri-vation and the seasonal affective disorder some Alaska residents—especially the transplants—suffered. She pitched in and helped.

Grandpa's accident was a case in point. Mom was dealing with it the best way she knew how. Getting Grandpa the best treatment they could. Visiting him as often as possible, though the forty-five-mile drive from their home in Wasilla to the nursing home in Anchorage took an hour each way.

Robyn tried to focus on her anger once more. She stopped before the front door and practiced the words she had planned to say. "What were you thinking, Mom? Telling a stranger we're considering selling our home when Grandpa doesn't even know yet."

Oh yes, those words would cut deep. In her own ears, she sounded rude, disrespectful, and childish.

Tears flooded her eyes, and she flopped down on the sofa.

When her mother came in twenty minutes later, Robyn met her with a tender heart. She threw her arms around her. "Mom, I'm sorry I was mad at you. Can we talk about this?"

"Of course." Her mom took her coat and gloves off and sat down beside her. "I know it's hard for you to think about moving away from here. This has been your only home."

"Yes. But I—"

Mom held up one hand. "Haven't you ever wondered what it would be like to live someplace else? Someplace. . .easier?"

Robyn stared at her. "You mean, outside Alaska?"

"Yes."

"No." Robyn let out a puff of breath and looked away. The conversation had nose-dived so fast she felt dizzy.

"I thought a lot about it on the way home," Mom said. "I realize I shouldn't have mentioned to Mr. Sterns that we might sell our property before the family had discussed it thoroughly. He caught me by surprise when he said he was looking at land and thinking of moving up here, and I just. . . let it fall out of my mouth. That was wrong of me."

Robyn shook her head. "I thought maybe you were just tired of the dogs and never having any money."

Her mother laughed with a sniff. "Honey, I love dogs. It's true, sometimes I wonder how we'll get by, and I do get sick of vacuuming up dog hair, but our life here has been pretty good these last twenty-five years, don't you think? What you can remember of them, that is."

"Well, yeah." Robyn reflected that she had never known anything else. What if she'd grown up in Pennsylvania, or some other place that had even less snow? She would still love animals, of that she was sure. But what if she'd never had the opportunity to go dog sledding? "If you and Grandpa really think we should move, then I guess we should. But I can't imagine being happier somewhere else. And Grandpa. . . do you think he would even consider moving south?"

"You're probably right. He'd hate it." Mom sat for a moment, staring down at the rug. Then she smiled. "I don't know how God is going to work this out, but I believe He will."

"So. . ." Robyn eyed her cautiously. "You're willing to tell Mr. Sterns that we don't want to sell this place?"

"Yes. Unless Grandpa wants to sell it. It's half his, after all."

Robyn nodded. "Thank you."

Her mother held out her arms, and Robyn hugged her.

"Mom, I know keeping the kennel going has been hard on you. You've worked constantly since Dad died, and I appreciate that."

Her mother turned and grabbed a tissue from a box on the end table. "There have been some difficult moments. I won't deny that. The financial worries have been stressful. But, you know what? Even when I'm worrying, I know that's wrong. God doesn't want me to wear myself out worrying. What do you say we pray about this together?"

"Yes. And maybe tomorrow I can go with you to Anchorage, and we can talk to Grandpa and see what he thinks."

"That's a good idea. In fact, why don't I call the store tonight and see if it's possible for me to work an earlier shift tomorrow? If I could get out, say, by three, we could drive into town and see Grandpa and eat supper in Anchorage."

"Can we afford it?"

"Well, I was thinking fast food, not a fancy restaurant."

Robyn nodded. "Yeah. Let's do it. I'll get Darby to feed the dogs their supper."

"Can she handle it alone?"

"I think so. I'll have the meat ready and leave her lots of notes."

Her mother laughed and seized her hand. "Let's pray now."

Chapter 5

Rick made a house call at a dairy farm on his way to the clinic Tuesday morning. He also stopped to see a client's injured Irish setter. Heading once more for the animal hospital, he realized he would drive past the hotel where Philip Sterns was staying. On a whim, he drove into the parking area and strolled to the lobby.

At the desk, he told the clerk he was looking for Sterns.

"I'm sorry, I can't give you his room number," the young woman replied, "but if you'd like, I can call his room and see if he's in."

Rick hesitated. What would he say?

"Oh, there he is now." The clerk nodded toward the elevators.

Rick swung around and saw a thin, middle-aged man step out and head toward the main entrance.

"Thanks." He hurried to catch up with him. "Mr. Sterns?"

"Yes?" The man stopped walking and turned toward him.

"Hi. I'm Rick Baker." He extended his hand, and the man shook it. "Uh, I understand you're looking for property in the area."

"Are you a real estate agent?"

"No." Rick smiled sheepishly. "Actually, I'm a veterinarian. But I do know someone who's in the real estate business—the agent who helped me find my place in Wasilla last year."

Sterns eyed him curiously through his glasses. "And how did you get my name?"

"I'm sorry. I probably should have started with that. I'm a neighbor of the Hollands."

"Ah." He relaxed visibly and Rick felt more confident.

"Cheryl and Robyn are friends of mine, and they mentioned they'd had a visitor who was looking for property. Since I work close by, I thought I'd drop in and see you'd found an agent to work with."

"Yes, as a matter of fact, I'm on my way out to meet with one now."

"Oh, well, you're all set then." Rick felt a little silly, but he was glad he'd gotten a look at the man. He was sharper than Rick had suspected, given Robyn's description.

"Wasilla is one of the areas I'm considering when I relocate," Sterns said. "Perhaps you could give me the agent's name. If I don't find what I want down here, I may do some serious looking up there."

"Sure." Rick wrote down the name of the agency for him.

"Do you treat the Hollands' dogs?"

Rick nodded. "When they need it. They're a healthy lot."

"So, as far as you know, their dogs wouldn't have any problems? I'm looking at some of their adult females and one male, Tumble."

"Oh, yes, I know Tumble. He's in great shape. I don't know a kennel with a better health record." Rick eyed the man once more but could think of no way to get useful information from him without arousing suspicion.

"The girl, Robyn," Sterns said, frowning. "She seems reluctant to sell them."

"Robyn loves her dogs, but she's a businesswoman. If she thinks it's best for her kennel, she'll sell you the dogs you want. If not, then she'll offer you others of comparable quality." Rick stepped back. "I'd better head on over to the animal hospital. Nice to meet you."

Sterns nodded and walked out the door. Rick inhaled deeply. He should have asked Joel's assistance first, and not tried to meet Sterns. If the man was underhanded, he'd be suspicious now. And Rick had admitted that the Hollands had talked about him. That might not sit so well. He wished he'd thought of a way to get out of revealing that.

He pulled out his cell phone as he walked to his pickup. Sterns passed him in a red rental car. Rick waved, but Sterns ignored him.

"Hey, Joel? This is Rick Baker. Are you able to access databases to find out some background information on someone from another state?"

※

Robyn drove toward Anchorage with her mother beside her.

Mom was content to let her drive and was even happier when Aven phoned. After chatting for about ten minutes with him, she put the headset on her phone and passed it to Robyn.

"Hey," Robyn said. "What's up?"

"You're not driving in heavy traffic while you talk, are you?" her big brother asked.

"No, I'm on the Glenn Highway, and traffic's light."

"Okay. I guess you heard Mom telling me about this guy who's interested in the land."

"Yeah, I did. What do you think about that?"

"I told Mom to do whatever she thinks she has to do."

"I agree, mostly. If we really need to sell, then she and Grandpa should do it. Mom and I talked a lot last night. I think the question is, do we need to be thinking about this now?"

"Well, Caddie and I are agreed that we should try to help you if we can."

"No, that's not right. You shouldn't be helping support us." Robyn looked at her mother, and Mom shook her head adamantly. "Listen, you've sent us part of your pay ever since you joined the Coast Guard. But you have your own family to think of now. It's time for us to stand on our own feet and for you and Caddie to invest your income in your own family."

"Well. . .we'll talk about it when we come for the race. But keep me posted on this guy, okay? Because if you don't want to sell the land, you need to be firm, and if that upsets him and kills the sale of the dogs. . ."

"We can handle it," Robyn said, but she wasn't sure how. She passed the phone and headset back to her mother.

"You know what, honey?" her mom said to Aven. "We're going to talk this over with Grandpa tonight. After we've discussed all the options, we'll be able to make a better decision about it."

Robyn sighed and tried to concentrate on the road.

"You know," Mom said after she had hung up, "when Rick called this morning and you were in the shower—"

"What about it?" Robyn asked. She'd scurried as quickly as she could to take the brief call. Rick had inquired about her grandfather and their plans and then signed off to drive to work.

"We chatted for a couple of minutes, and he mentioned that he's still going to church in Anchorage, but he wants to stop driving that far, even though he'll miss his friends there."

"Really?" Robyn stared at her. Had Mom been doing a little snooping on her behalf?

"I invited him to visit our church any time. It wouldn't surprise me if he showed up some Sunday."

Robyn said nothing but wondered how she would handle things if Rick walked into their church on Sunday. She was glad for the warning.

Twenty minutes later they reached the nursing home. Grandpa was eating an early supper from a tray.

"They say they'll have me up and eating in the dining room within a few days," he said after greeting them. "I'm not sure I want to."

"What's wrong?" Mom asked.

"I think they need a new cook. Cheryl, I miss your cooking. Did you bring me anything?"

Mom laughed and opened her tote bag. "Robyn made some brownies this morning while I was at work, though when she had time, I don't know. She's busy all the time without you there to help her."

"That's right." Robyn passed the plastic container of brownies to him. "We're in high gear, getting ready for the race. I need you, so hurry up and get better."

He fumbled with the container, and Robyn leaned over to help him open it.

"So what's going on at home?" Grandpa asked. "Didn't you have a buyer coming yesterday?"

"Yes, he came," Cheryl said.

"How many dogs is he taking?"

Robyn smiled at his assumption. "He wants four, but I don't want to sell one of them."

"Which one?"

"He's got his eye on Tumble."

"What? You can't sell Tumble." Grandpa pushed up on his elbow and scowled at her. "Did you tell him you'd sell our top stud dog?"

"No, Grandpa. I didn't. But of course he saw Tumble when we went into the yard, and he took to him. He said he'd read about us before he came, and he might have had the idea in his mind all along to make an offer for Tumble."

"Well, he can't have him."

Robyn looked at her mother.

"Fine. We'll tell him that Tumble is absolutely not for sale. But, Dad. . ."

"What?" Grandpa lay back on the pillow, not entirely mollified. "That's what comes of having that Web site. Everybody and his brother can look on there and see our best dogs."

"That's advertising," Robyn reminded him.

"Yes," her mother added. "A lot of people look at that site. The pictures of the dogs are the next best thing to seeing the actual dogs. I think it's brought in quite a bit of business."

"You think we should sell Tumble?"

"Not necessarily, but. . ." Mom cleared her throat. "You know things have been tight lately. I may be able to get a few more hours per week at the store, but. . ."

"No," he said. "We don't want you working more. I hate that you have to work away from home. If Dan was still alive, he wouldn't hear of it."

Mom pressed her lips together and looked toward the window.

"What?" Grandpa said again. "Is it worse than I know about?" When Cheryl still didn't meet his gaze, he turned to stare at Robyn.

Her breath caught, and she started to speak but stopped. Were their financial straits as bad as Mom thought they were? She wished she could say with certainty that everything would be all right, but she didn't dare.

After a long moment, Grandpa sighed. "I see. It's me. My medical expenses. Well, I tell you what, I can walk out of here today. I don't have to stay in here six weeks, or even two weeks, no matter what that therapist says." He threw back the bedclothes and thrust his legs over the side of the bed.

"No, Grandpa," Robyn said quickly. She reached to take his arm, but he had already pushed off the bed.

Almost at once his knees buckled, and he collapsed against her.

Mom stifled a cry and leaped to help Robyn get him back on the bed.

He lay there with his eyes nearly closed, panting.

"Let's not have any more stunts like that one," Mom said in a tight voice. "You need this treatment. I won't argue about it."

"You can't sell off all the dogs," he choked. "Robyn knows which ones she needs to keep and which ones to let go. Don't you, Robby?"

"Yes, Grandpa." She took his hand and squeezed it.

"Dad. . ." Mom's face radiated pain as she looked down at him. Her eyes glistened, and tears spilled down her cheeks.

"Don't cry," he said. "We'll sell a few dogs and we'll get by."

Slowly Mom sat down. "I guess this would not be a good time to suggest selling the homestead."

Grandpa stared at her for a long moment, then looked away. No one spoke for a minute.

"Grandpa, I don't think we need to think about that," Robyn said softly. "If the bills are too big, then I could get a job, too. And if we need to sell more dogs, we will, though I'd like to keep our foundation stock so that we can keep breeding. But if worse comes to worst—"

"She's right," Mom said. "I never should have considered it. I'll tell Mr. Sterns—"

"Who?"

"The man who's buying the dogs. I'll tell him we're not selling the house."

"Wait, wait, wait." Grandpa grabbed her sleeve. "The man buying the dogs—the one who wants Tumble—also wants to buy our property?"

Mom shifted uneasily. "He mentioned that he was looking for a place in the area. But I can see you don't want to consider that."

"What would we do?" Grandpa asked. "Where would we live?"

"I. . .don't know."

Robyn's throat constricted as she watched Grandpa's face. The unspoken thought hung in the air—that he might never go home to live with them again.

"I'd like to meet this fellow," he said.

"Oh, that's not necessary." Mom leaned forward, her brow furrowed. "I'll explain to him that I spoke prematurely. And I'm sorry. Truly sorry. I hadn't stopped to consider how you or Robyn would feel before I mentioned it to him."

"No, I'm serious." Grandpa nodded. "If things are bad enough to make you think like that, then maybe we do need to take drastic measures. And even if we're not selling more than a few team dogs to this man, I'd like to get a look at him. I'm a pretty good judge of character. I'd like to talk to him and make sure he knows how to handle good dogs. I won't sell—or let Robyn sell—Holland dogs to just anyone. I'd rather starve first."

Robyn's pride welled up, and she wiped an errant tear from her cheek. She'd seen Grandpa turn away a buyer once because he'd heard the man treated his dogs poorly. "I love you, Grandpa." She leaned down and kissed the top of his head.

Mom let out a sigh and managed a wobbly smile. "All right. Shall I call him and see if he can come here to meet you? He's staying nearby in a hotel."

"Sure," Grandpa said. "I'll put on my best bathrobe."

Robyn laughed. "I'll help you get ready. Anything you need, just ask me." She looked at her mother. "And thanks, Mom. I think we'll all feel better if Grandpa's in on this decision."

"You could handle the sale by yourself," Grandpa said grudgingly. "You know enough about dogs—what they're capable of and exactly what they're worth."

"Thanks for trusting me, but as you said, you're a pretty good judge of people."

"That's because I've been around so long and met so many of them."

Mom excused herself and went out into the hallway to call Mr. Sterns.

A staff member came in and retrieved Grandpa's supper tray.

"You okay?" Grandpa asked Robyn.

"Yeah. I was pretty keyed up about this, but Mom and I prayed about it last night. We agreed we needed to bring you in on it. I'm glad you're going to meet Mr. Sterns."

"What's he like?"

She shrugged. "I don't like him, but I'm trying not to pass judgment on him unfairly. He doesn't know a lot about dogs, and he's just getting into sledding. He wants to do some racing right away. I've got to wonder if he wouldn't work the dogs too hard at first."

"Hmm. That can happen." Grandpa opened the brownie box and held it out toward her. "Have one?"

"No, those are for you. We've got more at home." He took one and she replaced the cover on the box.

Mom came back, wearing a businesslike smile. "Mr. Sterns would be happy to meet you. He's having dinner with his real estate agent, but he can come by here around seven."

Grandpa looked at the clock on the wall opposite the bed. "Why don't you two go and eat? You've got almost two hours. You can get back in plenty of time."

Mom looked at Robyn, and she nodded.

"All right, but you have to promise not to try to get up alone."

He frowned at his daughter-in-law. "Me? Would I do that?"

Mom swatted lightly at his shoulder.

"We'd better go." Robyn jumped up. "See you later, alligator—and we're serious. Be good."

They drove around the corner for hamburgers and milkshakes. Robyn wondered if Mom was reluctant to spend even a few dollars for the meal. She tried to keep the conversation on pleasant topics and described how well Darby was doing in her sled driving lessons.

Mom waited in the nursing home lobby for Sterns while Robyn went to

Grandpa's room to make sure he was ready. She helped him get his robe on. He wanted to move to the armchair, so Robyn called one of the staffers to help her, and they got him situated. She had to admit, he looked stronger and more capable sitting in the chair than he had lying down.

As the staffer straightened the bedclothes, Mom led Philip Sterns in and introduced him to Grandpa, a strained smile on her face.

"So, you want to buy some Holland Kennel dogs," Grandpa said affably.

"Yes, sir. I made a list of three good breeding kennels before I flew up here, and yours was the top one. I knew the minute your granddaughter showed me your dog yard that I'd come to the right place."

"That right?"

"Oh, yes. Everything's shipshape. And your dogs have wonderful bloodlines. I read up on your dogs' performances. That Chick line is what I want."

Grandpa smiled. "Then I guess you know our Tumble is one of Chick's sons."

"He's a fine-looking dog, and I think he's perfect for my foundation stock."

"So you want to breed dogs, as well as race." Grandpa shook his head, still smiling. "That's ambitious."

"I know. But I never do things by halves."

"Well, sir, why don't you sit right down here and tell me about your experience with sled dogs. What sort of setup do you have in California?"

Grandpa knew the right questions to ask. Sterns soon relaxed and talked freely. After twenty minutes of talk about dogs, Grandpa brought up the property matter.

"Sounds like you might do all right if you start with well-trained dogs and have someone to advise you when you need it. But just so you know, I'm not ready to sell my property. My son and I bought the place twenty-five years ago, and it's home. Cheryl and I talked about it a little tonight, and I just don't want to sell."

"That's perfectly all right," Sterns assured him. "I've been out all day looking at land, and I've seen a couple of places that might do for me."

Grandpa nodded. "Well, Cheryl can hang on to your contact information in case we decide to sell later on, but for the time being, the Hollands are staying put."

The nurse entered the room with a clipboard in her hand. "I'm sorry, folks, but Mr. Holland needs some rest now."

"I'm sure he does." Robyn jumped up, ready to help get Grandpa back to bed if she was needed.

Sterns said to Cheryl, "I'll come up to Wasilla in the morning, then, and get the four dogs I'm buying, if that's all right with you."

"Uh, Mr. Sterns?" Robyn shot a quick glance at Grandpa.

"Yes?"

"We're keeping Tumble. Grandpa and I agree he's an essential part of Holland Kennel right now."

Grandpa nodded. "That's right. Tumble has never been for sale. But we can offer you one of his sons who would—"

A flicker of darkness crossed Sterns's face and he exhaled sharply. "I thought we had a deal."

Mom stepped forward with a look of alarm. "I believe you asked Robyn to think it over."

"You've wasted my time."

Robyn said hastily, "I'm sorry, sir, but we're keeping Tumble. We haven't advertised him for sale, and I told you yesterday I didn't want to sell him. If that means you don't want the three female dogs, either. . ."

He looked at her sharply then flicked a glance toward Grandpa, who sagged a little in his chair.

"Folks," the nurse said, "I really must ask you to leave."

Sterns locked gazes with Robyn again. "I'll let you know tomorrow."

Chapter 6

Sterns exited abruptly, and Robyn and her mother kissed Grandpa good night and left.

"Mom, I'm sorry things went badly in there," Robyn said as they walked toward the car.

"No, honey, don't be. You were wonderful. He was rude and made assumptions he shouldn't have made. I'll be glad to see the back of him tomorrow."

"Me, too."

Mom smiled at her as she unlocked the car. "Are you sure you want to sell him any of your babies?"

Robyn swallowed hard. "I think we have to. We need to order more meat for the dogs, and we'll have a lot of expenses while we get ready for the race. But I'm glad Grandpa wouldn't sell Tumble."

"So am I," Mom admitted. "He personally raised that dog, and I know Tumble is one of his favorites."

Robyn drove home and found Darby's note saying her father had driven her over and helped her feed all of the dogs their suppers. The temperature had dropped to ten below zero. Robyn made a brief round of the kennels and made sure all of the animals were snug in their shelters. She'd put extra straw bedding in the doghouses that morning, and all were settled down for the night. The puppies slept together in a jumbled pile in their communal shelter. She checked the padlock on the barn, reflecting that if Sterns didn't buy the dogs he'd picked out, she'd have to dip into her meager savings account to pay for the next shipment of dog food.

Snow began to fall as she went into the house. She took off her boots and work jacket near the back door.

Her mother, already in her bathrobe, sat at the kitchen table with a mug of tea. "Everything okay?"

"Yes," Robyn said. She walked to the stove and lifted the teakettle. It held plenty of hot water, so she opened the cupboard to get herself a mug. As she turned around, the glow of headlights swept over the walls.

"Someone's here." Her mother rose and walked to the window. "Looks like Rick's truck. I'm not dressed for company. Would you mind if I disappeared?"

"That's fine." A shiver of anticipation propelled Robyn to the front door before he even knocked. Over the last few days, Rick had paid a lot of attention to her and her family. Was it just neighborliness, or was her wish coming true? In the midst of the stress and sadness she'd encountered, Rick was the one bright spot of her days. But she didn't dare count on that continuing. If he backed off once this crisis passed, the disappointment would be too great.

⁂

Rick drove into the Hollands' yard at nine o'clock Tuesday night. Ordinarily he wouldn't call so late, but he knew Cheryl and Robyn had spent the afternoon and evening in Anchorage, and the lights were still on at their house.

As he climbed the steps to the front deck, Robyn opened the door. Her long, dark hair hung loose about her shoulders, and she wore black pants and a green sweater. Usually he saw her in jeans and a thick jacket, but this softer outfit gave her a decidedly feminine air.

His pulse quickened, and he smiled. "Hi. Is it too late? I just wanted to tell you what I learned today."

"No, come on in. We haven't been home long, and I was making myself some tea. Want some?"

"Sure." He followed her to the kitchen, unzipping his jacket.

She opened a cookie jar shaped like a husky and put a handful of cookies on a plate then fixed him a cup of tea to go with hers.

"How's Coco doing?" he asked.

"Good. She's one of the three Sterns wants to buy." Robyn made a face as though she'd tasted foul medicine. "Just thought I'd warn you, since you've gotten friendly with her."

Rick winced. "Did you plan to sell her?"

"I'm not against it. I'd rather sell some of the extra males that we've trained as team dogs, but he wants females, so. . . ."

"I came to talk to you about Sterns."

"Did your friend find out anything?"

He nodded, hating to bring bad news but knowing she'd feel somewhat vindicated for being uneasy about the man. "Joel discovered that Philip Sterns has been in prison in California for fraud and theft."

"You're joking." Robyn tossed her dark hair back and brought the sugar bowl over from the counter. "Do you want milk?"

"No, thanks. I told Joel I wanted to make sure the information he got was for the same man. He brought a picture of the guy over to the clinic for me to look at. It's him."

"How did you recognize him?" She sat down opposite him.

Rick hesitated. "I stopped at the hotel this morning, and I got a look at him. But Joel didn't find any outstanding warrants on him." He picked up his mug and sipped the hot, strong tea.

"What does that mean? He's not a fugitive?"

"As far as we know, he's done his time and he's free now."

She shook her head. "I don't know about you, but I feel as though we've had a narrow escape. Mom was actually thinking about selling the property to this guy."

"I. . .didn't know she owned it." Rick said quickly, "I don't mean to pry. I'd just assumed Steve. . ."

"Grandpa owns half." Robyn reached for a cookie. "Mom and Dad owned half together before Dad died. Grandpa had invested in the land with Dad when they first came here."

"I see." He could also tell that the situation was taking a toll on her. Her eyelids drooped, and she seemed to consider her words carefully. He wished he could assure her that everything would be all right, but he couldn't do that.

"We told Grandpa all about Sterns," she said, "and he wanted to meet him, so Mom called him. He came over to the nursing home. Grandpa told him the property's not for sale, and he was okay with that. But when I said we aren't selling Tumble either, he got kind of nasty."

"I'm sorry to hear that."

"Yeah. We don't like the idea of selling any dogs to him, but he walked out saying he'd let us know tomorrow if he still wanted Coco and the others." Her dark eyes held misgivings as she took a bite of her cookie.

"You could still say no."

"If he wants to buy and I told him now that I don't want to sell. . ." She shook her head. "He was a little scary tonight."

Rick wished he could do something concrete to comfort her, but the situation seemed beyond his control. He did know Someone with greater power though. "I've been praying about your situation."

"That means a lot." She smiled at him, and his heart lurched.

"I'm glad Steve and Cheryl don't see a need to sell the property. I'm sure God will find a way for your family to get through this rough spot." He was glad he hadn't jumped in with an offer to buy them out. That probably would have upset Robyn and her grandfather even more. It was just as well that his assets were tied up. He took a cookie and bit into it.

"Grandpa's determined to stick it out here," Robyn said. "He was shocked when Mom hinted at leaving Alaska."

"Well, maybe you should just wait and see what happens. The Lord knows what's ahead. I'm sure He's got something planned for the Hollands."

She nodded slowly. "Sterns is supposed to come tomorrow if he wants to buy. If not, he'll call. I'm not sure I'll wait around all day to see if he shows up. I've got a lot to do for the race."

"What's on your list for tomorrow?"

"Putting up markers on part of the race route. Of course, if we get a lot of snow out of this storm, I may have to wait."

"I don't think this will amount to much." Rick glanced toward the window.

"It's too cold for a really big snow."

"Well then, I'll probably try to get the hilly part marked tomorrow."

The opportunity to be with her and perhaps help her in a small way beckoned him. He asked casually, "Want someone to tag along?"

She arched her eyebrows. "What, you want to ride on my sled?"

"I've mushed in my time. Had a team before I went away to vet school."

"So, you're saying you'd go along if I supply you a team?"

"I guess that's a little presumptuous."

"No, it's not. We have an extra sled. If you're serious, it might be fun."

Rick smiled at her. "I haven't driven a team for a while, but I used to know what I was doing. It would be an honor to mush with you."

"Great. Hey, wait a minute. Isn't tomorrow one of your days in Anchorage?"

"They need me Thursday this week, so I switched." He frowned as he remembered Bob's and Hap's reactions when he'd told them two days a week in Anchorage was too much for him. After next week he was going back to Tuesdays only. They hadn't liked it one bit. Rick had even told them that his goal, as much as he liked them, was to stop working at Far North altogether and put his energy into his own practice.

"So you're free all day?"

"I could go with you in the morning. I've got a few barn calls I need to make after lunch, but if you're sure you trust me to drive some of your dogs, I'd love to go out on the trail with you."

"Sure. Call me by eight. If the weather's not good, or if Sterns has scheduled a time to come, I'll tell you. Otherwise, we can go then."

"Sounds good." Rick finished his tea.

"Want some more?"

"No, I'd better head home and get some sleep. I have to hit the trail in the morning, and the boss musher is strict about punctuality."

She laughed, and Rick's anticipation level soared. If he could have imagined the perfect way to spend his free morning, sledding with Robyn would have been beyond the most appealing thing he'd have come up with.

He leaned across the table and squeezed her hand. "Thanks for trusting me. I may be too keyed up to sleep."

"You'd *better* sleep. I don't want you falling asleep on the runners tomorrow."

❖

The next morning, conditions were perfect for sledding. Robyn hurried to feed all the dogs and make sure the equipment was ready. As she worked, her thoughts bounced continually to Rick. His generous offers of help lately gave her spirits a boost, and the fact that he wanted to go sledding with her. . .just thinking about it made her breathe faster. He must like her as more than a client and neighbor. The way he'd looked at her last night had propelled her dreams into high gear.

At about seven thirty the back door to the house opened and her mom came out to the dog lot.

Robyn's heart sank. "Did Mr. Sterns call?"

"No. I just wanted to check with you before you take off. What should I do if he comes while you're out?"

Robyn checked her relief and considered her mother's situation. "If he doesn't call in the next hour, Rick and I are going to head out. We should be back in a couple of hours though."

"Yes, but I don't want to be here alone when he comes."

When it came down to it, Robyn didn't blame her. She'd feel the same way. "Maybe you can try to call him when we're ready to leave and see what he says."

Mom went back into the house.

Robyn laid out harnesses for four dogs each for her and Rick and got out both lightweight sleds. She decided to give Rick the newer one, as the old one was more fragile. And she would give him four strong but calm dogs. She would take four of her client's dogs herself.

Rick called promptly at eight, and she found herself grinning as she answered her phone. "Come on over. I'm good to go."

"Sterns hasn't contacted you yet?" he asked.

"Nope, and I've got the sleds out."

"I'll be there in ten minutes."

She went into the house. Mom wasn't due to go to work until one o'clock, and Robyn found her in the kitchen.

"Thought I'd bake apple crisp and take some to Grandpa tomorrow."

"Good idea. I bet he'd like some licorice, too."

Mom smiled. "Don't know how he can stand that stuff, but I'll pick some up this afternoon." She jotted it on the shopping list that hung on the refrigerator door.

"I've got to put in another order for meat for the dogs," Robyn said, watching her face.

"Okay." Neither of them spoke of how close they were cutting their finances. *When the race is over*, Robyn told herself, *we should be okay for a while.*

More than two weeks still lay between them and the Fire & Ice, and all the entry fees were in the bank. They never spent any of the money from the race for anything other than race expenses until the event was over, but usually they made a profit of a couple thousand dollars.

"So, Rick's on his way over," Robyn said. "Do you want me to try to call Mr. Sterns?"

"I guess I can do it."

"Okay. If he's on his way, of course we'll stay."

Mom took her phone off the counter and pushed a few buttons. "I'm getting his voice mail." She waited a moment then said in her best "leave a message" voice,

"This is Cheryl Holland. We just wondered if you planned to come up to Holland Kennel today or not. Please let us know. Thank you very much."

She closed the connection and gulped.

Robyn walked over and kissed her cheek. "Thanks. You did great."

She went out to the dog lot, and Rick soon joined her. His first words were, "Did you get ahold of Sterns?"

Robyn shook her head. "We haven't heard a word from him. Mom called his cell phone, but he didn't answer."

"Well, cell service is spotty at best outside Anchorage."

She nodded. "So, are you ready to mush?"

He grinned. "I am so ready. Who's on my team?"

"I'm letting you take Max. He's your leader. And Bandit, Dolly, and Spark."

"Who do you get?"

She picked up the first set of harness. "Oh, I'm taking four of Pat Isherwood's dogs."

"He's the guy who had the appendectomy?"

"Yes. He's paying me good money to keep them in shape for him. I try to take all eight of his dogs out two or three times a week. This past week has been tough though. I took the other half of his team out Monday, but they'll need to go again tomorrow, and no excuses."

Putting the dogs in harness with Rick helping her was an interesting experience. Despite the cold temperatures—only ten degrees this morning—Robyn found herself blushing when their faces came close together as they bent over the same dog. She'd always been independent, even more so since her brother left home. She lived in a fairly remote location and had braced herself long ago for the possibility that she wouldn't find a husband out here.

Although more men than women lived in Alaska, she'd increased the odds against finding a match by choosing not to go to college. Instead, she'd stayed home and worked in the dog business. That seemed most practical after her father died, and she loved dogs and sledding. She knew she wanted to continue Grandpa Steve's kennel business, and her mother had reluctantly agreed. But in taking that path, she had isolated herself to some extent. Her contacts were mostly through business and church now, and she'd decided not to worry about it.

"Hey, you really do know what you're doing." She laughed and straightened as Rick adjusted the harness on Bandit. "Go ahead and get Max. I'll start getting my team hitched up."

The last thing on her checklist was to alert her mom. Rather than leaving the team while she trudged to the house, Robyn called her on the cell phone.

"Are you two leaving now?" Mom asked.

"Yep, we're all set. I don't know if you'll be able to get me when we leave here, but if you do hear anything, try to give me a call."

"I will. Be safe, honey."

Robyn laughed. "Well, I've got a doctor with me, just in case."

Rick laughed, too, as she put her phone away and zipped the pocket. "You're sassy this morning."

"I feel good. Don't you? New snow, terrific dogs. . ."

"Great company," he finished.

She felt her cheeks warming again and untied the snub line for her team. Ignoring his flirtatious smile, she stepped onto the runners of her sled. "Ready?"

Rick nodded as he stowed his own line.

Robyn turned forward. "Hike!"

⚓

Rick couldn't remember when he'd had a better time. Robyn led him first over trails he knew well, but then they veered onto land he'd never traveled. They stopped every time the race trail changed course, or any place a hazard occurred, like a sharp drop-off or rocks hidden beneath the snow. Robyn had packed different colored ribbons for marking the way and warning signals. Their brief stops gave the dogs short rests.

Rick had thought he was in good shape, but keeping up with Robyn challenged him. He watched her jump off frequently and run behind her sled, amazed at her energy.

"Hey, watch your team," Robyn called at a stop an hour into their trek.

Rick had forgotten to set his snow hook. The minute he stepped off the runners, the dogs had leaned forward, ready to take off. "Whoa!" He jumped back onto the sled, putting his weight on the runners and reaching for the snow hook.

Robyn laughed. "Don't bother. I'll get this one. It won't take a minute." True to her word, she quickly positioned the markers where the trail took a turn and regained her position behind her team.

At the next stop, Rick was determined to prove he wasn't an absolute greenhorn. He set his hook and made sure the lines were taut before letting go of the sled.

"Not bad." Robyn tossed him a roll of plastic ribbon. "I want to mark this curve because of the rocks there. If someone runs into them, it's bad news. We've had more than one sled wreck at this spot."

Since no trees grew nearby, he held stakes she had set in the snow while she packed more of it tightly around them. "We'll need to have someone check them the day before the race," she said. "I get volunteers to run short stretches of the route that day until the whole trail is covered. It breaks the trail if we've had new snow and gives us the assurance that all the markers are still in place." She clumped the snow tightly around the last stake. "There."

Rick stood when she did. "This is fantastic. Thanks so much for letting me go with you."

She smiled up at him. "I'm having fun."

Her rich brown eyes sent him a message that made him believe she really was enjoying this morning as much as he was. He thought he knew her well enough now to interpret her moods. Had things gone beyond friendship?

Her glowing cheeks and bright eyes drew him. Now might be the time to kiss her. Or would that be too forward? He'd known her a year, but they'd spent only a little time together, most of it in the past week. He wanted to let her know how he felt—but did he really understand that himself?

He liked everything he knew about her, and each new revelation confirmed his impressions of her character. She was diligent and loyal. She loved the Lord. She cared deeply about her family, its heritage, and its well-being. And she was very pretty. But there was still so much to learn. If he told her now what he thought, would he regret it?

He leaned toward her, his heart pounding. As he reached for her, she sobered and hesitantly raised her arms. He pulled her closer. Robyn came into his arms but turned her face away, resting her head against his shoulder. His heart tumbled. Did she do that to avoid a kiss? Maybe it was too soon. But she stayed in his embrace for a moment.

Then she laughed, a sudden, contented burble.

He pulled away and eyed her cautiously.

"I'm sorry. It's not funny, but. . ." She tossed her head, her lips curved in amusement.

He tried not to let his apprehension come through in his voice. "What?"

"It just hit me how hard it is to hug someone in January gear in Alaska." She smiled up at him. Something about her expression told him she'd found the experience enjoyable.

He nodded. "We may have to repeat this experiment when we're in a warmer place."

Her smile widened. "We'd probably better head back, in case Mom's got company." She pulled out her phone and checked it. "Just as I thought. No service out here."

"Let's go." Rick hurried to the back of his sled and reached for the snow hook. She hadn't protested his comment. As they took the trail back, he found himself looking forward to kissing her and hoping that time came soon.

The dogs pulled them back toward the Holland Kennel yard at a smart trot. Rick believed those on his towline could have kept going all day and loved it. As the miles flew by, his thoughts drifted back to their embrace. Robyn was right—parkas weren't the best attire for courting.

Cheryl came out the back door of the house as they came to a halt and ran to where Robyn hitched her team leaders. "I'm so glad you're back!"

"What is it, Mom? Did Mr. Sterns show up here?"

"Not yet, but six of our dogs are missing."

Chapter 7

Six dogs? What do you mean?" Robyn couldn't process what her mother told her.

"I've called the police. I didn't know what else to do." Mom wrapped her arms around herself and shivered. "I don't know how this could have happened. I'm sorry."

Robyn put her arm around her mother. "You're freezing. Go inside. We'll put the dogs away and come right in."

Rick had tied his team with a snub line and walked slowly along the yard, looking at the ground. "These look like fresh snow machine tracks," he called.

"Yes, they were pulling a trailer with a box or cage on it." Mom's eyes swam with tears. "I would have heard them, but after Mr. Sterns called, I decided to do some vacuuming, and when I shut it off, I heard the motor out here, but it was too late. By the time I got to the window, they were already pulling out."

"Wait," Robyn said. "Sterns called you?"

"Yes. About twenty minutes after you left. He told me he'd come around noon. I tried to get you, but I couldn't get through, so I started cleaning up the house. I decided it was a good time to. . .well, that doesn't matter. The thing is, when I heard the motor and ran to the kitchen window, I saw this snow machine with a trailer leaving the yard and going out that old woods road. I figured someone had just driven through, even though we have it posted not to. I was a little mad, but it happens."

Rick had come over and stood beside Robyn, listening.

Mom went on, "Then I saw that one gate was open."

Robyn swung around and looked at the enclosures. "Both gates are closed now."

"Because I shut the one to the male dogs' yard. It was wide open. I knew you wouldn't leave it that way, so I ran out to look. Tumble was gone. And you'd said you were taking some of Pat Isherwood's dogs out this morning, so I knew that meant you didn't take Tumble for your leader."

"Right," Robyn said. "And Rick had Max leading."

Her mother nodded and her face crumpled. "When you called me right before you left, I looked out and saw that you each had four dogs in your team. I had wondered if you would take Tumble in case Sterns came while you were gone, to make sure he didn't try to take him, but I could see that you didn't. So I ran through the lot to see what other dogs were gone. I counted fourteen missing, so besides the eight you had out, it looks like six were stolen."

Rick reached out and touched her shoulder. "When will the state police be here?"

"Any time now."

"Sounds like you did the right thing. Why don't you go in and put the kettle on? Robyn and I will take care of the teams and be in shortly."

She nodded, and her face quivered. "I feel so. . .angry. Angry and stupid."

"Don't," Robyn said softly. "We'll get them back." She wished she believed that.

Her mother turned and trotted toward the house.

Robyn looked at Rick. "What do you think?"

"It's very odd. Sterns calls and says he won't come around for three hours or more, and then thieves come into the lot in broad daylight and steal six dogs."

Robyn nodded. "Yes, including Tumble, the dog he was so angry about not getting. Let's put these mutts away and make a list of who's missing."

They quickly stripped off the dogs' harnesses and piled them on Robyn's sled. When all of the dogs they'd exercised were tethered to their kennels, Robyn walked around the lot. She'd already realized the six missing dogs included two of Patrick Isherwood's team, Wocket and Astro. Tumble and three other Holland Kennel dogs had also been taken.

"Odd," she said, looking over the female dogs' enclosure. "If it was Sterns, why didn't he take the three females he wanted to buy?"

"Better yet, why didn't he take *any* females?"

"Hmm." Robyn looked back toward the other side of the lot. "Maybe they didn't want to waste time. If he knew he wanted Tumble, he'd go for him first and grab whichever other dogs were closest. That way he could get in and out quick."

"Do you think they watched us leave?"

"Maybe. And maybe they didn't realize Mom was in the house. You'd think they'd have heard the vacuum, but not if they waited back in the woods; and when they came out, their own motor would drown it out."

The reality hit her, and she pressed her hands against her churning stomach. "This rots."

Rick came over and stood in front of her. She couldn't help looking up into his sympathetic eyes. In today's cold sunshine, they were the color of swirled caramel. At any other moment, she'd have pondered the embrace they'd shared on the trail, and how she was sure Rick would have kissed her if she'd encouraged him. But she couldn't think about it now. Not with Tumble and five other dogs hijacked out of her lot. "What am I going to tell Patrick?"

Rick gritted his teeth. "The truth. I'd wait until the officer gets here though. See what he thinks your chances are of recovering the dogs. Then give Patrick a call and tell him exactly what happened."

Rick stood by while Cheryl and Robyn talked to the trooper, Officer Glade, in their living room. He wished he could do more, but both women assured him they valued his support.

"This is all the information I have about Philip Sterns." Cheryl handed Glade the sheet of paper on which she'd carefully listed Sterns's name, phone number, and the hotel where he'd stayed in Anchorage. Robyn was able to add the license plate number of his rental car.

"Are you certain it was Sterns who came here today and took the dogs?" Glade asked.

"No, not at all." Cheryl spread her hands helplessly. "He's the only one I could think of. He'd expressed interest in our stud dog, Tumble, and he was angry when Robyn and Steve said they wouldn't sell him. I can't help thinking he may have decided to just take what he wanted."

Glade took a few notes.

Robyn hauled in a deep breath. "But, Mom, he didn't take the other three dogs he wanted." She turned to the trooper. "Mr. Sterns wanted to buy the one male—that's Tumble—and three breeding females. But the six dogs that were stolen were all males. If he really wanted to start a breeding kennel, why take six males?"

Rick thought that was an excellent question. Of course, Sterns may have simply been in too much of a hurry to be choosy, but as Robyn had told him earlier, he knew exactly where Coco and the other dogs he'd picked out were tethered.

"Was the dog yard locked?"

Robyn shook her head. "We lock the gates every night, but since it was daytime and Mom was here, I didn't bother this morning. I latched them securely after we took the team dogs out, but no locks."

Rick stepped toward Glade. "Officer, I did a little investigating on Robyn's behalf yesterday. She'd told me about the situation with this potential buyer. I have a friend in the police department—perhaps you know him. Joel Dawes."

"Sure, I know Dawes." Glade eyed Rick with new speculation. "You talked to him about this business?"

Rick hoped Joel hadn't done anything beyond his clear-cut duty in helping him. No way to get out of telling the trooper now though. "I asked him to do a quick check on Sterns, and he did. He found out the man has a criminal record in California. In fact, he's spent some time in the California Correctional Center."

"All right," Glade said. "I'm going to my vehicle and call this in. We need someone in Anchorage to contact his hotel and see if he's checked out. If he has, we can find out fairly easily whether he's left Alaska. It shouldn't be too hard to find a man traveling with six dogs."

"Is there anything else we can do?" Cheryl asked.

"Just stay calm. After I call this in, perhaps Miss Holland could show me the kennels and the snow machine tracks. I may be able to tell whether they were waiting for you and Dr. Baker to leave this morning."

Rick nodded, glad he hadn't followed the tracks on impulse. He might have ruined some evidence.

"We'll put our boots and coats on," Robyn said. "Whenever you're ready, just come and tell us."

Glade went out to his car, and Cheryl went to the kitchen to start a pot of coffee.

Rick took Robyn's hand and drew her toward the sofa. "Come here for a minute. I wondered if you'd like to pray about this together."

The cloud lifted from her face. "Thank you. I'd like that a lot."

They sat down, and Rick bowed his head. He wished he had the perfect words to say, the ideal way to make things better for Robyn, but all he could do was pour out his heart. "Lord, thank You for sending Trooper Glade out. You know where those dogs are and who is responsible for this. I ask now that You'd keep them safe and comfort Robyn and Cheryl. If it's in Your plan, please let the thieves be caught and the dogs returned."

He didn't expect Robyn to pray, too, but when he said, "Amen," she said softly, "Lord, please keep the dogs safe and let us get them back. Especially Pat's dogs. Thank You."

She squeezed his hand and released it. He opened his eyes. Her smile was a bit wobbly, but she seemed calmer.

They stood, and Rick glanced out the window. Glade was getting out of his truck. Beyond his vehicle, an SUV turned in from the road.

Rick caught his breath. "Robyn?"

"Yeah?"

"Isn't that—"

"I don't believe it." She turned toward the kitchen door. "Mom! Come in here quick! Philip Sterns just drove in."

"Either he's got a lot of nerve, or he's innocent." Mom stood between Robyn and Rick, peering out the front window.

"Should we go out?" Robyn felt as though she was watching a crime drama through the glass.

"It looks like Trooper Glade is going to ask him a few questions," Rick said.

Robyn looked up at him and scowled. "I don't know about you two, but I want to hear what he says."

Rick chuckled. "What do you say, Cheryl? Shall we join them?"

Mom was already pulling on her jacket. The three of them walked out to the driveway together.

"Mrs. Holland! Robyn!" Sterns's mouth drooped as they approached. "The officer just told me what happened. I'm so sorry."

Robyn decided to keep her mouth shut. If she voiced her thoughts right now, it wouldn't be pretty, and it might compromise the trooper's investigation. Mom, however, stepped forward with a regretful smile.

"Thank you, Mr. Sterns. At least the three dogs you spoke for weren't taken."

"Oh? I'm glad to hear that. I assume you still want to do business? I came ready to pay for them and take them with me." He took out his wallet.

Mom turned and said to Robyn, "You want to go ahead with this, don't you?"

Robyn wished she could have more time to think about it. Since her roster of female dogs had not been depleted, she supposed it was all right—if Sterns wasn't behind the theft.

"I. . .guess so." She reached out and took the money, knowing that sealed the bargain. "I'll get you a receipt."

"I've got cages in the vehicle. Should I drive around back to the dog yard?" Sterns asked.

Trooper Glade said, "I'd rather you didn't do that, sir. I'm not done looking at the evidence out there."

Cheryl said, "Is it all right for my daughter to go into the female dogs' enclosure and bring out the three dogs this gentleman is buying?"

"I suppose so," Glade said. "While you do that, I'd like to ask Mr. Sterns a few more questions."

"Of course. And if you'd like, you can talk inside. It's quite chilly out here." Mom arched her eyebrows and Sterns nodded.

"Thank you," Glade said. "Perhaps that's best."

Sterns held out his key ring to Robyn. "The cages are in the back of my rental."

"I'll help you," Rick said.

Robyn felt immense relief. Selling a dog always saddened her, but under the circumstances, she was afraid she might break down and cry. That or say something she'd regret later. "Thanks."

Together they walked around the house, while Mom took Glade and Sterns inside.

"Are you okay?" Rick asked.

She puffed out a breath of cold air. "As well as can be expected, I guess."

"I know what you mean." He shook his head as she unfastened the door to the shed. "I don't like it."

Robyn reached inside and grabbed three leashes off the hook near the door. She handed him one. "Me either. Based on what little we know right now, I still think Sterns is behind this mess. But without proof, I couldn't see a good reason to call off the deal."

She clipped her leash to Coco's collar then unhooked her tether line. Holding the end of the leash firmly, she knelt beside the dog she and Grandpa had raised from a pup and hugged her. "Bye, girl," she whispered. "I hope he's good to you."

Coco whined and licked her face. Robyn felt tears welling in her eyes and knew there was no sense prolonging the moment. She rose and handed the end of the leash to Rick. "Can you take her, please? I'll get Rosie."

He waited while she repeated the procedure with the second dog. When she stood, he smiled mournfully. "Is it always this hard?"

"Sort of. But I usually don't think I'm handing them over to a thief. We make sure they'll have a good home."

"And you're not sure this time."

She shrugged helplessly. "The setup Sterns described sounds terrific. . .assuming he's telling us the truth. But if I refuse to let them go now. . ."

Rick nodded. "He could get really nasty, I suppose. But if you want to say no, I'll stand behind you."

Her mouth skewed into an involuntary grimace and she looked away. "I can't ask you to take the heat for me. And you have patients to see this afternoon. You can't stay around and guard Mom and me if we make him mad."

"You could announce it while the state trooper's here. I'd think that would deter Sterns from doing anything rash."

She bit her bottom lip and considered that. "Thanks. I appreciate everything you're doing today. Just having you here is a big help. But I think right now we should smooth things over. I don't want to put Mom in a situation that's worse than the one we've got right now. And besides—" She hesitated, but looking up into his caramel-colored eyes and seeing the sympathy he radiated, she knew she could tell him anything. "We really need the money."

"I thought maybe. But I hate to see you do something you don't want to do." Rick sighed then pulled out a smile. "Okay, I'll support your decision. Robyn, I care about you and your family. I'll do anything I can to help you."

She tried to smile, but her lips trembled too much. A fresh memory of his awkward embrace on the trail sent a dart of yearning to her heart. The possibility that Rick liked her beyond their casual friendship delighted her, but she couldn't spare the time to think about that now. Instead, she sniffed and got out a muffled, "Thanks."

Rick's smile twisted as though her pain had reached him, too. "You want to get the last dog, and we'll take them out to Sterns's vehicle?"

When all three dogs were loaded in the cages in the back of the rented SUV, they went inside. Mom sat on the edge of Grandpa's recliner in the living room and smiled wanly when Robyn and Rick came in.

Robyn cocked her head and listened. The two men were talking in the kitchen.

"I gave them coffee and left them alone," Mom said, rising. "I suppose I should get ready for work."

Robyn went to the desk in the corner and found her receipt book. She hesitated only a moment then wrote out the document for Philip Sterns. She crossed the living room and stood in the doorway. "The dogs are loaded, Mr. Sterns."

He turned around to smile at her, and she handed him the receipt. "Thank you. Officer Glade and I were just discussing the incident that took place here earlier. I want to tell you personally, I had nothing whatever to do with this. I hope you don't think otherwise."

Robyn found it hard to meet his gaze. "Right now we're still in shock. We don't know what to think."

"I guess you can go, Mr. Sterns." Glade closed his notebook and stood.

"I assure you, I'm happy to cooperate," Sterns told him. "It's a shame someone stole that beautiful dog, Tumble. If there's anything else I can help you with, I'll be happy to do it."

Glade nodded and looked at Robyn. "I'm going out to look at the tracks now. Can I go out this door?" He glanced toward the back door that led into the dog lot.

"Yes. Would you like me to come out with you?"

"I'll go take a look. Maybe you can step out after you've seen Mr. Sterns off and show me where each of the stolen dogs was kept."

When the door closed behind him, Robyn faced Sterns. "Have you booked passage for the dogs to California?"

"Actually, they're staying here in Alaska."

Robyn couldn't hide her surprise, and he smiled. "I've found some property outside Anchorage. I'll board the dogs at a kennel near the city while I go back to California to wind up my affairs there. I'm returning in two weeks to close on the house I'm buying. Unless, of course, you and your grandfather have changed your minds about selling this place."

"No, thank you. I hope the dogs will be happy with you and that you have good times together."

"That's gracious of you. Perhaps we'll see you at some race or other." He walked through the living room, said good-bye to Rick, and went out to his car.

Robyn drew a deep breath and let it out slowly.

"You holding up all right?" Rick asked.

"Kind of."

Her mother entered the room from the hallway that led to their bedrooms. "At least that's over," Mom said. "What are we going to do about Pat Isherwood's dogs?"

"After I show Trooper Glade what he needs to see, I'll call Pat. I can't put it off."

"I suppose not. Well, I don't have time to eat lunch. I need to get to the store."

"I'm not sure I can eat anyway," Robyn said. "Want me to make you a sandwich to take with you?"

"No, that's all right." Cheryl turned to Rick. "I'm so glad you were here when this happened, and when Mr. Sterns came. I admit I was a little frightened to see him again."

"I'm glad I could help," Rick said. "Robyn, do you mind if I go out to the kennels with you?"

"Not at all. Thanks."

Glade came slowly along the path from the old woods road, studying the snowmobile's trail as they walked across the yard.

Robyn smiled grimly as they met near the dog enclosures. "This is the female dogs' enclosure. No dogs were taken from here, though the three Sterns just bought were all in here. When Mom told us about the theft, I looked around a little. Of course, we had to put away the teams we'd taken out. I couldn't tell for sure, but I don't think the thieves came into this enclosure."

Glade nodded, still searching the ground. "It looks to me as if they stopped the snow machine over there." He pointed to the other gate. "And I'd say there were two of them, though Mrs. Holland didn't specify she saw two people. But she was looking at the back of the rig, with the trailer between her and the snow machine."

"True," Robyn said. "I'm sorry we messed up the footprints and all."

"Well, you couldn't leave your teams out, I suppose."

"I didn't go too close to the kennels where the six dogs were stolen on purpose. I thought you might want to look over the ground for evidence. I'll take you in there now if you want."

The dogs began to yip as she opened the gate. "Shush," Robyn called, and for the most part, they did.

Rick and Glade followed her into the male dogs' enclosure.

The dogs that hadn't been out for exercise that morning jumped and whined as she passed them. Tumble's absence struck her suddenly with the force of a meteorite. His tether line lay slack on the snow, and his kennel sat empty and silent. A painful lump rose in her throat. "Tumble was here."

"He's your best dog?" Glade asked.

She nodded. "He's our primary stud dog. We sell the pups and collect stud fees. And he's a terrific leader, too."

"How much is he worth?"

She put her hand to her lips and blinked back tears. Would it come down to this—placing a number on Tumble's life for the police and the insurance company? "I. . .let me think." She named a figure and shrugged. "Maybe more. But that's taking into account what he could earn for us and the prestige his record brings to the kennel."

Glade wrote it down and studied the ground around Tumble's doghouse. The thief's footprints were indistinguishable from Robyn's on the packed snow.

She showed him the next empty kennel. "This dog belonged to a client, and so did the one beside him. I have eight of Patrick Isherwood's dogs here to train while he recovers from surgery."

"How many of the stolen dogs were his?"

"Two."

"The other four were yours?"

"Yes, sir." Robyn eyed Rick while the trooper wrote it all down. Rick's confident demeanor and sympathetic smile encouraged her a little, but the entire situation still ripped her insides to shreds.

When Glade had inspected all of the empty kennels, Rick said, "Officer, we still wonder about this Philip Sterns. The whole situation is off-kilter, with him wanting to buy dogs and getting angry over the male, then showing up today to buy the three females shortly after the others were stolen."

"I agree," Glade said, "but I don't have enough evidence to arrest him. I did get the name of the kennel where he said he would board the dogs he bought, and you can be sure we'll check into that."

"You know about the microchips, right?" Robyn asked. "For identification."

"My dog has one," the trooper said.

"Well, so do all of these dogs. We put them in our puppies and any dogs we buy that don't already have them. Patrick's dogs have them, too."

"That's good to know." He made a notation then glanced up. "Does Sterns know about them?"

"I. . ." She felt her face color. "He must. It's common knowledge. But I don't recall specifically discussing it with him. I should have, but I've been so upset about this—him wanting to buy Tumble, and now having six dogs stolen. I'm afraid I didn't say anything to him about it."

"That could work in your favor." He put his notebook away. "We'll do everything we can, Miss Holland."

"Thank you," Robyn said. "We're talking about a huge loss to the business, as I'm sure you realize."

Robyn and Rick walked around to the front of the house with him. When he'd driven away, they went inside.

Cheryl sat curled up in Steve's recliner, sobbing.

"Mom?" Robyn rushed to her side. "I thought you'd left."

"I'm sorry, honey." Mom reached for a tissue and dabbed at her eyelids. "I shouldn't have stopped long enough to think about things. I kind of lost it, I'm afraid. I know we've done everything we can, but I feel so horrid! It's my fault."

"Don't say that." Robyn sat on the arm of the chair and hugged her mom close. "If Sterns is behind this, then it's my fault if it's anyone's. I'm the one who made him mad, not you."

"But right in daylight, of all things, when we have so many dark hours they could have done it in."

"I know." Robyn rubbed her mom's back and caught Rick's eye. He gave her a sympathetic smile but looked as though he wished he were elsewhere. Robyn continued to stroke Mom's shoulder. "They probably watched the house for a few days and thought you worked every morning. If they came by the old woods road today, they'd have seen Rick and me hitching up the teams, but they couldn't see that your car was in the garage. When we left, they assumed the house was empty and they could do whatever they wanted."

"This isn't your fault, Cheryl," Rick said, "or yours either, Robyn. It's the thieves' fault. No one else's."

Robyn knew that he was right in an elemental way, but she still felt guilty and responsible.

"Do you think they'd have taken more dogs if we hadn't come back when we did?" Rick asked.

"I don't know." Robyn frowned, thinking about the possibilities.

"I upset Grandpa, too," Mom persisted. "It was stupid of me ever to mention selling the property. When Sterns talked about buying the place, it just popped into my mind as a possible solution to all our financial troubles. But it wouldn't be, really. I can see that now."

"Oh, Mom. Stop beating yourself up. I love you so much." Robyn squeezed her, feeling her mother's chest wrack with each breath that was more of a sob. "Look, do you want me to call the store and tell them you'll be late?"

Her mother sniffed and straightened. "No, I've already asked them several favors in the last week. I've got to go in today. But tomorrow we'll go to see Grandpa again, all right? Can you go with me?"

"Of course."

"I'll be at the clinic tomorrow," Rick said. "If it's any help, I could drive you ladies to Anchorage with me. If you want to stay in town all day, that is."

Mom wiped her face and glanced in the mirror near the front door. "Ick. I'm a mess. Rick, thank you. Why don't you settle that with Robyn? If she thinks it would be inconvenient, we'll take the car. Now, I've got to run." She bustled out the door, wiping her eyes with the tissue.

Rick glanced at his watch. "I'd better get going, too. I need to drive to a farm on the Palmer Road. Will you be all right?"

"I suppose so. I locked all the gates when we came out of the yard. You can bet I'll never leave them unlocked again, even when I'm right here in the house."

Rick paused, looking down at her, and she suddenly remembered again the hug he'd given her while their dog teams waited on the trail. Her cheeks went hot. In spite of all that had happened in the last two hours, the affinity between them mushroomed to occupy almost all her thoughts.

And yet, she wondered if she ought to let her feelings go too far down that trail. Rick still commuted to Anchorage. Would he give up his small-town practice and go back to the larger clinic? Just because he was helping her now didn't mean he would always be around.

"I'll call you later," he said softly. "And I'll be praying that the police find the dogs. Think about whether you want to ride with me tomorrow. I'll leave around eight."

"Thanks."

He reached out and rubbed his knuckles gently over her cheek. "It's going to be okay."

She nodded.

He went out quickly and closed the door.

She stepped to the window and watched him get in his truck and drive away. Her heart longed to be with him. Would his attention last?

Other things vied for her concentration. More than anything, she dreaded calling Patrick, but she couldn't put it off. Sending up a quick prayer, she pulled out her phone.

Chapter 8

That evening, Rick drove to the little church Cheryl had told him the Holland family attended. He didn't know if they would be there tonight—after today's events, going out for the midweek Bible study and prayer time would take an effort of the will. But maybe that was best. Without Robyn there to distract him, he might have a clearer mind and make a better assessment of the church.

Three dozen people sat in small groups, sprinkled about the auditorium, talking softly. Rick spotted Robyn and her mother almost at once, in the fourth row. The leap his heart took surprised him a little.

He paused near the door for a moment before walking down the aisle. He couldn't slip into a seat near the back and let her find out later he'd come in without speaking to them. But would she welcome his presence?

That was silly. Of course she would. But was she ready to let her fellow church members see him single her out?

He walked hesitantly down the aisle.

"Well, hi, Dr. Baker." A man whose cattle he treated regularly stood and shook his hand. "Glad to see you here."

"Thanks. Thought I'd visit and check it out." Rick felt foolish but quickly reminded himself of his purpose.

"You're welcome any time."

He nodded and moved away, hoping he'd conversed long enough to be polite. The service would start any minute, and he didn't want to be caught standing in the aisle.

Robyn looked up when he paused at the end of her pew.

"Hi."

She smiled and moved over. "Did you see all your patients this afternoon?"

"Yes." He settled beside her and whispered, "I wasn't sure if you'd be here, but I wanted to visit this church. The Lord's helping me arrange things to spend less time in Anchorage, and I've asked Him to show me a place to worship near home, too."

"That's great. I hope you like it here."

Cheryl grinned at him. "Hi, Rick."

He smiled back and faced the front as the pastor moved to the lectern.

Rick was very conscious of Robyn sitting beside him during the Bible study. She listened intently and found her way around her Bible with ease. And she smelled great.

After a while, he was able to rein in his thoughts and concentrate on the pastor's words. He found himself liking the man and the message, which came directly from Romans chapter 10.

When the time to give prayer requests came, the pastor said, "The Hollands have asked for prayer for Grandpa Steve and also for their business. They had an incident this morning at the kennel, and six of their dogs were stolen. The police are working on it, but pray that the dogs will be found. This could make a big difference to the business, and some of the dogs were special friends. Robyn tells me two of them belonged to someone else and were here for training."

Robyn kept her head down as he gave the report. Rick wished he could encourage her. He wanted to give her hand a squeeze, at the very least.

As the pastor moved on to another request, she glanced up at him. Her dark eyes held a sheen of tears.

"You okay?" he whispered.

She nodded. "Thanks for being here. God knows where the dogs are, but. . . having you here helps."

Warmth spread through his chest. He sat back, silently giving thanks to the Lord for leading him here tonight.

⁑

The next morning, Robyn hurried to feed the dogs and get showered and changed for the trip to Anchorage. She made sure all the gates were securely locked. Even so, she hated to drive off and leave the homestead unoccupied all day.

When she was ready to go, just after eight o'clock, she joined her mother in the living room.

Mom was talking on the phone but signed off and gave her daughter a wan smile. "That was Trooper Glade. The kennel owner in Anchorage confirmed that Sterns is boarding three sled dogs with him."

"It's a reputable concern," Robyn said grudgingly. "I thought I'd heard of them, and I checked out their Web site last night. It looks like a decent place."

Her mother eyed her cautiously. "Are you sure you want to go today?"

"Yes. I haven't seen Grandpa for two days. Besides, I've got to pick up the vet logs and time sheets for the race."

"Okay. We can make the bank deposit in town, too."

"Got it right here." Robyn patted her leather shoulder bag, where the cash Sterns had given them for the dogs rested. "Let's go. I'd like to be home by suppertime if we can."

In the car, Mom drove down the Glenn Highway in silence. The sky was still dark, and the mountains were black hulks in the distance. After a while, she glanced over at Robyn. "You could have ridden into town with Rick."

"No, we needed our own wheels to do all our errands."

"You like him, don't you?"

Robyn swallowed hard and looked out the side window. What she felt for Rick had burgeoned in the past week to more than mere liking. But how could she explain that to her mother?

"I mean, we all like him," Mom persisted, "but it seemed to me yesterday that there was something a little extra between you two. And then he showed up at church last night."

"Yeah. I like him. A lot."

"That's great. He's a good man."

Robyn inhaled deeply and let her breath out in a puff. "Do you think. . .I mean, I've thought for quite a while now God might want me to be single."

Her mother laughed softly. "How long has this been going on, honey? You're only twenty-four."

"I know, but I'm not exactly in a high-circulation area. Who do I meet? The same people at church week after week, and a few dog lovers."

"Huh." Her mother shook her head, her lips pursed in an almost-smile. "I guess it would be hard for God to bring the right man for you to Wasilla."

"You know what I mean." Robyn scrunched up her face and gritted her teeth.

Mom laughed. "Yes, I do, but for the last year you've had a handsome, intelligent, single man living next door to you. Haven't you ever thought about Rick as eligible until the past week?"

"Well, sure, but. . ." Robyn turned away again, her old insecurities taking over. She'd never figured she had a chance with Rick. "I wasn't going to chase him."

"Of course not. But since the day of Grandpa's accident, he's been coming around a lot."

"Yeah." *More than he had the entire previous year*, Robyn thought. She'd first started hoping he would notice her last year, when he helped with the Fire & Ice sled race. But he was always on the go—running to Anchorage to the vet clinic or working at his own new practice down the road. She saw him only now and then, when a dog needed attention. Things had definitely changed in the last ten days.

They went to the bank first, then to the nursing home. Grandpa's face brightened when he saw them. "Hey, how you doing? My two lovely girls!"

Both kissed him and sat down to talk.

"Only a couple of weeks till the race," he said. "I gotta get out of this place."

"You're getting better," Mom said. "The nurse told me so."

"Well, they'd better let me go home before race day, or I'm going to know the reason why."

Robyn suppressed a laugh. It wasn't funny—if he couldn't go home, they *would* know the reason.

After half an hour, she stood. "I've got some errands to run, Grandpa. I'll come back for Mom in a couple of hours."

"What are you doing?"

"Picking up supplies and paperwork for the race."

"Hey, have you got all the vendors lined up?"

"Darby Zale and her mother are doing that. They've done a fantastic job, too. And Anna's got all the volunteers scheduled."

"Did you get enough people for all the checkpoints?"

"Yes, we did."

"And Rick is still going to do the vet exams at the start?"

"Yes, Grandpa. Mom can tell you who's doing what. I need to go get things done."

After quickly completing several of her errands, Robyn headed toward the newspaper office. The sun had risen, which made her feel more energetic and made it easier to find her destinations. As she nosed into yet another parking spot, her cell phone rang.

Rick's warm voice greeted her. "Hey! I guess you got to town all right?"

"Yes. I'm just going into the newspaper office. They promised us advance coverage for the race, and I brought them some information. I want them to see my face, so they won't forget about the article."

"Sounds like a plan. Say, how about lunch?"

"Together? Uh. . .you and me?"

"Yeah. Your mom's welcome, too, if she wants to come."

"Well, we were planning to eat with Grandpa at the home, but. . ."

"Of course."

Robyn sucked in a breath that seemed a little short on oxygen. "If you're serious, I'll ask them if they'd mind."

"Great. There's a place close to the nursing home. I could meet you there. I'm seeing patients until noon, but I could get over there by twelve thirty."

Robyn soon arranged the plan with her mother, who sounded thrilled that the two young people were getting together for a meal. Robyn called Rick back to tell him she'd be there.

She took her file folder into the news office and chatted for a few minutes with one of the reporters, who took notes and promised that the article would run the following week.

Leaving the office, Robyn noted that she had only a half hour before she was to meet Rick. She took out the list of Anchorage kennels she'd put together the night before, from Internet searching and the Yellow Pages. No time to visit any of them before lunch, and her stomach had begun to perform forward rolls every time she thought about seeing Rick again. On a lunch date. Deep breaths.

She got to the restaurant before he did. After looking around the parking lot to make sure he wasn't there, she walked to the shop next door and asked if she could hang a flyer for the race in their window, where other events were posted. The icy cold glass tingled her fingers as she taped up the flyer.

She got back to the restaurant as Rick parked his pickup. He climbed out and grinned when he saw her near the entrance. Suddenly Anchorage in January felt like a tropical beach. Robyn was sure her face turned scarlet.

The restaurant was full, but they waited only a few minutes before a table opened for them.

"Get your errands done?" Rick asked after they'd given their orders to the waitress.

"Yes, mostly. I need to pick up the trophies, but the shop is near the highway, so I think Mom and I will stop there on our way home."

"Everything's coming together for the race, then."

"Yes." She frowned, feeling she must have overlooked something. "Every year it rushes up at us, and we have a thousand details to take care of, then suddenly it's over."

"Sounds about right. Have you thought about security?"

"Quite a lot since yesterday. We decided to hire someone to watch the dog lot that day."

"Too bad it had to come to that."

"I know, but if we go off all day and leave the place unprotected…and the whole world will know we're over at the race."

"Are you taking any dogs?"

"I usually have a few of our best ones hitched up and showing off at the race to advertise. Darby and my brother, Aven, will be helping." She clenched her jaw for a moment. "Of course, Tumble was going to be our poster child for the kennel. If we don't get him back…oh Rick, I'm so discouraged."

"I guess it's hard not to be."

"The police don't have any leads yet, or if they do, they haven't told us. Mom talked to Trooper Glade this morning, and all he did was assure her that Sterns actually took the dogs he bought to the kennel he said he'd use." She looked up as the waitress appeared with their plates. After the woman had set them down, Robyn smiled across the table. "Would you like to ask the blessing?"

"Sure."

After he'd prayed, they began to eat, and Robyn steered the conversation to his work. She enjoyed hearing about the four-footed patients he'd treated that morning.

"It's been awhile since I examined a ferret," Rick concluded. "And a woman brought in the most beautiful Persian kittens."

They ate for a few minutes. He took a sip from his coffee and set the cup down. "Hey, things are going to be okay. You know that, don't you?"

"Thanks. I admit I'm still fretting over the dogs. Especially Tumble and Pat's two dogs."

"We'll keep praying," Rick said.

Robyn ate the last bite of her sandwich and opened her bag. As she took out a piece of paper, the waitress approached.

"Dessert, folks?"

Rick raised his eyebrows and smiled at her. "Piece of pie?"

"No thanks, but you go ahead if you want."

"No, we're all set," Rick told the waitress. She totaled the bill and laid it on the table. "So what's that?" Rick nodded toward the paper Robyn had unfolded.

"It's a list of kennels in the area. I want to go by that place where Sterns left Coco and the other two dogs."

"Why? The police said it was legit, and I mentioned it to Hap Shelley this morning. He says the couple who own the place are honest and treat the animals well."

Robyn frowned. "Call me stubborn if you want, but I'd like to see it for myself."

"Okay, Stubborn. But let me go with you."

"Can you do that? I thought you had to get back to the clinic."

"It's not far from here." He looked at his watch. "Plenty of time."

She left her car in the restaurant's lot and climbed into Rick's pickup with him. She was surprised when, just a few minutes later, they entered a residential area and pulled in at a house with a kennel sign out front.

Following signs, they walked around the house. A din of yapping erupted, and several dogs in fenced runs leaped up and barked at them.

A woman met them just inside the entrance. "May I help you?"

Robyn cleared her throat. "Yes, I'm Robyn Holland, and I'd like—"

"Of the Holland Kennel in Wasilla?"

"Yes." Robyn stared at her.

The woman smiled. "One of my clients recently bought some dogs from you. They're beautiful."

"Why, thank you. That's why we're here, actually." Robyn peered toward the door that led to the kennels and dog runs.

"Did you. . .want to see the dogs?" The woman frowned.

Rick stepped forward. "We just wanted to inquire, since we were in town, and make sure they'd arrived safely and are adjusting well."

She nodded, eyeing him thoughtfully. "Have we met?"

"I'm Dr. Rick Baker, from the Far North Veterinary Hospital."

"Of course." Her expression cleared.

"Miss Holland is extremely particular about making sure the dogs she sells are well cared for," he said. "I told her this is one of the top kennels in Anchorage."

"Thank you. I can assure you the dogs are all fine. They seem to be settling in well. Mr. Sterns expects them to be here for a couple of weeks."

Robyn nodded. Probably the woman had security rules that wouldn't let just anyone walk in and visit dogs that belonged to other people.

"I…I also wondered if you'd had any other dogs come in yesterday or today that might be…" She looked down at the floor, unsure how to proceed.

The woman said carefully, "The police were here this morning, looking for stolen dogs."

Robyn nodded, attempting to hold back tears that sprang into her eyes. "We had six dogs stolen."

"I'm so sorry. We've only had two others check in within the last twenty-four hours, and they're both repeat clients. But if anyone shows up with several well-cared-for huskies, I'll let the police know."

"Thank you." Robyn pulled the list of kennels from her bag. "Could you please tell me what you know about these places? I thought perhaps we should call them and ask if anyone had brought dogs in…."

The woman took the paper and studied it. "I know these folks, at the Aspen Kennel. That's a good one. And I think Bristol is all right. This one…" She touched one name and glanced into Robyn's eyes. "I don't know much about the Galloway Kennel, but what I've heard…." She shook her head. "They've been in business a few years, but I wouldn't take my dog there." She ran down the list, making a few comments about each one. "This one's new, and I don't know anything about it. Never heard of this one." Finally she handed the paper back. "Sorry I couldn't be of more help."

"I appreciate it." Robyn took a card from her pocket. "Here's my card for the Holland Kennel. One of the stolen dogs was Tumble, our primary breeding male. If you hear anything—anything at all that you think might have to do with our situation—could you please call me?"

"Sure. I hope you get your dogs back." The woman pocketed the card. "Rosie is out in her run now. I think Mr. Sterns's other two dogs are inside napping. But if you step outside and look through the fence at run 4, you should see Rosie."

"Thank you." Robyn turned and went out. Rick followed her to the metal mesh fence, and she looked across the expanse, over the head of the Brittany spaniel leaping and barking at her just inches away in the first run. Sure enough, Rosie stopped trotting along the fence of her enclosure and barked at Robyn and then stood whining, her nose pushed into the mesh. Robyn clenched her shaking hands on the fence.

"We'd better go," Rick said softly.

She nodded, unable to speak. She didn't want to upset the dogs. Already, Rosie might be fretful because she'd seen her former owner. Robyn trudged to the pickup.

Rick opened the passenger door for her and offered his hand for a boost up. When he got into the driver's seat, he smiled apologetically. "Ready to go back?"

She swallowed hard. "Yeah, just take me back to my car. Thanks."

"You can tell your grandfather that these three dogs are in good hands."

She bit her lip and said nothing, but she knew she wouldn't go straight back to the nursing home.

"What's the matter?" Rick asked.

She looked up into his gentle brown eyes. "I think I'll drive over to the Galloway Kennel."

"What for?" He eyed her for a moment then reached for her hand. "No, Robyn, don't."

"What if they're over there? I can't not look. She made it sound like it's the worst kennel in town. If Tumble's in there. . ."

Rick sighed. "What's the address?"

She told him, and he started the engine.

"You're. . .taking me there?"

He said through gritted teeth, "It'll be quicker if we don't go back to the restaurant first. And I'm not letting you go alone."

Chapter 9

Almost half an hour later, they located the Galloway Kennel. Rick parked at the curb a hundred yards beyond the building.

He ought to call Far North and alert them that his lunch hour would probably stretch to two. It wasn't something he liked to do, but then, he almost never did it.

"This is a pretty bad neighborhood." He stared out at the littered sidewalk and dilapidated buildings.

Robyn raised her chin. He'd come to recognize that as a sign that she wasn't giving up. With a sigh, he got out of the truck and went around to open the passenger door for her. They went in together.

A bell on the door jingled, and a woman came from an inner room, where several dogs were barking. The warm smell of dogs and bedding met them.

"Hi," Rick said. "We're looking for some dogs that were stolen yesterday from a breeding kennel in—"

"Stolen? Why are you looking here?" The woman rested her hands on her hips and glared at them.

Rick gulped and glanced at Robyn. Wrong approach.

Robyn said, "We're contacting all the kennel owners in the area. The police are looking for these valuable dogs, but we thought perhaps business owners could help us, too. If you'd be on the lookout for—"

"Are you insinuating that we would have stolen animals here? This is outrageous."

Rick spread both hands. "No, ma'am, you don't understand. We only—"

"Oh, I understand. I understand plenty. Go on. Get out of here."

He looked at Robyn. She gritted her teeth and shrugged.

"Let's go." He reached for her arm and guided her toward the door.

When they were outside and the door shut behind them, she let out a pent-up breath. "Of all the—"

"I'm sorry." Rick walked beside her toward the pickup. "I jumped right in and said the wrong thing. I should have let you do the talking."

"Now we'll never know if they're in there."

"Maybe not. But we can ask the police to come by and take a look."

She nodded. "I guess."

Rick opened the door and helped her into the truck. Once inside, he hesitated to start the motor. "What now?"

She eyed him cautiously. "You're up for more adventure?"

"Well, I sort of feel like I'm the one who blew it." He consulted his watch. "If there's another one that's not too far from here, we could try one more. I promise to be more diplomatic this time."

"Or sneakier."

"That might work."

She smiled then. It was worth the wait, especially when she reached over and squeezed his hand. "Thanks for being here. Facing her alone would have been scary. And I do think we should ask the police to question her. As soon as possible."

Rick took his cue and pulled out his phone. He tried Trooper Glade's number. When he got no response, he rummaged in the glove box for an Anchorage street map. He handed it to Robyn, and she pored over it while he dialed his friend.

A minute later, he was able to tell Robyn, "Joel Dawes said they'll send someone out here this afternoon. I think we can count on it. And he'll let us know the outcome."

"Good." Robyn pointed to her crumpled list. "The kennel closest to this one is a new one. That lady at the first place said she didn't know anything about them. But that might be a good place to hide some hot property, don't you think?"

"Maybe so."

He drove a few miles and found the location. He and Robyn climbed out of the truck and stood by the tailgate, looking over the run-down one-story building. Paint was peeling off the siding. The front held no windows, and the door had a handwritten sign that read BARKLAND KENNEL—PICKUP HOURS 9 TO 11 A.M. AND 4 TO 6 P.M. Barking and whining came from the back of the property.

"Maybe we should let the police handle this one, too." Rick glanced hopefully at her, but her jaw was still set. "I can try Trooper Glade again. Even if they didn't come until tomorrow. . ."

"The dogs could be taken out of Alaska by then."

"Well, yes."

Her brows drew together in a scowl. "And the police aren't going to want to spend hours searching every kennel in town. I'm sure they have violent crimes that are much more urgent."

"No. They'd send someone. This is like grand theft, isn't it? Those dogs are valuable. I'm sure if I talk to Joel, I can convince him that it's important to send someone here as well as to that Galloway place."

"But if our dogs aren't here, they wouldn't go and search all the other kennels on the list."

"Is that what you plan to do?" This was getting out of hand. He'd had no idea she was so determined. No way could he blow off the clinic for the whole afternoon and escort her to half a dozen more kennels. "Robyn, I can't go around to them all with you. If I'm gone much longer, the clinic staff will send the police out to look for *me*."

The set to her mouth rebuked him. Pain and anger filled Robyn's heart right now, and it spilled over into the lines of her face and the stiff set to her shoulders. Without her saying a word, he knew she wanted to see justice done and to recover the dogs, not just for her family but for Patrick Isherwood, too.

"Did you call Pat Isherwood yesterday?" Rick asked.

"Yes."

"How did he take the news?"

She winced. "He didn't like it, of course. I assured him the other six dogs he left with us are locked in. I even asked Darby and my friend Anna to stop in today and make sure everything's okay while we're gone."

"But you feel as though you've got to find those dogs yourself, not leave it up to the state police." She didn't answer, but her stricken face roused new longings in him. He wished he could protect her from violence and crime, and beyond that, from feelings of inadequacy and failure.

"I'm going in." She stepped forward, and he grabbed the sleeve of her parka.

"Let's think about this for a minute. You know that if we walk in and ask to see the dogs, they won't let us."

"You may be right. So? Do you have a better plan?" Her dark eyes sparked with resistance.

Rick wanted to take the hurt and anger away. Not only to return the dogs to her, but to assure her that this would never happen again. It was beyond his power, but she had come to trust him, and for the last couple of days she'd relied on him in small ways. If nothing more, she might let him bear some of the stress for her.

"Let me go in and ask to see the kennel," he said. "They might recognize you."

Her puff of breath formed a white cloud in the cold air. "Or you. You were with me yesterday."

"All bundled up in a parka. Not this jacket, I might add." He patted the front of the wool jacket he'd worn to the clinic. "And they might know your face from any number of places. There's a fetching picture of you on the Holland Kennel Web site, for instance."

She blinked twice and looked away. "If you think you can distract me with flattery, forget it."

He smiled. "All right, I'll save that for later. But it's true, Robyn. They might recognize you. And have you considered that the thieves might be people you know?"

Her lips twitched. "Someone else in the dog business?"

"Maybe. Or someone in Wasilla who knows a little about your routine."

Her gaze sought his again. "So, you think we're wasting our time looking in Anchorage? What do you suggest we do?"

"Since we're here, let's go ahead and check this one. There's just one vehicle in the parking lot." He nodded toward the ten-year-old pickup sitting in front of the kennel. "Probably the owner is the only person here, or an employee. No customers right now."

"So?"

"So, what if I go in and inquire about possibly leaving a dog here for a week when I take my vacation. While I'm in there, you can sneak around the back of the building. From the sound of things, they've got some pens or tethers out there. You wouldn't be able to see any dogs that are inside, but you could at least check out the outdoor accommodations."

She nodded. "Better than nothing, I guess." She pulled her hood up and arranged it over her dark hair.

He smiled down at her. Now wasn't the time to mention it, but the image of her sweet face peering out at him from within the circle of faux fur with her brown eyes wide and her cheeks flushed stirred him. Sometime when they were in a quiet, warm place and didn't have to worry about dogs or criminals, he would tell her how lovely she was.

Had no man seen her beauty before him? It was unthinkable. But why, then, was she still single? Had her independence kept the suitors away? Perhaps her close-knit family deterred them, or her success in business intimidated them. Her seeming assurance might put off some men, he supposed, but he knew she had a wide streak of insecurity that she hid well.

Of course, he made a huge assumption there. Perhaps she had been courted and he knew nothing about it.

"I'm leaving the truck unlocked." He said it even as he made the decision. "I want you to be able to get in quickly if you need to."

She nodded. "Okay."

"Be careful," he said. "If anyone sees you, it's all right to tell them you're with me and you wanted to see the dogs. But I'm planning on you staying out of sight. I'll meet you back here in ten minutes."

"Got it," she said.

He hesitated, then bent and kissed her cool cheek. When he pulled away, she was watching him with something like curiosity in her chocolate brown eyes. Sometime he would really kiss her, and maybe that would knock the questions out of that simmering gaze.

"Go on," he said. "Get to the side of the building and give me a minute to go in and get the guy talking."

⁑

Robyn tiptoed along the side of the kennel building. She ducked low beneath the small window toward the back of the wall. As she approached the rear corner, she looked back toward the street. Rick was out of sight.

She peered around the corner and saw a large, fenced enclosure. Within it, a dozen or more dogs of different sizes and breeds ran free. She couldn't see any shelter for them other than a lone pine tree that rose near the back of the lot. The dogs had no bedding to lie down on. She ducked back quickly, before they saw her.

Already they were barking—one thin hound wailed continuously from a far corner and several more sporadically joined in. She hoped they weren't left out there too long in the snow with nothing to lie on.

She took another peek. Beyond the large enclosure was another fenced area. This one seemed smaller, though it was hard to tell from her position. Inside she saw a couple of dogs that appeared to be chained to tree trunks. They lay inert on the ground. One looked like a German shepherd–husky cross. Her heart squeezed painfully. Were her dogs and Pat's in this place? She focused on the dog nearest her—a small beagle cross in the big enclosure. It was so thin she could see the outline of its ribs, and it whined without a letup. Shuddering, Robyn scrutinized the other dogs. She realized she was looking for Tumble, but if he'd been among the pitiful assortment, she'd have recognized him at once.

A loud spurt of barking erupted from inside the building, and the dogs outside took up the yapping. Some of them ran toward the back of the building and threw themselves against the fence.

She concluded that the dogs inside had begun making a ruckus because of Rick's presence, and those outside chimed in because they wanted to be part of whatever was going on. Even the ones in the far enclosure sat up and peered toward the building. Robyn decided that it no longer mattered if the dogs saw her. They couldn't possibly make more noise than they were making now.

She ran along the fence, focusing on one dog after another. None of them looked remotely like the glossy, well-fed huskies she had lost. She circled behind the pen and along the edge of the second enclosure. Her steps dragged as she realized most of the dogs within had visible injuries. Some had scabs and scars on their legs and faces. One had red lacerations on its hip, neck, and front legs. None of the wounds were covered. Looking at the hurting dogs turned her stomach and stoked the fire of her anger. She wondered if the animals out here belonged to the owner or were long-term boarders. But this was a new kennel. How had they gotten so many customers? No people in their right minds would leave pets here if they glimpsed the pitiful scene out back.

She came to the edge of the building on the side opposite where she'd started. This side held several windows. Banking that Rick would keep the owner talking in the front, she decided to take a chance and look in.

Inside, she saw a row of screened doors fronting dog cages, three deep. The animals inside yelped and whined, some pressing against the fronts of their cages. Off to her left lay an open door, and through it she glimpsed Rick standing near a desk. She quickly turned her scrutiny to the dogs in the cages. She couldn't see them well, but one particular bark, deep and insistent, rang a chord in her heart. It sounded like the bass voice of Hero, one of her largest sled dogs.

As the caged dogs moved about, she could make out their silhouettes through the mesh fencing of the enclosure doors. She stared at the cages one by one until she spotted one where the big occupant's pointed dark ears stood up above a black-and-white muzzle.

Hero!

In a flash of certainty, she knew it was him. Soon she picked out two other cages she thought likely held dogs from Holland Kennel. The others weren't within sight but could easily be on the side of the room nearer the window.

A quick look toward the open doorway made her catch her breath. Rick was backing away from the desk, nodding. As she watched, he moved out of her line of vision. She'd better head for the truck.

She glanced back toward the yard behind the building. If she took the time to go all the way around the back, Rick would be upset, wondering where she was. And the owner might look out back to see why the dogs out there hadn't settled down. She decided to chance running across the front parking lot.

Before she acted, movement inside caught her eye. She flattened herself at the edge of the window and watched a man in coveralls enter the room with all the cages. He opened one of the lower tier cage doors and clipped a leash on the occupant's collar. When he led the dog out, Robyn gasped. The husky he'd chosen was one of Pat Isherwood's lead dogs. He led it across the room and opened the back door. The dogs in the fenced yards barked and howled louder. The man came back with the leash slack in his hands.

Robyn felt sick. Had he turned Astro out with all those other dogs? What if they fought? Some sled dogs lost their manners when they met strange dogs and weren't under the owner's control. They might get aggressive—or the other dogs in the pen might. Some of the valuable huskies could be killed. The man stopped near another cage and turned his back to the window. Time to move.

She ducked low beneath the window frames and dashed to the front corner of the building. Rick stood beside the pickup, staring toward the wall where she'd begun her foray.

When she left the cover of the kennel and ran toward him, he turned, his eyes wide. She scurried to the passenger side of the truck and dove in. Rick hopped in on his side and gunned the engine.

"Wait! He's got them."

"What?" The incredulity in his expression was almost comical. His mouth hung open and his eyebrows disappeared under the lock of hair falling over his forehead.

"I saw Astro, and I'm pretty sure Hero's in there, too. He took Astro out the back. I think he put him in the pen out behind, with about twenty other dogs. They're all loose in there. Astro will probably get in a fight. They could kill him. And the worst thing is, I think he was going to put the others out there, too. Hero, especially, might get aggressive."

"Let's get down the street where he can't see us if he looks out. Then we'll decide what to do." Rick put the truck in gear and drove away. By the time Robyn had her seat belt buckled, they were half a block down the street. "Why would he put valuable dogs in a pen with a bunch of others?" he asked.

"I don't know. Some of the dogs outside look sick and emaciated. And some of them have injuries."

"It doesn't make sense." Rick pulled in at the curb and turned to face her. "If he stole those dogs to sell, why take a chance on them getting sick or torn to pieces?"

She had no answer.

"Okay. Tell me everything."

His patience made her want to scream. "We need to call the police."

"Agreed," Rick said. "But are you sure he has them all?"

"No. He may have sold some. I think I saw two others of ours though. There are a lot of dogs in cages in the back room."

"I figured that. Heard them yelping and saw the stacked cages. It's not a good situation. I'm surprised anyone brings a dog here to board."

Robyn sucked in a deep breath. "We need to get the cops here fast."

Rick took out his phone and punched a few buttons. "Joel? This is Rick. Hey, we've located some of the stolen dogs. They're in a kennel here in Anchorage." He gave his friend the address. "We need you to send someone fast. We're afraid the dogs will be hurt. The fellow seems to be putting them together with a lot of strange dogs. Well, I don't know. I didn't see it myself, but Miss Holland did. And she's positively identified at least two of the stolen dogs, with possible IDs on two more."

Robyn tried to send him a silent message of thanks. A minute later, Rick hung up and sighed. "He says they'll need a warrant. That could take awhile."

"Can't they just come ask to take a look? Those dogs are in danger."

"Tell me exactly what you saw."

"Well, out back there are two pens. In the one I went to first, at least ten or twelve dogs were running free."

"I thought you said twenty."

She frowned. "I might have."

"Well, is it ten or twenty?"

"Yes. Somewhere in there." She looked away. "I'm sorry. I know I'm upset, but I'm not hysterical. I didn't count the dogs, okay? I'm guessing there were at least ten, possibly twenty, but no more than that. Probably twelve or fifteen."

"Okay. And how did they look?"

"Some were lethargic. Some barked constantly."

"I heard."

Robyn nodded grimly. "One at least was horribly skinny. Some of them looked okay so far as their physical conditions went. I looked them all over, and I could see right away that none of them were ours."

"What kinds of dogs?"

"Uh. . .mutts, smallish dogs. A beagle, and one that might be a coon hound.

One I thought was a Scottish terrier. It's hard to tell with some of them. They haven't been groomed, and their hair is long and matted. Some mixed breeds."

"Small dogs though."

"Well. . .some. All types. I hadn't really thought about it."

Rick set his jaw firmly and checked the rearview mirror.

"So, anyway," she said, less agitated than before, "I could see that beyond it there was another fenced yard, so I walked around the perimeter of the fence. In the second pen, the dogs are tethered. There were only six or eight in there, and they weren't happy. One was chewing at the post he was hitched to. A couple were just lying in the snow. When they saw me, they barked, so I hurried around to the far side of the building, where I could hide if anyone came out the back door."

"What type of dogs in that part?"

"One looked like a husky cross. A couple of pit bulls. One I think is part German shepherd."

"So, big dogs. No little lap dogs."

"Not in that pen. And each was hitched up so they couldn't reach each other."

Rick's face had gone grim, and he focused on something far beyond the truck's windshield.

"What?" she asked.

"Just thinking."

"I could tell. Wanna share?"

He smiled but sobered almost immediately. "If they steal a top sled dog, they can't run him in races. Not in Alaska anyway. Someone who knows him would see him—because you would plaster Tumble's picture all over the place at every sled race in the state."

"I sure would. If we don't get some results today, that's exactly what I plan to do. Someone will recognize him for sure, and Hero, too, if they show up at a race."

"And they couldn't breed Tumble. How could they advertise him?"

"They could change his name."

"Yes, but it would take a couple of years for them to get any results that they could brag about. You can't just steal a breeding animal and make money by breeding him right away without revealing his identity. You have to give him time to build a new reputation. So what's the point? If they want Tumble's progeny, it would be a lot less risky to bring a good female to your kennel for breeding."

What he said made sense. Robyn held his thoughtful gaze for a long moment. "All right. So either they're going to sell them out of state, or—"

"In which case, they should have had them out of here by now, not stashed in a third-rate kennel."

"What then?"

Rick's mouth twisted as though it pained him to say the words. "What if they're planning to put them in fights?"

Chapter 10

Robyn raised her chin. "Not Tumble."

"Yes, Tumble. Hero. All of them. They took all males. Aggressive, territorial males."

She lost her assertive air and lowered her jaw, taking in a gasp of a breath. "Those dogs. . ."

"Yes?"

"The ones that were tethered."

"What about them?"

"They looked like they could have been in fights. The others, running loose in the other pen—why would they want the little ones?"

"Those might be legitimate boarders, to cover up for the illegal part of the business."

"But why would he turn Astro loose with those dogs?"

"Are you sure he turned him loose, or did he hitch him up in the other pen, where the dogs are tethered?"

She hesitated. "I don't know for sure. He came back so quickly, I assumed he'd let Astro loose. But why would he do that?"

Rick said carefully, "Maybe to see how he acted with them. To watch whether he picked a fight or not."

"You're saying they have those small breeds and mutts to. . ."

"Bait dogs. To teach the fighting dogs to go after them. Some people use cats or rabbits."

"That's awful."

"I'm not saying that's what they're doing, but it sounds like they've got one pen of smaller dogs that aren't well cared for, just waiting to be used for whatever purpose, and another pen of battle-scarred dogs that could be fighters who've been injured or are getting past their prime."

"Wouldn't they just. . .do away with them?"

Rick ran a hand over his eyes and up through his hair. "I don't know. I hear a lot of things at the clinic. It's a terrible practice, and it's illegal, but it does happen. Dog fighting, betting. And sometimes they steal pets to use as. . .training aids."

Robyn shivered. "They wouldn't do that with our dogs, would they? Valuable sled dogs?"

"More likely they're trying to replenish their fighting stock."

She shook her head. "I can't believe that. I don't *want* to believe it."

"Then don't. At least until the police tell us otherwise." He reached over and took her hand. "I'm sorry. I wish I hadn't said anything about it."

"No, that's what you were thinking and I need to know what we're dealing with. Thank God we found them today." She frowned and was silent for a moment. "When I saw the man go back inside, I thought he was going to get another dog from his cage."

"Maybe he was just going to put some of them out for some fresh air while he cleaned the cages." Rick looked back down the street behind them. He couldn't see the kennel building, but he was sure he'd see the owner's pickup if it left the parking lot. "What if I go back and take a look in those pens?"

"If he saw you, he'd recognize you. And those dogs will put up a fuss if you go near the fence."

He faced front. "True, but if I'm careful, it may be worth the risk. I just want to see if he put the rest out there, and if they're engaging with the other dogs."

As he watched her, trying to gauge her reaction, her face flushed and her muscles tensed. Tears glistened in her eyes.

Rick shook his head. "What am I saying? I know it's best if we wait for the police."

She turned quickly toward the window, shoved her hand into her jacket pocket, and pulled out a tissue.

He wasn't sure what to say or do.

"I hate this." She sobbed and held the tissue to her eyes.

Rick took a couple of deep breaths and tried to form a response that she wouldn't reject. He slid over as far as his seat would allow him and touched her shoulder. "Hey. It's going to be okay. The police are coming."

She hiccupped and wiped her face again. "Crying makes me mad."

That brought a little smile to his lips. "I can see that. You don't like feeling helpless, do you?"

She shook her head almost violently, and her hood fell back.

Rick stroked her shoulder through her padded jacket. "We've found the dogs, and we're going to get them back. All of them."

She nodded and sniffed.

"It's all right to cry a little. You've had a lot going on. Your grandpa, and the race. . ."

She sobbed again, bigger this time, and his pulse raced. Had he made things worse?

"Oh, Rick, I'm afraid that the race will be a fiasco."

"Why should it? That's silly."

"No, it's not. I've never had to host it without Grandpa. There's so much to remember. I keep thinking I'm forgetting something crucial. Will I be able to pull it off? Mom helps when she can, but her biggest contribution is putting food on the table so I don't have to worry about that and can concentrate on the business."

"The race is going to be better than ever this year."

"You're just saying that. We're talking about the family name and reputation here. The kennel's success or failure. You know my worst fear?"

"Why don't you tell me?"

"My fear is that Mom's fears will come true. That we'll have to sell the dogs and get drudge jobs in the city." Her shoulders heaved. "With my luck, there'll be a blizzard on race day."

Rick suppressed a smile and bridged the gap between the bucket seats, pulling her head over onto his shoulder. "Shh. Stop being a gloom-and-doomer. The race will be terrific. Your brother's coming to help, remember? Your mom and I will be there. Grandpa Steve may even be able to come home to see it, even if he can't help out."

She collapsed against him, still sniffing and plying the tissue, but quieter now. He wondered if she was capable of accepting the kind of help she needed.

"You've got friends helping, too," he went on softly. "Anna and Darby and the folks over at Iditarod Headquarters."

"I do." Her small, shaky voice sounded very unlike confident, independent Robyn's voice.

"Yeah. You've got tons of friends, and a terrific roster of volunteers." He kissed her hair. "Sweetheart, it's going to be fine. You'll see." He shifted slightly on the uncomfortable edge of his seat. "Hey, look!"

Robyn sat up and followed his gaze. A police car had turned in at the end of the street and rolled toward them.

Rick opened his door and jumped from the truck, waving at the officer. "I'm Rick Baker," he told the trooper through the open car window. "I called for help about the stolen dogs."

"Trooper Straski. You've actually seen the dogs in the suspect's possession?"

"Yes, sir."

"Where is it?"

Rick straightened and pointed. "Just down there, on the right. About halfway along the block."

"Okay, we've got another officer on the way, and we've put in a request for a search warrant."

"So, will you talk to the man now?" Rick asked. "You don't have to wait for the warrant, do you? Because I'm a veterinarian, and from what we've seen, I suspect that man may be involved in a dogfighting ring."

"We'll talk to him. Where are the dogs in question?"

"Last we knew, one was in a pen behind the building with several other dogs. The rest were still caged inside. But the owner may have been transferring them all out to the pens."

"And you're the dogs' owner?"

"No, Miss Holland is. She's in my truck."

Straski glanced toward Robyn. "And what are you to Miss Holland?"

"Her neighbor. I'm Dr. Rick Baker, with Far North Veterinary Hospital." Rick figured the officer would recognize the name of the large practice, so he dropped it instead of his smaller Wasilla clinic's name.

As he'd expected, the trooper's eyes flickered. "I'm going to pull over and speak to Miss Holland."

Robyn got out of Rick's pickup and gave the trooper a shaky smile. "Thank you for coming so quickly. We're afraid those dogs are in immediate danger."

"I understand, ma'am. You're the owner?"

"Yes, I own four of the stolen dogs. Two others belonging to a client of mine were stolen yesterday as well, out of my kennel yard. Trooper Glade took all the information."

"Yes, ma'am. Can you show me your identification, please?"

Robyn looked at Rick and fumbled for her wallet. He sensed her frustration at the delay and gave her a tight smile.

When the trooper had examined her driver's license, he handed it back to her. "As soon as another officer gets here, we'll go and speak to this man. There was only one person at the kennel when you went there?"

"That's right," Rick said. "I went inside, and Miss Holland stayed outside. She looked around the back of the building and saw the dogs in the pens."

"Some of them looked as though they'd been mistreated," she said. "Not like pampered pets that had been dropped off for care while their owners were on vacation."

A second police car approached. Rick was glad when Glade got out and walked over to join them. "Miss Holland." He touched the brim of his hat. "Dr. Baker, isn't it?"

"Yes, sir."

"Hello." Robyn's expression held genuine relief. "I'm so glad to see you again."

"I heard the call saying you'd located some stolen dogs, and I asked for the assignment."

"Thank you. They're just down there." She pointed toward the kennel and caught her breath. "Rick! Isn't that the owner's truck?"

Rick jumped to her side and looked down the street. The beat-up green pickup was pulling out of the kennel's parking lot.

⁂

The green truck hadn't come more than a few yards toward them when the driver hit the brakes and backed up hastily, turning around in his parking lot. With a squeal of tires, he roared off down the street in the opposite direction.

"He saw the police cars," Robyn wailed, but the two troopers were already in motion. Glade reached his vehicle first and took off after the kennel owner. The second officer was close behind, with his strobe lights flashing.

Rick stood close beside her, watching. "They'll get him. Let's drive down to the kennel and wait there."

"All right." She'd like to be closer to the dogs. They climbed into Rick's truck, and she paused with her hand on the seat belt's buckle. "What if some of his buddies come to the kennel while we're there alone?"

Rick shrugged. "We'll play dumb. Come on. Let's see if any of your dogs are still there."

He turned the truck around and headed back to the kennel.

Robyn hopped out and bounded toward the door. "Locked."

She pulled a face at him, but Rick only shrugged. "When the police bring the warrant, they'll go in and get your dogs out. But they could be out back in the pens."

"That's right. Come on." She ran around the far side of the building and the length of the wall to where the fenced area began. The dogs inside started barking.

Robyn scanned the enclosure with the tethered dogs. They lunged to the ends of their chains, snapping and growling at her and Rick. Only one had the noble carriage of her huskies.

"There's Astro." She pointed. "At least he's hitched up, away from the others."

Rick studied the large Alaskan husky. A peak of black hair stuck down into the white of Astro's face, between his eyes. He strained at his chain and barked, lunging toward Robyn.

"Hush, boy," she called. "It's okay. We'll get you out of there soon."

"See any others you recognize?" Rick asked.

Robyn shook her head, wishing she could say yes. If the others had been sold or moved to another location, the police might not be able to trace them.

"Let's walk around the back and take a closer look." He held out his hand and she grasped it.

Slowly they circled the pens together and came to the side she'd first visited that afternoon. One dog paced back and forth without seeming to notice them, though several others barked continually and another lay chewing at his paw.

Rick exhaled shortly and shook his head. "They're showing signs of stress all right, and some look malnourished."

"Sad, isn't it?" Robyn hated to see animals neglected or in pain.

"I'll say. Most of them need medical care." Rick looked toward the building. "This can't be a legitimate kennel. I hate to say it, but I think my first instinct was probably right. It's a front for a fighting ring."

Robyn cringed at the thought. It meant more dogs in danger, and many maimed and killed in the past. "I hope the police catch everyone connected to this miserable outfit." She stood watching the dogs and praying silently.

"They probably shut down and move to a new spot periodically and use a different kennel name each time to make it harder for the police to catch up with them." Rick looked at his watch. "Hey, I'd better call Far North again. I should have been back over an hour ago."

"I'm sorry," Robyn said. "It's my fault."

"Don't worry about it. This is more important, and I'm sure the other vet on call can handle things and explain to the patients' owners."

He made the call, and Robyn considered calling her mother but decided to wait until she had more information. It would be wonderful to be able to tell her and Grandpa that they'd found Tumble.

About ten minutes later, Glade drove into the parking lot. "We got him. He hit a parked car, but no one was hurt, and we stopped him in an intersection. We called for backup right away. They're still untangling traffic, but I figured there were enough officers there to handle it. I wanted to make sure you knew—there are several dogs in cages in the back of that truck."

"Are the dogs all right?" Rick asked.

"We think so. One of the other troopers will drive the truck back here. Maybe you'd take a look at them, Dr. Baker."

"Sure."

Glade looked at Robyn. "And you can tell us if any of them belong to you or your client."

"Thank you. One of Mr. Isherwood's dogs is still chained out back of this building, in a pen with some other dogs. We couldn't see any of my family's dogs or Mr. Isherwood's other one though. Will we be able to look inside the building as well?"

"As soon as the warrant gets here." Glade checked his watch. "That should be soon."

She smiled ruefully at Rick. "Again, I apologize for keeping you away from your work."

"It was worth it. We not only found out where your dogs went, but we stumbled on a lot of other dogs that need care."

"I guess I should call Mom," Robyn said. "I hoped to know more by this time, but she'll be worried if I don't check in with her soon." She took out her phone and walked a few steps away.

Her mother answered on the second ring.

"Hi, it's me," Robyn said.

"Honey, where *are* you? You can't be still with Rick."

"Yes, I am. He's right here. Mom, you'll never believe it. We found the dogs."

"What? All of them?"

"Well. . ." She gulped, wishing for a completely positive report. What if she was wrong and none of the Holland Kennel dogs were in the building or the truck?

"I haven't had a close-up look at any of them yet, but we've found Astro for sure, and very likely some of the others. Maybe all of them."

"Where are they?"

"Astro is chained in a pen with some other dogs behind a crummy kennel building. We're pretty sure the others are here, too. The police are bringing a warrant to search the place, and they've arrested the guy who was running it."

"What? Slow down and tell me everything."

The green pickup, with the front fender on the passenger side crumpled and the headlight spilling shards, pulled in off the street.

"Mom, I've got to go. They have some dogs for me to look at and see if I can identify any of ours. I'll call you later." She walked over to join Trooper Glade and Rick.

Straski brought the truck to a halt in the parking lot and climbed out.

"Ready to do a canine lineup, Miss Holland?" Glade asked.

"I sure am."

They walked to the back of the truck. Rick said, "Officer, the Far North Veterinary Hospital is prepared to take some of these dogs in for medical care if you need a place."

"I'm sure we will," Glade replied.

Rick nodded. "We can take fifteen. But there are more than that out back, and another batch inside the building."

"Can you give me a list of other places that might take some?" Glade asked.

"Sure. I can recommend other veterinary practices and one or two *good* kennels."

Trooper Straski opened the back gate of the truck and called to Glade, "Want to help me lift these cages down?"

Rick hurried to help them, and soon the first cage sat on the pavement.

Robyn knelt beside it and peered in at the dog. "Oh, he's scared."

"Do you recognize him?" Rick asked.

She couldn't tell for sure through the small openings in the plastic cage. "Can we open the door?"

"We'd better get a leash first," he said. "If these people do train them to fight, the dogs might be aggressive when they come out of the cages."

"I think I saw a leash in the truck cab." Straski went to get it and returned with a red nylon leash in his hand.

"Okay," Rick said, taking the line. "Robyn, open the door slowly, and if he lets me, I'll clip the line to his collar. If he has one."

"What if he tries to attack you?" Glade asked.

Rick looked up into Robyn's eyes. "If I say, 'Shut it,' do it fast."

"Got it." Slowly she opened the cage door a couple of inches. The dog inside cowered at the back of the cage.

Rick bent cautiously to peer inside. "It's a white dog, smaller than Astro. Siberian husky, I think."

The dog let out a low whine. Robyn knelt, and he moved aside so she could look in. "Wocket!" A laugh bubbled up her throat. "That's Pat's other dog. He's small, but he's got heart and stamina."

"All right!" Rick grinned at her. "You can at least give your client good news today."

"Shall we leave him in the cage for now and look at the others?" Glade asked.

"Good idea." Robyn stood. "Rick, we may need to have you bring them home in your truck. We brought Mom's car into town today."

"Piece of cake," Rick said.

Glade had his notebook out but looked up from his writing. "I don't have a problem with you taking them in the cages if you want, Dr. Baker. You can return the cages to us when it's convenient—within the next few days."

"Thanks," Rick said. He and Straski hefted the next cage out of the truck. "This guy's heavier."

The dog in the cage shifted its weight and barked.

Hope clutched Robyn's throat. It sounded like the deep, insistent bark she'd heard every morning for the last two years when she went out to feed the male dogs at home.

"I think it's Hero."

"Okay. Let's play it safe and slow." Rick bent down, ready to grab the dog when the door opened.

Robyn couldn't help bouncing on her toes and smiling. "Ready?"

"Ready."

She cracked the door open, and the dog barked again. As soon as she saw his muzzle and ears push through the crack, she knew. "It's him! Take it easy, boy. It's me, so calm down."

Rick clipped the leash to Hero's collar.

She swung the door wide, edged around the cage, and dropped to her knees on the pavement. Hero catapulted into her arms and put his forepaws on her shoulders, the better to lick her face.

Robyn laughed and hugged him. "Okay, okay." She rubbed her face in his ruff of fur and stood. Hero jumped up on his hind feet and again rested his front paws on her shoulders.

"Oh, yeah," Rick said. "Somebody's glad to see Mom."

"He won't want to go back in the cage now," Robyn said.

Rick looked toward his truck. "I could put him in the cab of my pickup until we're ready to leave."

She nodded. "We can't let him loose, but I don't want to stuff him back in that cage until we have to. Come on, fella."

Rick unlocked his truck, and she led Hero to it. He hopped into the cab readily, and she stroked his thick fur.

"We're only going to leave you in here for a little while. I'll be back. And you can see us the whole time." Reluctantly, she shut him in.

Rick's smile was a bit lopsided. "He'll be okay."

"I know. I just hate to confine him again."

They went back to the confiscated truck. The two troopers had another cage ready to open. Inside was another of Robyn's dogs, Rounder. She let him prance around her on the leash for a few minutes and then put him back in the cage.

Only one more cage remained in the truck. Robyn gulped and eyed Rick. His troubled eyes mirrored her own dismay. They still lacked two stolen dogs, Tumble and Clipper.

When the troopers lifted the cage out of the truck, a low, guttural snarl issued from within. Robyn caught her breath. She couldn't imagine that noise coming from either of the two unaccounted for Holland dogs.

"Let's think about this," she said.

Rick leaned over the cage and peered into one of the slots. Snapping and growling caused him to jerk backward. "I think it's a bulldog."

Chapter 11

O h, great," said Glade.

"An English bulldog?" Robyn asked.

"That or a pit bull, but he looks heavy."

"A couple of years ago we raided a dogfight," Glade said. "They were using bulldogs. Had a Rottweiler, too."

"Let's not open the cage." Robyn stood back, eyeing it warily.

Rick exhaled heavily. "Well, counting Astro, we've found four of your six."

"Here comes the warrant," said Straski. "Maybe your other two are inside."

"Let's hope so." Rick stepped closer to Robyn. "How are you doing? Are you cold?"

"A little." She flipped the hood of her parka up and stuck her hands in her pockets. The temperature had fallen several degrees since noon, and the sun was already falling toward the horizon.

"You and your mom will have to drive home in the dark."

Robyn shrugged. "We expect that this time of year."

As Straski took a radio call, two officers got out of the newly arrived cruiser and handed Glade a folded paper.

"Here's your warrant. You want us to stay?"

"Yes. We may need you to help us line up emergency care for several dozen mistreated dogs." Glade opened the paper and scanned it. He nodded, refolded it, and tucked it inside his notebook. "All right, I've got the suspect's keys here. Let's see how many mutts are in the building."

Straski walked over to Glade. "That call was from Joel Dawes. He said to tell you that they've been questioning Keeler. He claims someone brought the dogs to him yesterday, and he didn't know they were stolen. Supposedly the man said he wanted to board them for a few days until a sled race."

"Oh, right," Glade said. "Then where was Keeler taking them today?"

"No clue." Straski grimaced. "Dawes says to check his files and see if there's paperwork on the dogs in question. If there's any truth to Keeler's story, we should find the name of the person who brought them, which he's conveniently forgotten. But if Keeler went out to Wasilla and nabbed them himself, or if he's in it with whoever did the actual theft, we won't find it."

"Right. Or else we'll find falsified records." Glade unlocked the front door and opened it.

Rick and Robyn followed him and the other officers inside. Immediately a cacophony of barking erupted from the back room.

The tall trooper walked to the doorway and the noise level increased. "There's got to be two dozen dogs in there." Glade had to yell to be heard over the din.

"And that's not counting the ones out back," Rick said.

Glade squared his shoulders and took a deep breath. "Suppose you start writing that list of kennels and vets for me, Dr. Baker. Straski, you make a quick survey of the records out here. The rest of us will help Miss Holland see if her other dogs are in those cages."

They found several leashes hanging on nails inside the room. One by one, Robyn glanced into the cages and eliminated the dogs. At last she came to one that held an Alaskan husky, and her heart soared. "This is Clipper. He's mine."

"Is it safe to let him out?" Glade asked.

"Yes, he'll be fine."

The dog emerged from his confinement yipping and wagging his tail.

"Hush, now," Robyn said, but her smile almost split her face. Only one more. *Thank You, Lord,* she prayed as she stroked Clipper's fur. *Please let us find Tumble, too.*

Fifteen minutes later they opened the last cage to reveal an Irish setter. Robyn's stomach twisted.

By this time, Rick had completed his calls and stood beside her. "I'm sorry," he said softly.

Glade frowned. "The one that's still unaccounted for—he's your top dog, right?"

Robyn nodded, unable to speak past the painful lump in her throat.

Glade riffled back through his notes. "And your most valuable. I don't know what to tell you, Miss Holland. We'll go through the pens out back to make sure, but I'm starting to think they got him out of here quickly."

One of the other officers said, "Could be they had a private buyer for him. Or maybe he was so tough looking, they took him straight to a fighting ring."

Robyn shuddered, and Rick slipped his arm around her. While she usually thought of herself as a self-sufficient woman, she welcomed his strength and warmth today. Knowing he truly cared about her and the dogs shored up her spirits.

"Let's look out back," she said to Glade.

Half an hour later—at almost four thirty—Robyn and Rick left with a sheaf of paperwork and five dogs. Astro, Rounder, Hero, Wocket, and Clipper rested in cages in the back of Rick's pickup.

As he drove directly to the restaurant where Robyn had left her car after lunch, she took out her phone and called Patrick Isherwood. "This is Robyn. I have some good news."

"You found the dogs. Tell me you found them."

She smiled. "Yes, we did. Pat, I'm so sorry this happened. But Astro and Wocket

are fine. Astro has a small laceration on his front left leg, but it's superficial. We'r
in Anchorage, and a vet is going to thoroughly examine them. Then we'll take ther
home. They'll be back at Holland Kennel tonight."

"Bless you! I don't know what you did to find them, but I sure do appreciate it.'

"Thanks." Her voice cracked a little. "The state police have arrested one man, an
more may be charged. I'll call you again tomorrow and give you all the details."

While Rick pulled into the restaurant's parking lot, Robyn inquired abou
Patrick's health and signed off. She blew out a long breath, thankful he hadn
pressed her too closely about her own dogs. She didn't want to have to say it alou
yet, or to think the unthinkable—that Tumble might be lost forever.

"I'm so thankful we found most of them," she said to Rick. "I know you wer
praying the whole time."

"I was. I still am." He got out and opened her door. Slowly they walked towar
her car. It had been a long day, and she felt like a wrung-out dishrag. Even so, sh
hated to end her time with him. "Thanks so much for being there. For everything

"I'll have them home in a couple of hours." She noticed fine lines at the corner
of his eyes and realized he was tired, too.

"Take your time." She gazed toward his truck. The dogs stayed quiet in thei
cages. She wanted to go take one last look at each of them, but that wasn't neces
sary. Rick would take the best possible care of them until they returned to their ow
spots at Holland Kennel.

"I don't want to keep them caged any longer than I have to," he said. "And it
cold. Even though we put blankets over the cages, I don't want to leave them in th
truck long. I'll take them out at Far North and feed them and give them some wate
And I'll look them all over in good light for wounds or any other problems."

"Astro's the only one we know of with an injury," she noted, "but if you see an
serious problems and feel any of them need overnight care, call me."

Rick nodded. "I think Astro did that on the chain. Scraped his leg. Poor guy wa
pretty wound up, and very excited to see you. I don't think they hurt him intentionally.

"Ha. But they would have put them in a situation where they had to fight fo
their lives." Robyn scowled and shook her head.

"The police have no proof of that yet," Rick said.

"Well, the troopers did find a list of phone numbers for people who are know
to be involved in dogfighting. Trooper Glade said so."

"Yes. And it's likely Keeler was delivering the dogs in his truck to someon
connected with that. But they'll need more evidence before they can press charge
Meanwhile, they can charge Keeler with accepting stolen merchandise—"

"Merchandise!" Robyn snorted. "These dogs aren't merchandise. And I sti
don't understand why they don't charge him with theft."

"Patience," Rick said. "They're searching his house tonight. If they find a sno
machine and trailer there. . .well, who knows what will come of this. But it may hav

een someone else who stole the dogs and took them to Keeler. He might be just a
niddle man."

"He's not as ignorant as he claims."

"Agreed." Rick smiled down at her. "Hey, you're shivering. Get that car warmed
ıp and go pick up your mom. I'll bring the dogs to your house later."

"Thanks, Rick. I don't know how I would have made it through today without
ou." She stood on tiptoe and kissed him on the cheek, feeling very bold. The look
n his soft brown eyes melted her heart.

"I'm glad I could help." He waved and headed for the pickup.

⚜

Robyn paid special attention to the recovered dogs the next day. All of them seemed
iealthy, and already Astro's wound looked better. Rick had treated it with an antibi-
)tic salve that tasted bad enough to keep the dog from worrying at it.

Her mother didn't have to work, and they'd both stayed up late, settling the
logs into their kennels after Rick brought them home.

Robyn went into the barn after feeding them all breakfast and opened her
raining notebook. As she looked over her notations on which dogs had been exer-
ised that week, she realized she was woefully behind on her training program, both
or Patrick's dogs and her own team. The stolen dogs should have a light workout,
he decided, except for Astro. After that, she'd take out a bigger team for a serious
raining run.

She took down the harnesses, checking her notes to be sure she got the correct
ize for each dog. Instead of having a set for each animal, she used color-coded har-
iesses in four sizes and kept a list in her notebook of which size fit each dog. Along
vith the four harnesses, she set out a short towline, four tuglines that clipped to a
ing at the back of each harness, and four short necklines that connected each dog's
ollar to the towline.

As she gathered the pile of lines and set them on her plastic toboggan, her
nother opened the barn door. "Trooper Glade called, and he's on his way here. He
,ays he has some new information on that man Keeler."

"Okay. I was going to go mushing, but I'll wait."

Her mother nodded. "I figure it must be important or he'd have told me over
he phone instead of coming out here."

Robyn tidied up her work area in the little barn and went into the house. Mom
vas puttering about the kitchen. Robyn sat down at her computer and checked her
email. Several people had written to her with questions about the Fire & Ice 100
ınd the shorter races that would be held the same day while they waited for the
ong-distance mushers to complete the course.

"Mom, Dennis Cooper wants to know if we can board his team the night
»efore the race. He's staying at the Grandview, but he needs a place for eighteen
logs, just for one night."

Her mom shook her head, her eyes widened. "Two weeks from today. Wow. can't believe how fast it's crept up on us. I guess we have room. You'd know bette than I would."

Robyn frowned and opened a spreadsheet on the screen. "We're taking Beck Simon's team. We'll be really crowded, but I don't blame them for wanting thei dogs in a locked enclosure. We can shorten the tethers and squeeze in a few mor for one night."

"Some people will sleep in their trucks and stay near their dogs," Mom said.

"Yes, but it's been brutally cold. Today's the first day we've had above freezing i weeks. If it's cold that night, people and dogs could get pretty uncomfortable."

Mom walked over to the desk and set a cup of hot tea down beside Robyn. "W could bring the puppies in for the night and put Dennis's team in the puppy yard.

"Hey, that's a thought. I'll tell Dennis we can take his bunch, but that's it, okay If anyone else calls or emails, tell them we're overflowing. And thanks for the tea.

Glade arrived a short time later, and Robyn welcomed him into the livin room.

"We've done some more checking on Philip Sterns," he announced.

"Could you connect him to the theft of the dogs?" Robyn asked.

"No, nothing solid. If he's behind it, he hired someone else to do it. He alibie himself in Anchorage that morning and has credit card slips from buying gas an lunch on his way here."

Robyn sank back in her chair and let the air *whoosh* out of her lungs. "When w heard he had a criminal record, I was sure he was up to no good."

Glade took out his notebook and flipped a few pages. "It looks as though h plans to make a fresh start here in Alaska, where few people know about his crimina past. We'll watch him, but for now we've got to give him the benefit of the doubt.

"I understand," Robyn said.

"What about Keeler?" her mother asked. "Did you get any more informatior out of him yet?"

"Some." Glade leaned forward and tapped the notebook with his pen. "Th files at the kennel gave us some names, and some of the names are familiar to us."

"Did they tell you who took our dogs to him?" Mom asked.

He shook his head. "I strongly suspect Keeler was in on the theft. He'd entere the dogs in his ledger as new arrivals, but with a dummy client name and address.

"You searched his house, didn't you?" Robyn asked.

"Yes, and we found some circumstantial evidence." Glade turned to her mothe "Mrs. Holland, we found two snow machines and a trailer at Keeler's house, as wel as several dog cages. That's not unusual in itself, and he does run a kennel. But I like to show you some pictures of the equipment and see if you recognize it. I knev you had Internet service, so I wonder if we can take a look at some photos I postec on the police page this morning."

Robyn took him to the computer, and Glade quickly brought up the Web site and keyed in the necessary coding to access the photos.

Mom studied the pictures pensively and shook her head. "I can't be sure. And I didn't get the license plate number. The color seems right, but I was looking more at the people on the snow machine."

"I've asked you this before, but was there one person or two?"

"I think there were two. I'm not a hundred percent sure. I saw them from behind as they drove away. I had the impression of a large person partially blocking my view of a smaller person sitting in front of him. I think it was the colors of their clothing that made me think it, because I couldn't distinctly see a second person." She shook her head. "I'm sorry."

"Based on the footprints we found near the snowmobile tracks, I think there were two people here that day, too." Glade looked at Robyn. "And you haven't found anything else since I was here Wednesday?"

"Nothing. I bought some extra locks in Anchorage yesterday though. We'll be extra vigilant between now and the Fire & Ice."

"That's the race your business sponsors?"

"Yes. It's two weeks from tomorrow."

"Well, I hope everything goes well for you." Glade stood and zipped his jacket. "I'll call you if we get any solid information in this case."

"The cages we used to bring the dogs home are out back," Robyn said. "I can take them now, if you'd like."

Mom grabbed a jacket and followed them out the back door.

Robyn led them to the five stacked cages.

"Some of those were on the trailer the day the dogs were stolen."

Robyn looked at her mom. "Exactly like this?"

Her mother frowned. "I think so. Gray with red trim. Yes, I think they were just like these."

Glade ran a hand over the top of one cage. "These are probably sold in a lot of places."

"Yeah, it's a common brand," Robyn said. "Probably a lot of kennels use them."

"Well, it's a little something to add to the file we're building."

When he had left, Robyn returned to the dog lot and stood outside the fence, looking in at the male dogs. Wocket, Max, and the rest whined and wriggled, eager to join her for a run in the snow. She prayed in silence, thanking God for returning the lost dogs to her. Their financial situation hadn't changed in the long run, though the cash from the dogs Sterns had bought would help some. In two weeks they'd know how much profit they realized from the race. But she felt at peace. God would take care of her and Mom, and Grandpa, too. In her mind, having the five powerful dogs back in her care was proof of God's love. Even though she feared she would never see Tumble again, God knew where he was. If it was part of God's plan for her and the business, Tumble, too, would come home.

She hurried to the shed and got the toboggan with the harnesses. In just a few minutes, her team of four was hitched to the new sled. She unclipped the snub line, grasped the handlebar, and called, "Hike!"

⁂

Late that afternoon, when the sun dipped low toward the mountains, Rick drove from his humble office in downtown Wasilla to the Hollands' house. Cheryl directed him around to the back. He stopped at the edge of the dog lot and smiled.

Robyn and Darby were playing with several yearlings in the puppy enclosure.

"Hello, ladies."

"Hi, Dr. Baker," Darby said. "Look at what Bobble can do." She touched the puppy's head to focus his attention then moved her hand in a circular motion. The puppy flopped on his side and rolled over.

Rick laughed. "That's terrific. How long did it take you to teach him that?"

"This is only my third session working on it with him." Darby took a treat from her pocket and tossed it to Bobble, who caught it neatly in his mouth.

Behind him, the back door to the house opened. "Darby, your mom just drove in," Cheryl called.

"Thanks, Mrs. H." Darby made a face at Robyn. "Gotta go. I'll see you at the meeting tomorrow."

"Okay. Thanks for helping." Robyn opened the gate just wide enough for her and Darby to squeeze through without taking any pups with them.

"Thanks for my mushing lesson," Darby called over her shoulder as she ran around the corner of the house.

"She's a good helper." Robyn bent over the gate and put two padlocks in place. Her loose dark hair spilled out of her hood and hid her features from him until she straightened. "She's going to be a great musher, too. I expect her to win the Iditarod or the Yukon Quest someday."

"I hope I'm there to see it. Are you busy?" Rick asked. "Is it time to feed this motley crew?"

She smiled. "Not yet. In about an hour."

"Take a ride with me?"

"A sled ride?"

Rick chuckled and reached to brush back a strand of her hair. "No, I meant in my truck. If we hurry, we can get up on the ridge behind my house and see the sunset."

"Sure. Just let me tell Mom." Her flicker of a smile left him with an impression of shyness as she jogged to the back door.

She was back a moment later, and he reached for her hand. They walked together in silence to the pickup in the driveway. His own property was only a quarter mile down the road, and he turned in at the gravel drive to his log home. The house was silent as they drove past it, but smoke oozed from the chimney.

Rick shifted into four-wheel drive, and they bounced up the hill behind the house on the track he'd packed with his snow machine. The shallow snow had compressed enough for him to drive to the top of the ridge without danger of getting stuck.

When he stopped the truck, he put it in park and left the engine running. The view of the town and the highway couldn't be beat, and he traced the part of the trail he could see, where the racing teams would compete for the trophy in two weeks. But the distant mountains and snow-covered plains glistening in the late rays of sunlight drew his gaze and dazzled him. As he and Robyn watched without speaking, dusk shrouded the mountainsides in deep purple and gray. Pink, gold, and red reflected off the peaks.

Robyn sighed. "I could never leave Alaska." She cast a quick glance his way, and her forehead crinkled, as though she feared she'd said the wrong thing.

"I love it here, too," he said. "Especially out in the wild. I was smothering in Anchorage. That's why I moved out here last year—to be closer to the land but still near enough to civilization that I could earn a living."

Her expression cleared and they sat in silence, watching the colors spread and change. As the shadows of night overtook them and the mountain peaks dulled to shades of gray, she stirred. "When the race is over, I hope I'll be able to get out on the trail more myself."

"Maybe we can take another run together soon." Rick smiled at the memory of their sledding adventure earlier in the week. It had started as a perfect day. Cheryl's news of the theft had derailed it fast though. He hoped they would be able to spend more days together—carefree days. And soon.

Robyn smiled up at him. "I'd like that a lot. You're pretty good at mushing."

He pulled in a deep breath and decided now was the time to express the burden on his heart. "Robyn, I've been praying for you and your family. I want you to know that I'm confident God has some solutions for you. To your financial situation and your grandpa's health problems. God knows all about it. He already knows how He's going to resolve those things."

She put her fingertips gently to his cheek. "Thank you." Her gaze flickered away but came back to him. "Do you think I did the wrong thing yesterday? To chase around hunting for the dogs, I mean."

"I hadn't even considered it. That's not at all what I meant."

She nodded, her eyes wide and attentive. "I was afraid afterward that I'd overstepped some boundary."

"I don't think so. We'd all been praying about it. God used your persistence to bring the dogs home. If you hadn't gone looking for them, perhaps He'd have used another means. Or maybe He'd have let them all slip away and never be found. We don't know, do we?"

"No, we don't. You're right—the Lord knew all along He would take us to them and let us bring them home. I've tried to rest in Him about Tumble and the other unresolved issues. I'm so thankful we got five of them back. And I'm glad you were there, too. When I told Mom about it, she was horrified at what I'd done. She kept saying, 'If you'd gone there alone, that man might have killed you.'"

"I doubt that," Rick said, but the thought sobered him. "Robyn, I love the way you are."

Her eyelids flew up, and he chuckled.

"I love your passion for the dogs, and your confidence in your skill. But I also love the fact that you can be impulsive now and then."

She laughed. "Are you sure?"

"Okay, not *too* impulsive. But, yeah. Yesterday I was a little frustrated when you wouldn't give up the search. But I admired you for that, too. You're really something, and. . .and I like that something."

Her cheeks took on a becoming flush.

He held her gaze for a long moment. "There's something I want to tell you."

Her eager gaze encouraged him to go on.

"I'm tired of running back and forth to Anchorage."

She frowned and her lips parted. "You. . .just said you love it out here. You're not going to move back there, are you?"

"No. I need to stop working at Far North. It's not fair to the folks in Wasilla. I want to have a full-service hospital for the animals here and be open every day, with the assurance that pets can stay there if they need recovery time and monitoring."

"What are you going to do about it?"

"I've told the partners at Far North that it's too hard for me to keep coming into town. I'm going to stop seeing patients at the clinic altogether at the end of the month."

"What did they say?"

Rick toyed with his key ring. "Hap and Bob aren't thrilled with that, and I admit I've enjoyed working with them. I learned a lot during the five years I was in practice with them. But it's time."

"Will they bring in a new doctor to take your place?"

"They'll have to," Rick said. "Bob plans to retire next year. But I'm not going back."

Her smile reached deep inside him, and he blurted the rest of his plan. "I'm thinking of advertising for a partner, too."

"Really?"

He nodded. "There's enough business, and if we have two doctors, one of us could always cover emergency calls. I'd need a bigger building. I've looked around some, but I haven't found anything suitable that I could rent, and my current landlord doesn't want to add on to the building I'm renting." He hesitated then shrugged.

"I'm thinking of building an animal hospital beside my house."

"Wow. Are you sure you'd want to be that close to it?" Robyn sat up straighter and gazed down the hill toward his log home.

"I don't know. It would be convenient, but I can picture it becoming burdensome, too. I'm praying about it. I'd like to have a place big enough for some kennels and an area where I could treat large animals."

Her face took on a glow of excitement in the twilight. "That would be terrific. But expensive."

"I know. I think I can swing it within a couple of years. And I know exactly what I want for the building." He pointed down the hill to a flat area across the driveway from his house. "Right down there. That's where I want it. The bank is looking at my loan application. This is my home now, and I want to build my business here, too."

"I think that's wonderful." Her dark eyes caught the gleam of the last rays of sun off the snow.

Rick reached for her without another twinge of hesitation. As the long darkness settled about them, he kissed her, delighting in her response. He no longer wondered if she might be the right woman for him. Rick had found his home and the one he hoped would share it with him.

Chapter 12

The *Anchorage Daily News* ran its article about the Fire & Ice race on the following Wednesday. Robyn had granted permission for them to lift photos from the Holland Kennel's Web site.

"Hey, this looks great," her mother said as Robyn came in from giving the dogs their breakfast.

Robyn poured herself a cup of coffee and joined her at the kitchen table. "Let me see."

Together they perused the article.

"That's one of their pictures from last year's race." Robyn pointed to a photo of Pat Isherwood crossing the finish line with his arms raised over his head in victory.

"They took the one of you from our site," Mom said. "I've always liked that one."

Robyn grimaced. "I should put some new ones up, I guess. That picture's about three years old. Oh, look here. They pulled the one off the 'puppy page.'" The photo near the bottom of the story showed Grandpa Steve in the dog lot, his arms brimming with husky puppies.

"This is a fantastic article," her mom said. "They never gave us this much publicity before."

"Maybe the news about the dog theft last week helped." Robyn shuddered. "Makes me feel kind of weird."

Robyn's phone rang, and she answered it.

"Hey, Robyn," Darby squealed in her ear. "Did you see the paper?"

"We're looking at it now."

"Isn't that Bobble on the right in the picture with your grandfather?"

Robyn laughed. "It sure is. Coming over after school?"

"I'll be there."

Darby clicked off and Robyn closed her phone, but her mother's phone rang almost immediately.

"Hello? Who?" She made a face at Robyn. "I think you want to speak to my daughter." She held her phone out and hissed, "It's someone from the *Seattle Times*."

"The Seattle. . . ?" Robyn gulped. She'd half expected to hear from the weekly papers or the *Mat-Su Valley Frontiersman*, but not the huge daily paper in Seattle. "May I help you?"

A woman's voice said, "I saw the story in the *Anchorage Daily*, and I'd like to interview you."

Robyn stared at her mother and said into the phone, "You want to know about next week's race?"

"Well, sure, you can tell me about that, but I mostly want to know about you. The woman who runs Holland Kennel and chased down the thugs who stole her sled dogs."

"Uh. . ." She held the phone away from her face. "Mom, they want to interview me."

Her mother pushed her chair back. "Go for it, honey. People outside Alaska will hear about the race."

Any publicity would be good for the business, Robyn told herself, though she disliked having the spotlight shine on her. She gulped and smiled. "I guess that's all right," she told the reporter. Of course, it was silly to wear this plastic smile when the woman was fifteen hundred miles away. She felt like an idiot. She lost the smile in a hurry, before Mom turned around and saw it.

⁂

Rick closed the door of his small veterinary office at five o'clock on Saturday. He checked his hair in the rearview mirror before heading for the Hollands' house. Maybe he should stop at home first and clean up a little. But Robyn had said to come as early as he could. Her brother, Aven, and his wife had arrived, and Rick was invited to share supper with the family.

Robyn met him at the door and drew him into the house. A tall, dark-haired man in uniform rose and waited for her to introduce them.

"Rick, this is my brother, Aven," Robyn said with a smile and a fond glance toward the young man.

Rick extended his hand and shook Aven's, feeling as he did so that Robyn's brother was assessing him.

"Glad to meet you," Aven said. "Mom and Robyn have told us a lot about you."

"Nothing bad," Robyn said quickly.

Rick smiled. "I've heard a few tales myself. I think the family's glad to have you home."

"They're staying all week, until after the race." Robyn couldn't seem to stop grinning. Rick loved seeing her so happy. She looked toward the hallway as a pretty young blond woman wearing black pants and a red sweater entered the room. "Oh, and this is Caddie, my sister-in-law. Caddie, this is Rick Baker."

"Pleased to meet you, Dr. Baker." Caddie took his hand.

"Oh please, let's not go all formal or I'll have to learn your ranks," Rick said.

Aven and Caddie laughed.

"Agreed," said Caddie. "Let's not go there. I just changed out of my uniform, and I'm ready to relax for a few days and be just plain Caddie."

Rick doubted she had ever been considered plain, and the pride in her husband's eyes confirmed that.

"What are your jobs for the race?" Rick asked as they settled down to talk.

"I'm the jack-of-all-trades," Aven said. "I've worked on every one of these races since Dad and Grandpa started it twelve years ago—except for last year and the year before. Couldn't get leave. But I've missed it, and I worked it out months in advance so that Caddie and I could be here for this one."

"I agree with Aven," Caddie said. "I'll do whatever is needed. Someone may have to explain things to me, since I've never gotten involved in dog sled racing, but I'll take lots of pictures, and I'll help wherever I can."

"Don't worry," Robyn said. "We'll put you to work."

⁜

On race day Robyn could hardly contain her joy. The start area near Iditarod Headquarters came to life at five a.m., when volunteers opened the check-in and service booths and the contestants began readying their teams. As race director, Robyn dashed from one task to another. The six o'clock starting time approached at lightning speed. All the checkpoints were manned by several volunteers, and all the drop bags of extra supplies, equipment, and food for the dogs and mushers had been delivered to the stops along the route.

As usual, the Fire & Ice trail would begin and end in an open area near the Iditarod Headquarters building. Trucks, booths, contestants, volunteers, and spectators turned the grounds into a temporary, dog-centered city, not unlike some of the tent cities that had sprung up during Gold Rush days.

"Slow down, girl," Grandpa called as Robyn passed where he sat in a wheelchair, near the starting line.

She laughed and paused to kiss his forehead. "I'm so glad you're here, Grandpa."

"I wouldn't miss this for anything." He pulled her closer and added, "And I'm not going back to that place."

"I hope you never need to." She tugged his hood up over his knit hat. "I'll help you with your therapy every day."

"Robyn, a photographer's here from the *Frontiersman*," Aven called. "Do you have time to speak to him?"

"Uh, not really." Robyn lifted her hands helplessly. "Point him toward Billy Olan. He's one of the favorites today, since Pat Isherwood isn't well enough to race yet. Oh, and Rachel Fisher's team looks good. She and her dogs are very photogenic."

Aven led the photographer away, and Robyn blew out an exaggerated breath.

"Aw, you're photogenic, too, Robbie." Grandpa grinned up at her.

"Thanks. I love getting publicity for the race, but I hate having the attention focused on me."

"Hey, you're still going to let me hand the trophy to the winner, right?" he asked.

"Yes, of course." She squeezed his thin shoulders. "Are you cold, Grandpa? I can help you go inside for a while if you need to warm up."

"Not yet. I'm warm as toast." He held up one hand, clad in a hand-knit woolen mitten. "Your mother made sure of that this morning."

Robyn laughed and hurried to the registration area.

The volunteers greeted her.

"All of the mushers have checked in," Anna said, handing her a clipboard.

"Great." Robyn scanned the list. The forty-eight dog teams comprised a record number of contestants. Rick and his old partner, Dr. Hap Shelley, had examined all the entered dogs the day before. Now the mushers harnessed their teams and gathered near the starting line.

"We've got three entries who've previously run the Iditarod," Anna said with a dreamy smile, "and so far I've seen two Iditarod winners in the crowd."

"I hope there'll be more before the race starts," Robyn said. "I'm counting on at least four." More good publicity when the big-name mushers turned out to support the race.

Aven dashed to the booth. "Robyn, Mom wants to know if we have any extra booties handy."

"Booties?"

"For Erica Willis. She had a slight mishap on the way here and some of her equipment got wet. Her dogs need eight dry booties."

"Sure." Robyn told him where to find the needed accessories for the dogs. "Oh, and did all the drop bags get delivered to the halfway point? I never got confirmation on that."

"We're all set," Aven said over his shoulder as he hurried away.

"How you doing?"

She whirled and found Rick standing behind her. "Terrific. How about you?"

"Ditto. This is great fun."

"It's a madhouse," Robyn conceded, "but I love it."

He handed her a loose-leaf binder. "All prerace vet checks are complete. Hey, isn't that—"

Robyn turned to look at the man who'd snagged his attention. She caught her breath. "Philip Sterns."

"Thought so."

She and Rick waited as Sterns wove through the crowd toward the booth. It took him only a couple of minutes to locate them. "Miss Holland. Good to see you again."

"I'm surprised to see you here, Mr. Sterns," she said.

He smiled and nodded at Rick. "I returned from California yesterday and thought I'd come up here to watch the race. Maybe get some inspiration for training my new team." His brow furrowed. "Say, have you heard anything about those dogs you lost?"

Robyn studied his face for a moment. "Yes. We got most of them back."

"Oh? That's good news." He looked around as though expecting to see the dogs popping up out of thin air. "Did you get that magnificent Tumble back?"

Robyn glanced at Rick. His sympathetic gaze told her the interview was painful for him, too. "No, actually we recovered all of them except Tumble. The police are still hoping to find him."

Sterns nodded, his eyes wide. "I wish you the best."

"Thank you. Now, if you'll excuse me, the race is about to start."

The teams entering the 100-mile race gathered near the start area. Ormand Lesley, the race marshal, called the time for the first racer, and the team took off to the sound of much cheering. At two-minute intervals, the other teams set out over the trail in the predawn darkness.

Robyn wished she was driving a sled today, following the trail away from the crowd, out into the quiet tundra.

The spectators cheered each team on its way then settled down to watch the shorter races.

As soon as all of the teams in the 100-mile race had left, Rick approached Robyn again. "Guess I'd better jump in my truck and get to the halfway checkpoint."

"Have fun." She wished she could go with him and watch the teams come into the rest stop one by one, but she was needed here. "We'll see you later."

He smiled at her. "Save me some coffee."

She waved and grinned as he drove out. The sled teams would all take a two-hour rest at the fifty-mile point, and during that time, Rick and another vet would examine each dog. If all were in good condition, after their mandatory halt they could head on back to Wasilla and the finish line.

By ten o'clock, the sun had risen and the temperature climbed to a comfortable twenty-five degrees. People took their folding chairs and waterproof cushions to the edge of the trail where the other races would be run during the time that the long-distance teams were gone.

Robyn didn't expect the winning team to cross the line before mid-afternoon. The record time for the Fire & Ice, not including the required two-hour stop, was seven hours and twenty minutes. But that was not a terribly fast time, and it was always possible someone would knock the record to smithereens. They probably wouldn't see any sleds come in until well after three, but everyone would start to get keyed up and watch the trail eagerly from two o'clock on.

During the morning, short runs for teams of four, six, and up to ten dogs were held on shorter trails nearby. Each team completed two heats, and their times were added together. In each class, the dogs' route was as many miles long as the number of dogs allowed per team. A two-dog class for children ages twelve and younger was a favorite feature of the day's program. That class ran only a mile for each of its two heats.

People ate lunches they'd brought or bought snacks from the vendors. One of the past Iditarod winners gave a talk about the historic race inside the headquarters building, and spectators viewed the exhibits there and visited the gift shop.

All too soon the sun began to lower in the west. Robyn hoped the first teams of the 100-mile race would come in before it set. Pictures of the finish would be better, and the spectators would get a bigger thrill from the event if they could see well.

At two forty five, Ormand Lesley called her via radio. Cell phones just didn't make the grade where the race went.

"The leaders just passed the last checkpoint," Ormand said. "It's Olan and Fisher in a tight race."

Robyn's pulse quickened. If Rachel Fisher won, it would be a coup for Holland Kennel. She wouldn't be the first woman to capture the trophy, but half her team was sired by Holland dogs, with four of Tumble's offspring among them.

"They're ten miles out," she announced to those nearest her. "Olan and Fisher leading."

Darby jumped up and down and clapped her gloved hands. "Oh, I hope Rachel wins it. We haven't had a member of the local sled club win for three years."

Robyn smiled. "Yeah. It sounds like she has a good chance."

The buzz mounted as word got around. Robyn went to the speaker and made the official update. "Folks, we'll be seeing the first finishers in just a few minutes."

Spectators hurried to get refreshments before the real excitement began. The participants in the shorter races tended their dogs and put away their equipment.

Aven and Caddie found Robyn. "Hey," her brother shouted. "Want to come in the truck to where we can see the lake?"

"I sure do." They would be able to see the teams coming across the frozen lake from a hill a short distance away. Robyn looked around. "Where's Grandpa?"

Caddie said, "Your mom took him inside to warm up and have something to eat, but they'll be out here when the leaders come in. Aven promised to radio in when we see them."

"Oh, let me come, too." Darby seized Robyn's arm and bounced on her toes.

Robyn laughed. "All right, but you'll have to sit on my lap."

The four of them piled into Aven's pickup. In just a couple of minutes they gained the vantage point and looked down on the windswept lake.

Caddie shivered. "It's getting cold, now that the sun is going down."

"I see them!" Darby pointed, and they all followed her gesture, squinting against the glare of sun on snow.

At the far side of the lake, a team of sixteen dogs ran down the bank and onto the glare ice. The sled's runners had barely hit the surface when a second team appeared and plunged down the bank after them.

Robyn held her breath.

"Who's leading?" Aven asked.

"I can't tell. Should have brought binoculars." Robyn frowned in concentration.

"I've got a zoom lens." Caddie held up her camera and peered through the viewfinder. "Can't read the bib number."

"That's Rachel!" Darby grabbed Robyn's hand and laughed. "See her red hood? It's Rachel for sure. Billy Olan's wearing dark green."

They watched in silence as the two teams skimmed over the lake. Billy's fourteen dogs gained slowly on Rachel. As his leaders came up to her sled and veered out around her team, Rachel bent low. The watchers faintly heard her call to her dogs. They put on a new burst of speed and maintained their lead all the way across the ice, though not increasing it.

When they reached the near side of the lake, Rachel's team bounded up the bank and out of sight into a stand of trees on the shore. Billy's team ran after her.

"Let's go back," Aven said. "We don't want to miss it when they cross the finish line."

They squeezed into the truck. Robyn took the radio and called her mother as they barreled down the hill to the paved road and back to the race's finish area.

Mom and Grandpa were just coming from the headquarters building, and Robyn ran over to update them. "Mom, I think Rachel might win it. She was barely ahead of Billy when they crossed the lake. I'm so excited for her!"

"I'll be disappointed if she loses now," Darby said.

Grandpa looked eagerly toward the finish line. "No matter where she places, she's run a good race."

"Yes. I'm thinking she and Billy might both break the race record." Robyn chuckled in delight. "I hope that guy from the *Frontiersman* is still here."

"He's inside eating doughnuts," Mom said.

"Yes, I let him interview me about the history of the race." Grandpa nodded and leaned on his daughter-in-law's shoulder. "Come on, Cheryl, I need to get back to my chair and sit down."

The crowd stood three-deep along the lane roped off to form the finish. Grandpa sat to one side just over the line, with the rest of the Holland family close by. The throng roared and cheered as the teams came in, but the dogs trotted on until they crossed the line and the mushers called, "Whoa." Caddie and the news photographer snapped away with their cameras.

Rachel Fisher brought her team in just seconds before Billy Olan's. Rachel set her snow hook and fell into her excited husband's arms.

Aven used the portable speaker to draw the people's attention and handed the microphone to Robyn.

She waited for the crowd to quiet. "The winner of this year's Fire & Ice 100 is Rachel Fisher of Wasilla."

Cheers erupted once more.

"Her leaders are Canby and Soot. Her trophy will be awarded tonight at the banquet. And in second place, we have Billy Olan of Talkeetna. His lead dogs are Buster and. . ." Robyn checked her clipboard. "And Sitka."

Out of the corner of her eye, she saw a police car enter the parking area.

Chapter 13

Robyn couldn't help feeling a tiny bit annoyed as her anxiety level climbed. They didn't need police officers making the people nervous. Probably they were just checking to make sure everything stayed orderly with a crowd this size.

The trooper got out of his vehicle and sauntered toward them.

Robyn thrust the microphone into her brother's hands. "Take over. That's Trooper Glade, the officer who investigated the dog theft."

She walked quickly toward Glade, thankful to hear Aven launch into an update on the other contestants: "We've just received word by radio that a third team is within a mile of the finish."

The crowd's attention was diverted in the opposite direction from Robyn and the trooper as they strained to spot the next team.

"Hello." She held out her hand and Glade shook it. "Is there any news for us?"

Her mother joined them and greeted Glade.

"I do have a bit of information that should interest you. I'm sure you remember the man who bought some dogs from you the day of the theft."

"Philip Sterns," Robyn said, nodding.

"Yes," the trooper said.

"He's here."

Glade's eyes widened. "Here, as in right here this minute?"

Her mother turned and scanned the spectators. "He's been here all day, hobnobbing with the racing folk. I last saw him over on the right side of the finish line."

"Do you know what his vehicle looks like?" Glade asked.

Mom shook her head.

"Probably a rental again," Robyn said. "I didn't notice it when he arrived."

"Are you sure he's still here?"

"Ninety-nine percent. I saw him about three minutes ago."

"All right," Glade said. "Hold on a sec. I'm going to call this in. If you see him moving toward the parking area, please alert me immediately."

He walked toward his car, and Mom said, "What do you suppose this is about?"

"No clue." Robyn chewed her lower lip.

Behind them, the crowd began to clap and shout as another dog team sped toward the finish.

A few minutes later, the people hushed again and Aven announced the third-place finisher.

Glade again got out of his car and came toward them. "Sorry to leave you ladies in the dark, but I wanted to be sure my backup is nearly here. I expect another officer in about ten minutes." He looked at Robyn. "You met my backup at the kennel the day we recovered the other dogs—Trooper Straski."

Robyn pounced on the one word that gave her hope. "*Other* dogs?"

Glade grinned. "We found the last one."

"You—" Robyn seized her mother's wrist and looked over her shoulder. "This has something to do with Sterns?"

"It has a lot to do with Sterns. We figured your lead dog had been passed to a fighting promoter or sold out of state already, but we decided to check a few more kennels, just in case. But nothing turned up. Until today, that is."

"What happened?" Robyn asked.

"Remember the kennel where Sterns parked the other dogs he'd bought from you?"

"Yes. Rick and I talked to the owner the day after the theft."

"She called our switchboard yesterday and asked for an officer to come around."

"Tumble was there?" Robyn stared openmouthed at her mother and shook her head. "He certainly wasn't there the day we went in."

"That's right. I believe the kennel owner was totally innocent. She said Sterns came back for his three dogs a few days ago and asked if she could take them again this weekend while he drove up here for the race. And he said he'd added a fourth dog and would leave all of them, if she had room."

"I left her my card and asked her to call me if she heard anything about Tumble or stolen sled dogs," Robyn said.

Glade smiled in sympathy. "We'd also told her to call us if anything suspicious happened. Maybe she knew you'd be busy with the race today."

"You mean she just accepted his word and let him leave the dog without any questions?" Robyn asked.

"She said she recognized Tumble immediately because she'd looked at his pictures so many times over the past two weeks. Sterns showed her a veterinarian's certificate, saying the dog was up-to-date on his shots, but it had a different dog's name and registration number, though the general description was close enough to get by. She didn't let him know she suspected it was Tumble."

"Good for her," Mom said.

Glade nodded. "After he left, she got on your Web site and compared the pictures of Tumble to the new dog he'd brought her. The resemblance was enough to make her call us."

"You're certain it's Tumble?" Robyn asked.

"Absolutely. When Straski compared the pictures of your missing lead dog with the real thing, he could see it was either Tumble or a ringer. Since you'd told us the day he was stolen that your dogs all had microchip implants for identification, our next step was to get someone to read the microchip. The Humane Society was able to help us, and we verified that it really is your dog." Glade stiffened, focusing on something behind them. "Heads up. I think I see Sterns moving this way."

Mom's eyes widened. "What do we do?"

"Nothing. Just stay calm, and don't turn around unless he comes over here and speaks to one of us." Glade glanced over their heads. "He sees me."

"Well, those hats aren't exactly camouflage," Robyn muttered.

Glade cracked a smile. "Oops. He's changed course and is heading for the parking lot. Excuse me, ladies." He jogged away from them, and Robyn turned to watch. Sure enough, Philip Sterns was walking swiftly past a row of parked vehicles.

"Go get Aven," she said to her mother. She followed Glade slowly, watching as the trooper angled to intercept Sterns.

A familiar pickup entered the parking lot just then, and Robyn caught her breath. Rick was returning from the halfway checkpoint, which meant all the mushers had left there. He pulled in slowly and scanned the rows of cars.

Sterns reached a dark green SUV and opened the driver's door. Glade hurried across the lot, but Sterns already had the vehicle in motion and backed out of his parking space.

Robyn watched helplessly from her vantage point forty yards away. If only Rick knew what Glade had just told her.

Glade's shout reached her ears, but Sterns paid no attention to him. He quickly shifted the transmission and plowed forward with his SUV, forcing Glade to leap aside to avoid being struck down.

Rick's pickup went into a quick reverse and turn. Robyn's heart leaped. He must have seen what was happening. As he positioned his truck sideways across the lane between parked vehicles, she sent up a frantic prayer.

Sterns barreled toward him but hit the brakes at the last possible moment. Instead of slamming into Rick's pickup, the SUV slowed, skidded on the snowy surface, and gently smacked the pickup's rear passenger-side fender. Rick's truck spun a quarter turn in the lane, and both vehicles came to rest.

Before either man could get out of his truck, Glade reached Sterns's door. "Get out of the vehicle! Keep your hands high."

Another police vehicle came into the lot and stopped just beyond Rick's truck. Trooper Straski got out and hurried to help Glade.

Robyn walked over to where Rick was climbing out of his pickup. "What's going on?" he asked. "I saw that guy almost run Glade down and figured I could block the exit, but I didn't realize it was Sterns until just now."

"They've found Tumble. And they've got proof that Sterns was involved."

Rick's jaw dropped and he opened his arms.

She launched herself into his embrace.

"Thank You, Lord." Rick hugged her, then stood back and looked toward the side of his truck. "Looks like I'll need to call my insurance company."

"I'm just glad you showed up when you did," Robyn said, "and that you reacted quickly enough to stop him. If he'd gotten out onto the road, it could have meant a high-speed chase."

Rick exhaled heavily. "Yeah. That wouldn't have been so good."

Aven came running from the area near the finish line with Caddie and his mother close behind. "What's up?" Aven called. "Did the police get him?"

Robyn looked over to where Glade was putting Sterns in the back of his cruiser. "They sure did."

"One of us had better get back to the booth," Caddie said regretfully. "We left Darby to announce the teams as they come in, and things are happening fast over there."

"I'll go back with you," Aven said, smiling down at his wife, "but we want all the details later, you hear me?" He fixed Robyn with a phony glare, and she was able to raise a smile.

"Don't worry about that. We'll tell you every little thing tonight."

"Grandpa's probably going nuts," Mom said, looking anxiously toward where they'd left him.

"We'll probably have to tell this story several times." Robyn grimaced. "You can tell him they've found Tumble and caught Sterns and that I'll give him the blow-by-blow as soon as I can."

Aven and Caddie hurried back toward the race area.

Straski approached Robyn, her mother, and Rick. "Well, folks, this could have ended worse."

"Yes," Mom said. "Thank you so much."

Straski spread his hands. "I'm the latecomer." He nodded at Rick. "I understand you did some fast thinking and driving, Doc. Good job. If you'll step over here, I'll take your statement. We've called for a tow truck from town to come take Sterns's vehicle away." He eyed Rick's truck. "Yours looks drivable."

"Yes, I intend to drive it to a garage for an estimate," Rick said.

Robyn and her mother added what little they could to the officers' reports with their accounts of Sterns's appearance at the race.

"Why on earth did he come here today?" Robyn asked.

Glade shook his head. "You got me. Maybe he wanted to establish himself as a friend of yours—a satisfied customer—so you wouldn't suspect him anymore."

Rick said, "Or maybe he was establishing an alibi for another crime."

The officers were silent for a moment then Glade said, "Interesting theory. Maybe we'd better check around and see if any major thefts happened today—especially where sled dogs are concerned."

"When will you question him?" Robyn asked.

"He's already talking." Glade looked at his notes. "I told him I'd picked Tumble up at the kennel this morning and that we've arrested three people connected to the Barkland place. We've got strong evidence they've been supplying dogs for fighting. When I told him all that and named the men who actually stole your dogs, he admitted he got Tumble from them."

"He hired them to steal the Hollands' dogs?" Rick asked.

"He hasn't confessed to that. . .yet," Glade said. "He'd like me to believe they contacted him and he saw himself as Tumble's rescuer."

"Oh, right. That's why he told us he'd found him." Robyn shook her head in disgust.

"He will confess," Straski put in. "I talked to headquarters about fifteen minutes ago. Keeler named him as his client. Seems Sterns hired Keeler and his friends to steal Tumble. He told them they could have any other dogs they nabbed—he only wanted the one breeding male."

"Where's Tumble now?" Rick asked.

Robyn's pulse surged. "Yes, is he still in Anchorage?"

Straski grinned. "Step this way, madam. I have a passenger who's eager to see you."

Robyn grabbed Rick's arm to compensate for her wobbly knees. "You. . .have him here? Now?"

Straski laughed and turned toward his state police truck. He opened the back and rummaged for a moment. He took out a leash, rummaging a bit more as Rick and Robyn approached. When they were only a couple of yards away, he said, "Come on, fella. It's okay."

A whine emerged from the back of the truck.

"Tumble?" Robyn almost couldn't believe it was true, but when his furry black-and-white face poked out of the cage and he yipped with joy, she laughed. "Yes! Come on, Tumble."

The dog jumped down from the back of the truck and into her arms. She scooched down and hugged him, fluffing his fur. Tears filled her eyes.

A moment later she felt Rick's hand on her back. "What do you say I go tell your brother and ask him to make an announcement?" Rick asked.

"I'd like that." Robyn stood and held the leash firmly with both hands as Tumble pranced around her. "Ask him to tell everyone that Tumble has come home."

❖

After the awards banquet, the school cafeteria where the event was held emptied quickly. Soon the parking lot emptied.

Rick dived into the cleanup with the other volunteers. He managed to catch Cheryl alone for a moment when she went to fetch her father-in-law's coat and hat. "I don't know if Robyn told you, but I'm planning to expand my practice here in Wasilla," he said.

"She mentioned it. I think it's wonderful." Cheryl smiled. "Everyone here will be glad to know you're in town anytime they need you."

"Eventually I want to build a bigger facility and maybe even bring in a partner to work with me, but for now I think full-time hours and possibly adding a receptionist will move me forward."

He could tell the exact moment she latched onto his idea. Her eyes lit and she stared at him for a moment before speaking. "A receptionist?"

"Yes. I wondered if. . .well, I know you have a job, but I think you'd be an asset to my practice, Cheryl. I need someone to answer the phone, schedule appointments, keep records, and occasionally help me with the animals. Starting the beginning of February."

She was still staring at him. "Do you mean it?"

"Of course."

She laughed and hugged him. "Did you know how much I hate my job at the store? Standing up for hours on end?"

"Well, you could sit at least half the time, I'm sure. And when I build the new animal hospital, you'd be a lot closer to home. I plan to put it next to my house."

"Oh, Rick. I think. . .no, I *know* I adore you. Thank you so much."

Contentment worked its way through him. "I don't know what they pay you, but I'd try to at least match the hourly rate—"

"You had me with 'an asset to my practice.'"

He laughed. "Great. We'll talk over the details soon."

"I'll look forward to it."

"Mom?" Robyn made her way toward them. "Grandpa wants to know what's keeping you."

Cheryl threw a knowing glance at Rick. "I'm going to let this handsome veterinarian tell you." She hurried away.

Robyn watched her. "What's up? She looks radiant."

He chuckled. "Hope you don't mind. I just offered your mother a job."

"A job?"

"As my receptionist."

Robyn stood still for five long seconds. Rick was afraid she was upset, but slowly her lips curved upward. She leaned toward him. "Thank you. That's the most wonderful thing you could have told me, now that Tumble is found."

Rick reached for her hand. He hoped he'd have the courage to tell her a few more things soon. "Come on. Let's get this job done," he said.

The volunteers stripped the tables and tidied the serving area.

Aven and Caddie stayed until after nine o'clock, but finally Robyn pulled her brother aside. "Take your wife home. She looks exhausted."

Aven looked over at Caddie, a deep furrow creasing his brow. "She does look beat. But we're almost finished here."

"I'll help Robyn lock up," Rick said. "We'll probably be only twenty minutes behind you."

"Okay." Aven looked at the pair uncertainly.

Rick winked at him. "We'll be fine. We just need to box up a few things and load them in my truck."

"All right. Want us to take Tumble?"

Rick looked over to where the dog was snoozing on the floor under one of the tables. He'd had his time in the spotlight earlier, and the race-goers had lavished attention on him. Rick fully expected to see Tumble's photo on the front page of tomorrow's newspaper.

"Sure," Robyn said. "Hitch him up in his kennel, would you?" Rick had taken her home earlier to feed all the Hollands' dogs, but she hadn't wanted to leave Tumble there so they'd brought him back. He'd behaved himself and sat quietly during the dinner.

Robyn called to him. He jumped up and trotted eagerly to her. "Go with Aven." She patted his head and smiled into his trusting eyes. "You big lug." She stooped and kissed the dog's forehead.

When Aven and Caddie had left with Tumble, Rick began packing up the last few things. "All of this goes to your house, right?" He gestured to the dishes and leftover paper plates and cups remaining on the nearest table.

"Yes, and those extra napkins. Oh, and Anna left her purse. I called her as soon as I found it, and she said she'll come pick it up tomorrow."

"And Patrick's taking his dogs home at last?"

"All eight of them go in the morning. I'll miss them."

Rick closed up the carton he had filled. "You'll lose a couple more soon, too, won't you?"

"Yes. I had two people come to me today and ask if I had team dogs they could buy." She smiled, but her eyes drooped.

"Sounds like business is doing almost too well."

"Yeah. It won't hurt us to thin out the ranks a little though. We'll have more puppies in spring, and I'll have a lot of youngsters to train. And Clay Brighton wants me to do some initial training with a litter of yearlings he has."

Rick nodded. "I'm proud of you."

"Thanks. I hope Grandpa feels well enough soon to start helping me again. I guess you heard Trooper Glade say we might be able to get back the three dogs Sterns bought. They're putting them in official custody at the kennel in Anchorage until after Sterns's arraignment. Aven thinks we should pursue it, and he's offered to help out if we suffer financially because of it."

"He's a good guy, your brother."

"The best."

A few minutes later, Rick began carrying cartons to the truck while Robyn held the door for him. At last the hall was cleared.

Robyn walked to the light switches. "Well, that's over for another year."

Rick put his arm around her and walked her to the door. A beam of light came in through the glass from a security light outside. "Tired?"

"Yeah. But not as tired as Grandpa."

"I hope he didn't overdo it today," Rick said.

"Me, too." Robyn fumbled with the key ring in her hand. "I'm a little concerned about Caddie, too."

"Oh? Something I don't know?"

"Maybe. She's expecting in August."

"Wow. I didn't know that." Rick couldn't help grinning. "That's terrific. Aven seemed awfully happy, but I just figured that was his normal, sunny personality."

She laughed. "I've never seen him this happy. Caddie's the best thing that ever happened to him."

Rick touched her cheek and looked into her eyes in the dimness. "I love it when you laugh. You're so beautiful then." He gulped. Would she think that meant he didn't find her beautiful at other times? Because he did, always. "Robyn. . ."

She didn't speak but arched her eyebrows and waited.

He hesitated only a heartbeat. "I love you."

She caught her breath and he pulled her into his arms. He kissed her as he'd wanted to for weeks, holding her close and running his hand through her thick, glossy hair.

"I love you, too," she whispered when he released her.

"There's so much we need to talk about."

"Whenever you're ready."

He pulled her close and held her for another minute, then took the keys from her. They stepped outside and he locked the door.

⁂

In mid-April Rick arrived in the Holland Kennel dog yard as Darby finished her mushing lesson. He helped Robyn and Darby unhook the three dogs from the sled and put them away. As he pushed the sled, laden with harnesses, toward the shed, a snowball hit him in the back and he jumped about a foot off the ground.

"Gotcha!" Darby laughed.

He whirled in time to see her bend for another handful of snow. "Oh no, ya don't!" Rick scooped up enough to pack a quick snowball and lobbed it at her.

Robyn joined in and caught Darby on the arm. For a couple of minutes they exchanged shots, with Robyn alternating her aim between him and Darby.

At last, Rick held up both hands, laughing. "I surrender."

"Okay, Dr. Baker, I'll let you go this time, but only because I need to get home. Don't forget who's the champ though."

"Right. I'll get you next time. If there's enough snow left."

Darby headed for the driveway. "Thanks, Robyn. I'll see you tomorrow at church."

Rick helped Robyn put the equipment away in the shed. "The snow's going fast. Pretty soon you'll be training with the ATV again."

"I know." She smiled ruefully. "Grandpa wanted to drive again today. His last sled ride for the season. I let him take one ten-year-old dog inside the fenced yard. I feel so bad that we can't turn him loose with a team anymore."

"Maybe he'll get distracted this summer, helping you and working with all those new puppies."

"I hope so." She smiled up at him. "Where are we going tonight?"

"That new restaurant on the Goose Bay Road."

"Great. Anna says it's really good. Give me fifteen minutes to change?"

"Sure." They walked to the back door, and Rick held it open for her.

"Hi, Rick," Cheryl said as they entered the kitchen. She and Grandpa Steve sat at the kitchen table together.

"I'm going to change, Mom, and then we're going out to eat."

"Join us for a cup of tea while you wait, Rick?" Grandpa asked.

"Thanks, I'd like that." He removed his gloves and unzipped his jacket. Robyn headed off to her room, and Rick sat down beside her grandfather.

"Twelve of Tumble's new pups are reserved. Can you believe that?" Steve's eyes glittered. "We've only got four more babies, and Robby wants to keep two of them."

"I guess you'll stay busy this summer."

"You bet I will, Doc. Robyn plans to run the Iditarod next year, and I've been going over her plans with her. Gotta make sure all her equipment is just right, you know."

Rick nodded. "I'll be there to help."

Cheryl placed a mug of tea before him. "It's a big venture."

Grandpa nudged the sugar bowl Rick's way. "It is, but she can do it. She's a spunky girl. If she's not in the top ten, I'll eat my mukluks."

Rick laughed.

They were still discussing the big race when Robyn swept into the room wearing a calf-length skirt, an aqua sweater, and tall boots. "What are you yakking about now, Grandpa?"

"Our plans for the Iditarod, that's what."

She patted his shoulder. "That's right. We've got lots to do, haven't we?"

Rick stood. "Ready to go?"

"Yes." Robyn stooped to kiss Grandpa and blew her mom a kiss. "We won't be late."

"Well, we might be," Rick said.

"Oh?" She eyed him suspiciously.

"I'm not worried," Cheryl said. When Robyn turned to get her coat, she winked at Rick. "Have a good time, kids."

An hour and a half later, when they left the restaurant, the sun was just going down.

Robyn sat beside him in the truck, relaxed and dreamy. "What a beautiful night." She gazed out toward the mountains. The clouds glowed pink and lavender.

Rick drove to the lakeside park and stopped the truck where they could look out over the still-frozen expanse. "Hope you don't mind. I wanted to talk about something in the restaurant, but it seemed a little too popular."

"Yeah, it was crowded. The food was good though." She looked up at him with serious, dark eyes. "What did you want to tell me?"

"Not tell you. Ask you." He reached in his pocket and took out a small, square box. "I. . .I got you something when I was in Anchorage Monday. That is. . ." He hauled in a deep breath. Time to start over. "Robyn, I. . ."

She was staring at the little box. Slowly, her eyelashes lifted and she met his gaze but said nothing.

"I love you," he whispered.

Her lips quirked into the gentle smile he adored. "I love you, too."

He nodded, wondering if his no-frills plan was the best after all. Robyn wasn't a lace-and-roses girl, but it wouldn't have hurt to buy some flowers.

She sat quietly beside him. Most women would have pounced on the box by now, squealing and crying. Not that she didn't care deeply, but she waited for him to do this his own way. So, what was his way?

The simple approach. He reached for her hand. "Will you marry me?"

Her sharp intake of breath left him in suspense for several seconds. Finally she exhaled.

Had he asked her too soon? She'd known for months how he felt. Was she wondering about all the things he'd pondered the last few weeks—what their home and businesses would look like, for instance, where all her dogs would reside, and how they'd make sure Grandpa Steve could live at home as long as possible?

"Yes."

"You will?"

"Nothing would make me happier than to be your wife."

He kissed her tenderly, nearly exploding with thankfulness and anticipation. The questions faded into the fast-falling dusk.

He drew back and placed the box in her palm, closing his hand around hers. "I made some guesses—educated ones. I hope you like it. But if you don't—"

She sprang the catch and held the box up close to her face. "Oh, Rick, how could I not like it?"

He helped her remove the ring and slid it onto her finger. "It's Alaskan gold and amethyst."

"It's perfect." She curved her arms around his neck. "Thank you for picking it."

He kissed her again.

"Mom and Grandpa will be so happy," she whispered in his ear.

"Yeah, they are."

She leaned back. "They are?"

"Uh. . .yeah. Your mom saw the box on my desk, and. . .I hope you don't mind. They're waiting for the official word."

She smiled and stroked his cheek. "Let's go."

Epilogue

On a bright July day, Rick and Robyn stood together before their pastor at the little church in Wasilla. In the front row sat Cheryl, Steve, Aven, and Caddie. On the other side were Rick's parents and sisters, who had flown in for the wedding.

Anna and Darby stood beside Robyn at the front of the church. Because of her impending due date, Caddie had gently refused to be a bridesmaid. Rick had called on his brother and Bob Major for the occasion.

Friends, neighbors, owners of Rick's patients, and people in the sled dog business filled the church. Several renowned mushers slipped in anonymously before the ceremony, though the reporter from the *Frontiersman* spotted a couple of Iditarod winners and snapped photos of them entering the church.

Robyn held a lacy handkerchief to her eyes for a moment. Why should she cry? She was barely leaving home. She'd be living a quarter mile down the road from Mom and Grandpa, in Rick's snug log home. The dogs would stay at the Holland Kennel, and she could walk over every day to work with them.

Her mother had blossomed in her new position as receptionist at the Baker Veterinary Practice. She'd surprised and delighted Rick by organizing his records and transforming the atmosphere of his little office from chaotic to peaceful. When the new animal hospital was built, Rick and Robyn fully expected her to reign as office manager.

"What token do you give this woman?"

Robyn realized her thoughts had wandered.

Rick spoke up firmly. "A ring."

They both turned to gaze down the aisle. Darby's little sister, Katy, came proudly down the aisle with her eyes glittering. Wearing a snow-white harness and leash, Tumble walked beside her, lifting each foot daintily and gazing at the people in the pews.

When they reached the front of the church, Rick's brother knelt and detached a small box from Tumble's harness and handed it to Rick. He winked at Robyn and handed the box to the minister.

The pastor opened the box and revealed their wedding rings. Katy led Tumble to the side. She stood beside Darby and Anna and signaled to Tumble. He sat down and panted quietly, looking over the crowd.

A few minutes later, the vows were complete. Robyn gazed up into Rick's tender eyes as the pastor said, "You may kiss your bride."

As her husband bent and kissed her, Tumble let out a low bark. Darby and Katy both reached to pat him.

"Hush," Darby whispered. "You'll see her every day."

POLAR OPPOSITES

Dedication

To my newest grandchild, Abigail Faith, I can't wait to get to know you.

Chapter 1

Cheryl Holland left her car in short-term parking at the Anchorage airport and hurried toward the terminal, zipping her jacket. Late October winds held a biting promise of snow.

She wished she'd asked her son-in-law for a photo of the passenger she was supposed to pick up. But an emergency call had come in, and Rick had rushed out the door of the veterinary hospital calling over his shoulder, "Oh, Cheryl, I'm supposed to pick Oz up at eleven. Can you possibly. . . ?"

"Sure," she'd called blithely. In the past year, she'd become Rick's right-hand man, gal Friday, and jack-of-all-trades, rolled into one. And she loved it. But it would be nice to know what the new veterinary partner looked like.

"Maybe he'll carry his instruments in a medical bag like Rick's." She strode past the airline check-in areas and a gift shop selling Native Alaskan art. "Great. Now I'm talking to myself." A woman heading the other way eyed her cautiously, and Cheryl smiled. "Hello." *Note to self,* she thought. *Don't talk to yourself in public.*

She paused below a flight board and searched for Oz Thormond's flight from Seattle. At least she'd found the number scrawled on Rick's notepad. The one thing she knew about Dr. Thormond's appearance was that he would look nothing like the young veterinarian whose photo she had posted on the Baker Animal Hospital's Web site a month ago. That was Dr. Brad Irwin, the new vet school grad Rick had hired to work with him and possibly become a partner in the business. The same bright-eyed young veterinarian who had decided at the last possible minute that he didn't want to live in Alaska after all and had walked away from the job offer.

Cheryl still steamed about that. She'd worried a little about Dr. Irwin's youth and inexperience, but Rick had reminded her that he couldn't pay a lot at first. As the practice continued to expand, he would raise Dr. Irwin's salary. She'd also cautioned him that the young man from North Carolina might find Alaska a little overwhelming. And cold.

Rick had scoffed.

Until Brad Irwin had dumped the job offer with no warning.

"That's right," Cheryl said. "I hinted that he ought to have made the guy sign a contract, too. My son-in-law is entirely too trusting."

A man searching the ARRIVALS board shot her a sidelong glance. Cheryl favored him with a cheery smile and a bright, "Hello. Sorry about that."

"No problem. My son-in-law's not the greatest either."

She laughed. "Oh, Rick's terrific. But he assumes everyone else is as honorabl as he is." She spotted the number for Dr. Thormond's flight. On time and landin in ten minutes. The baggage claim area would be the place to find him. She smile at the disgruntled father-in-law and walked away.

Okay, no more talking to myself. I'm looking for a man who graduated from vet scho with Rick, so probably early thirties. She smiled as she remembered Rick's euphori when he'd learned Oz would come.

"Cheryl, this is fantastic! I told you that I asked my friend last summer to com work with me, and he couldn't. He was all tied up doing bear research at zoos in th Lower 48. Well, guess what? He's got a grant to come to Alaska and take part in polar bear project on the North Slope. And when he's not doing that, he wants t live here in Wasilla and join my practice. My first pick for partners, and he's actuall coming."

Her daughter, Robyn, had been as overjoyed as Rick, and the two of them ha quickly adjusted their plans. Cheryl had promptly deleted Dr. Irwin's photo and bi from the Web site, but Rick gave her nothing with which to replace it.

"It's happening so fast, he probably doesn't have time to do that. He's movin up here in two weeks. We'll get the info from him when he gets here."

She'd had to be satisfied with that. On the home page of the site, she posted banner announcing Dr. Oswald Thormond's imminent arrival, all the time wonder ing if this new arrangement would fall through, too.

She found a vacant seat between two deserted baggage carousels for Alask Airlines and pulled out her cell phone.

Rick answered her call immediately.

"I'm at the airport, in baggage claim. How will I know this guy?"

Rick laughed. "He'll be the one with the wide-eyed stare and the big grin. Blu eyes and— Oops, gotta go. Sorry, Cheryl."

She considered making a DR. THORMOND sign to hold up, but she had n materials. Passengers began filtering into the area from the gates above. She scruti nized each man who entered. They all clustered around the nearest carousel. Withi five minutes, fifty or sixty people had gathered. A digital sign over the farther carou sel flashed to life, declaring, SEATTLE AA FLIGHT 5790. As a group, the passenger moved over to the second carousel.

Cheryl eliminated anyone who was not traveling alone or had been met b someone else. She spotted a sober young man with glasses and a moustache on th other side of the moving belt. Possibility. She watched him closely as suitcases bega flowing along the carousel. He had a wheeled carry-on and a soft briefcase tha might hold a laptop, and he now waited for checked bags. Time to approach him.

She sucked in a deep breath and rose. Before she could push her way to his sid the young man hauled a huge camouflage bag off the belt. She quickly skirted th crowd. When she was halfway around, she saw him exiting toward the parking lo

Okay. So that wasn't him. Disappointed and less confident than before, if possible, he turned back and stood at the edge of the crowd, seeking a man who was looking for someone. After all, Oz would expect Rick to be here, and he'd search the crowd for him, wouldn't he?

A rugged young man in camouflage pants and a hooded sweatshirt stood alone but periodically scanned the crowd. But he was too young. Wasn't he? She wavered. Maybe he had a boyish face for his age.

Blue eyes, Rick had said. She'd have to get closer to be sure.

She edged around the people who huddled three deep about the loop of the carousel, losing sight of her quarry for a moment. When she spotted him again, she was within a few yards, but he was turned away, arranging his carry-on atop the large suitcase he'd just retrieved.

Cheryl walked closer and cleared her throat. "Dr. Thormond?"

He ignored her, struggling with the strap to his smaller bag.

"Excuse me," she said louder. "Are you—"

He looked up at her with curious and very brown eyes.

"I'm sorry. You're not Dr. Thormond, are you?"

"I wish. I've got two more years of med school." He straightened and gave her pleasant nod then turned toward the exit.

Cheryl sighed and let her posture droop. Maybe she should just wait until the crowd dissipated and see who was left.

She started back to the set of chairs, but a couple with two young children had claimed them. Instead, Cheryl shrank back toward a wall of brochures touting local attractions and again scanned the travelers.

One in particular caught her eye, but not because he was a young, hip veterinarian. The gentleman—and Cheryl knew instinctively that he *was* a gentleman from his bearing and the way he courteously worked his way through other passengers to the conveyor—looked about fifty, with wings of white accenting the lush, dark hair at his temples. She watched him covertly as he set down his carry-on bag and swung a large wheeled suitcase off the belt. He waited for another, giving her the opportunity to study him further. He was just too handsome. *If only,* she thought.

She made herself search again for a much younger man. Blue eyes. . .early thirties. . .No one of that description leaped out at her. Edging around behind the crowd, she realized she neared the handsome man's position. Oops. No thirty-somethings over here. She'd better turn back.

Before she could act on the thought, the people parted and the man she'd admired from a distance halted two steps from her. "Sorry," he said with a smile.

She couldn't help staring up into his vibrant, very blue eyes. "Oh, excuse me." She stepped quickly to one side.

He nodded. "Thanks. I'll just get this mountain of baggage out of the way while I wait for my ride."

He parked himself nearby and looked over the heads of the thinning throng. After five minutes or so, only a dozen travelers were left. Cheryl was very aware of the man still waiting patiently with his bags. She glanced over at him and he smiled.

"I suppose I should have the person I'm meeting paged," she said.

"That's an idea. I could ask them to page my friend, too. Rick was always punctual in school. He must have had an emergency."

Cheryl froze, her stomach doing an odd flip. "Rick? Not Rick Baker?"

The man focused on her and nodded. "Yes, actually."

She felt a flush wash over her cheeks. "You must be Dr. Thormond."

"Yes, I. . ." He smiled and held out his hand. "If I'm not mistaken, we're waiting for each other."

"I'm Cheryl Holland, Rick's mother-in-law. And you're right. He did have an emergency this morning."

The gentleman shook her hand and held on to it, gazing into her eyes. His dark eyebrows drew together. "No. You can't be. Rick's *mother-in-law*? Absolutely impossible."

Cheryl stepped back, releasing his hand. "Oh, I assure you it's true. Rick married my daughter, Robyn, last summer, and—"

"Yes, yes, Robyn. I've heard all about her and her sled dog business. Sorry I couldn't make the wedding. But. . ." He eyed her, cocking his head a little to one side. "Pardon my astonishment, but I'm finding it hard to believe you're old enough to be Rick's mother-in-law."

After the split second it took to absorb that, coming from the lips of a devastatingly handsome man in her own age bracket, Cheryl laughed. "I can see we're going to have an interesting time of it at the practice."

"Are we?" he asked.

"Yes. You see, I'm not only Rick's mother-in-law, I'm his receptionist and aide-de-camp."

His tentative smile broadened. "I must say, I like the way things are shaping up."

She couldn't look into those twinkling eyes any longer. In the four years since Dan Holland died, she hadn't engaged in a single conversation she would consider flirtatious. It felt good in a way—exciting, affirming that she hadn't become shriveled old widow. But a few moments' banter was one thing. Did she expect an ongoing flirtation in the office? That was the furthest thing from her desire. Time to establish a more professional relationship if she intended to work with this man on a daily basis.

"Well, Dr. Thormond, if you have all your bags, let me help you get them to my car. The drive to Wasilla takes forty-five minutes or so. Did they feed you on the plane?"

"No, I slept most of the way from Seattle. I don't suppose there's a café where we could stop on the way?"

Cheryl laughed. "There's a wide variety of restaurants, sir. Anything from burgers to Thai food. I even know a place famous for Alaskan dishes—sourdough biscuits and reindeer sausage."

He raised one hand to his heart. "That sounds wonderful, but I doubt we could properly appreciate a place like that in less than a couple of hours. Perhaps we'd better stick with something quick and directly on our path. I'm good for Thai food, if you are."

"Excellent choice. We pass right by a good place."

Cheryl insisted on taking one of his smaller bags, and they wended their way out to the short-term parking lot.

"I thought about renting a car right away, but Rick advised me to wait. Said he's got a vehicle I can use for a few weeks until I get my feet under me and see what I want."

"Probably my daughter's Jeep. I think that's wise. Rick has a pickup, completely stocked with his veterinary equipment. You may want to get a similar rig eventually."

They reached her car, and she unlocked the trunk. While Dr. Thormond lifted his bags into it, she reminded herself again that today was the day to set the tone for her working relationship with him. "Professional," she said under her breath.

"Excuse me?" His eyebrows arched, and his lips quirked, just waiting to smile again.

"Nothing. Sorry." She quickly unlocked the doors and slid into the driver's seat, telling herself silently, *And no more talking to yourself, Cheryl. That's an order.*

⚏

Oz faced Cheryl Holland across the table at the restaurant, and two things struck him at once. He was very hungry, and she had a shy streak. The hunger issue had been addressed, and their orders would arrive in a few minutes. As to her reserve, she seemed friendly enough, but she had trouble making eye contact now that they were seated close together, face-to-face. Just a matter of drawing her out, he supposed.

"So, tell me about the rental cabin Rick found for me to stay at. Have you seen it?"

"Yes. In fact, we had it ready for. . ." Her face went a becoming pink. "I'm sorry, this is a little embarrassing. But you know we had another veterinarian lined up for this position?"

"Oh yes, Rick told me about it. He asked me to join him way back last summer. At the time, that looked impossible. So he went ahead and hired someone else. Then the guy ran out on him."

"Right. I just. . .didn't want you to think you were our second choice or anything. Rick wanted you from the start, but when that couldn't happen, he hired this Dr. Irwin. We found housing for him and did a lot to prepare for his arrival. Rick was very disappointed when he backed out—we all were. But then we prayed about it together. The next day Rick told me he'd called you to get your advice and you were considering coming to Wasilla after all."

"Not often we get a second chance at an opportunity we've muffed." Oz watched the change in her face as she warmed to the topic. Cheryl animated was well worth watching. He smiled at her. "This is going to be a great adventure. Rick and I got along famously in school, and I'd give up a lot for the chance to work with him. But to do that *and* have the ability to do polar bear research. . .well, it's a dream come true for me."

Cheryl smiled back. She'd definitely relaxed a bit. "I admit I was surprised when I first realized *you* were Dr. Thormond. I expected a younger man—someone Rick's age. He didn't have a photo, and he hadn't described you very well."

Oz chuckled. "I went back to school and began the career I'd really wanted for twenty years."

"That's wonderful. What did you do before vet school?"

"I was in corrections."

Her jaw dropped, but she recovered quickly. "Prison work?"

"That's right. It started out as an expedient course of action. My father died, leaving my mother destitute. I took the job that would pay me the most short-term—as a guard at the county jail. I'd finished college, but not grad school. I gave up the dream for two decades."

The waitress brought their plates and they looked at each other.

"I'm guessing you're a lady who prays before she eats."

Cheryl's soft brown eyes widened. "Well, yes, I am."

Oz chuckled. "Rick wouldn't marry a woman who wasn't a genuine believer, and I figured the chances were good that her mom was, too. Shall we?"

They bowed their heads, and Oz offered a brief blessing for the meal and thanks for his safe journey. When he looked up, Cheryl's face was pensive as she spread her napkin in her lap. The spicy smell of ginger and cashew chicken made his mouth water, and he reached for his fork.

"You stayed in corrections for twenty years?" she asked.

"Nearly. I went from the county jail to a federal facility, where I eventually became a supervisor. But even though I wasn't one of the inmates, I felt the confinement. Wanted to get outside more. And I'd dreamed of working with animals since I was a kid. Working with the prisoners gave me a measure of satisfaction—I was giving back to the community, so to speak. But it wore me down emotionally. Made me cynical."

"I suppose it would."

"It struck me that it wasn't too late to go to grad school and get the credentials. That was about twelve years ago, and I've never looked back."

Cheryl smiled and gave a little nod, as though his explanation satisfied her doubts. "Working with animals is very therapeutic. It kept our whole family going after my husband died."

"In what way?" Oz asked softly, aware that he was getting a peek behind Cheryl's outward demeanor. She'd represented the veterinary practice so far today, but this was personal.

"Robyn and I—and my father-in-law, too—were devastated when Dan died. My son, Aven, is a Coast Guard officer. Of course, he came home on leave. But after Aven went back to his ship, Robyn and Steve and I sat down and made plans. My husband had worked for an oil company, and he drew a good salary. Without that, we had to support ourselves. We decided to build the kennel—which had been more or less a hobby—into a first-class business. Robyn trains sled teams for the best now, and world-class racers are buying Holland Kennel puppies."

"Rick's told me a little about it. He's really proud of her."

"Yes. I took a part-time job outside, but we got by, and now the business is something we're all proud of." They ate in silence, but a few minutes later, she lifted her teacup and looked at him over the rim. "I'd love to hear more about your bear research."

He liked her unaffected friendliness, and even her slight reserve. She showed the interest that made a good listener. Instinct told him she was good at her job and Rick's office ran smoothly. Alaska looked better and better.

"I've spent the last three years doing bear research at zoos," he said. "Polar bears have always intrigued me, and they're very different from other species. I've traveled to northern Canada and Siberia to study bear populations. This year I applied for a couple of programs, and what do you know? The Alaska Department of Fish and Wildlife contracted me to do wildlife research in February, and I'll go out with a team of geologists on a privately funded trip at the end of March."

"Wonderful."

"I'm excited about it. After I got that news, Rick contacted me again with his offer. He says he can give me time off from the practice to continue my research, so I jumped at it."

"I'm glad you have a chance to follow your passion."

"Yes, and earn a living, too." Oz laughed and took a sip of his coffee. "I can hardly wait to get up to the North Slope."

"Would you like dessert?"

They both looked up at the waitress.

"What do you say?" Oz raised his eyebrows and smiled at Cheryl.

"Not for me, thanks, but go ahead if you'd like."

"I guess we're all set," he told the waitress. He reached for his wallet.

"Oh, this is a business expense," Cheryl said. "Rick told me to put it on the credit card for the practice."

"We have a credit card for the vet practice?"

She laughed at his expression. "I guess we're not quite as primitive as you thought."

"To be frank, I figured Rick was broke. He told me about the new building and everything."

"You'll love it. And he did take some loans for that, but our receipts are good. I'm sure you'll want to discuss the details with him, but I can tell you that he doesn't seem worried about his financial future. Which is nice for me, as an employee and a mother-in-law. We're all proud of the way he's built the business."

"I can't wait to see it." Oz pushed his chair back. "Shall we?"

They went to the car, and Cheryl put the key in the ignition. No response came from the engine.

Her face fell. "Hold on."

"Flat battery?" Oz asked.

She reached down and fumbled on the floor beneath her seat then opened her door. "No, this happens all the time. I can fix it." She pulled a lever to pop the hood and climbed out.

Oz wondered if he should offer to call a service station.

Metallic tapping came from beyond the raised hood. Cheryl lowered it with a thud and got in. When she turned the key, the engine roared to life. She smiled at him apologetically. "I really need to go at those terminals with a wire brush. They're quite corroded." She put the gearshift into reverse. "I guess I know what I'll be doing after supper tonight. Sorry about that."

Oz couldn't think of a suitable reply, so he sat back and admired the scenery. Mountains towered in the distance to his right, and as Cheryl headed out of the city, ranks of peaks unfolded in the distance. He'd heard so much about Alaska, but the reality dwarfed all the tales. Already he knew he would love the land. A tiny, rodent-like anxiety gnawed at his satisfaction. What about the twenty-hour nights in winter and the subzero temperatures for weeks on end?

"I hope you like your cabin." Cheryl pushed back her short, curly hair and shot him a sideways glance. "It's only big enough for one person, but I suppose it will do until you find something better."

"I'm sure I'll find it suitably rustic, yet comfortable." He grinned at her, and she smiled back.

He was really here, in the land of glaciers, dog sleds, and women who fixed their own cars. That flutter of doubt had shadowed him since he'd accepted Rick's invitation two weeks ago, but he'd never faced it head-on. He didn't intend to either. The adventure was on.

Chapter 2

Cheryl tried to concentrate on her work the next morning, but that was difficult, knowing Oz Thormond was touring the Baker Animal Hospital with Rick as his guide. Whenever they entered the hall, she could hear their deep voices. Oz's enthusiastic laugh punctuated Rick's account of his headaches while seeing the new facility built.

The front door opened, and Cheryl turned toward it, expecting a pet owner with an unscheduled patient in need of medical care.

Instead, Robyn walked in. "Hi, Mom! How's it going?"

"Terrific. Dr. Thormond seems impressed."

"Isn't he great? I like him a lot." Robyn's dark eyes danced. "He and Rick spent the evening catching up and telling me tales about their days in vet school. Sounds as though those two had as much fun as a couple of kids in an amusement park."

"Really? Rick strikes me as a serious young man, although I know he has a playful side." She tried to imagine Oz Thormond pulling practical jokes and cutting up. She shook her head. "I like Dr. Thormond, too, but I don't see him as a delinquent. He was at the top of their class, Rick tells me."

"He's smart all right. I didn't mean that they did anything awful. But together, they seem to enjoy life more than the average person does."

"Hmm. Maybe it's not such a good idea for them to work together."

"Are you kidding?" Robyn perched on the corner of Cheryl's desk. "They'll get twice the work done, with half the stress. You'll see."

"Yes, I will." Cheryl decided not to mention the added stress she felt whenever Oz's laughing blue eyes settled on her. The very thought sent an unwelcome warmth to her cheeks, and she shoved her wheeled chair back and stood. "So, what are you here for, young lady?"

"I'm going out to a kennel with Rick this morning."

"Oh yes, the Bensons'. He's going to vaccinate two litters of puppies and check a dog that we had in here last month with a fractured tibia."

"Right. Ron Benson has a breeding female shepherd for sale, and I thought I'd take a look."

"You'd add a German shepherd to your breeding stock? Since when?"

"Oh, I don't expect to buy her. But I haven't had much time with Rick this week, and it'll be fun to ride along with him. Besides, I called Grandpa to see if he wanted to go with us."

"And?"

"We're picking him up in a few minutes."

"Great. It'll do him good to get out." Grandpa Steve Holland sometimes got bored when left alone at the home place, where he lived with Cheryl. The house lay a quarter mile down the road, and Robyn maintained her business of raising and training sled dogs there. She went over every day, and Grandpa helped her around the dog yard as much as he was able, but he loved to get out and see folks beyond the family circle. Cheryl did her best to keep him active, and she appreciated Rick and Robyn's efforts to get him out of the house frequently.

Robyn glanced at her watch. "Maybe we'd better remind Rick."

"Yes. We have scheduled patients, starting at ten. If you want to get back before then, you should leave soon."

Robyn leaned toward her. "Before you do that, what do *you* think of Oz?"

"He's terrific, but. . ."

"But what?"

Cheryl grimaced, trying to sort out her feelings. Did they really matter? "He won't last a month."

Robyn's eyebrows shot up. "Why do you say that? So far, he loves it here."

"Yes, but. . . Oh, I don't know. He's always lived in the city, and he's not used to the cold and the long winters."

"Mom, he's originally from upstate New York. They have snow there."

Cheryl shrugged. "I hope I'm wrong."

She hoped so intensely. But she faced the truth. Being around Oz made her giddy, like a sixth grader with a new crush. But no way would this man be a permanent part of her future. He was a suave, educated bachelor from the city, cultured and used to fine things. His wristwatch probably cost more than her car. Before coming to Wasilla, he'd been employed by the San Francisco Zoo, and before that the Philadelphia Zoo.

She was a country girl who'd grown up making do without a lot of things that people like Oz considered necessities. She saved her bread bags to reuse them and tried not to drive into Anchorage more than once a month to save gas. The mother of two grown children, grandmother of a darling baby boy, she valued her family above all else.

Polar opposites.

True, Rick had assured her that Oz was committed to staying at least a year. Which meant that next fall he'd probably pull up stakes again and move to wherever he could get another study grant. Nope, she wasn't going to allow herself to get used to having him around.

The men's voices grew louder as they came out into the waiting room where Cheryl's desk sat.

"Oh, hi, honey." Rick grinned at Robyn. "Ready for our adventure?"

"Yes, and I called Grandpa and he wants to go."

"Great. Let's go get him. Oh, Cheryl. . ." Rick turned toward her. "I'm going to let Oz settle in. He wants to set up his computer and unpack those crates of books that arrived the other day. But he says he'll handle any emergencies that come in while I'm gone, so don't hesitate to call on him. Otherwise, I expect to be back in time for my first appointment at ten, and Oz can shadow me and get a feel for how I work."

"Okay, that sounds fine."

"Bye, Mom. Catch you later." Robyn kissed her cheek and bustled out the door with Rick.

Oz still stood behind her.

Cheryl couldn't see him, but every nerve was aware of his presence. It was almost like standing with her back to a fireplace in a chilly room and letting the warmth of the blaze gradually thaw and then toast her. She turned slowly. "I'll put some coffee on if you'd like."

"Thank you. The jet lag is catching up with me. I must say I'm delighted with the size of my office and the exam rooms."

She smiled. "Rick spent months planning this building and getting advice. He said he intends to work here another forty years, and he wanted to get it right."

"He did a great job." Oz looked around the waiting room and chuckled. "I admit I'm glad you're here. When Rick said he was taking off for a couple of hours, my first thought was, 'Oh no, someone will come in with a cat that needs immediate surgery.' I've spent the last three years working with exotic animals, and the last six months mainly doing research. Haven't treated everyday pets for a long time."

"I'm glad you're here, too. I've done this for over a year now, but I still get nervous when Rick's not here and an injured animal comes in."

"I'm sure you do a great job of calming the owner down and making the patient comfortable."

"I do my best." She took a step toward the hallway. "We have a small kitchen back here. Did Rick show you?"

"Yes, he did."

"I'll start the coffeepot, and you can help yourself whenever you want. We also have a refrigerator for people food, as opposed to the ones for pet food and medicine."

"Wonderful. If I can just remember which is which, I won't have to worry about some husky getting my ham sandwich for lunch."

"Or you getting a salad with a cat food garnish." They both laughed. He was way too easy to talk to. This side of him reminded her of Dan Holland, though he looked nothing like her late husband.

Four years, she thought as she measured the coffee. *Dan has been gone four years.* Could she let go of him enough to let someone new into the deepest part of her heart?

She heard whistling coming from the hallway and paused to listen. Apparently Oz had mastered the twitters and trills of myriad birdcalls and threw them willy-nilly into his rendition of "North to Alaska." She'd have to be careful, or she'd let herself like the new guy too much. But as she walked back to her desk with a bounce in her step, she found herself humming along.

⁂

Oz set the last of his medical books on a shelf and stood back to catch the effect. With his framed diplomas on one wall and a photo of him with a grizzly bear he'd treated at the San Francisco Zoo hanging over the file cabinets, he was almost done moving into his new office. Most of his personal items had gone to the rental cabin, but he'd bring a few knickknacks here to make it his own space. Maybe the antique dueling pistols he'd bought in Russia last year.

He ran his hand over the surface of the walnut desk. Not too shabby. Rick had spent a lot to make sure his new partner would like working here. Had the time come to settle down for good? Wasilla was a bit provincial, compared to his usual haunts, but Anchorage wasn't far away, if he got a culture craving.

The phone on the desk emitted two quick beeps and he picked up the receiver. "Hello?" Nothing. One button blinked red at him. He pushed it. "Hello?"

"Dr. Thormond, this is Cheryl. A client just called, and her dog had a collision with a motorcycle. She's bringing him in with a fractured leg and possible internal injuries. Since Dr. Baker is out, can you handle it? ETA about ten minutes."

"Uh. . .sure. Take the dog into the first treatment room?"

"That would be Rick's room. Would you like to see Thor in your own treatment space?"

"Certainly. Do we have a file on Thor?"

"Yes, we do. He's a Great Dane, about three years old, and is up to date on his immunizations. I'll bring you his file. Would you like to meet Mrs. Nickerson with me? For a large dog, we usually take the stretcher out to the parking lot."

"Of course."

He hauled in a deep breath as he returned the phone to its cradle. This was going to be a lot different from his work with zoo animals. And so much for Rick being the dog expert. His first patient. Oh well.

Cheryl tapped on the door and entered carrying a manila file folder. "Here you go. He's a healthy dog. Too bad he ran out into the street."

"What happened to the biker?"

"Road burns. He wasn't going very fast, and he was wearing his helmet."

"Good for him."

"Mrs. Nickerson said the young man was quite upset about Thor's injuries, but it wasn't his fault." Cheryl gave him a sympathetic smile. "You're supposed to take over the large animal end of the practice so Rick can concentrate on dogs. Sorry about this."

"Well, it's a *large* dog."

She chuckled. "I'm glad you see the humor. You'll get a good initiation to our stretcher routine."

Oz flipped the file open and scanned Rick's notes on the dog's past visits. "Thor doesn't seem to have had need of anesthesia until now. Let's have some local anesthetic ready, in case we can use that, but we'll probably need to put him out." He gave her the dosage, based on the dog's weight.

While she hurried to set out the medication, syringe, and a set of sterile instruments, Oz scrubbed up and put on gloves. When they were ready, Cheryl wheeled the stretcher from the treatment room into the hallway and out through the waiting room. A beige minivan pulled into the parking lot as they reached the front door.

"That's Allie Nickerson." Cheryl pushed a large button on the wall, and the double doors swung open.

"I'm impressed that Rick sprang for so much technology."

"He wants to give the best animal care in Wasilla. He does, too."

Oz smiled at her fierce loyalty. He pushed the stretcher outside and down the ramp. A woman with long, dark hair in a ponytail leaped from the van and opened the slider door behind the driver's seat.

Cheryl called, "Allie, this is Dr. Thormond, Rick's new partner."

The woman threw him a distracted glance. "Hello."

Cheryl let Oz handle the stretcher and went to the door of the van. "Oh my. I'm sorry this happened."

Oz set the stretcher's brake and stepped up beside Cheryl.

The big dog lay listlessly on the middle seat. His coat was caked with congealing blood on his right side, and his hind leg had obviously sustained a compound fracture.

"Let me lift him, ladies. One quick move will be easiest on him, I think."

They stepped aside.

Oz leaned into the van and rested his weight on his left knee. "Hi, fella. I know you feel lousy. I'm gonna help you." He slid his right arm under the dog's head and neck.

Thor growled, low in his chest.

"Okay, maybe we should give him a tranquilizer first." He backed out of the vehicle.

"I'll get it." Cheryl hurried inside.

For the next forty-five minutes, Oz concentrated on the patient, but he noted that Cheryl never left his side while he examined the Great Dane and operated on his fractured leg. She seemed to know which instrument Oz would need next, and when she hesitated once, he gave her precise instructions. She complied with a minimum of delay. He'd had some qualms about the lack of a well-trained veterinary technician to assist in times like these, but she more than met his expectations.

When he'd finished, he peeled off his gloves.

Cheryl gently bathed the blood from the dog's side with warm water. "Shall I give Allie an update?"

"I'll go out and talk to her. Thor's going to need a prolonged recovery, but I'm hoping he'll have full use of that leg back." He pulled off his protective mask and goggles.

"Do you want me to stay with him until you come back?"

He nodded. "Thanks. After I talk to Mrs. Nickerson, we can move Thor to the recovery area and she can see him." He opened the door. Rick hurried down the hallway toward him. Oz called over his shoulder to Cheryl, "Looks like Rick's back."

A flicker of relief tempered the satisfaction that ran through Oz. His first surgery in Alaska was performed on one of Rick's canine patients. He'd just as soon his friend looked the dog over and made sure he hadn't missed anything.

"Hey, Ozzie! Allie just told me you were putting Thor's leg back together. How'd it go?"

"All right. I just finished stitching him up. He's still groggy, but I haven't put the cast on. Thought I'd leave that for you."

Cheryl looked up as they entered. "Hi, Rick."

"How's he doing?"

"Great."

"Internal injuries?" Rick asked.

"Nothing major." Oz put the chart in his hand. "I haven't updated this, but you can see the medications we used."

Rick frowned over it for half a minute. "Looks good. Just what I would have done. We'd better not cast it until that swelling goes down."

"Yeah. Do you want to talk to Mrs. Nickerson?" Oz asked.

"No, you did the surgery. Go ahead." Rick held the door for him.

Oz nodded and headed for the waiting area with a smile. He'd forgotten how great it felt to tell an owner her pet would recover. Treating domestic animals had its perks.

Allie rose, her face pale with strain. "How is he?"

"He's doing well." Oz took a seat and gestured for her to sit down beside him. "Thor came through the surgery fine, but he'll need several weeks of rest. We're going to put a cast on his leg, probably tomorrow. Dr. Baker will take over his care now, and he can advise you on that, but I'm hopeful that Thor will make a complete recovery."

"Thank God." Tears spilled over her eyelids and ran down her cheeks.

Oz reached over to the end table and grabbed a box of tissues. "Here you go. There's nothing to worry about. You'll be able to go in and see Thor in a few minutes, and then we'd like to keep him here at least overnight. When the swelling is down and the cast is on, you'll be able to take him home."

"Thank you so much, Dr. . . ." She blinked at her tears and gazed up at him. "I'm sorry. I've forgotten your name. But thank you."

"Oz Thormond." He smiled and rose. Cheryl stood in the hall door, watching him. Oz walked over and asked softly, "Is Thor ready to see his owner?"

"Yes, we put him in a low recovery bed. I'll take her in."

"Thanks. And, Cheryl. . ."

She looked up at him with raised eyebrows. Her brown eyes shone with compassion.

"You did great," Oz said. "Thank you for all your help in there. Rick must be very grateful to have an assistant as capable as you are."

Slowly, her smile curved her lips. As she approached Allie, Oz acknowledged that his first day on the job, while challenging, was looking pretty good, and Cheryl's presence played an important part in that.

Chapter 3

Grandpa Steve came from his bedroom, walking slowly but steadily.

"You all set, Cheryl? We don't want to be late."

She smiled and rose from her armchair. "I'm ready. But you don't have to worry about being late, Dad. It's only next door."

"I know, but I want to meet Rick's new partner. Come on." Steve took his jacket from the closet and pulled it on.

Sometimes living with her father-in-law brought Cheryl a lot of headaches, but for the most part, they got along. He'd helped her and Dan get established when they moved to Alaska, and she found satisfaction in helping him as he grew older. They'd always been good friends, but since Dan's death, they'd drawn even closer. Because of her care, Steve was able to continue living at home.

She took his arm as they went down the front steps. For the hundredth time she wondered if she ought to see about having a ramp built on the house. Right now, he was doing fairly well, but he'd spent some time in the hospital and rehab last winter, and some days he was shaky on his feet.

They made it safely to the car, and Cheryl drove the short distance down the road to Rick and Robyn's house. She parked behind the pickup in their driveway. "Dr. Thormond must have arrived. Robyn's Jeep is right over there."

"Is he going to get a car of his own?" Steve undid the seat belt and reached for the door latch.

"That's the plan, but Rick told him to take his time and make sure he gets what he wants. He'll probably want a truck or a van."

The door of the spacious log cabin opened, and Robyn skipped down the steps.

"Hey, Grandpa! How are you today?" She kissed him and took his arm as they headed for the house.

"I'm good. I'm always good. Where's this hotshot new vet we've got? I want to see him."

Robyn laughed. "He's inside, and he wants to meet you."

A minute later the two shook hands.

"Oz," said Grandpa. "What kind of name is that? Are you from the Emerald City?"

"No, sir. It's my mother's fault. She named me Oswald, and I've been stuck with the nickname since the cradle."

"Aha." Grandpa looked him up and down. "Well, it doesn't seem to have harmed you any."

"Supper's ready," Robyn said as she led them to the round dining table. "Oz, let's put you there, beside Rick. So how do you like your new digs?"

"It's great. Small, but comfortable. And I think I'll like having the woodstove for backup heat." Oz took a seat between Cheryl and Rick.

Robyn set a pan of lasagna on a trivet and sat down between her husband and Grandpa. Rick reached for her hand.

"Let's ask the blessing." He held out his other hand to Oz.

Grandpa clasped hands with Cheryl and Robyn. "We always do this. Keeps Robby from grabbing a bite while we pray."

Robyn made a face at him.

Cheryl had already grasped Steve's hand. She felt her cheeks heat up as she reached out to Oz and quickly bowed her head. She tried to hold his hand lightly, but not so loosely that he'd think she didn't want to touch him. But too firm a grip might be construed as boldness.

She hardly heard a word of Rick's brief prayer. Instead, she thought about Oz's warm, strong fingers clasping her hand. She still wore her wedding ring. Had he noticed that, and what would he think about it? Since Dan had died, she hadn't seriously thought of beginning a new relationship, but she wasn't totally against it. Of course, a new man entering her personal life would have to meet a high standard. So far Oz had passed all her imaginary tests on professionalism. The jury was still out on adapting to the climate and culture. He'd prayed over lunch the day she picked him up at the airport. How many men would have suggested it when eating out with a stranger?

Rick said, "Amen," and she opened her eyes. Though she was thankful for the meal, the distraction of holding a handsome man's hand had all but eliminated her thoughts of prayer.

Oz released her hand slowly.

She didn't look at him but reached for the salad bowl. Enough of this woolgathering.

"Now, Doc," Grandpa said, fixing Oz with a sober gaze, "have you ever driven a sled team?"

Oz grinned. "That's one of the few things I've never driven. I did ride on a reindeer sled once, but I didn't get to drive."

"Well, you'll have to learn. When you get a day off, you come over, and Robby and I will fix you up with a sled and team."

"Sure, anytime." Robyn smiled at Oz. "When you want a lesson, come on over. I'm sure Grandpa would be happy to boss you around. He does it to me all the time. And it's a good idea for you to get a couple of lessons in case you ever need to drive a sled."

Rick reached for Oz's plate and held it up so Robyn could load it with lasagna. "You know, in winter we use snow machines in the business a lot. More than dog sleds. Sometimes that's the only way to get around to the remote farms and kennels."

Oz nodded. "I did learn to use one of those when I went to Russia. We were doing research on the Siberian ice sheet. Talk about remote! If your machine doesn't run, you've had it."

Grandpa leaned forward, his eyes glittering. "You'll have to tell me more about that. You know, when Danny and I first came up here, we'd never seen a snow machine before, but Danny was keen on getting one right away. He got an old, used Ski-Doo, and he took Cheryl off to see the lake. Well, wouldn't you know it, that thing conked out on him. He was going to walk back on the trail they'd packed and come get her with a dog team, but guess what?"

"Cheryl got the sled running," Oz said.

Grandpa frowned. "No. But that's a pretty good guess. You tell him, Cheryl."

She looked over at Oz and held the salad bowl out to him. This shopworn family tale was far less exciting than Oz's bear tracking in Siberia. "Dan had stopped the machine, and it wouldn't start again. Turns out it was a poor connection to the battery, is all. A family of Tlingit Native Alaskans came along, riding a couple of sleds. They helped us out and got us going again. That's when I decided I needed to know more about engines."

"And she's been our designated mechanic ever since," Grandpa said with a laugh. "Keeps the snow machine and the snowblower and lawnmower running. Not bad when it comes to minor things with her car either. I'm glad she likes it. Someone had to know how to keep the vehicles running, and personally, I'd rather spend time with the dogs."

Cheryl smiled and shook her head. "It's not that I'm so crazy about engines, but someone around here needed to be practical. And those folks who helped us became friends of ours. They still stop in to visit when they come to town." She decided it was time to turn the conversation. Enough about her grease-monkey tendencies. "Oz was telling me that he'll be heading for the North Slope in February."

"Is that right?" Grandpa asked. "I don't guess the mama bears are coming out of their dens yet."

"It's a little early, but we'll get out over the ice pack and tag a lot of adults. And I'm going on a different trip at the end of March or the first part of April. It's usually easiest to locate mothers with new cubs then."

"Maybe you'll be around to help out with the Fire & Ice race here in January and the start of the Iditarod in March," Grandpa said.

"I'm planning on it. I want to jump into the culture here and contribute to the community." Oz smiled across the table at Robyn. "Rick's told me how hard your family works to put on the Fire & Ice. And how hard you're training to run some races yourself. I know he's proud of you."

Robyn shrugged. "I hoped to do the Iditarod this year, but it's going to have to wait. I'm doing a couple of shorter races."

"By next year this time, you'll have your Iditarod team training." Rick winked at his wife then turned back to Oz. "She works harder than anyone else I know. She's wanted to do the Iditarod for a long time, and we really hoped it would be this year. But I trust her judgment. She trains teams for other people, and she'll know when she's got the right dogs."

"We'll all be there to help you and cheer you on," Cheryl said.

"Thanks, Mom." Robyn looked eagerly at their guest. "I'm going to help Rick at the dropped dog station in Anchorage during the Iditarod again this year. That might be something you'd enjoy helping with, Oz."

"What is that?"

"It's where the dogs that are dropped from teams along the trail go to wait for their owners to pick them up after the race."

Rick nodded and handed him a plate of sliced garlic bread. "Sometimes dogs get sick or are injured along the trail, and the musher has to drop them from his team. Somebody has to give them the treatment needed and make sure they're well cared for until the race is over."

"Sounds like an interesting way to support the race," Oz said. "Maybe it will distract me from those long winter nights we'll be getting."

"By then, daylight hours will be lengthening again, but yeah, anything like that helps." Robyn glanced around, and apparently satisfied that all her guests had been served each dish, she began to eat.

Cheryl let the talk flow around her. Dogs, sledding, veterinary patients.

"Back in the old days. . ." Grandpa began, and she stifled a laugh. With a new audience, Steve would probably trot out all his old stories. But that was okay. Oz seemed to have a patient disposition. One more point in his favor. Did his numerous good points outweigh their differences yet? Of course, he'd been to Siberia, and who knew where else. He'd get cabin fever here during the long winter and leave when his research was done.

"Stop it," Cheryl said under her breath.

"Excuse me?" Oz smiled tentatively at her.

"Oh, nothing. I'm sorry."

"She talks to herself," Robyn said.

Cheryl gritted her teeth as her cheeks warmed. "It's a habit I'm trying to break."

Chapter 4

On Sunday morning Oz attended church with Rick and Robyn. Cold winds blew in from the mountains, promising snow, and for the first time he wore his ultra-warm parka.

He wasn't sure what to expect at the nondenominational church. The structure was much smaller than the one he'd attended in San Francisco, but its members included people of different races and varied ethnic backgrounds. He went with Rick and Robyn to a classroom for Sunday school during the first hour, and they introduced him to the class's leader, Sam Kwon, a young man about Rick's age.

"We're glad to have you here." Sam grinned as he shook Oz's hand. "How do you like Alaska so far?"

"I love it. Had my first mushing lesson yesterday."

"That's terrific," Sam said. "I hope I'll see more of you."

"Is he Korean?" Oz asked Rick as they settled into the third row. "The name sounds like it." He gazed at Sam again, puzzling over the leader's features.

Rick grinned. "His mother's Korean, but his father was born here. Part Russian, part Native Alaskan."

"Aha. Interesting. I hope I'll have a chance to get to know him better."

"No doubt about it," Rick said. "He and his wife, Andi, are good friends of ours, and they're very outgoing."

Oz looked around the class of about thirty people. "Where's Cheryl?"

"Oh, she teaches a primary class. You'll see her after Sunday school, I expect."

Oz couldn't help mentally comparing Cheryl to the women he was used to in the city. He liked so many things about her: She took care of her father-in-law, helped out wherever she was needed at the vet practice, drove a Ski-Doo with the best of the Alaskans, and taught a children's class. She might lack the polish of his old acquaintances, but he wasn't sure that was a drawback. He opened his Bible, determined to listen to Sam and not daydream about the lovely, tough, compassionate Cheryl Holland.

After the class, she greeted them warmly at the back of the church auditorium.

"Good to see you again," Oz said.

"Thank you." She wore a brightly patterned skirt, a knit top, and a cranberry jacket. Oz had already noted that the church people didn't waste fuel overheating the building, and she'd dressed appropriately.

"Mom, where's Grandpa?" Robyn asked.

"He has a cold, and I persuaded him to stay home and rest."

"I hope it's not serious," Oz said.

"I don't think it is, but it's windy and cold today. I didn't want him getting chilled."

They followed Rick and Robyn down the center aisle.

"How did your class go?" Oz asked.

She smiled at him. "Great. I had eleven children this morning."

He let her enter the pew after Rick and sat on the aisle beside her. Around them, the rows filled quickly. The service was less formal than his usual fare, but that didn't bother him. He liked being surrounded by enthusiastic people who put their hearts into their singing.

Rick and Robyn had both assured him that if he wasn't comfortable at their church they wouldn't be insulted if he chose another. But he liked this one—the friendliness, the worshipful atmosphere, and the plain exposition of God's Word.

Cheryl caught his eye as they stood for the final hymn. She opened her mouth as if to speak then closed it with a slight smile.

Did she wonder about his reaction to her home territory? She was too polite to ask. Even though he'd never belonged to a church like this one, he knew the answer to her unspoken query.

He leaned toward her. "Feels like home here."

Four weeks later, Cheryl concluded that Oz had settled into the routine of the office. When she answered the phone, many patients' owners asked for him by name. He'd met dozens of residents and their pets and livestock. Business had picked up so much she was training a friend to man the desk and schedule appointments so she could assist the veterinarians more. Three couples had issued dinner invitations to Oz. He'd told Cheryl with a laugh that if he wasn't careful, his social calendar would be full every weekend.

He seemed to take the late fall weather in stride, too. Eighteen inches of snow had fallen over the valley. Instead of complaining, he'd called a young man Rick had recommended and hired him to plow his driveway. Then he'd set up another dog sledding lesson with Robyn and Grandpa Steve. He'd also taken a snow machine jaunt with a client whose horse he had treated.

Cheryl grudgingly revised her original estimate. Oz showed self-sufficiency she hadn't expected. He'd stayed more than a month. In fact, his first words to her that morning were, "I'm beginning to feel like an Alaskan."

His jaw sported dark stubble that morning. She took note—it only added to his masculine attractions—but she refused to comment. Not for a minute did she believe he'd forgotten or neglected to shave. He was following Rick's example and growing a beard for the winter. The two men had arrived within moments of each other amid falling snow and grabbed shovels from the utility closet to finish clearing the walkway.

It was the first Monday in November. While they shoveled, Cheryl placed a copy of the day's schedule on each man's desk, as she did every day. Today Oz's entire morning was scheduled with barn calls. Rick would see patients in the office while Oz traveled around to vaccinate livestock and check on ill and injured horses and cattle. That was all right. She'd be able to concentrate better and get more done while he was out of the office. In spite of her good intentions, she found herself keeping track of him when he was in the building and listening for his voice. Not today. She'd continue training Angela to man the front desk and catch up on her filing.

About ten o'clock, Angela fielded a call and turned to Cheryl for help. "It's Hal Drake. He wants a doctor to come to his ranch."

Drake was a regular client with a large herd of beef cattle. "Put him through to Rick," Cheryl said. They didn't give out the doctors' cell phone numbers unless it was urgent.

A woman and her twelve-year-old daughter came in with their cat in a plastic cage.

"Have a seat," Cheryl told them with a smile. "Dr. Baker will be right with you." She walked down the hallway to inform Rick that his next patient had arrived.

When she looked into his office, he was hanging up his phone. "Guess I'd better call Ozzy on his cell. Sounds like we have a big problem out at the Drakes'."

❖

"I've done what I can for now," Oz said, examining an Arabian horse's front leg. "Her pastern's swollen, and it seems tender. Keep doing the cold packs. I'll come by tomorrow, and we'll see if it looks any better."

"All right, thanks." The owner was a young woman whose family owned four saddle horses. The mare had stumbled and wrenched her pastern earlier that morning, and Cheryl had added the stop to his list of calls.

He set the mare's hoof gently on the floor and straightened his back. "Just keep her in the barn tonight and let her rest."

"Thanks. I will."

As Oz headed for the pickup he'd bought the week before, the sun was just rising, although it was after ten o'clock. His phone rang, and he fumbled in the pocket of his jacket for it.

"Oz, it's Rick. We have another barn call for you, and this one sounds serious. A beef rancher who's a regular client has one cow dead and several others symptomatic with an undiagnosed illness. I'll head out there as soon as I finish with the patient I'm treating now, but we may both need to be there."

"Sure. How do I get there? I'm at the Lilleys' place now."

"Why don't you swing by and pick up Cheryl? She's a little skittish around cattle, but she's helped me once or twice. She's great at keeping the records for you and running back and forth to the truck."

"Okay, if you're sure. I'll come back right now."

"Yeah, I think that's best. From Mr. Drake's description, we might need an extra pair of hands. Angela's here, and she can cover the desk while we're out."

On his short drive to the animal hospital, Oz found himself anticipating working closely with Cheryl. She'd helped him a few times with animals he'd treated at the office. She stayed calm and seemed to know what to do before he asked. Rick had chosen well when he picked his office manager.

When he reached the practice, Cheryl jogged down the steps carrying a large tote bag and climbed into his truck. "Hi. Turn left out of the parking lot. It's four or five miles."

Oz took the pickup out onto the road, a little surprised at her terse directions. "Thanks for coming."

"I hope I can be of some help. I can record tag numbers and dosages for you. Just don't ask me to herd cows."

He smiled. Her mouth was set in a grim line, and he guessed Rick had understated her feelings toward cattle.

⁑

How did I get into this? Cheryl bounced along with Oz in the truck, up the long farm lane. If the farmer's situation hadn't sounded so urgent, she'd have said no. She was surprised Rick had offered her services. Since when did he think she was an expert at assisting with treating sick cattle? She'd helped him once and nearly lost a finger to an inquisitive cow. Instead of greeting patients in the comfortable office, she'd soon be standing in a barnyard in the ten-degree wind.

"I shouldn't have agreed so quickly," she muttered.

"Did you say something?" Oz looked over and smiled at her.

"No, but I'm really not on very good terms with cows. And these belong to the big, shaggy variety."

"That's right. Scottish Highlands, Rick said. They have very long hair."

"And very big horns."

He chuckled. "They're quite docile, I understand. I've never been close to one myself."

She gulped. At least she had thermal mittens and hat, besides her warm parka and high boots.

"If it makes you feel better, the owner usually helps if I need someone to hold an animal still," Oz said. "If you can keep handing me instruments and filling in the records, we'll do fine."

Even with his vivid blue eyes holding her gaze for a moment, Cheryl couldn't quite believe him. She loved animals, but cattle at close range put her on edge. She should have simply refused to go. On the other hand, if she could hold it together, her presence would save him time and headaches. She determined to make this trip worthwhile if it killed her. Which wasn't out of the realm of possibility, given those wicked horns on the beasts. She let out a long sigh.

"Not thrilled about this, are you?" Oz asked. "Sorry."

"Oh, please, it's not the company. Yet."

He laughed. "I know, I know. It's them." He nodded toward the fence that ran alongside the lane.

They'd approached the farm buildings, and several dozen cattle awaited them, milling about in a large holding pen. One especially large and hairy specimen fixed them with a doleful gaze and lowed.

"Chin up," Cheryl told herself. "You can do this."

"Yes, you can." Oz brought the truck to a halt before the barn and smiled over at her.

"Oh. Sorry. I didn't mean to say it out loud."

"It's okay. If you need a pep talk while we're working, just say so, and I'll be happy to give you one."

"Okay, now I feel silly. It's the horns, mostly. And the hooves. Cows' hooves can be very sharp, you know."

"Oh yes." He grinned as he opened his door and climbed out of the truck.

"Well, we're here to save sick animals. I'll try to focus on that." She didn't wait for him to come and open her door. This wasn't a social outing after all. It was work. She jumped down and pulled her clipboard from her tote bag.

She wondered, not for the first time, if her son-in-law was trying his hand at matchmaking. She already suspected Grandpa Steve of that when he'd tried to persuade her to give Oz his dog sledding lessons. She'd quickly quashed that idea, pointing out that of all the family she was the least skilled in mushing, though she was competent. Oz would be much better off with Robyn as instructor.

When Rick had told her Oz needed her to guide him to the Drakes' ranch, she'd watched him for a moment, looking for anything that would betray a smugness or self-satisfaction. She couldn't detect any insincerity. He'd had the decency to thank her and say, "You don't mind, do you? I suppose I should have asked you before mentioning it to Ozzy."

And she'd said, "No, it's all right." So she couldn't blame Rick that she was now walking to the fence where Hal Drake, his wife, and three ranch employees stood bleakly waiting for Oz's opinion. She refused to consider the possibility that she had accepted the challenge in order to be near Oz. He had nothing to do with it. She was here for the Drakes and their animals. And she'd do a good job. Period.

Oz entered the pasture and walked over to the corner, where the others stood near a dead Scottish Highland cow.

Cheryl stayed outside the fence, a few feet away. That was close enough, in her book.

Chapter 5

I t looks like red nose." Drake raised his hands helplessly. "Can't see how that could be. We vaccinated every animal last spring."

"I'm going to take some lab samples, and we'll find out for sure," Oz told him. "Meanwhile, you need to isolate any that look sick."

He walked over to the fence. "Cheryl, I'm going to get my instrument bag. Can you grab a box of latex gloves out of the back, please? And I'll need supplies to take some fluid samples."

When they reached the truck, she began gathering what he needed. Efficient, as always. He called Rick's cell phone, and his friend answered on the first ring.

"Hey, buddy. Looks like IBR, but they vaccinated. Have you got anything that will help?"

"We've got some vaccine on hand, but not enough. If that's what it is, we'll need more."

"Right. I think I'd better take samples from the dead animal and bring it back to look at under the microscope."

"Do you want me to run it in the lab, while you examine the other sick cattle?"

"Might be a good idea. Why don't you stay there and treat any patients who come in? Set up the scope, and I'll send Cheryl back with some samples. You can call me as soon as you're sure what we've got."

"Okay," Rick said. "That's probably the most efficient way to do it."

"Until I know for sure what we're dealing with. . ." He signed off.

Cheryl closed the rear window on the truck cap. "I think I've got everything you need."

"Did you hear what I told Rick?"

"Yes. I'd be happy to take the blood samples back to the office."

"Thanks. I think that's best."

He got his bag from the front of the truck and they walked back to the fence. He went through the gate, and she handed him a pair of gloves over the top. Drake and his helpers had gone to check on the rest of the herd and weed out any showing symptoms. Oz put on his surgical gloves and began taking samples from the dead cow, thinking of other diseases that could cause symptoms similar to those of IBR.

Cheryl put the identifying labels on the vials.

"I'll get a couple more samples from cattle that are showing symptoms."

259

Her brow furrowed, and the corners of her eyes drew down. "Doesn't look good, does it?"

"Nope."

A few minutes later, he laid the last vials in the cooler and shut the lid securely. "Have Rick call me, okay?"

"Sure."

"And pray. They've got three hundred cattle here. If this is a contagious disease, it could devastate them."

Cheryl nodded soberly. "We'll let you know as soon as we can. And I'll be praying every minute."

✣

Cheryl kept busy doing online research while Rick made slides and examined them. The disease they suspected was a nasty one. She kept thinking about how well Oz had handled the situation. She'd enjoyed the chance to watch him in action. He worked quickly and confidently and moved with ease among the cattle. He'd seemed at home on the ranch, in spite of his metropolitan background. She'd misjudged him. Oz could adapt to any situation and enjoy it to the hilt.

After fifteen minutes, she went to the door of the small laboratory near the back of the building.

Rick was still hunched over the microscope. He pulled away from the eyepiece and jotted something in his notebook.

"Got a diagnosis?" she asked.

"Yes. It's IBR all right. Drake must have gotten a bad batch of vaccine." He looked over his shoulder at her. "Guess I'd better call Ozzy." He stood and stretched. "Pull all the vaccine we've got, and I'll order more."

She went to the refrigerator and took out a case of glass vials.

"Hey, Oz," Rick said behind her. "You were right on the money. Can you ask Mr. Drake what drug company he got his vaccine from last spring?" He paused, pacing back and forth in the small room while Cheryl checked for more bottles of the medicine. "McPhail Pharmaceuticals? Does he have the paperwork with the batch number? Great." He leaned over the desk and jotted more notes.

In Cheryl's Internet research, she'd discovered that infectious bovine rhinotracheitis was a virus that caused respiratory infections in cattle. If the Drakes hadn't separated the ill cattle from the healthy ones soon enough, the entire herd could've been affected. Besides breathing difficulties, it could lead to numerous problems including eye infections, spontaneous abortions in cows, and even the brain infection encephalitis.

"Yeah, we'll have to notify the company and see if anyone else has had trouble with that batch of vaccine." Rick ended his phone call and came to look over Cheryl's shoulder. "That's all we've got?"

"Yes. Enough for a hundred and forty doses."

"Well, we'll have to inoculate the entire herd. It won't cure them, but it will keep any that aren't infected from getting the disease. I'd better call some other vets and see if anyone has more vaccine we can borrow."

"Angela and I'll make the calls. You need to get to the Drake ranch with what we've got."

"You sure?"

"Yes. Any vet who's got some will be happy to donate it and will probably come and help you administer it. If I can't find enough in Wasilla, I'll call Anchorage."

"Great. And if the vets don't have it on hand, try some of the other farmers." Rick put his arm around her and gave her shoulders a squeeze. "I knew I was getting a gem when I hired you."

Cheryl smiled at him. "Thanks."

She immediately sat down to phone other veterinary practices in the Wasilla-Palmer area. Within an hour, she and Angela had obtained promises of 180 more doses of the needed vaccine from two local veterinarians. Before sending them to the Drake ranch with the medicine, she had them confirm that their vaccine was not from the same company as that which Drake had used earlier.

She phoned Rick with the news that the other vets had come through for them. "Dr. Kane and a tech from Dr. Rodriquez's office are on the way."

"Terrific."

"How's it going?" she asked. "Can I come help you, or would I just be in the way?"

"Come ahead, if you want to get filthy. I've got forty more doses of vaccine from our batch to administer. Ozzy's treating the six affected animals they've isolated. It's not pretty, but you could mix up disinfectant for him and fetch and carry between the truck and the barn."

Cheryl hurried to gather a few items and pull on her warm outerwear. This time she felt no reservations about joining Rick and Oz at the ranch, though it meant spending a chilly November afternoon waiting on smelly, sick cattle. Was her love of animals expanding to include bovines, or was it the satisfaction she found in helping the veterinarians in the field? She even reflected that it might, after all, have something to do with a certain vet who was out there treating the cattle without regard to his own discomfort. She wouldn't analyze that too deeply.

She drove to the take-out window at a fast-food place on the way and loaded up on coffee and sandwiches. Driving out of town, she marveled at the colors the late November sun painted on the snowy mountains. They were down to about four hours of sunlight each day now, and she loved getting out of the office during the brightest hours.

When she pulled in at the ranch, she could see Rick and Dr. Hilda Kane in the middle of a herd of cattle, confined in a small pen near the barn.

"Hey! How's it going?" she called.

"Not bad," Rick said. "Only about fifty more to go."

"I've got hot coffee and burgers, if you can take a break."

"Don't say that in front of these beef cows," Dr. Kane said with a laugh. "But that sounds good."

"We'll be there in a sec," Rick told Cheryl. "Ozzy's in the barn. He'd probably love to have some black coffee about now."

Cheryl took two of the covered cardboard cups from the holder and carried them into the barn. She found Oz with Mr. Drake, examining a yearling steer. "Hot coffee," she said brightly.

"Oh, bless you, Cheryl." Oz straightened and stripped off one latex glove. "Black?"

"As the mud on your nose. Or is that manure?"

He wiped his nose with his sleeve and reached for the coffee.

Cheryl laughed. "There you go. Would you like some, Mr. Drake?"

"No thanks. My wife's been out twice to tell me my dinner's getting cold."

"Maybe you should go eat," Oz said.

"Maybe I will. You must be hungry, too, Doc."

"I've got sandwiches for him and the others in my car," Cheryl said.

Drake nodded. "All right then, I'll get a bite. You think we're gonna beat this, though, don't you, Doc?"

"I do. We're doing everything we can. When we're done revaccinating, it will be up to you to watch for more affected animals and get them out of the herd as quickly as you can."

"Reckon the boys and I can do that."

"And you can't slaughter any animals for sixty days. Don't forget."

"Don't worry, I won't." Drake headed for the house.

Oz leaned against the wall and sighed. "Coffee never tasted so good. Thanks."

Cheryl smiled up at him. "Do you really think you've stopped the infection?"

"Can't say for sure. Rick's been on the lookout for more symptomatic cattle while he inoculates the herd. We haven't found any new cases for the last hour. But only time will tell. This thing's nasty. It can resurface weeks, months, or even years later." He raised his coffee cup again to drink. Fine lines showed at the corners of his eyes and mouth.

"Tired?" she asked.

"Yeah, and the day's only half over." He shook his head. "Guess my age is catching up to me."

"I've got burgers in the car. They should still be warm."

"Oh, you said the magic word."

They walked outside together. Rick, Dr. Kane, and a young man Cheryl didn't know were washing up in a bucket of water and disinfectant on the tailgate of Rick's pickup.

"Hey, Cheryl," Rick called. "I saw that you'd brought enough lunch for an army, so I invited Hilda and Jerry to join us."

"That was my plan." Cheryl handed out wrapped sandwiches. "Hope everybody likes coffee. I've got extra cream and sugar here if anyone wants it."

"Thanks," said Jerry. "I was just heading out on my lunch hour when Dr. Rodriquez asked if I could come here and bring you some extra vaccine."

"Let's go in the barn," Oz said. "It's quite warm in there."

They found seats inside on hay bales. The temperature felt almost balmy. The three vets and Jerry launched into a discussion of the cattle's prognosis as they ate.

Cheryl sat back and listened, sipping her coffee. She looked up at one point. Oz winked at her.

Her heart lurched. "Very blue eyes," she whispered, so low that no one could hear.

Even so, his eyebrows shot up, and those blue orbs seemed to twinkle.

On the way home, she somehow wound up riding with Oz again. She tried to tell herself that Rick had arranged it, but she and Oz hadn't objected.

Her admiration for "the new guy" had grown today, but her own self-confidence had plunged. The stark differences between her and the man she'd come to admire nagged her.

She hadn't left Alaska for more than twenty years, and she wasn't sure she ever wanted to. But Oz was a world traveler. Educated. Her own high school diploma and one year of college hadn't bothered her before. She'd left school to marry Dan, and when he'd gotten the offer for the Alaska job, they'd gladly left behind all they knew.

But now her low-key, small-town life seemed boring and inadequate compared to Oz's exciting international adventures. She'd loved her family, raised her children, and helped in the family business. A big night out for her was a trip to the huge bookstore in Anchorage. How could someone like Oz find her interesting?

Admitting that she wanted him to find her interesting sobered her.

The sun shone on the glittering landscape as they drove back toward the office. The wind picked up handfuls of loose snow and swirled them across the road to pile up in drifts against the ridges left behind by the snowplow.

"You were a lot of help," Oz said.

"Thanks. You were terrific. I could almost see how you do the polar bear research. I guess it's not that much different from what you did with those cattle today."

"There are some parallels. But you can't just walk up to a bear and stick it with a needle the way you can a steer."

They rode in silence for a few minutes until her curiosity got the better of her. "How do you get close to the polar bears?"

"Usually we fly over and tranquilize them from the air."

"Is that what you'll do when you go to Barrow?"

He nodded. "Yes. In February, if we get a good window on weather, I'll go up for a couple of weeks, and we'll use a helicopter to get out on the edge of the ice sheet. When we see a bear, we'll tranquilize it. Then we'll land and tag it, take samples, and put a radio collar on it. But in the spring, when we concentrate on the denning area, we'll do things differently."

"You told me you want to tag cubs."

"Right. I hope to go when the mamas and babies first come out of their dens. That's my late March trip. I want to tag a significant number of cubs if I can."

"When you put a radio collar on a bear, how long do you follow it?"

"Over its lifetime, if we can. Polar bears can live more than twenty years. But we can't put collars on the little ones. They grow too fast, and the collar would choke one before we could get back and change it. If we make it too loose, the cub slips it off. So we usually collar the mother."

That made sense. "How long do the cubs stay with her?"

"More than two years. Then mama drives them away and starts a new family." Oz pulled into the parking lot.

Cheryl reached for her clipboard and gloves. "I'll call the clients you didn't get around to today and explain."

"Thanks. I'll try to see them all tomorrow." Oz pulled the keys from the ignition. "I've decided I need to get my pilot's license. Is there a flight school in Wasilla?"

Cheryl froze and stared at him. "Do you have to?"

"No, I don't suppose it's really necessary, but it seems the best way to get around this state. I hear Alaska has more licensed pilots per capita than any other state."

"That's true. And fewer miles of roads." She gave a little cough, but the heaviness in her chest didn't budge. Flying was safe, everyone said. Safer than driving a car on Alaska's sorely limited highway system. But the fact that she'd lost Dan in a small plane crash outweighed all the statistics anyone could throw at her. "I...I don't know." She avoided his piercing gaze.

"Well, it's just something I thought might come in handy." Oz kept his tone light and opened his door.

Cheryl jumped out quickly and headed for the office. If Oz had wanted to squelch the possibility of a romance, he'd done it effectively. Saving hundreds of woolly cattle and chasing polar bears with a dart gun she could live with. But she would not lose another man she loved in a plane crash.

Chapter 6

Several weeks later, Oz returned to the office after a long day on the road.

"Hello!" Cheryl turned from the bank of filing cabinets and smiled at him. "Does it feel like the shortest day of the year?"

"Ha! If you go by how tired I am, it's more like the longest."

Twilight had covered the valley three hours ago, and he'd made his last four barn calls in the dark.

"You should go home and rest."

"I will, after I restock my supplies and file my paperwork. Is Rick still here?"

"Yes. Our last patient left about ten minutes ago. Maybe he's writing reports."

Oz ambled down the hall and rapped smartly on the door of Rick's office. "You in there, Richard?"

"Yeah, come on in."

Oz opened the door. Rick was leaning over his desk, with several catalogs spread out on its surface.

"What's up?" Oz asked.

"Cheryl was going to reorder some supplies, and I realized our business has increased dramatically this fall. I'm trying to predict what we'll need over the next quarter. And I'm looking at the prices on those large-animal operating tables, too."

"It would be an extravagance," Oz said. "I think those things are solid gold."

"We'd have the only one in Alaska...." Rick stared off out the window, and his eyes took on a dreamy glaze.

"Quit that." Oz sat down on the corner of his desk. "I can operate on cows and horses where they're lying. Always have. We don't need to lay out umpteen thousand dollars for fancy equipment."

"It would make your job easier."

Oz shrugged. "I do 90 percent of my work in the field. You know that. We don't get racehorses that need tendon surgery in here."

"True." Rick closed one of the catalogs and shoved it aside. "Just dreaming."

"Well, if you're serious about making me a full partner, I'll put it to you straight. Don't spend all our profits on equipment we don't need."

Rick arched his eyebrows. "Of course I want you to be a full partner. Does this mean you've reached a decision? You'll stay?"

Oz ran a hand through his hair. "I don't think I've ever worked so hard in my life as I have here. But I love it. And the people I work with—well, you and Cheryl are the best. I mean that. And so long as you're willing to let me take a few weeks off two or three times a year for research—in addition to my vacation time, of course—then, yes. I can't think of anything I'd like more."

Rick grinned. "Terrific. We feel the same about you, Ozzy. So, can I announce this happy merger at Christmas dinner?"

Oz smiled and lifted a shoulder. "Sure. Why not?"

"We'll make it official after New Year's, if that's okay." Rick closed the rest of the catalogs and stood. "I'll ask the lawyer to draw up an agreement with the terms we discussed."

"Great. Hey, Rick, there's something else I'd like to talk to you about."

"Yeah? What?"

"You know the research trip I'm taking in the spring?"

"Yeah, that's coming right up, isn't it?"

"Well, for the first one, we'll do most of our spotting from a helicopter. But on the second trip—late March—I'll be in a totally different situation. I'm going with several other scientists. We'll be working on different projects for a couple of weeks. Most of the others are geologists. I'm the only biologist on that jaunt, and I'm supposed to bring an assistant to help with my research."

"Ozzy, I'd love to go, but I don't think we can both leave the practice for two weeks."

Oz sat up straighter. "Sorry. I wasn't actually thinking of you."

"Oh. Bummer." Rick laughed. "What were you going to say then?"

"I was thinking. . ." Oz frowned at him. "Is this where I should say, 'Oh, come on, I really need you,' and beg you to go?"

"No, I'm serious. I can't do it. It will be right after the Iditarod, and it's a busy time of year for us. . .lots of animal babies being born."

"Right." Oz hesitated, but there was only one way to get Rick's candid opinion. "I was thinking of asking Cheryl."

Rick sat back down, never taking his eyes from Oz's face. "You're serious."

"Well, sure. I need someone to help me in the field and with the record-keeping and to spot for me. They don't like you to go out alone in such a remote location. Cheryl's been terrific with the domestic animals. I can tell she's worked hard to overcome her"—he paused and groped for a word—"I wouldn't call it fear, but her apprehension toward cattle."

Rick laughed. "She has gotten over a lot of her uneasiness in working with large animals. She still respects them, but she's not afraid to get into a corral with a dozen cows anymore. I credit you with that—hauling her around on so many barn calls."

"She's terrific. I couldn't do without her on a lot of cases." Oz waited, eyeing him thoughtfully.

Rick pulled in a deep breath. "Sure. I guess it's okay. Angela's doing quite well on the desk." He glanced up at Oz. "That's another thing Cheryl's been good at—training her substitute receptionist."

"Yeah, she's good at a lot of things." When he looked back at Rick, Oz couldn't help noticing that his smile reached from ear to ear. "What?"

"Nothing. Need any advice on what to get her for Christmas?"

"Oh man! I meant to order something a couple of weeks ago and I forgot. What do you think I should get her? I've got something on the way for you and Robyn, but..."

"Chocolate's good." Rick shoved up out of his chair. "And speaking of my beautiful wife, I'm heading home. How about you?"

"I'm going to stay a little while and do some paperwork. But maybe I'd better think about going to Anchorage tomorrow night and doing some shopping."

"Candy...books...flowers..."

Oz scowled at him. "Flowers? Are you nuts? That's not a Christmas gift. What are you getting her?"

"Robyn picked out a bracelet and a quiviet shawl."

"Ah. And for Robyn?"

"A new stud dog for her breeding kennel."

"Oh. Guess that's not something Cheryl would want."

Rick laughed. "I don't think so. A little pricey for a coworker, too. But if you're serious about taking her to the North Slope, you might consider a snowsuit. I'm not sure if she has a good one. I can ask Robyn if you like."

Oz stood and picked up his clipboard. "Maybe I should see if she's interested in going first."

"Yeah. Whatever." Rick nodded and strode toward the door. "See you in the a.m."

Oz went to his office, thinking over the conversation. Chocolate? Cheryl rarely ate sweets, as far as he knew. Books? Maybe a cookbook or something on gardening. He'd learned she liked those activities.

He could hear her moving about in the waiting room. Was she really the right person to take along on the research trip, or was his attraction to her coloring his decision? Maybe he should ask for a university student or another veterinarian—someone with more scientific training.

A rustle at the doorway made him turn. She stood there smiling, wearing her rose-colored sweater and black slacks. Her vibrant expression, as usual, made him feel as though he belonged here.

Would he regret coming to a place where he felt accepted as part of the family? Forming a closer bond with Rick, whom he loved like a younger brother? Caring about Cheryl and Robyn and Grandpa as though they belonged to him, too?

"I'm going home, Oz. Can you lock up when you leave?"

"Sure."

"Is there anything I can get you before I go?"

"No, but..."

She waited, her eyebrows arched and an expectancy lighting her expression.

"Uh. . .I was wondering." He swallowed hard. Maybe he'd better spend some more time with her and get a better feel for her commitment to the job. He didn' want to ask her now and regret it later. After all, he'd only known her for a couple of months.

"Yes?"

What sort of outing could they enjoy together? He stood and walked toward her. "Do you ski?"

"Not much. I've been cross-country skiing several times, but if you mean the alpine kind, it's not my forte."

"Ah." Chuck that idea. She probably didn't want to hear about his past weekends at Aspen and Sun Valley anyway. "Well, I've had several mushing lessons, and I wondered if you'd like to go sledding with me Saturday. Robyn said she'd loan me a team anytime, and I'm sure she'd do the same for her mother."

Cheryl sobered and looked away. He thought for a moment she'd refuse. When she turned her gaze back to him, her smile had changed. It was smaller and softer now. Almost shy, like that first day when she'd had lunch with him on the way here from the airport. "That sounds like a lot of fun."

He looked down at her for a long moment. He'd asked her for a date. An employee. His best friend and almost-partner's mother-in-law. Was he nuts? Gazing into her shimmery brown eyes, he felt very sane. "Great. I'll fix it with Robyn."

"Of course that's Christmas Eve, but if we go early. . ."

"Yes. We'll want to take advantage of the daylight, such as it is." He flicked an involuntary gaze toward the window. Full darkness cloaked the gorgeous view of the mountains.

She nodded, her smile back to the bigger one she greeted patients with. "All right then. Thanks for asking me, and I'll see you tomorrow."

She left, and he let out a long, slow breath. Was this what he wanted? Somehow he felt that Rick and Robyn wouldn't object. In fact, Rick would probably jump for joy when he heard the news. But what if Oz decided after one date that he didn' want to pursue a deeper relationship with Cheryl? Would the entire Holland family hate him? The thought of disappointing Cheryl troubled him.

And yet. . .what if it worked? What if this was God's will in bringing him here? Oz felt a little guilty. He hadn't prayed before he'd asked her. Maybe this was all a mistake.

He sat down in his desk chair with a thud. He admitted he was attracted to Cheryl. What was not to like? But it might be a mistake to get romantic too soon. Or to let her think of romance. Better not give her anything personal for Christmas. Books, like Rick had suggested. That was the ticket. And he'd keep it on a strictly friendly basis Saturday.

Now that he'd asked her out, would it be difficult to separate business and pleasure with Cheryl? If he asked her to go on the polar bear research trip, that had to be business only. But that was three months away. What if they'd decided by then that they didn't like each other all that much?

He leaned back and put his feet up on the desk, careful to set his heels on the blotter, not the shiny walnut surface. Asking Cheryl out felt right, the way driving a truck and burning wood at his cabin felt right. He'd lived under primitive circumstances before, but only for a couple of weeks at a time. He liked Alaska, and the decision to stay and go partners with Rick was another thing that felt right.

He couldn't imagine winding up in an uncomfortable situation. But it could happen if he and Cheryl started something and then one of them backed off. They could end up miserable and having to work together every day. He hated that idea. But then, he'd never seriously considered getting deeply involved with a woman again. Maybe he should follow his original plan and keep it friends only. Things hadn't escalated too far for that.

Still, he hadn't felt this content since before Jo died, more than ten years ago. Even then, he'd been unhappy in his career. He was ready to settle down again, as incredible as that may seem. His restlessness and eagerness to move on to the next project had waned, and he wanted to stay here. Yes, he still got excited when he thought about his research, but he'd also have Wasilla to come home to when it was done. That thought sent a warm glow all through him. He'd found home.

Lord, give me wisdom where Cheryl is concerned, along with the business and everything else in my life.

There. If he kept that attitude foremost in his mind, he wouldn't let his emotions get out of hand. He lowered his feet to the floor and opened the folder of notes he'd made at his barn calls.

Chapter 7

Driving a team of four huskies full of energy, Cheryl followed Oz's sled along the trail. She'd driven this route dozens of times in the past. She used to exercise teams regularly when Dan was alive, but she rarely went sledding anymore. Robyn and Grandpa Steve had taken over the kennel after Dan died, and she'd divided her time between her outside jobs and maintaining the home.

It felt good to be out in the crisp air. The temperature had climbed to thirty degrees, and with the sun shining down the valley, it felt almost warm. She lowered the zipper on the front of her parka halfway to let some air in.

Ahead of her, Oz approached a bend in the trail on the hillside above Rick and Robyn's log home. When they rounded the curve, they'd be able to look down on the veterinary clinic.

"Gee," Oz called to his dogs.

Cheryl didn't pay attention at first, but when he yelled, "Gee!" louder and a bit perturbed, she snapped her gaze forward.

"I mean *haw*," Oz called. "Haw! Oh, rats!"

The dogs had swerved off the trail to the right, and the sled bounced up over a ridge of snow. Oz flew off the back, his arms flailing, and landed in eighteen inches of powder. The dog team continued on, curving around downhill, toward the clinic.

If the dogs hadn't been loose, Cheryl would have stopped to laugh and pull Oz out of the snow. Instead, she steered her own team after his, calling, "Whoooooa Tumble! Whoa, boy!"

She trailed his team for a hundred yards, calling all the time to the leaders, until Tumble, Robyn's prize breeding male, usually very savvy on the trail, slowed to a walk then stopped. The rest of the team followed his example.

"Stay, Tumble," Cheryl called as her own team pulled alongside them. Tumble stood obediently. Cheryl set the snow hook on her own sled then plodded through the loose fluff to Oz's rig and took his hook from where it hung below the handlebar. She pushed it into the snow then stepped on it firmly with one foot. "Hike."

The two leaders—Tumble and his harness mate, Keet—stepped forward a little, and the other dogs followed, pulling the towline taut. "Good boy," Cheryl called. "Line out."

Tumble lay down in the snow, and the rest of the team copied him.

"What can I say? I don't know my right from my left."

270

She turned around.

Oz slogged through the snow toward her. Tufts of snow clung to his hat and beard. His sheepish smile warmed her.

"More likely you don't know your gee from your haw. I can help you with that."

"Oh? You mean there's hope for me?"

"Definitely. We did it for Robyn when she was about five years old, and it worked like a charm."

"What's that?"

"I took a permanent marker and wrote a *G* on the back of her right glove and an *H* on the left one. On each side of her handlebar, too. I don't think she ever made that mistake again."

"I hate to admit it, but I think I need it until my brain adjusts to the new terminology."

She nodded, trying to keep her expression neutral, but a laugh burbled up from deep inside her. She tried to swallow it, but she couldn't. It burst out as a whoop. "You sure did look funny, flying off into the snow."

Oz grinned. "I'm glad I provided so much entertainment. And thanks for stopping my team."

"You're welcome. They probably would have just gone home, but you never know. They might have run out into the road, looking for a shortcut."

He eyed the placid dogs thoughtfully. "It still seems like I ought to have reins or something."

"Nope. Just your voice. That and the dogs' training are all you've got to control them with."

"Gives me a new appreciation for the people who trained them. . .and for the dogs. Especially the dogs."

"They're awesome. Very intelligent. My advice is to give each a kibble, and we'll head for home. How does hot chocolate sound?"

"Great, if you have time."

"Sure. The kids aren't coming over until suppertime. I know the sun's going down, but we've got a couple of hours. Let's go put these mutts away and sit by the fireplace for a while."

The glint in his blue eyes set her stomach fluttering. She wouldn't have admitted it to anyone, but for two days she'd been thinking about what would happen after their sled run. Oz and a mug of cocoa in front of a snapping log fire. Of course, Grandpa would be there, too. Elderly in-laws were almost as good at killing romance as children. But Oz had opted to spend the entire day with her. At suppertime, Rick and Robyn would join them, and they'd celebrate Christmas together. Oz spending the holiday with her and the family meant something—how much, Cheryl wasn't sure yet.

"You ready?" she asked, ignoring how cute Oz looked with little icicles in his dark beard.

"I think so." He went to the back of his sled and stood with one foot on the brake and the other on the runner nearest his snow hook.

Cheryl stood on her sled's brake and leaned down to pull her hook from the snow. They wended homeward through the sparse woods with her team leading. She stopped them a quarter mile from the dog yard and pointed. Oz's team halted behind hers. They stood for a moment, gazing out over the valley as the rays of the sun hit the distant mountain peaks, scattering scarlet, orange, and purple shadows across the summits.

Cheryl hauled in a deep breath and zipped up her parka. *Thank You, Lord. That is one gorgeous sunset.* She turned forward and called, "Hike!" Her leaders bounded forward, toward home.

⁜

As the dog teams trotted into their home yard, Robyn came from the small barn. Darby Zale, the teenager who helped her with kennel chores, watched them from inside the puppy pen.

"Whoa," Oz called, and this time his dogs obliged him by stopping neatly, with the leaders' noses a couple of yards behind Cheryl's sled runners.

"How was your run?" Robyn asked, approaching his team.

"Great." Oz took care to set the snow hook correctly before he stepped off the back of the sled.

"We had a fantastic view of the sunset," Cheryl said.

Oz walked forward to unhook the leaders. Robyn was already unclipping Tumble, and Darby helped Cheryl with her team.

"You don't have to do that, Robyn," he said. "Your mom and I had all the fun. We can put away our dogs and equipment."

"I don't mind."

He wondered if she was evaluating the dogs to see if he'd run them too hard. He glanced over at Cheryl. She grinned at him as she walked with one of her dogs toward the pen where Robyn housed all her grown female dogs. Cheryl could have gotten some laughs by telling how he'd messed up his commands and tumbled into the snow, but she didn't. He appreciated that. He'd have laughed it off if she did tell the story, but somehow it made him like her more that she protected his fragile male ego. Maybe after a day or two, he'd tell the tale himself, but right now his elbow still smarted from the landing, and he'd rather choose the moment when the memory wasn't so fresh. He passed Robyn on his way into the male dogs' pen with Keet.

"Hey, Mom," she called, "after Darby and I feed the dogs, I'm going to take Grandpa over to our house for a little while."

Cheryl paused after hitching the gate to the other pen. "You don't need to do that."

Oz noted her dismay. Was she upset that Robyn was attempting to leave them alone for a while?

"I want to show him something. We won't be gone long." Robyn looked at her watch. "In fact, by the time we feed the dogs, I'll only have about an hour before Rick and I are due here for supper and the Christmas tree."

"Well, get to it then," Cheryl said. "Ozzy and I can put the sleds away."

Robyn and Darby hustled about the yard as he and Cheryl finished putting away the teams and hung the harnesses in the little barn. Floodlights illuminated the dog yard, and the two young women efficiently distributed dog food, meat, and fresh water to the forty-odd dogs currently in Robyn's care.

Cheryl showed him where to stow his light sled, and they left the barn together. "How about that hot chocolate?" she asked. "I need to check the stew, too, but I'm ready to relax for a few minutes."

"Sounds good." He followed her in through the back door of the house. He'd only been here a couple of times, with Rick. The kitchen smelled great, and it looked more modern and better equipped than the one in his cabin.

Grandpa Steve stood in the dining room doorway. "There you are, Cheryl. Did Robby tell you I'm going over to her place with her?"

"Yes, she did."

"Did she tell you why?"

"No." Cheryl eyed him as she might a toddler who never ceased asking questions. "Why are you going?"

"To get your Christmas present." Grandpa's face beamed. "Robby's been hiding it for me for almost a month over there."

Cheryl laughed. "And here I thought you'd forgotten to get me anything."

"Oh no. Never." Steve turned to Oz, still grinning. "She's a good girl, but it's hard to keep secrets from her. She cleans everything, so I have to find ways to hide stuff I don't want her to see. How you been, Doc?" He held out his hand, and Oz shook it, laughing.

"Great. Sounds like you've found a good solution to hiding presents. How are you doing, Mr. Holland?"

"Steve. Call me Steve. I'm doing good."

Cheryl lifted the lid of a Crock-Pot, which sent a mouthwatering wave of steam billowing. "We're going to have some cocoa, Dad. Do you want to join us?"

"Is there time, before Robyn's ready to go?"

"I think so. I'll make sure it's not too hot, so you can drink it quicker." She bustled about, setting out mugs and powdered hot chocolate mix.

"Can I help with anything?" Oz asked.

"No thanks. I'm all set. Why don't you and Dad go sit in the living room? Oh, if he doesn't have the fire going, you can start that."

Oz followed the old man through the dining room. The table was set with gleaming china. A brass bowl in the middle held huge pinecones and red Christmas tree balls. In the living room, a plump Christmas tree stood sentinel over a mound of wrapped packages near the wall opposite the fireplace.

"Have a seat." Steve centered himself before an armchair and sank slowly into it. A blaze flickered low on the hearth. "Mind if I add a couple of sticks?" Oz asked.

"Go right ahead, young man."

Oz bent to pick two short logs from the woodbox. "Did you build this house, sir?"

"What? Oh no. Danny and I bought it when we first came here. A family had it, but they were pulling up stakes. Danny and Cheryl had Aven. That's Robyn's brother. Robby was born here. Well, not here. At the hospital in Anchorage. But we've been here more than twenty-five years."

Oz stirred the half-burned wood and added his logs then took a seat nearby. "That's a long time. Any regrets?"

"Not a one. Well, of course I could wish that my wife had lived to come up here with us, or that Danny had survived the—" Steve broke off and waved one hand. "That's in the past. No, I don't have any regrets. This is a good place to live and raise kids. Dogs, too."

Cheryl came in carrying a tray. She stopped before Steve. "There you go. Take your 'Grandpa' mug."

Steve laughed and reached for it. "Aven gave me this at Christmas about twenty years ago. I'm amazed I haven't broken it yet."

They sat chatting and sipping their chocolate. The firelight glinted off Cheryl's short brown curls. In the soft lighting, she looked younger than her fifty-plus years.

"So far I feel pretty good this year," Steve said. "Now, last year, that was a different story. They thought I'd had it."

"Oh, Dad, that's not true." Cheryl shook her head and turned to Oz. "He did give us a scare last year, but he's been doing very well. I'm proud of the way he's helped Robyn with the dogs this fall." She looked back at her father-in-law. "You've made a lot of progress. Getting out and exercising has a lot to do with that. I'm so glad you're feeling well."

"I wouldn't say I always feel well," Steve cautioned. "I've got some arthritis, for sure. But I can still get around with a bucket of dog chow, and on a good day I can buckle a harness strap. Thank God for modern medicine."

"I don't know how the pioneers did it," Oz said.

"Isn't that the truth." Steve sipped his cocoa.

Robyn entered through the kitchen. "Hey, Grandpa, are you ready to go? The dogs are all settled for the night, and Darby's gone home."

"I'm ready." Steve set his mug aside and reached for her hand. He let out a low groan as Robyn helped pull him up out of his chair.

Oz stood, too.

"We ought to get you one of those chairs that lifts you up," Robyn said to her grandfather.

"No, don't." Cheryl frowned at her over her mug. "The more he does on his own, the better. If you make it too easy for him, he won't be able to do anything."

"Oh, you're cruel," Steve said, leaning on Robyn's arm as he shuffled toward the coat closet. "You'll make me keep working in the kennel till I can't get out of bed."

Having just heard him claim he was still good for a day's work, Oz laughed at the old man's play for sympathy.

"Ha!" Cheryl said. "We couldn't keep you out of the dog yard if we wanted to."

"Mom's right. And I couldn't get along without you." Robyn took his jacket from the closet and held it for him.

"I'll expect you two and Rick back here in an hour or so," Cheryl said.

When Robyn and Steve had left, they sat in silence for a moment.

"I understand your son and his family will arrive tomorrow," Oz said.

"Yes. Aven could only squeeze out two days, but they're coming." Cheryl's smile lit her whole face. "I can't wait to hold my little grandson again."

"Will I see them at church?"

"I doubt they'll arrive until noon or later, but you'll join us for dinner, won't you?"

"Oh, I don't want to intrude. You were gracious to include me in your family time tonight, but—"

"No buts, Oswald. You're far from home, and we want you with us."

He laughed at her unexpected use of his first name.

She leaned forward and scowled at him as she had her father-in-law. "Unless you have plans elsewhere, we'll expect you here."

"All right, I give up. I'm sure there won't be a finer table spread in Wasilla."

She relaxed and sank back in her chair. "It will be informal, but I think I can guarantee good food and fellowship."

"What more could a man ask?" He caught her gaze, and they sat looking at each other for a long moment. The fire snapped.

"What about your family, Oz? I know your parents are gone. Don't you have siblings?"

He shook his head. "I had a brother, but he died when..." He cleared his throat, suddenly fighting tears. "He died in a motorcycle wreck when he was twenty-five."

"I'm so sorry."

They slid into silence again, watching the fire. Was this the time to tell her about Jo? Maybe not. Things had already gone mournful, and he wasn't comfortable with that. Besides, Rick had probably clued her in already that he'd lost his wife. She'd never asked, which made him think she knew at least the basics. He didn't want to discuss it now. Time spent with Cheryl should be full of peace and contentment, with a spark of hope.

After a minute, he stirred. "Let's not get all gloomy. This is going to be a wonderful holiday."

She reached for her mug. "Yes. I've been blessed, seeing my children start their families. And Dad—he's really come a great way since last year. I'm so thankful."

"Cheryl. . ."

"Yes?" She looked at him, a tentative smile hovering at her lips.

"I had a lot of fun today."

"So did I."

"I wondered. . ." He paused then shrugged off his own reservations. "I wondered if you would consider going on the trip with me in March. The one where we'll use ground transportation and tag the bear cubs."

Her jaw dropped. She sat staring at him, holding her mug in both hands.

"Me? You're asking *me*?"

"Yes."

"But. . .I am *so* not qualified."

"I think you are."

"Didn't you tell me that all the other people on the trip will be scientists?"

"Yes, but—"

"Are they bringing along secretaries?"

"Uh. . ." He gritted his teeth. "I don't know. Probably not."

She shifted in her chair and set the mug down. "Wouldn't you rather have another vet along? Someone who knows about bear biology and habitat and all that?"

"No."

That silenced her. His face suddenly warmed, more so than he could account for from the heat of the fire or his beard. "I'm not sure exactly who is going, other than Michael Torrence and Annette Striker. They're geologists. I met them on my Russian trip. Their job will be taking core samples from the ice sheet."

"Annette? So, there'll be at least one other woman along."

"Yes. I wouldn't ask you to go if it were all men."

"But why? Why me and not some grad student or another zoologist?"

"Because I think you'd be an asset to my project. We work well together, and you've already shown you're willing to save my bacon if I fall into a snowbank."

She chuckled, and a knot in his chest unraveled.

"I just don't know what to say. I feel so inadequate."

"Think about it." He sat forward and held her gaze. "I need someone else with me—it's a two-person job. It's true I could ask for someone from the university or the big veterinary hospital where Rick used to work in Anchorage. There are probably a dozen qualified people who'd jump at the chance to go. If you decide you really don't want to, I'll start putting out feelers. But I'd rather take someone who understands the way I work and who can read my handwriting."

She laughed again. The battle was nearly won.

He said quickly, "Besides, if you say no, my Christmas gift is wasted."

"What? You're crazy! What Christmas gift are you talking about?"

"It's out in my truck."

"Well." She eyed him pensively. "I guess it's a good thing I got you something."

They both laughed, and it felt good to share the moment with her—a moment that held no sadness, only satisfaction and a bit of speculation. The trip would be business, but it would also be a test of their friendship. Could she see that? He thought she could.

Cheryl's eyes narrowed suddenly and she stood. "Come on into the kitchen. I need to put the biscuits in the oven." He followed her, carrying their empty mugs, and leaned on the counter, watching her work.

She washed her hands and deftly combined the flour, shortening, milk, and baking powder into a spongy dough. She flopped it out of the bowl and kneaded it rhythmically on a butcher block. "How are you doing with the light deprivation?" she asked.

He looked up from her hands into her eyes. "Good. At least, I think so. Getting out in the sunlight helps. Like today. I didn't feel at all depressed, if you don't count the moment I realized I'd let my dog team get away."

"There's hope for you then."

How big a role did Cheryl play in his lack of melancholia? Quite a lot, unless he was mistaken. "Of course, the winter is young. What about you? Do you feel blue in the winter?"

"Sometimes." She gave a little laugh and tossed her head. "But then, sometimes I get that way in summer, too, so it's probably not Seasonal Affective Disorder."

"That's understandable. You've been through a lot."

She pressed her lips together and avoided his gaze while she patted the dough into a thick round on her breadboard. She opened a drawer beneath the counter and took out a biscuit cutter. Swiftly she cut a dozen circles from the dough and popped them into a pan. When she lifted the pan and held it out, Oz straightened. "Would you please put this in the oven?" She looked up at him. Her eyes glistened.

And he'd been so determined not to let past griefs color their day. "Cheryl, I'm sorry if I—"

"I'm okay."

He nodded and took the pan of biscuits. The oven was already hot, and he slid it in, onto the rack in the center, and closed the door.

Behind him, she said, "I just. . .you know. Sometimes I think about Dan. Holidays are hard. But I'm thankful for what God has given me. For a while, I wasn't sure Robyn and Dad and I could stay here. Things were tight after the insurance money ran out. But you know, God never forgets His children."

Oz stepped over close to her. "That's true. I'm glad you've felt His care."

She nodded and ducked her head again as she shaped the remaining dough. "I shouldn't have brought it up. No sense going into the sad widow mode and bringing you into the morass."

He sucked in a deep breath. "Look, since we're being frank, there's something you should know. I don't really want to tell you, because I pictured this day as a happy time, without any gloom and doom. But if we're going to. . . Well, I guess I should lay everything on the table."

She raised her eyebrows, her hands still on the dough. "You don't have to tell me anything."

"I. . ." He'd almost said, "I want to," but that wasn't true. If his conscience would let him, he'd never tell her. But the time seemed right, and he knew he'd feel guilty if he didn't. "It's just a matter of record. I wasn't totally honest about why I changed careers. I was married. For two years. Way back, before I knew Rick."

Silence hung between them for about five seconds.

Cheryl picked up her biscuit cutter. "I knew you'd been married, but. . . Okay. Why did you go to vet school?"

"It's true I'd always wanted to be a veterinarian. But Jo—my wife—served on the police force in Buffalo, and she was killed while she was on duty. I. . .decided to get out of the line I was in. I couldn't take it anymore, going into the jail every day and seeing men there who'd committed crimes and felt no remorse whatsoever. Before Jo's death, I was able to keep it in perspective, but when I became a victim. . ." He sighed. "I took some time off, and then I decided to go back to school."

"I'm so sorry."

He nodded, not looking at her.

She wiped her floury hands on a dish towel and touched his arm. "Ozzy. . ."

He swallowed hard and turned his gaze on her troubled face.

"Are you sure you're ready. . . ? I mean, it's not like we've been dating or anything, but—"

"Today was a date. Wasn't it? It was for me."

She nodded slowly. "Yes, it was for me, too. My first date in thirty years. But if you'd prefer not to think of it that way. . ."

His throat ached, and he moved turtle-like to cover her hand with his. "I do want to think of it that way. It's been more than ten years since she died. It's been tough, but yes, I'm ready to move on. What about you? It wasn't so long ago that Dan died."

"No. Four years is all. It seems like yesterday. And a hundred years ago."

He wanted to pull her into his arms, but he held back. Better to go slowly and prayerfully. Instead of rushing into something they'd both regret later, maybe they could ease their friendship into something stronger. He squeezed her hand and released it. "I know exactly what you mean. Thank you."

She sniffed. "I actually feel better, now that we've talked about it."

Oz was able to smile then. "I do, too."

While she cleaned up the counter, he slipped out to his truck and retrieved the packages he'd prepared for the family and slid them under the Christmas tree. He'd either settled on the perfect thing for Cheryl or a hopelessly wrong thing.

A few minutes later, Rick, Robyn, and Steve breezed in, and they sat down to supper. During the blessing, Oz once again felt a part of the family circle as Steve and Cheryl gripped his hands. They all included him in the conversation and told him some of their holiday traditions. But when they gathered about the tree, Oz began to feel out of place. He should have begged off.

The gifts that the Bakers and Hollands presented to each other were not extravagant, other than the new dog Rick had purchased for Robyn. He brought it in from the kennel with a huge red bow about its neck.

After they'd all exclaimed over its fine points, however, Cheryl banished it to the dog yard. "Huskies are not house dogs."

"Okay, Mom." Robyn took it out with good grace and returned to distribute more gifts.

Grandpa seemed pleased with the box of dried fruit Oz had ordered for him, and Cheryl obviously loved the new food processor she found in Steve's package for her.

Oz opened a small gift box from Cheryl and discovered a high-quality compass inside. He assured her it would come in handy on his dog sled runs and snowmobile trips. He tucked it into his pocket, knowing it would travel with him to the North Slope, even if she didn't. Rick and Robyn gave him a wool sweater with Native Alaskan designs knit in. From Steve he received a book on Alaskan history.

Rick handed Oz's package to Cheryl. He found himself holding his breath.

She carefully removed the paper and smiled. "Thank you. This seems significant." She held up the two books on polar bear habitat and anatomy so the others could see them.

He longed to explain his reasoning to her and tell her that they were readable yet scholarly treatments and that he didn't want to pressure her, but he thought she'd love the experience if she went.

Instead he just sat there, watching her face. The smile never quite left her mouth as she showed the books around. When she handed them to Rick for a moment, she looked over at Oz. She nodded slowly, thoughtfully, gazing into his eyes.

"Thanks." She only mouthed it, but he gathered in the single word and hoarded it. She liked his choice. And she was thinking about going with him.

He exhaled and winked at her. Cheryl laughed like a giddy bobby-soxer, and Oz knew irrevocably—he would never again leave Alaska for long. He was staying. Oh yes, this was home.

Chapter 8

There's a wolf down there on top of the mountain." The flight instructor, Clyde Hart, pointed out the side window of the plane. "Bank around so you can see him."

"Uh...okay." Oz thought about what the simple maneuver entailed. It was only his third lesson in the dual-control Cessna, but he loved the freedom he felt soaring above the frozen landscape. They'd flown up the Knik Glacier and were heading back to the Palmer airport now, where Clyde kept his plane.

Half a minute later, Oz had turned and headed back over the rocky mountaintop. The barren summit was covered with snow, except where outcroppings of rock thrust upward. The dark animal stood out in stark relief, trotting across the white expanse.

Oz had seen wolves before, on his Siberian and Canadian research trips, but usually in clusters around a kill. He'd never seen one traveling alone in the wild before. "Cool. So, what now?"

"We'd better get home before it gets dark," Clyde said. "Unfortunately, this time of year flying hours are limited."

"When can we go up again?" Oz asked. He banked again and spotted Pioneer Peak off to his left. Palmer straight ahead. Now that the Hollands' mid-January sled dog race was over, he had his Saturdays free.

"How about next week, same time, if the weather's okay? We'll be able to stay up a little longer."

Oz nodded. "Good. I'll call you the day before to confirm."

He radioed in to the small airport. Another plane had just landed, but there was no other incoming traffic at the moment. His heart thudded as he squared up for the runway. This was always the scariest part. The adrenaline spurted every time he got ready to land.

"Relax," Clyde said. "You're doing great. Check your rpm's."

Oz eased the throttle back and moved the yoke forward a little to keep the air speed above a stall. His gaze darted over the controls. Everything right? He could still power up and go around. No, it looked good. He nosed up just a hair to drop the speed and held the plane straight, holding his breath. The wheels hit the runway all at once and he exhaled.

"Perfect." Clyde slapped his shoulder. "Just like a surgeon. I find you medical guys are all precise. Everything's just so on the landing or you abort and try again."

Oz applied the brakes as the Cessna rolled down the runway.

"Next time we'll do some touch-and-go landings," Clyde said. "After you've done a bunch of those, you won't be so nervous coming in."

"If you say so. I love flying. I just hate landing."

"That's going to keep you super careful. When you've got twenty hours or so under your belt, you'll stop dreading the landing and be able to enjoy the ride more."

On the drive from Palmer back to Wasilla, Oz turned his truck's headlights on. A rim of pink still iced the mountains in the west. He put on his headset and called Cheryl. "Hey, it's Oz. Any messages for me today?"

"No emergencies. Cathy Sennett would like you to call her about her quarter horse's leg."

"Something wrong? I thought he was getting better."

"I don't think so, but she needs reassurance."

Oz glanced at his watch. "Maybe I can run out there now and take a quick look. I told her he'll need a couple of weeks of rest though. I hope she hasn't ridden him yet."

"Okay. And I scheduled two barn calls for you on Monday morning. I put them into the computer."

"Great. You should be relaxing on Saturday. Sounds like you're working as hard at home as you would in the office."

"It's okay." Cheryl hesitated. "How did your lesson go?"

"Terrific. We flew up the glacier, and we saw a wolf. We're going to practice more landings next week. Not my favorite part, but arguably the most important."

"Right. Well, I'll see you in church tomorrow."

Oz signed off, thinking that her voice sounded small and compressed. Maybe she was tired. He'd have to talk to Rick about Cheryl's extra work. Clients shouldn't be calling her at home. Maybe they could route the veterinary office's phone line to his or Rick's cell phone on weekends. That would keep Cheryl from feeling she had to keep working 24/7.

※

Cheryl sat for a long time at her desk on the evening of Friday, February 24, reconciling her bank statement and going over the financial records for Robyn's kennel business. The hoopla of the Fire & Ice race, sponsored by Holland Kennel each year, was a month behind them, and Robyn had paid off the last of the bills related to the event. Cheryl had kept the books for the business since the family started it. Maybe it was time Robyn took over or hired the accountant Rick used for the veterinary practice.

The back door opened. She felt the cold draft as Robyn and her grandfather came in from the dog yard.

"Do you want some coffee?" she called.

"Not me." Steve hobbled into the living room. "I'm beat. Think I'll lie down and watch a little TV."

"Are you all right?"

"Did I say I wasn't?" He kept going down the hall.

Cheryl watched his gait critically then swiveled to look at Robyn. "Is he really okay?"

"I think so. Just tired. He helped me clean out the dog pens. I mean, he really helped, not just supervised."

"Aha. Then it's probably just as well if he goes to bed early." Cheryl stood and stretched. "I finished going over your accounts. You did well on the race this year." She handed Robyn her open ledger. "Here's your bottom line. Not bad."

"Super. We had the biggest field ever for the Fire & Ice, and a lot of people entered the short races, too. More sponsors and vendors than ever before." Robyn sat down on the arm of the sofa. "Thanks for doing that, Mom. It's a big help."

"I was thinking maybe you should ask David Hill to do your books. You've got him preparing your tax returns anyway. Your business is solidly in the black. I think you can afford it."

Robyn cocked her head to one side. "I suppose you're right. Like Grandpa, I'm slow to make changes."

"Only in some things. The changes you've made in the breeding end of the business are good ones. And I just thought that, since I'm working full-time now, it might be a good time to make the transition."

"I'll talk to Rick about it. And, Mom, I appreciate all the work you've put in over the years."

"I know you do, honey." Cheryl slipped into the recliner opposite her.

"So...Ozzy's leaving Monday for his research trip."

"Yes. He's looking forward to it." Cheryl tried not to let her dismay show on her face.

"Are you upset that he's leaving? He'll only be gone two weeks."

"No. This is part of why he came here. They hope to catch and tag a lot of polar bears. It's just..."

"What, Mom?" Robyn leaned toward her, frowning. "I know you and Oz have gotten close."

"We're good friends," Cheryl said quickly.

"Sure. We'll all miss him." Robyn eyed her speculatively. "Mom, you care about him a lot, don't you?"

Cheryl licked her dry lips. It seemed a bit strange to have her daughter questioning her as to where her affections lay. But she'd always been open with Robyn, and being coy wouldn't help.

Her potential romance with Oz had seemed to stall for a few weeks after Christmas, in the whirl of preparations for the Fire & Ice. Oz had pitched in to help like a member of the family, but they hadn't had much quiet time together. He'd taken her out to dinner once since, but when all was said and done, their relationship hadn't progressed much. Now he was working toward his pilot's license. As the daylight hours increased, it seemed he spent every spare hour with his flight instructor.

"Yes, I do. I guess that's why I'm a little on edge."

Robyn's dark eyes focused on her sharply. "It's because he's flying to Barrow, isn't it? Not that he's going away, but that he's *flying* away. Like Dad did."

Cheryl's stomach twisted. "Honey, you mustn't say a word." Tears sprang to her eyes and colored her voice.

Robyn rose and stepped over to her chair. She stooped and slid her arm around her mother's shoulders. "It's going to be okay, Mom," she whispered.

Cheryl nodded and waved her hand helplessly. "I know. I feel so silly. Because I *do* trust God."

"He'll protect Ozzy."

"Yes."

Robyn hesitated then went to her knees on the braided rug beside the chair. "Mom, I know it's hard, but we need to remember, even if something happens, God is still in control."

Cheryl nodded and squeezed her hand. "I know. It's just remembering that night. Waiting and not knowing. And getting the call." Her tears splashed down her cheeks. "I try not to worry when he's having a flight lesson. In fact, I've purposely avoided knowing exactly when he's having them."

"But having his license will be a big help to him. He likes flying, and he'll be able to get around so much easier. Of course, he won't be the one flying the plane on his research trip."

"No, but then your father wasn't the pilot when his plane went down either." Cheryl clenched her hands. "I'm not sure I could take it if Oz's plane went down. And once they get to Barrow, they're going to take a helicopter out every day, if the weather allows it. Every single day."

Robyn's wan smile didn't reassure her. "I know. I guess it's a good thing Oz asked you to go on the later trip, not this one. You'll have to fly up there with him, but you'll be using snow machines once you get there, not a helicopter."

Cheryl shook her head. "I don't think it would worry me as much if I were with him. If he went down, so would I. And I wouldn't be back here wondering."

Robyn drew back and raised her eyebrows. "What? You're not afraid to fly, but you're afraid to let someone you love get in an aircraft? That doesn't make sense."

"When have I ever made sense?"

"Aw, come on. You're very efficient and practical. Rick says you're the best office manager he's ever known."

Cheryl managed a shaky smile. "It was wonderful of him and Oz to raise my wages at the first of the year. But I'll still worry about Oz doing all that flying, I'm afraid. And it'll be worse when he gets his pilot's license."

Robyn chuckled. "Mom, think about it. This isn't going away. What are you going to do if he buys his own airplane?"

"Do you think he will? He and Rick aren't clearing that much in the practice yet, are they?"

"I know they turned a solid profit for the year. Business is good."

"I'm glad for them. But. . .how would you feel if Rick bought a plane and started flying all the time?"

Robyn sobered. "I'm not sure. But the first thing I'd do would be to tell him if it bothered me. I'd talk out with him what happened to Dad and how it scares me a little to think. . .to think I could lose him that way, too."

"You're reading my mind, aren't you?" Cheryl studied her and reached to brush back a strand of her daughter's dark hair. "You look like your father, but you're so like me inside. I'm sorry about that."

"Don't be. I admire you. You've got spunk."

"Thanks. I think. But you're stronger than I am. Tougher."

Robyn inhaled deeply. "You really ought to tell Ozzy how you feel about him flying."

"No." She said it so quickly, Robyn's eyebrows shot up. "I can't do that to him—send him away knowing I'll fret about it."

"Okay, I'll tell you what. How about if you decide not to fret about it?"

Cheryl looked away. "Yeah. That's my goal. Psalm 37. I read it this morning, and I intend to read it every day while he's gone, to remind me not to worry. Because I know God doesn't want me to do that."

"Right. Maybe I'll come over to the practice every day at lunchtime. You and Rick and I can pray and eat lunch together. Angela, too, if she wants."

"That sounds good."

"But you won't tell Oz?"

Cheryl clamped her lips together and shook her head.

"You'd feel better if you did."

"No, I wouldn't. And he'd feel worse. He'd worry about me worrying." She stood and embraced her daughter. "Thanks, honey. I'm going to trust God in this—not just to keep Oz safe, but to keep me grounded, no matter what happens."

"All right. And I'll do everything I can to distract you. If I catch you biting your nails even once, I'll slap you silly."

⁜

"Guess I'd better get going." Oz grinned at Cheryl and Rick, unable to contain his anticipation.

Rick stuck out his hand. "We'll miss you."

"Thanks." Oz shook it and turned to face Cheryl.

"You won't decide you love it so much above the Arctic Circle that you won't come back, will you?" Her long lashes hid her eyes, but her lips twitched, holding back a smile.

"I hardly think so. We've gained a lot of daylight hours here, but I've got to regress to darkness at noon."

"You'll have some daylight up there, won't you?" she asked.

"Oh yeah, I was exaggerating. That's why they scheduled the trip now, not in January—not enough light then to make it worthwhile."

Rick smiled. "I guess it would be pretty hard to track the bears in the dark."

"Yeah, we're planning on six hours or more a day."

"We'll be thinking of you. Good luck spotting the bears," Rick said.

"We'll be praying for you, too." Cheryl's quiet tone made him focus on her. She'd set her jaw as though determined not to say anything out of line.

"Walk to my truck with me?" he asked softly.

"Sure. Let me grab my jacket."

She left the room and Oz put on his coat.

"We'll see you soon, buddy." He gave Rick a nod and walked down the hallway, pulling on his gray gloves. Angela was settling in at the front desk. She would free Cheryl up to assist Rick more during Oz's absence.

"Good-bye, Dr. Thormond," she called.

"See you, Angela." He nodded to the two pet owners sitting in the waiting area. One held a small plastic cage on her lap, and the other sat with a magazine on his lap and a malamute sprawled at his feet.

Cheryl met Oz at the door, and they walked across the parking lot together. At his truck, they stopped, and he faced her.

"I'm going to miss you."

She smiled. "Thanks. I know I'll be thinking of you a lot and praying for you."

"That's nice. Thank you." A sharp wind cut down through the valley. She hadn't put her hat on, and it lifted her curls and ruffled his beard. No sense prolonging the parting in the icy cold, but still. . . "It's been kind of crazy the last few weeks, getting ready for my trip and all."

"That's understandable."

"I hope we can find some time together after I get back. I'd like to spend time with you and. . .maybe just talk." The flying lessons had eaten up a lot of his time. It had seemed logical to take advantage of good weather, but it meant he hadn't spent the time with Cheryl that he wanted to. There was so much he didn't know about her.

She nodded, her brown eyes huge in her face. "I'd like that."

"Good." He almost wished he'd asked her to take him to the airport. Then she could meet him there when he returned, the way she had the first time he met her. But he'd already told them he'd drive his truck and leave it in long-term parking.

She'd be waiting here when he got back to Wasilla. He smiled down at her. "I'll send you a postcard."

That brought a chuckle. "I'd hold you to it, but I doubt they have postcards there. You'll be lucky if mail goes out at all during your stay."

"Ooo, I hope the weather's not that bad."

"Me, too." She went all sober again.

"Hey, you're not going to worry about me, are you?"

"No. I'm definitely not doing that. You've got the best security net in the universe."

"You've got that right."

"And besides, I have a lot more reading to do. I'm really getting into this polar bear thing."

"That's terrific. I'm glad you decided to go next month."

She shivered.

He'd better leave so she could go in out of the cold. He wanted to kiss her, but that seemed a bit premature. He reached out a gloved hand.

She'd shoved her bare hands into her coat pockets, but she pulled one out and squeezed his fingers.

Oz looked down at the black *H* she'd inked on the back of his left glove. They had so many memories to finish. "*H* for hug." He pulled her into a quick embrace. When he released her, she was smiling. Not the shy, secret smile. The big, joyful one. "Bye." He climbed into the truck.

She stood back and waved as he drove away toward the George Parks Highway.

⁜

On Friday morning the mailman brought a bundle of letters and a package to the door of the clinic and handed them to Cheryl. Snow fell outside, and she wondered how the weather was behaving seven hundred miles to the north.

She put the mail down on the desk where Angela sat and then turned to the waiting clients. "Dr. Baker is ready to see Cinnamon."

A middle-aged man lifted a cat carrier and followed her down the hall to Rick's treatment room. Rick greeted them and asked the man to set the carrier on the exam table. Cheryl closed the door so that the cat couldn't get away if it leaped off the table.

Ten minutes later, after Rick had vaccinated the cat and prescribed an ointment for a patch of eczema on its face, Cheryl walked with the owner to the front desk. "Good-bye, Mr. Allen. I'm sure Cinnamon will feel better soon, but be sure to call us if she doesn't."

"Thanks." He pulled out his checkbook.

She was about to turn away when Angela said, "Oh, Cheryl, there's some personal mail for you here."

Curious, Cheryl took the item Angela held out—a color postcard. "Thank you." Her heart fluttered as she walked quickly to the restroom and closed the door. The photo depicted brilliant green Northern Lights in full display over a rustic village. She turned it over and glanced first at the signature. Ozzy. She laughed aloud and read the message. He'd compressed his usually flowing script to fit the meager space allowed.

Hey, Cheryl!

You were wrong—they do have postcards here. This is Nuwuk, an Inupiat fishing village out on Point Barrow. We're socked in today with snow but yesterday collared five bears & tagged three yearlings. 17 below zero. See ya.

Ozzy

She read it over again and held it to her chest as tears filled her eyes. Not very romantic, but she didn't care. The fact that he'd bothered to find a postcard and managed to get it to her, probably by way of the first outgoing plane, meant more than a bouquet of hothouse roses would have.

"Thank You, Lord." She wiped away her tears and hurried to Rick's office to show it to him before taking the next patient in.

Chapter 9

Ten days later, Oz collected his luggage off the carousel in the Anchorage airport. Too bad home was still an hour away. Again he wished Cheryl was there, eyeing him cautiously and mumbling to herself.

He smiled at the memory. She'd worked her way to the top of his "Ten Reasons to Stay in Alaska" list, with polar bears and working with Rick vying for a close second.

Heading out of the airport, he passed displays of mounted Alaskan wildlife and native artwork. He paused before a case of jade and ivory jewelry. Wouldn't that beaded necklace look great on Cheryl? He'd have to give her a place to wear it, other than church. She didn't wear a lot of jewelry to the office. He squinted at the price tag. On the other hand, he could take her out to dinner about ten times for that amount. He tugged his roller suitcase over toward the wall and found a niche out of the foot traffic.

Taking out his cell phone, he punched in the number for the clinic. Probably Angela would answer.

"Baker Animal Hospital."

He grinned so hard his face hurt.

A passing woman glanced at him and raised her eyebrows as she walked on.

"Cheryl. It's Oz. I'm in Anchorage."

"Thank God!"

"How are you?"

"I'm great. We've all been praying for you. And we have a long list of non-urgent patients for you to see tomorrow if you can."

"I'll be ready." He glanced at his watch. "Can I see you tonight? By the time I drive to Wasilla, it'll be too late to come to the office."

"I'd love to see you. How about supper with me and Steve? Around six-thirty?"

"Sounds good."

⁜

Cheryl set the dining table for two. She did it every night, but this time she used her best china and set new candles in her brass holders. Should she light them before dinner, or would that be a bit much?

Robyn came in through the kitchen. "Wow, pretty snazzy. Where's Grandpa?"

"In his recliner. Thanks for having him over tonight."

Robyn laughed. "He wanted to stay and yak with Ozzy, but I think I finally got the message across that he can do that another time. You and Oz need some time alone."

Cheryl's cheeks warmed. "Oh, I don't know. . ."

"Stow it, Mom. I'm not buying it."

"But I told Oz on the phone that Grandpa Steve would be with us."

"Oh, and you think Ozzy will be horrified when he discovers that plan went awry and it's just the two of you?" Robyn laughed and walked through to the living room.

Cheryl surveyed the table in dismay. Was she making too much of this? Should she insist that Steve stay here and eat with her and Oz? Their friendship was solid, and she wanted it to remain that way. Would this look like a setup?

She snatched the tapers off the table and placed them on the windowsill. No candlelight. Maybe she should use her old ironstone dishes instead of the china.

Robyn and Steve came in. Steve had his jacket, hat, and mittens on.

"What are you doing?" Robyn asked, eyeing the plates Cheryl held in her hands. "Unsetting the table?"

"I decided it was too much. I'm going with the everyday dishes."

"You are not." Robyn wrested the plates from her and set them gently back on the table. "Hey! Where have those romantic candles run off to?"

"Oh, honey, I'm so nervous. Oz expects a nice, homey supper with me and your grandpa, and it will look like I've prettied up my spider lair for him and gotten rid of the chaperone. I don't want him to think I'm chasing him."

"Mom! You've got to stop this." Robyn stared at her. "You honestly believe he'll think you're vamping him?"

Cheryl grabbed the back of the nearest chair. Her cheeks felt as if they'd caught fire. "Well, I. . ." She clapped her hands to her face.

"Now, Cheryl, Oz Thormond is a sensible man. He's not going to get the wrong idea." Steve laid his hand on her shoulder. "You just relax and have a nice evening."

While he spoke, Robyn spotted the candles and swooped on them. She situated them precisely on the table. "There. Don't you dare take those off again."

Cheryl exhaled. "All right."

"And, Mom? Go put a dress on."

"What? No. That's silly. He won't—"

"A dress," Robyn repeated. "Come on, Grandpa. Let's vamoose."

Cheryl watched them out the door and looked down at her black slacks and powder blue sweater. Should she change? That smacked of overkill.

The front door opened, and Robyn stuck her head back inside. "What are you waiting for? Go get dressed. The green jacket dress. Now."

❖

Oz checked his appearance in the mirror and ran a comb through his hair. When did he get so gray? Maybe spending the last two weeks in sub-zero temperatures had done something to his hair. At least he didn't have to shave. His beard had come in full, almost lush. He rather liked it.

He looked down at his plain blue shirt. Maybe he ought to wear woodsman flannel. He didn't want Cheryl to feel uncomfortable if he came to supper overdressed.

His phone rang, and he snatched it off his dresser.

"Oz?"

"Yes?"

"This is Robyn. Welcome back."

"Thanks. How's everything?"

"Terrific. Are you headed to Mom's for supper?"

"Yes, I was just about to leave."

"Wear a tie."

He hesitated. "I beg your pardon."

"A tie. You know, those things men wear around their necks when they want to convince you they're civilized."

"That's what I thought you said. Are you sure?"

"Trust me on this one. Wear a tie."

"O. . .kay." He signed off and dashed to the closet. What was going on? Would Steve wear a tie to supper? Or did Robyn have something up her sleeve? Maybe the reporter from the weekly paper was coming to interview him about his research and she wanted him to look presentable for photos.

He picked the tie he'd worn with this shirt for the *Scientific American* interview. Should he wear a jacket, too? Robyn had been rather vague. He considered calling her back and demanding to know what was up. Was a tie enough for Alaska formal? Just in case, he snatched his corduroy sports jacket. Okay. Not bad at all.

He grabbed his parka, phone, and keys, along with a small bag from the airport shop where he'd finally decided on a gift for Cheryl.

At the Hollands' house, he parked his truck and picked up the small bag off the passenger seat. He took out the box and tucked it into his pocket. The big log house beckoned him with warm light spilling from the living room's front windows. Cheryl's car was the only vehicle in the yard, so this wasn't a press party. Good.

As he knocked on the front door, doubts again swept over him. What if Cheryl and Steve were kicking back in jeans? They'd think he was citified for sure. And they had to know he didn't come in from Barrow dressed like a college professor. Could he peel off the sports jacket and toss it in the truck before he went in?

Too late. The door swung open. Cheryl stood in the opening with soft light glowing behind her and her smile radiating welcome. "Oz. I'm so glad you're back. Come in."

She stepped aside and he entered, unable to take his eyes off her. The muted green dress she wore had simple lines but suited her perfectly. Around her neck hung a thin gold chain holding an oval locket. Her curls pouffed gently about her face, but it was those brown eyes that captivated him.

He reached for her hand. "You look terrific."

"Thanks. I hope you're hungry."

"Starved."

"Good. I made chicken pie." She took his parka and hung it in the closet near the door. Her glance swept over him, and she didn't say anything, but he was pretty sure he saw approval in her eyes and maybe just a tinge of anxiety.

She led him toward the dining room. The savory cooking smells made his mouth water.

"Oh, I should tell you, Robyn hauled her grandfather off for the evening. Sort of last-minute. I didn't know he was going when you called." She glanced over her shoulder at him, her brow slightly wrinkled.

"I'll have to catch up with him soon. He'll want to see some pictures from the trip."

"Yes. He's very interested in the polar bear project." She turned with a smile and a little heave of her breath and touched the back of one chair. "Why don't you sit here, and I'll bring in the food."

"Can I help?"

"Uh. . .well, sure."

He followed her into the kitchen. The tempting chicken pie sat on top of the range, brown and steaming.

She opened the oven and removed a pan of golden biscuits. From the refrigerator, she took a glass bowl of green salad and placed it in his hands. "Can you handle that and a basket of biscuits? I'll bring the pie, and I think that's it."

When they were seated at the table, she gazed at him with the shy, beneath-the-lashes look. "Would you ask the blessing, Oz?"

"Sure." Instinctively, he reached for her hand. She blushed a little and closed her eyes.

"Lord, we thank You for safety and for this food and for the company, major blessings all."

She smiled as she cut into the chicken pie and put a generous slice on his plate. "I'm getting very excited about our trip. Tell me how things went and what we'll focus on next month."

"To be honest, I can't wait to go back. We lost two days, due to weather, but I expected that. In fact, that's a pretty good record. And our tally of bears caught impressed the folks footing the bill with the grant."

"How many did you catch?"

"Nearly a hundred." He took a biscuit and broke it open. The flaky layers looked so tempting that he took a bite without even waiting to butter it. "Mmm, that's good."

"Thanks." Cheryl took some salad and passed him the bowl.

"Of course, a lot of the bears we got hold of were repeats from previous studies, but that's good in some ways. It lets us follow them and add to the data others have already collected on them. We put new collars on twenty-nine adults and tagged twenty of this year's cubs and seven older juveniles no one had caught before."

"Wow. That's a lot, isn't it?"

"It's a good number. With the repeats, we took tissue samples and measurements and recorded where we caught them so the data can be compared with past records. Three of the adults we collared had ear tags."

She nodded. "So, they'd been tagged as cubs, and now they're mature enough to be collared."

"Right." Oz took a bite of the chicken pie. The flavor made him think of childhood and Grandma's and good times. "You are such a good cook, Cheryl."

"Thank you." She blotted her lips with her napkin. "Do the hunters up there take a lot of tagged or collared bears?"

"Yes, quite a few. And they usually turn the equipment in. They know what we're doing can help them in the long run. Learning more about the bears' habits and distribution will help with managing the population. Most of the people are happy to help us."

"And do you think the bear population is shrinking?"

"Not enough evidence so far to be sure. There seem to be a lot in the area we covered. And Alaska has far fewer bears than Canada or Russia."

They ate for a few minutes in silence. Oz began to feel very comfortable as his hunger eased. Cheryl rose and retrieved a pot of coffee from the kitchen. He held out his cup, and she filled it.

"So when you and I go, we'll be going mostly after sows with cubs," she said.

"That's right."

"And we're the only bear people on this trip."

"Yes, the others are doing geological tests. We won't have anyone spotting bears from the air, which could make it a lot harder for us. We'll see. What we want to do is locate some of the females that were collared over the past few years and have given birth this year. We'll get some stats on them and the new cubs."

"Won't they be leaving land for the ice sheet about now?" she asked.

"They're starting now, but the ones with small cubs won't have left when we get there. We can't follow them out onto the ice. For this project, which is totally separate from the one I just came back from, we'll concentrate on maternity dens and new mothers, because we want specific information about the sows and cubs. Enough breeding sows in the area are wearing collars that I think we'll get a good sample. Other organizations who've worked within this bear subpopulation are cooperating. They give us their blessing as far as taking data from animals they tagged. It will help everyone to gather as much information as possible and share it."

"So, we'll send them our findings, and they can incorporate them into their studies, too?"

"Right. It's so hard and so expensive to do research in the Arctic that we have to cooperate whenever we can. The more we all share in the scientific community, the better."

She poured her own cup full of coffee and sat down again. "I'm still amazed that I get to be part of this. I don't feel at all qualified."

"You'll be terrific. And I can't think of anyone else I'd rather have along."

"It's the wildest thing I've ever done, but. . .I can't wait."

He grinned. "I know how you feel. It's going to be great. Just take the best cold-weather gear you can get."

When they'd finished the main course, she pushed her chair back. "I made some rather decadent brownies."

Oz patted his stomach. "Oh, please, no. Maybe later. I'm stuffed."

"Okay. If you're sure."

"This was fantastic."

"Would you like to sit in the living room then? We could take our coffee."

He rose and took his cup with him. She seemed to hesitate in the doorway then sat down on the sofa, hugging one arm tight. That must mean it was up to him—take the recliner opposite or the seat next to her. He compromised and sat down at the other end of the couch and turned to face her.

"You said you have pictures?" she asked.

"Tons. I brought the memory card from my camera, if you want to put it in your computer."

"Oh, let's." She sprang up off the sofa, seeming almost relieved at the prospect of doing something.

They spent the next half hour sitting shoulder-to-shoulder at her desk, with Oz narrating the slide show of his photos. Her questions probed deeply into the techniques they would use on their venture.

"Say, do you know how to shoot?" he asked.

"You mean, shoot a gun? Yes. Dan taught me when we first came here. Do you think I should brush up on that skill?"

"Wouldn't hurt. I mean, just in case. I've never had to shoot a bear with anything but a dart gun, but I did have to do in a wolf once."

She blinked twice and nodded slowly. "Okay."

"Is there a place we could practice safely? I could take you out on Saturday if you'd like."

"Sure. I gave Dan's pistol to my son, but—"

"I'll bring a gun."

"Great." She caught her breath suddenly and turned back toward the monitor.

Oz snaked his arm across the back of her chair. "Maybe right after my flying lesson?"

Her shoulders stiffened and her jaw clenched.

He watched her, confused, waiting for her to relax. Cheryl was so amiable. Surely she wouldn't be offended if he had his prescheduled lesson before their shooting date. "I...uh...set it up with Clyde so that we'll go up as soon as the sun's high enough. Is something wrong?"

"No. No, that's fine."

They sat in silence for a moment. Okay, the schedule wasn't the issue. Was it the mention of her husband that had put a damper on their conversation? Hard to believe that was it, but he couldn't think of any other explanation.

She pulled in a deep breath. "So. There are a few more pictures, right?"

"Yes. Cheryl, are you thinking about Dan?"

She whipped around and stared at him. "How did you know?"

Oz drew back a little, lowering his arm. "It just seemed like after you mentioned him teaching you to shoot that you shut down on me. I'm sorry if I brought up bad memories. You don't have to go shooting with me."

"Oh no, shooting doesn't bother me. I'm fine with that."

"Is it my timing then?"

She shook her head, setting her soft curls dancing, and laid her hand lightly on his sleeve. "No, that's fine. Everything's fine."

He eyed her cautiously. "You sure?"

"Very. And I'd love to do some target practice with you. Just call me Saturday, after you're done...done flying."

"Okay." She'd accepted another date with him. He ought to feel happier about it. He could see that she'd loved Dan profoundly. Everything he'd heard from Robyn and Rick bore that out. Could another man live up to those memories?

Chapter 10

The Holland family gathered around Cheryl and Oz at the Anchorage airport as they waited to board their plane to Barrow. Several hardy tourists and a few natives of the town would also be on their flight, along with the other scientists.

Cheryl entrusted her boarding pass to Oz and took advantage of the chance to hold her grandson, Axel, before they went through the security line. Her son, Aven, and his wife, Caddie, sat on either side of her, trying to catch up during the hour they had together. The young couple had arranged to make a quick trip up from Kodiak to see her and Oz off, and then would go home with Rick and Robyn to spend a couple of days in Wasilla.

"He's grown so much since Christmas." Cheryl grinned down at the seven-month-old baby.

"He sure has," Aven agreed. "Before you know it, we'll have him out mushing."

Caddie laughed. "Aven wants to get him a puppy already. I said let's wait a year or two."

"Say, Mom, did Dr. Thormond have to get permits to carry all the weapons he's taking?" Aven asked.

"Actually, he's only taking a dart rifle and one pistol, and they're in his checked luggage. The airline personnel are keeping an eye on them. Oz says they're used to people carrying guns for hunting trips and things like that, so he's not worried about it. He plans to buy ammunition for the pistol in Barrow."

Aven nodded. "Sounds good. Sometimes we get to take our personal firearms on deployment, if we're going someplace where we think we might get a chance to do a little hunting."

"Oz took me out a couple of times to practice, so I could use it if need be." Cheryl smiled at the memory of their target shooting. "Oz is an excellent marksman. He surprised me a little bit there." She looked up and saw that he was following their conversation.

"Have to be," Oz said with a grin. "Those tranquilizer darts aren't cheap, and if you miss, it can mean trouble."

"Oh yeah, I wouldn't want to duke it out with a polar bear." Aven eyed his mother with raised eyebrows. "You're the one who surprised me, Mom. When I heard you were going on this expedition, I couldn't believe it. You never liked to go camping in the winter."

Cheryl smiled and bounced Axel gently up and down. "Don't worry about me. We'll have enough gear to keep us comfortable. And I'll put up with a lot to have this experience."

"Yeah," Robyn said, winking conspicuously at her brother. "After all, it's for science."

Oz laughed louder than Cheryl thought was warranted at that, and she felt her face redden.

A bearded man approached them and looked around at Aven, Rick, Oz, and Steve. "Is any of you Dr. Thormond?"

"That would be me." Oz extended his hand.

"Grant Aron. I'm with the geological team on this project."

"Pleased to meet you. Call me Oz. And that lovely lady holding the baby is my assistant, Cheryl Holland. The rest are just riffraff who came to see us off."

They all laughed, and Oz stepped aside with Dr. Aron to discuss details of the trip. A few minutes later he returned to the family group. "Guess we'd better get through security. I know it's hard to leave the rug rat behind."

Cheryl reluctantly handed Axel over to Caddie.

"Have a wonderful time," Caddie said, kissing her cheek.

"Bye, Mom." Aven stooped to kiss her. "We'll be praying for you."

Robyn moved in for a big hug. "You have fun, Mom. I'm so proud of you."

Cheryl squeezed her tight. "Thanks, honey. And you take good care of Grandpa."

"We will."

Neither mentioned the fact that this would be Cheryl's first flight since Dan's crash.

Oz had made the round of handshakes. Cheryl quickly kissed Rick and Steve.

"Now, don't you tangle with those mama bears until they're good and sleepy," Steve said.

She laughed. "Don't worry. We'll be extra careful." She stole an extra second to hug the baby again and snatched up her carry-on.

Oz arched his eyebrows. "All set?"

She gulped, ignoring the forward rolls her stomach was taking. "Yes, sir. Let's do this."

They joined those waiting at the back of the line. Cheryl spotted Grant Aron a short distance ahead of them. As she neared the conveyor belt, she turned for one last wave. Robyn, Rick, and Steve waved. Aven and Caddie were busy gathering the baby's things. Cheryl gulped and stepped forward.

⚜

Oz looked out the window in his hotel room, but nothing had changed. The snow had begun a half hour before they landed in Barrow. They'd had no trouble landing, though Cheryl had seemed a bit nervous until the plane had come to a stop at the gate. But the storm had escalated into a blizzard that evening, and they'd been stuck in the hotel for two solid days. At least they'd had plenty of time to meet the rest of the scientists and check with the charter helicopter business that would take them to their base camp site. Now they just needed a clear day to get out there and set up the camp.

He paced the limited space in his room and glanced at the clock. Too early for lunch. Back to the window. Theoretically, the sun had risen a couple of hours ago, but the blinding snowfall made it impossible to tell.

His cell phone rang, and he grabbed it from his breast pocket. "Oz."

"Hi. It's Cheryl. Are you as bored as I am?"

"Possibly worse."

She chuckled. "I know this isn't very intellectual, but there's a checkers set down here in the lobby. What do you say?"

"I'll be down in two minutes flat."

"Great. I'll get us some coffee."

When he arrived in the lobby, she was seated in a niche that held two stuffed chairs and a small, square table near a window. She had the promised coffee in cardboard cups, and the checkerboard was set up. "Red or black?" she asked.

"Black—like my coffee." He settled into his chair and took a cautious sip. "Ah. Perfect. At least they have decent coffee here."

Cheryl took a drink and set her cup down. "Too bad about the weather. We won't get nearly as much done as we'd hoped."

"I know. But we can't reschedule, so there's nothing to do but tough it out."

"Well, I've made out a dozen postcards, caught up with my journal, and read every magazine in this lobby."

He laughed. "You're doing better than me. I've just paced and fumed all morning, I'm afraid."

"I've been praying that God will move this storm out."

"Me, too. Maybe we could pray together?"

"I'd like that. Sometimes just hearing another person's voice makes me feel better." She held out her hand without hesitation.

He grasped it and bowed his head. "Lord, thank You for bringing us here safely. Now, if it pleases You, we'd like a chance to carry out the work we came to do."

"Heavenly Father," Cheryl said softly, "we know You're in control. Give us what's best. We hope that's clear weather. And thank You."

They smiled at each other. Cheryl opened her mouth then closed it abruptly.

"What?" he asked.

"Nothing. Well, I was going to say something, but I decided it was better not to. I feel better, since we prayed about this situation."

"It's been pretty frustrating."

"Yes. To be honest, I started wondering if I'd made a mistake in coming."

"Oh, please don't feel that way. I'm so glad you're here to keep me company.

I can only take so much talk about mineral findings and ice core samples."

Her eyes picked up the gleam of the overhead light in the main part of the room. "I'm happy to be here with you, Ozzy. I just hope we're able to get out there and do the work, and that I'll live up to your expectations."

Oz looked toward the window, but the snow still swirled thickly. "Maybe it will clear off and we can go out tomorrow. We'll have plenty of snow for the snowmobiles to run in, but it might make it harder to spot the bears."

Grant Aron entered the lobby and looked around. When he spotted them, he walked quickly across the room. "Glad I found you. Nick just talked to the helicopter people. They said this is supposed to blow out tonight, and they can take out our supplies and equipment, except the snow machines, at first light. They said if we can run the snow machines out, it will simplify matters. They can take everything else in one trip. If they fly the snow machines, that will mean two extra trips, because they're so heavy."

"Well, it would save us a ton of money to do that, but it's forty miles."

"We can get there easily in a couple of hours, and they'll leave us extra gas for the machines."

"I don't know." Oz looked over at Cheryl. "What do you think?"

Her mouth had tightened, and her eyes contracted. "I. . . whatever you fellows think."

"Did you ask Annette?" Oz asked.

"She's game."

Oz nodded. "Okay, we'll talk about it."

"All right. I'll see you in the dining room later. No one's going out for lunch in this storm."

Grant walked away, and Oz turned back to face Cheryl. "You're not thrilled with this development."

"Actually, it's a toss-up for me. A half hour in a helicopter or two on a snow machine. And you know what? I think the ground transportation is winning. We wear extra socks, that's all."

"Okay." He studied her face. "Does flying bother you? I noticed on the plane coming up here you seemed a little on edge. Have you flown much?"

"Not really, and not for a long time."

"It's very safe."

She grimaced and picked up her coffee cup.

"Why do I get the feeling I'm missing something? This isn't the first time."

She sighed and set the cup down. After staring at the checkerboard for a moment, she licked her lips. "Okay. I'm guessing Rick's never told you how my husband died."

Oz's heart clenched and he caught his breath. "Oh."

"Yes."

"Helicopter?"

"No, a small plane. In Puget Sound." She waved her hand in the air above the checkers. "I'm not afraid of flying. Not much anyway."

"It's when other people fly that it scares you. I can see why." He reached back in his memory, putting together the pieces. "That's why you weren't enthusiastic about my flying lessons."

Her face crumpled. "I'm so sorry. I tried not to show it. The last thing I wanted to do was put a damper on your fun. You've enjoyed it so much!"

He left his chair and stood beside her, sliding his arm around her. "Cheryl, sweetheart, you have no reason to be sorry. Forgive me for being so oblivious to your pain."

She shook her head, but tears streamed down her cheeks. She fumbled in the pocket of her zippered sweatshirt and came out with a tissue. "Really, I'm glad you like doing it. Having a pilot's license will be a huge help to you. You can fly to patients who live far out in the bush, and if you want, you can fly to your research areas next year. You could even join the Iditarod Air Force."

"I might just do that. But I'd hate to think you'd be worrying while I did those things."

She huffed out a laugh that was more of a sob. "I won't. I promise. God is going to help me get past this."

"I'm glad. But it will probably never go away completely. I mean, every time I hear about an officer killed on duty, I get a little depressed, remembering what happened to Jo. It's part of our nature."

"Yes, but. . ." She wiped her face and smiled up at him. "I truly believe I can work through this and get to a place where I let the Lord handle it. I can't protect you—or my kids or anyone else—by stewing about it. So I'll leave it to Someone who can."

He bent a few more inches and brushed her lips with his.

She kissed him back, and his pulse picked up.

"That's the way to look at it," he whispered. "Thank you." He sat down again opposite her.

Her eyelashes were still dark from her tears, but her eyes glistened, and her cheeks were flushed a becoming pink.

"Okay," he said, "now I'm going to trounce you at checkers."

"Ha. That's what you think."

Chapter 11

The ringing phone on the nightstand woke Cheryl, and she groped for it in the darkness. "Yeah? Uh. . ." She tried to recall her room number.

"It's me, Ozzy. The weather's changed. The storm blew out to sea, and half the snow was swept away with it. How soon can you be ready to go?"

An hour later, all six team members had eaten breakfast and were ready to ride to the airfield, where their supplies were being loaded into the helicopter.

"I was hoping it would be a little warmer by now," Grant said, "but we'll take what we can get. We have a heater for each tent. Annette and Cheryl, your tent is smaller, so it won't take long to heat it. Just be sure you ventilate well. We'll only be forty miles from town, and if anything happens, we can call for the helicopter. We've got two satellite phones. I hoped for three, but they're expensive. We'd have had to give up some equipment for that. So we'll share. And Charlie has promised to keep his phone line open and come if we need him."

"So, we're all going on snowmobiles?" Annette Striker asked. She was closer to Robyn's age than Cheryl's, and her long, dark hair and flawless, olive-toned skin gave her an exotic air.

"We'll see what Charlie says," Grant told her. "I've got a rental outside. Ladies and gentlemen, if you're ready. . ." He gestured toward the door and they trooped out.

The men stood back to allow the women to climb first into a decade-old mini-van. Cheryl took one of the middle seats. Annette opened the front door and appropriated the passenger seat. Cheryl was mildly surprised when one of the other men, Michael Torrence, sat down next to her. Oz ended up in the back with the last of the geologists, Nick Weiss, and Grant drove.

Cheryl tried to follow the disjointed conversation. She'd learned all their names during their enforced stay in Barrow, but she was still sorting out their specialties and pet projects. Grant had taken leadership, ordered supplies, and organized their transport, but he had assured them all he was in no way to be considered the boss.

Nick, a graduate student in geology, would serve as Grant's assistant. He was the only one besides Cheryl who didn't have a Ph.D.

She'd begun calling the others "doctor," but Michael, a tall, blond man with a New England accent, had quickly put a stop to that. "We'll all work and live closely on this project. Let's stay with first names, if that's okay."

She didn't mind. It kept her from remembering every second that her higher education had ended after one year. She reminded herself that Oz had not chosen her because of her academic credentials but for her practical good sense and her work ethic. And he'd said they worked well together. That thought made her smile.

They reached the airfield in a predawn grayness at 7 a.m.

Their pilot, Charlie, was overseeing the loading of the last crates of gear onto the big helicopter. He waved them over and grinned. With his beard and fur-trimmed hood, it was hard to see his face, other than those gleaming white teeth. "Well, we finally got some flying weather."

"Is the chopper full?" Annette asked.

"We've got a little leeway." Charlie looked her up and down. "I can probably take two passengers. You want to fly?"

"Yes, please."

"Anyone else?" Charlie waved toward the three snow machines parked on the snowy tarmac to one side. "There's the transportation for the rest of you. Now, I can fly the machines out, if you want me to, but like I told Doc Aron, it will cost a lot more, and it will take more time in the long run."

"No, we'll be fine," Grant assured him. He looked at Cheryl. "Would you prefer to go in the chopper with Annette?"

She glanced at Oz, but he only arched an eyebrow. "No, thanks. I'd actually rather stay on the ground, if no one minds."

"I'll go in the chopper then," Nick said in his soft Kentucky tones. "Maybe Annette and I can get the small tent up before you get there, so you'll have a place to thaw out."

Grant chuckled. "You're just saying that because you never drove a snow machine before."

"Guilty." Nick winced. "I'm sure I'll learn quickly though."

"All right, let's load up and go," Grant said. "Cheryl. . ."

"She can ride with me," Oz said quickly.

She let out her breath, relieved that she wouldn't share a sled with one of the other men. Everything seemed new and a little scary.

Oz hesitated when they reached their snow machine. "Uh. . . I feel I should ask if you want to drive. You've put a lot more miles on snowmobiles than I have."

She smiled. "Thanks, but if it's all the same to you, I think I'll crouch behind you and let you take the wind in your teeth."

"If you're sure. . ."

"I'm sure. Besides, this way if something goes wrong, it'll be your fault, not mine."

He laughed. "All right then, m'lady, shall we embark?"

"You get on first."

He climbed aboard, and she straddled the seat behind him. She pulled her knit mask down over her face and peered out the eyeholes.

A few moments later, they were off, following Grant as he headed away from the airfield and out onto the open tundra. Michael followed on the third machine.

Cheryl hung on and enjoyed the scenery. In all her years in Alaska, she'd never traveled above the Arctic Circle. The rising sun dazzled her, sending rays of gold, peach, and orange over the drifted snow. She looked back and saw the helicopter rise and head toward them.

Oz guided their snow machine over ridges of crusty snow and across innumerable frozen ponds. He avoided the drifts and rough places whenever possible, but sometimes the machine thwacked down over an uneven patch.

She squeezed the handholds to keep her weight centered. When the terrain smoothed out again, she let go and flexed her hands. Her insulated boots and gloves kept her warm.

Long before they reached base camp, she tired of the ride. She'd have sore muscles in the morning from all the bumps they rocketed over without warning.

Several times Grant slowed to check his bearings then roared onward. They'd been out an hour when the helicopter flew back over them. Charlie hovered for a moment and waved, then sped for Barrow.

Cheryl began to regret not taking the shorter ride with Annette. Of course, Annette and Nick now had the joy of setting up tents in the snow. *I'm just as happy to be right where I am, Lord. And thank You.*

Ozzie's solid bulk broke the ever-present Arctic wind, and she appreciated her sheltered seat behind him. Now and then he looked over his shoulder at her. She always gave him a thumbs-up or a nod so he'd know she was okay.

After the first hour, icicles formed on his beard where it poked out beneath the mask portion of his knit hat. She wondered if his toes were cold. Her own remained toasty, but she wished she could stretch her legs.

At last Oz turned and pointed with exaggeration ahead of them.

She craned her neck to see over his shoulder. A small black hump had appeared on the horizon. "Is that the camp?" she yelled in his ear, over the drone of the engine.

He nodded vigorously.

Cheryl realized her hands rested on his shoulders. He leaned back against her for a moment. She tightened her grip in a quick squeeze before she settled back and grasped the handholds again.

Annette and Nick had set up the small tent for the two women. They had also put several crates of supplies inside. When the snow machines halted nearby, both were struggling to lay out the larger tent. Michael and Grant hurried to help them.

Cheryl jumped off the machine and staggered as she found her footing.

Oz swung his leg over and stood. He gave a little groan and flexed his knees with his hands pressed to the small of his back. "Man, I'm getting too old for this."

"Don't say that. It's our first day out." Cheryl turned her back to the wind.

"I know. I know." He chuckled and flipped his hood down, then pulled off the mask. "Whew. Feels good not to be pushing into the wind."

"I'm sorry. I should have driven for a while." She eyed him carefully, looking for signs of fatigue.

"I'm fine. But maybe you can find some coffee in all this organized chaos?"

Cheryl smiled. If one thing could make Oz feel at home out here in the snowy wilderness, it was a cup of hot, black coffee. She trudged over to where Annette was stretching out a tent flap.

"Hi. I don't suppose you and Nick spotted the coffee? I could start a pot."

"Fantastic. It's in our tent, beside the camp stove. I didn't have time to set that up yet."

"I'll get it." All those summers camping on the Kenai Peninsula with Dan and the kids would pay off handsomely now.

Cheryl hurried to the smaller shelter and ducked inside. In the semidarkness, she almost stumbled over the small heater. The interior was passably warm. She peeled off her gloves and threw them on the farther of the two cots. A small duffel bag lay on the nearer one, and she assumed that was Annette's way of marking her territory.

The camp stove, nearly identical to the one they had at home, looked like an old friend. She lugged it outside and commandeered a wooden crate to set it on.

"Here you go." She looked up. Nick stood nearby holding a metal rack. "It's the stand for the stove."

"Wonderful. I'll have some coffee for you guys in no time."

"Sounds good."

By the time she'd found and filled the coffeepot and set it on the burner, they had the larger tent up and were lugging the rest of the gear into it.

Oz turned her way and brought her dark green duffel over. "This is yours, right?"

"Yes, thank you." She reached for it, but he shook his head.

"I'll take it in for you."

"Thanks. The second bed."

He returned in a moment while she rummaged in a box of dishes for mugs.

"So, what do you think?" His vivid blue eyes sparkled.

"So far, I like it. Are we going bear hunting today?"

"Thought we might, after lunch."

Lunch, she thought. Were the women expected to do the cooking? Maybe she would have to do it, because she was the least educated and didn't have a scientific mission of her own.

"Hey, Cheryl," Michael called, "I've got a crate of canned stew here. How about I open a couple of cans and put it on the stove? Can you get the other burner going?"

She nodded, feeling a sudden liking for the lanky, blond man.

An hour later they had eaten, and Cheryl felt an eagerness to get on with the mission. The men pitched in to clean up and bear-proof the camp as much as possible.

Oz carefully selected the limited gear they could take with them on the snow machine. Cheryl put on a clean T-shirt and socks, in case those she'd worn all morning had absorbed sweat. She wanted to stay warm on this adventure, and she was determined not to complain if it killed her. When she went outside again, the wind had fallen, and the sun's rays now warmed her enough that she flipped her hood back and shoved her mask hat into her pocket.

Oz had a radio receiver sitting on the hood of the snow machine and wore earphones connected to the radio. He turned and smiled at her, but she couldn't see his eyes behind his sunglasses. "This is great. I'm picking up a fairly strong signal from a collared bear."

"We're not going out on the ice sheet, are we?" She glanced northward, toward Smith Bay and the Beaufort Sea.

"No, most of the bear population should still be on the land-fast ice or haunting the leads that have opened up near it. As the weather warms, the ice pack will move out from shore, but for now, most bears are sticking close to land because that's where the seals are."

She nodded. "Great. I've got my charts, notebook, and survival pack. Anything else I should bring?"

He reached out with his glove and touched her cheek. "I know the sun feels pretty good right now, but have you got your hat? It's bound to feel chilly when we start moving."

She patted her pocket. "Yes, sir, my cold-weather gear is all in order."

"Great. I've gone over the list, and I think we're all set. They're letting us take one sat phone today, since they plan to stick together on their first run. Let me just stow the radio." He put the receiver in a box of equipment on the back of the sled and climbed aboard.

Cheryl took her place behind him.

Nick and Grant had already started on their machine, with Nick in the driver's seat. He appeared to be taking a crash course in snow-sled driving from Grant. Michael waited near the third one for Annette to emerge from her tent.

Cheryl waved to him.

Michael returned her salute. "Good luck, and stay on the good side of those bears!"

Oz started the engine and put it in gear. Cheryl rather daringly rested her hands gently on his back for the first half mile. They came to a rough incline taking them closer to the coastline, and she reverted to clutching the metal handgrips provided.

What would the kids say if they could see her now? She looked toward the frozen sea, with the sun glittering on the drifted snow. Ridges of broken snow and ice littered their path, making the ride bumpy and uncomfortable again.

Oz stopped after about thirty minutes and let the machine idle while he got out the radio receiver. He put on earphones, and he grinned at her. "We're close. The signal's louder."

Cheryl looked around. "So there's a bear loose around here someplace?" All she could see was the rough snowfields and the ice sheet that covered the bay. A hundred yards offshore, a dark strip showed where a lead was opening in the ice.

"Let's get up on top of that hummock." Oz pointed to his right. "Maybe we can spot him from there. But if it's a sow still denned up with her cubs, she'll be harder to find."

Cheryl hung on as the machine toiled up the slope. Would the noise wake groggy bears or annoy conscious ones? A sudden uneasiness grabbed her. What if the knoll they climbed was a den? Surely Oz could tell if it were. Her neck prickled. She looked from side to side and behind them. Would her first encounter with a polar bear be too close for safety?

Chapter 12

Oz drove carefully, mindful of cottony spots that could be deep snowdrifts. He didn't want the snowmobile bogging down on them in bear country. The vastness of the tundra and the nearby ice shelf affected him more than it had when he worked from a helicopter.

He and Cheryl were down on the same level with the huge bears and could run across one without warning. Past experience had taught him all too well the fragility of life in this hostile environment. He hadn't told Cheryl about the graduate student they'd lost to an unexpected crack in the Siberian ice two years ago. He didn't intend to tell her either. But he would be extra careful since the woman he'd lost his heart to clung to the sled behind him.

He stopped the machine on top of a rough ridge of broken snow and ice. Cheryl stirred, and he felt the light pressure of her hands on his back.

"Are we getting off?" she asked.

"Let's take a good look around first and make sure we're alone."

She pulled her binoculars out from inside her thick parka and scanned the terrain to their left.

Oz looked ahead and to their right. "Okay," he said after a minute of silent watchfulness. "Let's see what the radio tells us."

She handed him the receiver.

"Southeast," he said. "Let's take it slow and easy. I think we're really close."

"At least we're downwind."

It pleased him that she'd thought of that. Polar bears had the best noses in the world. "Right. I'll stay on the flat as much as I can, but look for drifts and humps of snow where there could be a den."

He'd provided Cheryl with dozens of photos of bear dens to give her an idea of what they looked like. An undisturbed den might not give any more warning than a small breathing hole in deep snow. An abandoned den, however, would appear as a gaping hole or a snow cave, perhaps with claw marks around it. He turned to give the radio back to her.

"Look! There he is." Cheryl was staring off in the direction the beacon had indicated.

He whirled around and scanned the tundra. "Where?"

"Two o'clock."

Oz narrowed his search and focused on a patch of discolored snow. As he watched, it moved. "I see him. Big, isn't he?"

The bear lumbered toward the bay, on a course that would make him pass in front of the snowmobile about fifty yards away. Though the shaggy animal looked thin, he probably weighed close to a thousand pounds.

"Slow now," he said. "Hand me the dart gun."

He heard her quiet movements. A few seconds later, she slid the rifle forward.

He took it, never looking away from the bear. The large male continued his trek toward the bay. Oz sent up a silent prayer of gratitude.

"Is the heaviest dose loaded?" she asked.

"Yes, I put one in, just in case we needed it in a hurry." Oz put the gunstock to his shoulder and sighted in. He waited motionless for the bear to reach the point where his path would bring him closest to the snowmobile.

Cheryl kept still.

At last the moment came, and he fired.

The bear jumped and swiped at its shoulder with a massive paw.

Cheryl shifted a bit but said nothing.

Without moving, Oz said, "Five minutes or so. Pray he doesn't see us first." Their vulnerability struck him. If the bear should spot them and charge, he'd have to choose between making a run for it on the snowmobile—which he'd shut off—or pulling his pistol. And that probably wouldn't be enough to stop it.

"He's going on," Cheryl whispered.

The bear padded toward the ice, pausing every few steps to bat at its shoulder again and sniff the breeze. After shuffling fifty feet farther on its course, it lay down and rolled.

Oz laughed softly. "He didn't like that."

"Think the dose will put him out?"

"Oh yeah." He turned and smiled at her. "Patience, my dear."

"I can hardly wait." Her tone was anything but eager.

"Don't you want to see him up close?"

"Yes and no."

"Well, it makes sense to be cautious with a critter like this. But once they're out, they generally stay out while we do our work. Then we give them the antidote and back off. They come to within minutes. This drug is wonderful."

The bear staggered to his feet and plodded on a few more yards then weaved, his head bobbing.

"He's going down again."

"Oz?"

"Yeah?"

Cheryl held the binoculars over his shoulder. "I don't see a collar on that bear."

He froze for a moment, took the field glasses, and raised them. As he peered through them at the bear, he tried to remember if he'd noticed anything when it was closer to them.

"I can't tell," he said as the bear sank to its knees and elbows. "You know they're white, so other bears won't notice them. We'll have to wait and see."

"But if that's not the one giving off the signal we heard. . ."

He nodded and gave the binoculars back to her. "Then there's another one close by. Probably a denned sow." He looked all around, just to be sure he hadn't overlooked anything obvious.

The bear he'd darted lifted its head one last time then sprawled gracefully with its chin on its paws.

"Let's move in." He handed Cheryl the dart gun and started the engine. After driving to within ten feet of the bear, he turned the machine toward camp, so they could make a quick getaway if needed. "Stay here while I check him."

Cheryl leaned back, and he climbed off. He approached the bear. As expected, it didn't move. Oz walked around it to see if it lay comfortably in the snow, with none of the legs folded beneath it. He prodded it gently with his foot. The bear slept on.

He waved to Cheryl and she hesitantly approached. "It's humungous."

"Yup. And you were right. No collar."

Her eyes widened and she looked around. "You have the pistol, right?"

"Yes, I do. Okay, we're going to take vital signs first. Pulse, respirations, and body temp." Oz performed the tests, and Cheryl wrote down the results, staying a respectful distance from the bear's teeth and claws. Next Oz measured its length and girth. "He's kind of skinny," he told Cheryl. "Estimated weight, nine hundred fifty pounds. But he'll fatten up soon."

Next, he fixed white, numbered tags in both the bear's ears. Cheryl recorded the number, which was the same on both ear tags. "We use white because other bears don't seem to notice them," he said as he fastened the second one. "They've tried colored ones, and the bears tried to groom them off each other, like they would a bug."

She smiled. "What next? The collar?"

"Yes. Could you hand it to me, please?" Oz checked the battery and read off the serial number, then fastened the collar in place. "There. Now the tattoo."

She got the instrument out for him. He tattooed the same number that was on the bear's ear tags on the inside of its upper lips.

"One more thing," Oz said.

She nodded soberly and handed him the plier-like extractor. While she wrote the tag number on a plastic bag, Oz folded the bear's lips back on the side and removed the tiny premolar from just behind the bear's left canine tooth.

"How old do you think he is?" she asked, holding out the bag to receive the tooth.

"I'm guessing over twenty. But don't ask me how he kept from being caught all this time. This area's been monitored for quite a while now."

They packed up the tools. Oz reloaded the dart gun and double-checked the list on Cheryl's clipboard. "Okay, start the engine, and I'll give him the antidote." He administered the injection and hurried to hop on behind her. "Gun it, babe!"

She drove full throttle to the top of the rise from which they'd watched the bear and turned the machine sideways so they could both see the groggy animal raise his head and look toward the noise of the snowmobile.

"What if he comes after us?" Cheryl asked over the sound of the idling engine.

"He won't. He'll head for the sea."

"Okay. I'm just saying. What if?"

Oz wrapped his arms around her and gave her a gentle squeeze. "Then you hightail it for camp. They can swim for a hundred miles, but they can't run very far. They overheat easily."

"Think we could outrun him with this?"

"We won't have to." Even so, Oz found himself a bit on edge as they waited.

The bear shoved himself to his feet at last and lumbered slowly away from them, toward the ice shelf.

"Told you so." Oz nestled in against her hair.

"Will the drug affect him? Seems like I read it won't."

"No, there don't seem to be any long-term effects. It's been well tested and used for several years now. Once in a great while, a bear gets too big a dose, and then you have to resuscitate them."

"Just what I want to do—CPR on a bear."

He smiled. "At least we don't do mouth-to-mouth on them. But I'm careful with my dosage. I've only had to resuscitate one twice, and both times it was when someone else did the medicating."

"What about the other bear? The one that we heard the signal from before?"

"Oh, yeah." He gritted his teeth. Already it felt like he'd had a long day. He looked up at the sun then at his watch. "I guess we've got about three hours of daylight left. Shouldn't waste it."

She reached over her shoulder and patted his cheek. "Come on, Doc. Science awaits us."

Cheryl drove slowly along, below the rougher ridges of the snowscape. Hard to believe she'd touched a living wild polar bear. Oz kept watch with the binoculars as they rode, but she tried to stay aware of the area ahead of them, beyond her immediate path.

"Could be it's a sow still in her den," he reminded her. His breath tickled her ear. The sun was westering, and the temperature had declined a few degrees, but she didn't want to put her hood up. She loved having him ride behind her and occasionally brush her hair or give her a little squeeze. So much for her early resolution to keep a professional relationship with him. By now she knew it was hopeless, and her heart belonged to Oz Thormond.

"Hold it," he said close to her ear.

She eased the snow machine to a stop and looked to him for direction. He pointed toward the sea. A hummock of snow with a yellowish cast lay about two hundred yards away. She squinted. The sun sent long, low rays over the tundra to add cream and gray highlights. The hummock wriggled.

The object of her scrutiny suddenly came into focus, and she caught her breath. "Oh! She's got cubs!"

"Three, if I'm not mistaken." Oz took the strap from around his neck and handed her the binoculars.

"Aw! They're adorable. Can we get closer?"

"We have to." He frowned. "There's not much cover between us and them. Mama might not like it. I need to dart her and then wait for the drug to take effect. She might get protective when we get within shooting range."

Cheryl looked around. "If we go back west a ways and get behind some of those ridges, maybe we can get around beyond her without her noticing. There seem to be more knolls and drifts over there."

"Okay. But if the going is too rough, don't take any risks with the machine. We don't want a breakdown this late in the day."

She nodded, confident she could get him within a hundred yards of the bears without completely breaking from cover.

The short trip was more arduous than she'd expected, with rougher going and occasional breaks and deep cracks in the snow that she had to maneuver around. By the time they reached her goal, she feared the sow would have moved out of range. Oz got off the machine and took the dart gun from the scabbard. She followed him up a heap of frozen snow chunks, and they peeked over the top.

The sow and her babies rolled together playfully in the loose snow below them, only seventy-five yards away.

"Perfect," Oz said. "I should let you drive all the time."

"Can't we watch them for a while? They're so cute!"

"We need to make sure we're done and back to camp before dark."

"Right."

He shouldered the rifle and took aim.

"Don't hit one of the babies," Cheryl said, touching his arm lightly.

"I'll wait for a clear shot of Mom."

The sow cuffed one of the cubs playfully then rolled onto her back to let the three little ones nurse.

"They must have just left the den," Oz said.

"Can we examine the mother without tranquilizing the babies?"

"No, they've got claws and teeth, too. Besides, we want to tag the cubs. Can't do that without putting them out."

"Okay. Give me the dosage, and I'll get the darts ready for you."

"They must not weigh more than twenty pounds each."

He told her what he needed, and she went back to the snow machine. He had clearly marked the different syringes so they would not make a mistake. She took three of the smallest.

When she got back to his position, he lowered the rifle and turned. "Got a good shot at her, in her hip. She barely twitched. Once she's out, we can get down closer and do the cubs. They're so tangled up in her fur and with each other that I don't want to try from here and miss one or hit one twice."

Ten minutes later, the mother bear slept peacefully on the snow while one of her triplets continued to nurse and the other two wrestled with each other on her belly.

"Think she's out?" Cheryl asked.

"I don't know. She didn't lift her head like they usually do before they crash."

"Oz, maybe you should get closer and make sure she's breathing." The idea that the mother bear might be in distress while they laughed at the antics of her cubs made her feel ill and guilty. The animal's comfort and well-being always came first to a scientist.

Oz rose and made his way down the rough slope, carrying the dart gun, which he'd reloaded with the lower dose.

Cheryl hesitated then followed. If he needed to resuscitate that bear, he'd need help.

He was ten feet from the sow when she raised her massive head and blinked at him. Oz froze and raised one hand, the signal for Cheryl to stop. The cubs scurried around to stare and sniff at him. The mother bear moaned. Her left front paw lifted for a moment, in a casual wave, then plopped onto the snow. The bear lowered her head with a big sigh and lay still.

"Is she okay?" Cheryl hissed.

Oz stood motionless for another fifteen seconds. He turned, blowing out a deep breath, his eyes nearly closed. "She's good. Out cold now, but breathing steadily. Come on."

He quickly dosed the three cubs. While they recorded the mother's identification number, measured her, and tested the battery in her radio collar, they let the little ones waddle about.

One of the cubs crumpled to the ground leaning against Cheryl's boot.

"Oh, sweet!" She shot a glance at Oz. "Can I pick him up now?"

"Should be okay."

She sat down and cradled the cub on her lap. The second had collapsed beside his mother, and the third wobbled on his feet.

"I want one of these." She swept her cheek over his fur.

Oz laughed. "You know how cute those pups of Robyn's are in the spring, and how a year later they've turned into fierce, competitive canines?"

She nodded. "I know. They don't stay little and cute. I still want one."

"Hold on a sec." Oz fumbled in the pockets of his bulky jacket and took out the camera he used to photograph his "patients." He zoomed in on Cheryl and the cub and clicked away.

"Thanks," she called. "My kids wouldn't believe this otherwise. But will the mother get upset when her baby smells like a human?"

"I've never known them to reject the cubs after we handled them, but I did bring that little bottle of fish oil."

"Oh, right. I can put some of that on him, and she'll think he's dessert, right?"

"She'll groom him well, I'm sure. Okay, we don't have to take a tooth from Mama, because she gave at the last blood drive. Let's measure the little puffballs."

She rose and carried her new pet to him, and Oz quickly clamped the tags to the cub's ears. Reluctantly, Cheryl set the baby down and retrieved her clipboard so she could record the numbers. She held each cub in turn while Oz measured them, estimated their weight, tattooed their lips, and took blood samples.

"Okay, I'll give the little guys their antidotes first. Then I want you to get up the ridge while I dose Mama. I'll join you, and we'll watch the family wake up from their siestas and continue on their journey."

"Think they'll go on toward the sea tonight?"

He looked around, studying the terrain. The shadows spread long now. "I don't know. I'm thinking they're not far from the den, because we heard the signal for hours before we found them. They may have just come out for some recreation this afternoon, and she might take them back to the den for the night."

"I expect she'll be a little disoriented when she wakes up. I mean, they've lost an hour or more. The sun is lower. . ."

Oz nodded. "Let's watch until we're sure she's alert." He injected each cub with the antidote.

Cheryl stayed to pat them until they began to stretch and wriggle.

"Okay, off you go," Oz said. He stood over the mother, holding the syringe with her dose of antidote until Cheryl had carried the dart gun and medical case to the top of the ridge that hid the snow machine. She turned and waved, and he bent over the sow. A moment later he'd pocketed the syringe and loped toward her. He climbed the ridge and sank down beside her, panting. "Has she moved yet?"

"Nope."

They sat watching, with the lowering sun behind them. It colored the snow with magenta, peach, and mauve. The sow's fur gleamed orange as her cubs began to tug at her.

Oz slipped his arm around Cheryl's waist. "Nice family group."

"Yes." She smiled up at him. "Thank you so much for bringing me out here. I would never in a million years have come to Barrow if you hadn't asked me."

He smiled. "If my beard wasn't full of ice, I'd kiss you right now."

She didn't know what to say, but she dared to lean back against his shoulder. He lowered his head to rest on hers. "You'd better put your hood up. It'll drop to subzero fast once the sun's out of sight."

She flipped it up over her knit hat and snapped it in place. It felt good, and she realized then that her ears had been cold for some time.

"Mama's getting up," he said.

The mother bear pulled herself up on her front legs and looked all around. She leaned over to lick one of the cubs. A minute later, she staggered to all fours and edged the cubs eastward with her nose. They waddled along to a snowdrift and disappeared beyond it.

"So that's where their den is," Cheryl said.

"I think you're right. And we'd better head for ours."

Chapter 13

The next morning, all of the scientists rose well before dawn and were ready to leave the base camp by seven, as the sky lightened to the south and east. Nick and Grant headed their snowmobile northward to study the ice sheet. Oz insisted that they take one of the satellite phones, as they were the most likely to have a serious accident. Michael urged Oz and Cheryl to take the second one, since they'd be working with potentially dangerous animals. He and Annette took a southwestern path, toward a glacier where they would take specific geological samples for an oil company partially sponsoring their grant.

Oz meticulously checked over the medical supplies and safety equipment while Cheryl performed a checklist on the snow machine. None of the others seemed to think much about the possibility of mechanical failure, but it weighed heavily on her mind. She lifted the hood and checked all the fluids and connections.

"Making the Arctic safe for science?" Oz asked with a grin as he stowed the dart rifle.

"Somebody's got to."

He laughed. "You're right, and I appreciate it. You're probably the most experienced snowmobiler among us. Sometimes I tend to get lost in my mission and forget I'm also responsible for my own transportation and well-being on this trip. Usually someone else supplies and operates the helicopter or snowmobiles or a tracked vehicle. I'm just along for the ride until we spot a bear."

"Where are we going today?" she asked.

"I'd like to go inland a couple of miles and look for dens a little farther from the coast. The sow we caught yesterday was just emerging with her cubs, and there are bound to be dozens more at the same point in the maternity cycle. The more cubs we can catch, the better."

Cheryl opened the compact book of satellite maps they carried with them. "Okay, so this way?" She ran her finger in a direct southerly course from the camp.

"And maybe a little eastward as we go. Biologists who've tagged bears in this area in the last few years have concentrated more to the west of where we are. I'd like to collar some new bears and put lots of fresh DNA samples in the mix."

"Would you like me to drive? I'm short, and you can look over my head. You could use the time spotting bears and not having to watch out where you're going."

"I think that's a great idea. I'll admit, I thought about it before, but I didn't want to suggest it until you felt comfortable driving out here and realized what we're up against."

"Well, the terrain is rough in places."

Oz nodded and looked pensively toward the southeast. "Not to mention that it's randomly sprinkled with thousand-pound carnivores."

Cheryl smiled but had to disagree, in light of her recent studies. "Not so random. We both know there are places more likely than others as denning areas."

"True. But we could still run into some adult males heading for the sea ice anywhere on the North Slope. Hungry adult males."

"Yeah." She glanced toward the tent she'd shared with Annette the night before. "Hey, if you're almost ready, there's one more thing I need to do before we take off."

"What's that?"

"I left a pot of fresh coffee keeping warm over a low burner, so I could fill the thermos right before we go."

Oz's face melted into contentment. "I knew I picked the right assistant for this escapade."

Cheryl hurried to where they'd left the camp stove set up between the tents. She turned off the burner and filled the thermos, then closed the stove and collapsed the stand. No sense leaving it out where a heavy wind could grab it. She took the stove and stand into the tent. They'd cached all their food in locked metal containers and stowed them in a hole in a snow ridge fifty yards from the tents. If somehow bears got wind of the food, the team didn't want them ravaging the tents as well. Of course, there was no guarantee, and with no one left to defend the camp, anything could happen during their absence.

⁂

Oz hung on to the snowmobile and scanned continuously. He'd hoped it would be easier to spot bears on level ground than from the air. Many times he'd nearly missed them when searching from a helicopter because they blended so well with their surroundings. On the ground, they'd at least stick up higher than the tundra. But he and Cheryl had been out nearly two hours and had nothing to show for it.

He lowered the binoculars. They were hard on his eyes while the sun shone. Ordinarily, he'd wear his sunglasses now, but he couldn't use the field glasses effectively with them on. Instead, he got a magnified image of dazzling snow.

The panorama of a broken, white windswept plain made him feel small. They traveled through a rough area that was full of frozen ponds and pressure ridges of ice, but no mountains. He couldn't remember a more desolate landscape. They were driving into the wind now, and the icy blast on his face as they rode prompted him to unroll the knit mask he'd kept in his pocket and pull it over his head, then replace his hood. He leaned forward and rested his chin on the shoulder of Cheryl's parka. "Feel like some coffee?"

She slowed the snowmobile and stopped in the shelter of a drift. When she shut the engine off, the stillness settled over them like a heavy quilt.

"Wow. I wish there were such a thing as a Stealth snowmobile."

She chuckled. "What do you think? We haven't seen a thing so far."

"Let me try the radio again and see if we pick up any signals." He fiddled with it while she opened the thermos and poured the cup half full of black coffee. As he adjusted the receiver's position, he picked up a faint blip. "Hmm. If that's one of our bears, it's a ways away."

"Can you get a directional?"

"Maybe."

She handed him the coffee, and he took an experimental sip then a longer draft. "Thanks. That hits the spot. Have some, if you can stand it black."

"Maybe just a little." She sipped it and grimaced. "Yeah. That's the way you like it, all right. You want a granola bar?"

"Wouldn't mind. It's cold out here."

"I'm feeling it more today than yesterday," she admitted.

"I think the temp's dropped since we left camp. You okay?"

"Yes, for now."

They sat down on the snowmobile's seat and ate the high-calorie snacks, sharing a second cup of coffee.

"Well, shall we see if we can catch up to this bruin?" he asked.

Cheryl shoved the wrappers into a carrying bag while he stowed the thermos. "Can't go home empty-handed."

As they set out again across the trackless wilderness, his protective streak nagged at him. He tried not to think of all the things that could happen to Cheryl out here, fifteen miles from their base camp. He took up the binoculars again and studied every hummock of snow between them and the horizon.

⚓

They returned to base camp as the last rays of sun disappeared.

Annette and Michael waved from the cooking area between the tents. "We were getting a little worried about you," Annette called.

Cheryl walked toward them, staggering a little as she regained her land legs. "It took us forever to find the first bear. We only did three today."

"Sorry. Maybe you'll have better luck tomorrow."

"Do I smell chili?" Oz asked.

"Yes, sir," Michael replied. "Put your gear away and warm up. It should be ready in ten minutes or so."

The six of them ate in the men's large tent, sitting on cots and camp stools. Both kerosene heaters hummed steadily. It took Cheryl's feet a good twenty minutes to feel thawed.

"How are you doing?" Oz asked her as he stood to go for seconds.

"All right now, but I don't think my feet have ever been so cold."

"Let me take a look," Annette offered. "We don't want to risk one of us getting frostbitten."

"It was frigid out there today," Grant said. "We took a reading of five below zero this afternoon."

"Should be getting warmer by now," Nick said. He huddled on his cot wearing several layers of sweaters and his parka.

Cheryl felt silly to have the other woman examine her feet. She wanted to insist that they wait until they got into the privacy of their own tent, but Annette knelt before her and began peeling back her wool socks.

"They're still pretty cold." She cupped her hands around Cheryl's bare foot. "How's your feeling?" She ran a nail over the arch.

"I think it's okay." Cheryl smiled. "Your hands feel really warm."

Annette began to massage her foot. "Let's make sure your circulation's doing its work. You guys should have come back earlier."

"I guess you're right. We both got kind of stubborn and didn't want to turn back until we felt like we'd done a day's work. We opened the hood after we got done with the last bear and put our hands and feet on the engine to get them warm."

Oz came back with his replenished plate. "I don't think we'll go so far tomorrow, at least not if it's this cold. And we'll try straight south. Maybe the terrain is better for denning in that direction."

Cheryl shifted on the cot—whose, she wasn't sure—and leaned back on her elbows. "Thanks so much, Annette. That foot actually feels as if it belongs to me again."

"I don't see any discolored patches on your skin. Let's get the other one." Annette replaced the sock on Cheryl's left foot and reached for her right.

"You don't have to."

"I know, but I want you to be comfortable tonight."

"Yeah," Michael said, "she doesn't want you lying awake with frozen tootsies so that you'll hear her when she snores."

"I don't snore!" Annette sat back on her heels and glared at him.

"Oops, my mistake. Must have been Oz."

Annette sniffed. "Even if I *did* snore, it would have been a genteel snore you wouldn't have been able to hear in this tent, especially since you had your heater going." She peered at Cheryl's foot in the light of the lantern then began to rub it vigorously. "I don't see anything that looks like frostbite."

"Good. I wore extra socks, too." Cheryl let her continue for a couple of minutes then straightened. "Thanks so much. That feels much better."

"Do you girls want to play cards tonight?" Grant asked. He'd played endless games of rummy with Nick and Michael in the enforced evenings at the hotel and had apparently brought his deck into the field with him.

"No thanks." Cheryl rose. "I'm bushed. I think I'll wash my dishes and go to bed." To her surprise, Michael had suggested they clean up after themselves and they rotate cooking and washing the pans. Nick and Grant had drawn the KP duty tonight. Cheryl stuck her feet into her boots and clumped over to where Nick had set up the dishwashing station. When her plate, fork, and cup were clean, she rinsed them with water from a steaming kettle, dried them, and put them away. She turned to find Oz standing behind her.

"You sure you're all right?" he asked softly.

"I'm sure, but my bed seems very attractive right now."

He nodded. "Okay. I'll see you in the morning. And I promise we won't stay out so long if it's as cold as it was today." He gave her arm a gentle squeeze. "Sleep tight."

⁂

The next day, Oz rose in the darkness and began preparing coffee. When the pot simmered on the stove, he went to the cache for breakfast food. The locked coolers they'd buried kept canned goods from freezing as well as discouraged marauding wildlife.

As he approached camp with his arms full, Cheryl emerged from the women's tent, wearing a headlamp like the one Robyn and other mushers used at night on the trail with their dogsleds. She stood looking up at the sky for a long moment before switching it on. "Good morning." She hurried to help him.

"It's Sunday," he said.

"Yes. Will that make a difference in our routine?"

"Not much. We've got to use every good day we have. But I thought, since it's our turn to get breakfast ready, that we might be able to move things along this morning and maybe have time for worship before dawn. That way we don't have an excuse for setting out late."

"That sounds great. I'm glad you thought of it." She worked quickly, speaking only when needed.

Twenty minutes later, Michael joined them.

The coffee had perked, and they'd sliced canned ham and set out biscuits, cheese, and canned fruit on the folding table, with chocolate bars for the scientists to carry with them that day.

"You guys are the model of efficiency." Michael sliced open a biscuit and piled cheese and ham between the halves. "Annette and I may get off on time today."

"We're going to pray together, and maybe read a psalm, in the big tent before we go." Oz set a cup of coffee down on the table beside Michael's plate. "Anyone who wants to is welcome to join us."

"Thanks. Is it Sunday then?"

"That's right."

Michael shrugged. "I wouldn't mind, but I don't think Annette's much for church and prayer."

Annette came out of the women's tent, zipping her parka. "Another cold one, I suppose."

"Yes, and I'm wearing double socks again," Cheryl said. "I tried for triple, but that made my boots too tight."

"Well, take some of those instant hand warmers. There's a box of them somewhere."

"I put a few in our gear on the sled," Oz said. "We've got hot coffee ready, and all the breakfast sandwiches you can make and eat."

"Mmm. Coffee first." Annette took a mug from him. "Where's the sugar?"

While she doctored her coffee, the other two men joined them.

"Are you guys going out on the ice pack today?" Michael asked.

"Well, it's getting a little dicey. We'll have to see how it looks," Grant said. "The water's starting to open up between us and the offshore ice. Yesterday we went straight north, and the ice was still thick enough there. But if we're not certain about it, we won't take chances."

Michael nodded. "We're gaining an hour of sunlight a week up here this month. Things are bound to break up. Be careful."

"We will."

"Good. Well, since it's Sunday, Oz suggested a group prayer before we leave. I figure it can't hurt."

"Fine with me." Grant grabbed a plate and began fixing his breakfast in the lantern light.

Annette frowned but said nothing as she sipped her coffee.

"Man, it's cold." Nick shivered and reached for the coffeepot. "I move we adjourn this feast inside. No sense freezing out here until we have to."

Oz looked over at Cheryl. Again he regretted the discomfort she must be feeling on this expedition. "Why don't you go in, Cheryl. Enjoy your food, and I'll clean up."

"No, I'll stay and help you."

Oz hesitated. He could make a stronger appeal, but he didn't want to embarrass her in front of the others. Better to just hustle them to get the food they wanted and then put away the leftovers quickly.

"Okay. Anyone want to finish up this ham? I'd like to cache the tins and leftovers. If you want anything else, now's the time."

The others quickly replenished their plates and mugs then moved toward the big tent.

"We've got cleanup," Annette called over her shoulder.

"I know, but I don't want to leave anything out that might draw bears, even while we're eating," Oz said.

Cheryl swiftly helped him gather all the trash. Oz dumped the coffee grounds into the trash bag.

"Okay, you get inside and eat. And keep warm. I'll be there in a sec." Before she could reply, he scooted for the cache. Michael and Annette might be ready to pull out by the time he returned. If so, he wouldn't take it personally.

When he returned and entered the tent, Cheryl sat on a stool with her Bible open. The other three men sat on the cots, still sipping coffee, and Annette flipped through a sheaf of papers while she finished her breakfast.

"I always think about God when I get this far out, away from civilization," Grant said.

"I've heard that before—what you read," Nick said to Cheryl.

She looked up at Oz and smiled. "I was just sharing with everybody how I feel when I go outside and see the sky just crammed with stars—like this morning. We're miles and miles from any artificial light. Before I put my headlamp on, it was so awe-inspiring. Stars beyond counting."

"'The heavens declare the glory of God,'" Oz said.

"Yeah, that's what she read." Nick grinned at him. "Didn't know you were such a literature buff, Oz."

"It's the Bible, not literature." Annette didn't look up from her reports, and her voice held a tinge of annoyance.

"The Bible is some of the finest literature ever written," Oz said, "but it's a lot more than that. I believe it's God's Word."

Annette jumped up and pulled on her jacket. "Michael, I'm going to start loading our gear." She hurried outside.

"Is it me?" Oz looked around at the others, arching his eyebrows.

"It's not you," Grant said. "It's religion in general."

"I didn't mean to offend anyone." Cheryl's voice had lost its confidence.

"Hey, no offense taken here," Michael said. "I usually attend church on Sunday, and I wouldn't mind if you or Oz wanted to offer a prayer for our safety before we all pull out."

"Sure," Nick said. "I don't have a problem with that."

Oz nodded. "Thanks. Let's pray then." He caught Cheryl's eye, and she nodded slightly. Oz bowed his head. "Dear Lord, we thank You for bringing us here and allowing us to see and study Your magnificent creation. Give us safety and success in our missions, and bring us all here again tonight. Amen."

The others rose and wished them luck before dispersing.

Oz smiled over at Cheryl.

"I got my Bible out, and Michael asked about it," she said. "I didn't mean to start reading before you came in."

"Not a problem. Ready to roll?"

"Yes." She jumped up. "Just let me put this back in Annette's and my tent."

An hour later, they found their first bear of the day, a creamy sow traveling with a smaller bear.

"That must be a two-year-old," Cheryl called over the sound of their engine as they watched the pair.

"Yes, she'll be running him off soon and starting a new family."

By noon, they'd finished with those two bears and also caught and examined a female with two new cubs. They stopped to eat lunch on a choppy area of the glittering plain, with mountains just visible far to the south.

"I think it's warming up," Oz noted as he removed his gloves so that he could easily open a sandwich bag.

"Me, too."

"Toes warm?"

"Toasty." She ate in silence for a few minutes then smiled at him. "Well, today's a good day so far."

"It sure is. Only half over, and we've caught five bears." He popped the last bite into his mouth.

"Want the other half of this?" She held out part of her ham sandwich.

"Maybe later. I thought I'd have a granola bar."

She tucked the rest of the sandwich into its plastic bag and slid it into the pocket of her coat. "What would make this your all-time best day?"

He stopped chewing and cocked his head to one side. All sorts of thoughts flew across his mind. "You know, it would be hard to top being out here with you. And catching bears, of course. This is already one of the best days ever."

"Really? I mean. . .better than zoo work?"

"Much."

"Better than. . .I don't know. . .Siberia?"

"You're joking, right? We almost starved to death on that trip, and the—" He stopped just in time. He didn't intend to ever tell Cheryl about the time the helicopter had crashed on a snowfield or the student's drowning. "The biologist I was working with got sick and spent half the trip fighting off the flu. And that's only half of it." The other half could remain unsaid. He bit into the granola bar so she couldn't ask him another question right away.

She chuckled and flipped her hood back. The Arctic sun rippled on her rich brown hair, streaking it with auburn highlights. "I'm glad you lived to tell about it and came to Alaska."

He swallowed. "So am I." His voice went husky on him, and her eyes flickered. Oz slid one glove off again and reached for her. He ran his fingers into her shiny hair. "Very glad."

He leaned toward her and kissed her gently. When he released her, she looked up at him for a long moment then dove into his embrace, snuggling against the front of his parka.

"Ozzy, thank you for choosing me to come with you." He held her for a bit, wishing he could shed the parka. Oh well, the cold might actually be a benefit, forcing them to focus on anything but the physical in their relationship. He cleared his throat. "I've been thinking about it for a long time. About you and me, that is. I think I'm ready for—"

Movement in his peripheral vision grabbed his attention, and he stopped.

Cheryl must have felt his intake of breath. She pulled away from him. "What is it?"

"Easy. There's a huge bear about ten yards away from us."

Chapter 14

"Does he see us?" Cheryl asked.

"Oh yes."

Ever so slowly, she turned her head. To her credit, she didn't yelp or even gasp when she caught sight of the massive, yellow-white bear looming on a heap of crusty snow, staring at them. Her grasp on Oz's forearm tightened.

He shot up a barrage of prayer fragments. Which could he draw quickest—the pistol or the dart gun? If he darted the bear, it would take him ten or fifteen minutes to go down. And the pistol wouldn't stop a bear easily.

"Can you reach the keys? I'm thinking that if you started the engine, the noise might scare him off." Oz tried to keep eye contact with the bear, hoping it wouldn't notice her stealthy movement. "You can back this thing up, right?" He tried not to let even his lips move.

"Yes, but not very fast. So what do we do if he comes toward us when I start the engine? They say to wave your arms and yell."

"I don't think we can outyell the snowmobile. I'll make a dive for the gun."

After a pause, she asked, without looking at him, "Which one?"

Oz gulped and sent up another prayer. "Dart rifle, I guess."

The big bear opened its mouth and yawned. The sound of a bored bear couldn't keep Oz from noticing its oversized canines.

"Okay, I'm touching the ignition." Cheryl's voice shook.

"Do it. Just don't move toward him. I'll go for the dart gun. You ready? On three. One, two, three. . ." He whipped around and pulled the rifle from the scabbard. He always kept it loaded with the adult dose while they drove, but this bear must weigh twice what any of the females they'd caught did. Would he get a chance to reload?

The engine gurgled and roared to life. The bear reared on its hind feet and loomed impossibly big. Oz jerked the gunstock to his shoulder and fired. Cheryl eased the snowmobile back a few feet.

The bear let out a roar and clawed at its left shoulder, where the dart had landed. As the huge beast plummeted to all fours and down the snow heap, Cheryl stood suddenly and threw something. "Hang on!"

It took Oz a moment to realize she'd lobbed the half sandwich toward the bear. As the snowmobile zoomed forward, Oz rocked back in the seat, clutching the dart gun. They swept within ten feet of the bear as Cheryl cranked the tightest turn she could.

The bear jumped back but didn't run away. Maybe it was curious about that ham sandwich. Oz stared at the bear, mentally cataloging the shape of its head and the odd color of its legs.

Cheryl squeezed the throttle, and they roared farther away in a big arc.

Oz craned his neck to continue studying the bear for a few seconds. "He's not following," he yelled in her ear.

Cheryl backed off on the gas. The snowmobile slowed, and she turned it broadside so they could both look back without letting the machine face the bear. "Should we keep going? Or wait for him to go down?"

"The dose might not put him out. I was loaded for a sow at spring weight. That guy's got to weigh at least a thousand pounds. I'm guessing more."

"He's fatter than that first one we caught." Cheryl eyed the bear as it lumbered down off its perch and sniffed along the ground. "He's going for the sandwich. If you reload, we could go a little closer, until you're comfortable with the range, and you could hit him again."

"I don't know." Oz gritted his teeth, weighing the risk. "Right now we're far enough away that we could outrun him if he decides we're a sandwich machine. Remember, polar bears overheat really fast when they run."

She nodded. "So he couldn't chase us very far."

"Right. But I don't know *how* far. And if we go closer. . .he's got a taste of that ham now. I'm thinking it's too risky." All the reasons he preferred to stalk bears from a helicopter came back to him.

"But we've got to collar him! He's huge, Ozzy!"

"I know. And there's something else."

"What?" She turned and looked at him, her brow puckered in a frown.

"What color is he?"

"Cream? Yellowish, I guess. Hey! His legs look darker."

"Exactly. And did you catch a profile view?"

Cheryl caught her breath. "His head is wide, like a grizzly's."

"Exactly."

"Oh, Ozzy, come on! We can't not catch this guy. He's a grolar bear!"

⌘

Cheryl watched the bear shuffle along the snow, sniffing as though hoping for more sandwiches.

"I wonder if he ate the plastic bag. Oz, we have to put him down." She turned halfway around. "Get the gun ready. Come on! We can't miss this chance."

"Cheryl, sweetheart, calm down. Think about this. That is a carnivore we're talking about. The biggest land carnivore there is. And you want to ride right up close and pop him with a dart."

"We've caught three males since we started this project. What's one more?"

"I'll tell you. We saw the others before they saw us, and we sneaked up on them.

This one has not only seen us, he knows we taste good, and we've annoyed him."

"But this machine can go fifty miles an hour. You said yourself we can outrun him. I know we can."

"If he's half grizzly, maybe not. He might not have the genetics that would make him overheat. Besides, we don't want him to overheat and maybe die of heart failure."

She sighed. "Okay. I'll do whatever you say."

"Aw, Cheryl." He shook his head and wrapped his left arm around her shoulders, giving her a squeeze. "I love you too much to be reckless with your life. Right now, we're far enough away. But if we drove in another hundred yards and he came at us..."

His passionate speech was lost on her after the first few words. "Did you say... you love me?"

He laughed. "Of course. You're a smart woman. You must have figured that out by now."

She shook her head. She'd hoped. She'd wondered. But hearing him confirm her suspicions brought her a wave of tenderness and joy she hadn't expected out here in the frozen wilderness. Even when Oz had kissed her at their lunch stop, she hadn't quite been able to convince herself they were heading for a permanent relationship. "I...I love you, too."

He smiled and looked back toward the bear. "We'll have to discuss that in detail later. Right now, I'd better reload."

The bear ambled toward them, almost as if he were out for a leisurely stroll.

"Do you think he's feeling groggy?" Cheryl asked.

"I hope so, but groggy isn't good enough." He slid the rifle's bolt shut. "Okay, listen. If you can make a big swing like you did before and come around on his flank, I'll try it. I'm counting on him feeling the effects of the first dose by now. But I don't want to get too close. If he heads toward us, so I can't get a good shot, you get us out of there."

"Got it." She grinned at him. "Wait till Robyn hears."

⚜

Cheryl maneuvered the snowmobile slowly, so as to keep the engine puttering as quietly as possible.

Oz kept the dart gun aimed at the oddly colored bear, wondering how many kinds of fool he was. This shot should have been made from a hundred feet in the air above the bear, where there was no chance it could get at them, no matter whether the dart hit squarely or the dose was figured correctly.

The bear paused and turned, watching them as they circled, marking time but always facing them. The big bear seemed determined not to expose his sides for a clean shot into either shoulder or hip.

Oz held off, knowing each second he waited prolonged their danger. "Stop."

Cheryl obeyed immediately, bringing the machine to a halt.

"Keep your hand on the throttle. We may need to make a run for it." He glanced ahead. They had a clear path, should they need it.

The bear took a few steps toward them and paused to bite at his shoulder, worrying the spot where the first dart had hit him. Oz leaned his left elbow against Cheryl's shoulder to steady his aim.

"If I say go, you go, no matter what."

"I hear you." She sat perfectly still.

The bear rose on its hind feet and opened its cavernous mouth in a roar. Oz gritted his teeth and shoved down the impulse to flee. Once again, the mammoth bear twisted its head around to nip at its left shoulder, exposing the outside of its right foreleg and shoulder. Oz pulled the trigger. Again the beast roared. It dropped to a running position.

"Go!" Oz lowered the rifle and held on to the sled.

Looking back, he saw the bear run a few yards after them and stop. It turned its head and tried to reach the spot of the new injection.

Cheryl accelerated and they zoomed forward, over the rough snowfield, away from the bear.

When they'd gone a quarter mile, Oz tapped her shoulder. "Slow down and arc around where we can watch. He's not following."

She eased the snowmobile about. Oz could barely see their quarry now because of the choppy terrain.

"Should we go back?" she yelled.

"Let's give him ten minutes or so of peace. How's our fuel?"

"Good."

He nodded. "Keep the engine running." No use stressing the bear by approaching again and hoping the next charge would be another feint. He reloaded the dart gun and placed it in the scabbard then raised his binoculars. "I think it's just a matter of time now, but we need to be cautious. When he starts weaving, we'll go a little closer, but I don't want to upset him and ruin the advantage we have."

"Okay." Cheryl looked up at the sun then at her watch.

"We've got plenty of daylight," Oz said, and she nodded. It seemed hours had passed since he'd spotted the bear, but it was only two-thirty, and the sun would shine until almost seven.

"I know what you're thinking," Cheryl said.

"What's that?"

"That if we'd been in a chopper, we'd have had him easily, without the risk."

"There's some truth to that. But there are always risks. And honestly, in a helicopter, we might not have even seen him."

They waited in silence. The sun beat down, and Oz unzipped his parka. Spring was coming to the North Slope, no question.

"I guess the bay will be mostly open when we leave," Cheryl said.

"Probably. Grant said he didn't know if they could get out on the pack ice safely anymore."

"I hope they stayed on the land-fast ice today."

"Yeah, it's turned out pretty warm."

Cheryl stood on the machine's running boards. "Hey, can you see the bear?"

Oz rose and focused the binoculars. "I see him. I think he's down, but there are a lot of ridges between us. Let's go a little closer."

He sat down, and Cheryl drove slowly. When the bear was clearly visible, Oz clapped her shoulder. "Stop here."

The animal sat on the snow, licking its shoulder. It raised its head and looked toward them then lumbered to its feet.

Oz caught his breath. Had he made another mistake and approached too soon? A hundred yards of tundra still separated them, but they were pointed directly toward the bear again.

Cheryl turned halfway around on the seat. "He's staggering."

"Yup. Keep ready anyway."

The bear plopped down again and rolled over, batting at the air, then settled with its chin on its front paws. Just when it seemed quiet, it raised its head and stared at them.

"He's going out." Oz grinned in satisfaction. That final lifting of the head was a classic sign that the drug had done its work.

Gently the bear lowered his jaw again and rested. Its eyes closed.

"Yay!" Cheryl turned and raised her hand for a high five.

Oz complied, laughing. "Let me approach him first, just in case, but if I ever saw an unconscious bear, that's one right over there."

He got off the sled and took the dart gun, walking swiftly but with caution across the snow. Ten feet from the fallen animal, he stopped, overwhelmed by what they'd done.

The bear was huge, maybe the biggest one he'd ever caught. Even in the lean springtime, it must run more than twelve hundred pounds. Its fur morphed from creamy on its back and shoulders to yellow on its sides. Its lower legs were a mottled brown, and brown hairs also circled its muzzle. Instead of the elongated skull of most polar bears, its head was broader and its face flatter.

He stepped closer and prodded the bruin with the muzzle of the rifle. It continued its peaceful slumber. Oz exhaled and closed his eyes for a moment. "Thank You, Lord. I don't deserve this."

He turned and beckoned to Cheryl. She puttered in slowly and parked the snowmobile five yards from the bear, pointed toward camp.

Together they unpacked their equipment. "You think it's a real grolar?" she asked eagerly.

"I do, but the DNA we get now will be the proof. Take the camera and start getting pictures. This is historic."

Other hybrid grizzly-polar bears had been documented. The different types of bears were known to breed, both in zoos and in the wild. A hunter had killed one a couple of years ago, thinking it was all polar bear, and discovered after the bear died that it was part grizzly. But no one had ever examined, tagged, and collared a living grolar bear in the wild.

Scientists would have a heyday, tracking this fellow to see where he chose to wander. Would he take to the pack ice this summer, to hunt seals? Or would he stay ashore and favor the grizzly's diet of vegetation and fish? A million other questions came to Oz's mind as he worked.

Cheryl photographed the bear from every conceivable angle and clicked more photos to document Oz's work.

He measured the skull and girth meticulously and took several vials of blood. He removed the premolar tooth, which seemed large for a polar bear. Before putting the collar on, he tested it to be sure it would work correctly. "I've got to adjust this to the largest setting. This guy's neck is huge."

"All of him is huge." Cheryl brought him the ear tags. "I wish we could stay and follow him around."

"Yeah. I think he's around four or five years old." Oz touched a scar on the bear's face. "He's had at least one serious fight."

"This is so exciting. If he mates and has offspring. . ."

"Yeah. With the DNA, we'll be able to match it to his cubs, if there are any." Oz shook his head, still realizing what he was doing.

"Should we call someone outside on the satellite phone?" Cheryl asked. "How big is this?"

He paused with the ear tags in his hand. "I don't know. They're not going to come get him and put him in a zoo. At least, I don't think they would. I hope not. But collaring and tagging him will give us a chance to follow him for years. That's major. In fact. . ." He grinned at her. "In fact, the article we publish this summer will probably get us a grant to come back here next spring."

"We? Us?"

"Absolutely. I couldn't have done this alone. In fact, if you hadn't been driving, I'd probably have flooded the engine I was so excited, and right now I'd be the entrée he chased down your sandwich with. I expect you to help write the paper. And do the interviews with me."

"What interviews?" she asked.

"Listen to you. We can be on the Anchorage news next week, if we want, and it will escalate from there. Newspapers, magazines. . ."

"If we want?"

"Well, yeah. We have to decide whether we want to publicize this immediately or wait until we've analyzed all the data and written our scientific papers and our new grant proposal." The idea of continuing to work with Cheryl held a definite appeal. He could see himself working with her for a long time to come.

"Is there an advantage to waiting?" She glanced down at the bear. "Don't answer that now. We need to finish here and get this guy back on his feet."

"Right." Oz went back to work. He examined the claws, teeth, and other features that might exhibit a peculiarity of either the grizzly or the polar bear. When they'd done all the standard testing, sampling, and tattooing, he stood back. "It's funny, but I hate to leave him."

Cheryl nodded, watching the big animal's side rise and fall. "I know what you mean. This is special. Once he's awake and we leave, this part will be over. We may never see another grolar."

"Or is it a pizzly?" Oz chuckled at her widened eyes. "That's what they call hybrids with a polar bear father and a grizzly mother. A grolar is the other way around. Well, time to pack up the equipment, I guess."

Cheryl looked over her checklist. "I don't think we've forgotten anything."

"Just a picture of you with Gargantua." Oz reached for the camera and took several pictures of Cheryl next to the big bear.

They packed everything securely on the snowmobile, and Cheryl started the engine.

Oz injected the bear with the antidote and climbed on behind her. "Let's go."

She drove a safe distance away, and they watched until the bear pushed to its feet and walked unsteadily away, toward the northeast. Oz's slight sadness at seeing the magnificent animal leave them was tempered by the latent excitement he felt at the thought of finding this bear's cubs another year.

They arrived at the base camp just as the sun was setting, washing the snow with swaths of fuchsia and salmon. Cheryl parked the snowmobile and turned off the engine.

An unnatural silence lay over the camp. The other two snowmobiles were not in sight. No one had set up for supper. The tents stood dark and empty before them.

Cheryl twisted around and looked at him. "They're not back yet."

Chapter 15

Just to be sure, they checked both tents, but they were alone in camp. Cheryl met Oz outside, where they usually cooked.

"It's early yet," Oz said, but she couldn't stop the adrenaline that surged through her.

"Should we try to call them?"

"Yeah, why don't you try to raise them on the sat phone while I put away our gear."

He opened the box on the back of the snow machine, and she seized the phone.

"Take it in your tent, and I'll come get your heater going in there," Oz said.

She hurried inside and sat down on the edge of her cot. She fumbled for her headlamp and put it on so she could see to make the call.

Oz came in with the box that held most of their traveling supplies and set it on the floor. He lit the lantern first then the heater.

Cheryl's hands trembled as much from tension as from the extreme cold. She punched the numbers in wrong on her first try and had to start over. Finally she got it right. She stared across the tent at Oz, where he still knelt by the heater, listening. "No one's responding."

"That's odd. Try again?"

She severed the connection and held out the phone. "You try, please. I'm shaking so badly, I don't know if I can do it again."

He came over, took it from her hand, and laid it on the cot. He grabbed a wool blanket off Annette's cot and wrapped it around Cheryl's shoulders. "Get over by the heater. As soon as we make contact, we'll get some coffee heating."

She nodded and stepped over near the faithful heater, which glowed a comforting orange. She unzipped her parka but kept the blanket draped over her shoulders while Oz tried to call the geologists.

After a minute of silence, he pushed more buttons. "Yeah, Charlie? This is Dr. Thormond, with the scientific team."

Cheryl whipped around and stared at him. She hadn't really expected him to call in the cavalry so soon, but Oz was taking this as seriously as she did.

"Yeah, my team was a little late getting back to camp tonight, and we expected the other four to be here when we arrived, but it's deserted. Yeah... Uh-huh... Okay, I guess that makes sense." He signed off and laid the phone down.

"What did he say?" Cheryl asked.

Oz walked over and laid his hand on her shoulder. "He says to give them time to get back or at least call us. And if they're not here by dawn, he'll fly out here."

"Dawn? That's twelve hours."

He checked his watch. "Less than eleven, actually, but yes. Charlie can't search effectively in the dark, not knowing where they are."

Her lower lip trembled, and she clamped her mouth shut. Oz drew her into his arms. She clung to him, sliding her hands in under his open parka and pulling close to his solid, comforting warmth.

He patted her back rhythmically, through the layers of down, wool, and nylon. "Let's pray."

She nodded, her head moving against his chest. "Yes, please."

Oz let out a long sigh. After a moment, he said softly, "Heavenly Father, we're at a loss. Show us what to do. Please protect the others. We don't know what's delayed them, but it can't be good." After a few seconds of silence, he straightened. "I think I should go look for them."

Cheryl caught her breath. "That would be too dangerous. We don't know where they went. Shouldn't we stay in camp until daylight?"

"Ten hours is more than enough time for unsheltered people to freeze."

"I. . .I just don't know." Fingers of fear clawed at her stomach. "Do you think they're together? I thought they had separate plans."

"They did, but they may have stuck together, especially if Grant decided they couldn't go out on the icepack safely. He and Nick may have opted to tag along with Michael and Annette and run their experiments onshore."

"May have."

"The odds are good that they're together, or at least one team would have come back on time."

She didn't like that but couldn't think of an argument. "Why aren't they answering the phone?"

"I don't know. Maybe the battery died. Cold can do those things in."

"Yes, but we're all careful to keep the phones insulated."

Oz sighed. "I wish I had answers for you. But I think Michael and Annette were going to follow the coast east. Grant and Nick may have gone that way, too, looking for good, solid ice where they could get offshore. I can look for tracks."

"I'll go with you."

"No, you need to stay here. I'll take our phone. If they come back, you can use their phone to call me. And if their battery is dead, we have an extra one in our tent."

"But, Ozzy—" She gulped. It wasn't that she was afraid to stay alone. She'd done that many times. But to be alone for hours, wondering if he was safe. . . It would be too much like the night she'd waited for news of Dan. She remembered when she got the devastating news and learned of the men who'd gone out to help her husband and lost their own lives. Tears formed in her eyes, and a painful lump grew in her throat.

"What, sweetheart?" He stroked her cheek and tilted her chin up.

"I don't know if I can do it. Wait for you, I mean. And not know you're safe."

He pulled her close and held her tightly for a long moment. "Cheryl, I don't know what else to do, and I can't do nothing."

She sniffed and pulled away, brushing at her overflowing tears. "All right. I understand."

He eyed her carefully. "We have flares." She nodded. They always took a couple in their emergency kits. "I'll take some more with me. I'll set one off if I find anything."

"Okay. I'll go outside every five minutes and look."

"Every fifteen."

"No, every ten."

He smiled gently. "All right. And I'll leave you a couple. If you have news and you don't have a phone, put up a flare. I should be able to see it for a good many miles."

"Okay, but you have to keep looking back."

"Don't worry, I will."

She bit her lip. The stress showed in his sober expression. The ice in his beard had melted, and it glistened damp in the lamplight.

"Cheryl, I love you. And I will come back." He drew her to him and kissed her tenderly.

She kissed him back, hoping he could decipher her fear and confusion and understand how much she loved him and the ache that came as she agreed to let him go.

He squeezed her and stepped away. "Pray, sweetheart. And I'll see you soon." He left the tent.

She sat down stiffly on the edge of her cot, too numb even to think a prayer yet. A few minutes later, the snow machine's engine roared to life.

❖

She went outside into the bitter cold. Oz had been gone ten minutes. She peered toward the east. A reddish glow lit the sky. Her heart leaped, until she realized it was the aurora, putting on its ghostly show. Could she tell the difference if Oz set off a flare?

In her parka's pocket she'd stuffed a loaded flare gun and an instant hand warmer. She paced between the tents. He'd gone off without the promised coffee—without any supper either. She should have insisted he fortify himself before he left.

At least she could set up the stove and have hot coffee ready when he and the others came back. She hurried into the men's tent and got out the camp stove.

and stand. The dart rifle lay on Oz's cot. She paused, looking at it. Had he taken his pistol? He must have. She picked up the rifle and checked it. Loaded for bear. She smiled at that thought and shouldered it. At least she'd have a delayed-action weapon while she raided the food cache.

Another ten minutes must have passed. She studied the east carefully. The aurora still danced in soft pink and mauve ripples over the starry sky. Wispy clouds diffused the color into magenta and violet. Any other time she'd have marveled at the display. Tonight it was a distraction. . .maybe even a camouflage. She sought in vain for the starker, red-orange glow of a flare.

At last she turned her headlamp on and trotted toward the cache, holding the dart gun at the ready. The men had left a spade sticking in the snow near their hiding place and she quickly opened a hole and pulled out the first locked cooler. She'd forgotten to fetch the keys from the hook on the tent pole in the men's quarters.

She jogged back to get them, praying constantly and scanning the east, where the colorful sky met the snow-covered land. It was never truly dark here, unless a storm obliterated the night sky.

Once she had the keys, she headed back to the food, walking this time and breathing hard. She needed to start a regular regimen of exercise once she got home, so she'd be in better shape next year when she and Oz came back to look for those grolar cubs.

A half hour later, she had a pot of coffee simmering. She'd heated a can of stew and forced herself to eat half of it. It wouldn't do to let her anxiety keep her from eating. She paced between the tents, swinging her arms and stomping her feet frequently, sending up a continual stream of prayers. Her hands and feet numbed. She turned toward the heated tent for a warming session. As she stood before the heater and dropped her gloves to the floor, the thought she'd tried to suppress attacked her head on.

What if Oz didn't come back?

Chapter 16

Cheryl had been alone in camp nearly two hours. She'd wept, and she'd dried her eyes so the tears wouldn't freeze on her cheeks when she went outside again. She'd lectured herself, and she'd cried out to God. If only Oz hadn't taken the sat phone with him, she could call Charlie in Barrow and demand that he send someone out immediately.

She pulled on her knit mask and gloves once more and shuffled outside, carefully closing the tent door so the heat wouldn't escape with her. She turned eastward. The aurora had faded, except for one spot, where it shone brighter than ever far to the east and just a little south.

It took her a good half minute to make sense of what she saw and realize it was the light of a flare, reflected off the clouds. "Oh, thank You, thank You, thank You!"

She dashed to the food storage again and set about preparing plenty of nourishment for the entire team. She kept warm by cupping her gloved hands around the coffeepot and continued to stare eastward. Every few minutes she lowered her hood and pulled her hat up off her ears to listen, but she couldn't do that for long. In a frighteningly short time, her ears began to ache, and she covered them again.

At last she thought she heard an engine. She ran a few steps away from the stove, so its sputtering didn't mask other sounds. That was definitely a motor. Almost at once, a pinprick of light appeared in the distance. Five minutes later, a lone snow machine pulled into camp and stopped before the men's tent. She ran to it, rejoicing to see two riders and trying to identify them.

"Cheryl! Help me with Annette."

"Grant?"

"Yes." He held a hand up in front of his face as her headlamp's beam caught him in the eyes.

"Sorry." She reached up and switched it off. "Is Annette hurt? And did you see Ozzy?"

"Yes, this is his snowmobile. Help me get Annette inside, and I'll tell you all about it."

Grant had left the machine, but Annette still huddled on the seat.

"Of course." Cheryl hastened to help him.

Annette moaned as they took her arms and raised her off the machine. "Are we there?"

"You're here," Cheryl said. "It's warm in our tent. Come on, honey, we'll get you inside, and I'll bring you something hot to eat."

She and Grant walked on either side of Annette, with Grant bearing most of her weight. Cheryl opened the tent door, and they half carried her through. While Grant lowered her onto her cot, Cheryl closed the door and moved the heater closer. Annette groaned as Grant lifted her legs onto the cot.

"It's going to be okay," he said. "We'll take your boots and things off. It's warm in here, Annette. You're going to be all right." He shot an anxious look at Cheryl.

"I'll get her things off," Cheryl said. "You get warm. You must be half numb yourself."

"I am. Be careful of her left side. She's pretty bruised up, but I don't think anything's broken."

Annette's bootlaces were frozen in clumps of ice. Cheryl struggled with them for a minute and then pulled a knife from her survival gear and cut them. She eased the boots off. The wool socks followed. Annette's feet felt like blocks of ice.

Cheryl looked over at Grant, who had shed his parka and squatted by the heater, extending his trembling hands toward it.

"Grant, this looks really bad. What should we do? Warm water? Massage?"

Grant came over and touched Annette's feet. "No discoloration. Try massage. I'll go to the other tent and bring the second heater over."

"No, you stay here. I'll get it." Cheryl hurried to the men's tent, which she hadn't bothered to heat. No sense wasting fuel to warm the larger area when no one was there to use it. She carried the heater to the women's tent and set it up so the two units would warm Annette's sleeping area from both sides.

"Can you check the fuel and light it?" she asked Grant. "I'm going out and get that coffee and stew I fixed for you. I think you need it."

"No, you need to go back for the others."

"It will take me two minutes, and I think it's important."

He gave in, and she ran to fetch the hot food and coffee.

"Thanks," he said when she returned. "I think Annette's sleeping naturally. She needs to see a doctor, but I think she'll be okay. She was a good scout."

"What happened?" Cheryl asked.

"Nick and I spent most of the day out on the pack ice. We headed back to camp, and shortly after we got to shore, we saw a flare go up, a little to the southeast. Of course we rushed over there. Michael and Annette's snowmobile had fallen down into an ice ravine, and they couldn't get it out. Annette had managed to set off the flare."

"Didn't you have the sat phone? We tried to call you."

Grant shook his head. "They had it, and their gear dumped when the machine went down. The whole snowmobile rolled over several times and bounced down that crevice. They lost the phone. Nick and I got Annette out, but it took us almost an hour to get Michael up out of the hole. It was dark by then, and we couldn't start our snowmobile."

"I'm so sorry. What can I do to help?"

"Oz said that if we got back here with the snowmobile, we could hitch up the cargo sled and take it back for Michael. He's hurt bad."

"Of course."

Grant shook his head. "You know, I thought that extra sled was a waste of money and space in the chopper, but I'm glad now we've got it. They're out there trying to keep everyone warm. We were wondering if Nick or I should try to walk back to camp for help when Ozzy showed up."

"I'll go right now." Cheryl pulled her mask hat on.

"Are you sure? I'm feeling lots better now."

"Absolutely sure. You stay here with Annette. The thermos Oz and I use is over there. Fill it with coffee for me. I think I can hitch up the cargo sled by myself. If I need help, I'll come get you."

"Okay." Grant sounded doubtful, but already Cheryl had her hood fastened and her gloves on again. She hurried outside and moved the snow machine to the side of the big tent, where they'd parked the unused sled. It took her only a couple of minutes to hitch it to the back of the snowmobile. The six-foot bed would haul a prone man.

She didn't let herself think about the situation Oz, Michael, and Nick were in. Her only thoughts were getting there quickly and safely.

"No mistakes," she muttered as she drove the machine over to the women's tent. She checked the carrying box behind the seat. Oz had left the toolbox there, but the emergency kit was gone. They'd brought extra tools, and she ran to the men's tent, located them, and grabbed a couple of blankets off the cots.

As she ran back to the snowmobile, Grant came out of the other tent and handed her the thermos and a flare gun. "There don't seem to be any more flares in here. Maybe in the other tent?"

"I think Oz took them all. You keep that in case something happens here. Oh, where's the sat phone?"

"I told Oz to keep it. He's already put in a call to Barrow to tell them we need an emergency flight as soon as possible. Charlie said it would be awhile though. He had some minor problem with the chopper, but he was going to fix it first thing in the morning."

Cheryl stared at him. "Is he fixing it now?"

"I think so, but we don't want him hurrying and making a mistake." He smiled bleakly.

"Right." She gulped.

"Just follow the shoreline east. Oz will set off another flare when he hears your engine or sees the headlight of your snowmobile, to mark the spot for you. And be careful. There are ridges and crevices. If you go slowly, it will take you a half hour or so."

"Okay."

"I think you should take one of the heaters."

Cheryl hesitated. They were wasting time, but that could save lives. "All right, get it."

He brought it out, with a spare can of fuel, and secured it on the cargo sled with a bungee cord.

She revved the engine and headed away from camp. At once she felt tiny and alone. The stars glittered overhead, illuminating the endless snowfield. By now she knew the treacheries of the frozen tundra. Instead of running the engine wide open, she had to progress slowly. One advantage was that she knew this first stretch fairly well, and the tracks of other snow machines were easy to see.

"Lord, help me. Get me there safely, so we can bring the others back. And, Lord, please don't let me meet a bear now." Before she could utter an "amen," the eastern sky lit with a fresh orange glow. Adrenaline surged through her, and she hit the throttle.

"Thank You!" She pointed the snow machine's nose toward the flare. An ice ridge loomed before her, and she tried to slow. The machine hit it, and she flew into the air, clinging to the handgrips. They landed with a crash, and she bounced on the seat but kept her balance. The towed sled thudded behind her. She slowed, thankful to be alive, and looked back. The heater and other gear appeared to be still in place.

"Okay, that was not smart. Thank You, Lord, that I didn't wreck the machine." She took a deep breath, faced forward, eased the throttle in, and continued at a more prudent pace.

Oz and Nick lifted their arms and cheered, waving wildly and hoping she saw them in the glare of the third flare so she wouldn't overshoot their position and hit the same ravine Michael had driven into hours earlier.

Cheryl pulled up and swung around in an arc so that the snowmobile and the cargo sled paralleled their makeshift camp. She killed the engine.

Oz ran to her and pulled her up and into his arms. "Good job, babe! Fantastic!"

She hugged him. "I've got a heater and blankets and coffee. How's Michael doing?"

"Not good. I'm glad you're here." Oz let go of her reluctantly and went to the sled.

"Thanks, Cheryl," Nick called as he rushed to help Oz with the gear.

Michael lay still on a space blanket from one of the emergency kits, near Grant's malfunctioning snowmobile.

Oz brought the heater and set it up beside his prone form.

"Is he conscious?" Cheryl asked.

"No. Hasn't been since the accident, but he's breathing." He tried to downplay his frustration at not being able to do more for Michael.

Grant stood by holding the blankets. "Should I cover him? Maybe we could make a little tent with one of the blankets, to hold heat in."

"I think we should get him back to base camp as soon as possible," Oz said. "Cheryl, are you up to driving him back?"

"Nick should go. He's been out here longest."

"Couldn't we all go at once?" Nick looked from Cheryl to Oz. "Two can ride on the snowmobile. Can't Cheryl sit in the cargo sled with Michael?"

"I don't know if the machine can handle that load," Oz said. "Besides, we don't know what internal injuries Michael has. I think the less we move him the better, and if we lay him flat in the sled, there's no room for anyone else."

"Tell you what," Cheryl said, "I'll stay here with Oz. I brought hot coffee, and we've got the heater now. Nick, you take Michael on the sled. We'll wrap the blankets around him. Take it slow and easy. When you get to camp, Grant will help you get him into the small tent with Annette. Put Michael in my bed—there's no heat in you guys' tent. Then you can stay with Michael and Annette while Grant comes back for Ozzy and me."

"That will work," Nick said.

Oz didn't like that plan. He'd wait with a lot less anxiety if he knew Cheryl was safely back at base camp. He laid a firm hand on her shoulder. "Or you can go with Nick, and I'll just wait here for Grant."

"I'd like to stay." She looked up at him. Her eyes glittered through the holes in her mask. "We'll be perfectly safe now. Grant should be back here in an hour or two."

Oz opened his mouth to discourage her and closed it again. She'd earned the right to decide, and if she wanted to stay out here in the bitter cold for another hour or more, that was her prerogative. And it surely would be more pleasant with her here. "All right then, let's get Michael ready to go."

Cheryl maneuvered the cargo sled as close as she could get it to the injured man. The three of them lifted him on the space blanket and laid him carefully on a woolen one in the sled. Then they tucked the extra one around him.

"All right, Nick," Oz said. "Be careful."

"We'll be praying for you," Cheryl told him.

"Thanks. And Grant or I will come back as quick as we can for you." He got on the snowmobile and moved out with a jerky start.

Too late, Oz wondered if they should have sent the rookie snowmobiler off on such a crucial mission.

"They'll be okay, as long as he doesn't hurry," Cheryl said.

"I think he's too scared to do that." Oz reached for her hand. "Come on, let's get some of that coffee."

Chapter 17

They sat together on the seat of Grant's snow machine, facing the heater and taking turns sipping coffee from the plastic cup.

"Did you see the aurora earlier?" Cheryl asked.

"Couldn't miss it."

"It was amazing."

He wrapped his arm around her and slid closer. "I have to admit, I'm glad you're here and I'm not out here alone. I wish you had a more comfortable spot to wait though."

"It's a lot more comfortable than sitting back at camp wondering if you're alive." She winced, wishing she hadn't spoken.

Oz squeezed her gently. "I think I'm starting to understand you. Emotional security is much more important to you than financial or physical security."

She thought about that while he sipped the coffee. "Maybe so. I hadn't really considered it that way."

He handed her the cup, and she swallowed the last bit, which had cooled.

"Do you want some more?" she asked.

"Let's save it awhile."

She nodded. "You know what I've been thinking?"

"What?"

"We should raise the hood on this baby and see if we can get it running."

"Grant and Nick were trying when I got here, but I'm not sure they know as much about engines as you do."

Cheryl stood. "I don't know how many tools they brought along, but I grabbed a few things from the toolbox in your tent before I came."

Oz chuckled. "Why am I not surprised? And here I was wishing we'd brought a dog team instead of snowmobiles."

"We'd all have been home long ago if we were mushing." She switched on her head lamp and flipped up the snow machine's hood.

"Grant thought it was the battery," Oz said, "but the rope start didn't work either."

He opened the carrier behind the seat. "Their tools are in here. Tell me what you need, and I'll hand it to you."

She bent over the task without speaking for several minutes. "Hey, I think I found a loose connection." She turned and chose one of the wrenches he held. "Okay, give it a try."

"Maybe we should pray first."

"Already did, but another prayer wouldn't hurt." She smiled at him then closed her eyes.

"Lord, thank You. . .for everything," Oz said. "We'll leave this up to You."

Cheryl nodded. "Amen." She took the driver's seat and turned the key. The engine sprang to life.

Oz whooped and squeezed her shoulder. "Hallelujah! Now, how are we going to carry the heater?"

"Shut if off and let it cool a few minutes."

"Right. I'll carry it if I have to."

About halfway back to their camp, Oz spotted the light of another snowmobile heading toward them. They met Grant a few minutes later. He waved, circled around, and fell in behind them. Cheryl took them right up to the door of the men's tent, where Oz hopped off and carried the heater inside.

Nick burst in through the doorway. "You got it running." The young scientist's grin covered his whole face. He'd come from the other tent in his flannel shirt-sleeves and jeans.

"Not me," Oz told him. "Cheryl did it—totally Cheryl."

Nick whistled softly. "She's quite a lady."

"You got that right." Oz lit the heater and stood to face him. "You know, sometimes it pays to have a practical person along on the team. So, did you get Michael back here all right?"

"Yes. Grant helped me get him onto the cot. He doesn't look good though. I'd better get back to the other tent and watch him. Annette seems to be okay—she's sawing logs with the best of them. But don't tell her I said that tomorrow, or she'll bite your head off."

Oz smiled. "Cheryl already told me she snores. Doesn't bother me though. I don't have to listen to it."

"Where *is* Cheryl?" Nick asked.

"Probably out helping Grant put the equipment away. I'll go give them a hand."

Cheryl and Grant were just heading for the tents.

"I've got the heater going in the big tent now," Oz said. "You might want to come over to the small one for a while, though, and give it time to warm up." He took the box of gear Cheryl carried, and they went in together.

"So, Nick, what's the story?" Grant asked.

Nick was seated on a stool beside Michael. "Charlie called back and said he'll have a doctor here at sunup. That's not too long now."

Grant nodded. "Sounds good. I suggest we set up a rotation to sit with the patients."

"I'll take the first turn," Cheryl said. "You guys go get a little sleep. I'll come wake one of you in a couple of hours."

"Make it an hour," Oz said, "and wake me first."

"Sounds good to me." Nick rose and reached for his parka.

"It's been a long day for all of us," Grant said.

Oz stopped him before he went out. "Are you two all right? I haven't heard any complaints from you, but if you have any cuts or patches of frostbite, speak up."

"I'm fine, now that I don't have to go out in the cold anymore," Grant said.

Nick threw him an impudent smile. "Well, you have to get from here to our tent in twenty degrees below zero. But it's not far, Doc. Oh, and I'm fine, too."

"I wish we could do something for Michael," Cheryl said.

Grant went over and stood looking down at the unconscious man. "We checked him over and didn't find any external bleeding. I think he hit his head going down the crevice—he's got a bump—and Annette thought the snow machine may have rolled on him. She was terrified when we got there. I don't see what we can do, other than let him rest quietly." He and Nick exited and fastened down the tent door.

Oz and Cheryl stood looking at each other over the cot where Michael lay. "Feel like praying again?" Oz held out his hand.

She grasped it and bowed her head. Both offered brief, sincere petitions for Michael and Annette. When they'd finished, tears glistened in Cheryl's eyes.

Oz stepped around the foot of the cot and took her in his arms. "You going to be okay?"

"Yes." She sniffed.

"I can sit up with you, and we'll get Nick up after an hour."

"No, go ahead. I'm fine. I'll read a little."

He looked down into her face and brushed back one of her curls. "You are something, you know that? I never know what to expect. You charm bears and engines, and you make the best coffee above the Arctic Circle. And we still have some things to talk about."

"There's time," she whispered.

Oz nodded. "Yes. I'm very thankful for that." He kissed her and let her go.

⁂

The sun was barely up the next morning when they heard the beating of the helicopter's rotor. Cheryl hurriedly shoved her feet into her boots and grabbed her parka.

Grant, who was on watch, stirred and looked her way. "I guess Charlie got the chopper fixed."

"Yes. Is anyone else up?"

"I dunno. I've been sitting her since four-thirty. I got a few hours in earlier and thought I'd let the rest have a turn."

"Thanks. I appreciate that. I think I've slept like a log since I crawled into bed." She suspected it was her turn on duty, and Grant had taken pity on her. "I'll go see what's up." She ducked outside.

Oz and Nick emerged from the other tent as the big helicopter swept overhead and settled fifty yards away.

The wash of the wind from the rotors shoved against her, but she could tell the temperature had risen since she'd retired around midnight. She went to stand beside Oz and Nick.

The pilot shut off the engine, and the whirling blades slowed. Charlie and another man got out and walked toward them.

"I'm Dr. Roper. I understand you have a couple of people who need medical attention."

"Right in here, Doctor. Thank you so much for coming." Cheryl led him into the smaller tent. The other men stayed outside, and she could hear Charlie asking if they had breakfast ready.

"Michael is worse off than Annette," she said. "He hasn't regained consciousness since the accident."

Grant moved aside and let the doctor take his seat. He waited with Cheryl while Roper took Michael's vital signs and did a preliminary exam. He turned and asked, "Was either of you there when he fell?"

"No," Grant said. "My assistant and I came along not long after it happened."

Oz stuck his head in the tent doorway and beckoned to Cheryl.

She left Grant to answer the doctor's questions and joined him outside.

"Charlie's willing to fly a couple of us out to the ravine and try to lift Michael's snowmobile out."

"Wouldn't it be dangerous to climb down in there?" Cheryl asked.

"We'd put on a harness. He's got one in the chopper."

She nodded. "Well, I don't know how long it will take Dr. Roper to get Michael and Annette ready to fly to Barrow."

Charlie wandered over and nodded. "Morning, ma'am."

Oz said, "Nick's gone to the food cache, but I think I'll ask the doctor. Charlie says he can fly us there in ten minutes or so."

Cheryl stared at him. The trip last night had seemed endless. "Is it really that near?"

"I think it's about eight miles. It wouldn't have taken so long if the terrain wasn't so rough."

She nodded. "If you want to ask him, go ahead."

Oz went into the tent and came out in a surprisingly short time. "He says we should wait."

"It's okay," Charlie said. "I'll fly them in to the hospital and come back. You don't want to leave that machine down a crack until it gets snowed on or iced in. Now's the time to salvage it."

Oz nodded. "Thanks, Charlie. We want to retrieve it if we possibly can."

Nick walked quickly toward them between the tents, carrying one of the coolers. "What's the plan?"

Charlie said, "The doc's getting them ready to transport. I'll take them to Barrow and come back for you all."

Nick frowned at Oz. "Are we breaking camp?"

"I don't think so. That is, if you and Grant are willing to continue. We still have five days left. I'd hate to miss out on it."

"Me, too," Nick said.

Cheryl nodded. "I'd like to stay."

"Great," Oz said. "Charlie will come back and help us try to get the snowmobile out of the crevice."

Cheryl looked toward the women's tent. "Maybe we can get Michael's and Annette's gear ready while he's gone. Then Charlie could take their clothes and things to Barrow on his second trip." Cheryl prepared breakfast while the men went over their disorganized gear and helped get Michael into the helicopter.

Annette had awoken. She limped out, leaning on Nick's shoulder, and climbed into the chopper on her own. "If they let me, I'll be back," she called.

Charlie and the physician got in, and they lifted off.

Cheryl stood watching and waving with Oz, Nick, and Grant until the helicopter was only a speck in the sky. Cheryl turned away and noticed that Nick held a plastic grocery bag. "What's that?"

He grinned. "Something I asked Charlie to bring me when I talked to him last night." He opened the bag and pulled out a white bakery box. "I think the coffee's ready. Anybody care for a glazed doughnut?"

"Oh, man!" Oz glared at him. "Don't you know those things are bear magnets?"

Nick's jaw dropped. "I'm sorry. I just thought. . ."

Oz laughed. "I'm kidding. But since there's only four of us now, does that mean we get three apiece?"

⁂

Later that morning, all of the scientists and Cheryl flew out to the scene of the accident. Charlie had brought his son along. It seemed the young man, Barney, was always ready for adventure. The others watched from the ground as his father hovered and lowered Barney down to the disabled snow machine.

Rather than a crevasse in a glacier, the declivity was more of a steep-sided ravine in the tundra. The snowmobile lay upside down. Barney attached two cables to it, unclipped his harness, and stood back. Charlie raised the machine slowly and swung it out onto the level ground where Oz unhooked it. Then he flew back out over the ravine, and Barney clipped on and rode up to join them. He arrived on solid ground clutching a camera, a zippered survival kit, and a clipboard.

"Hey, fantastic!" Grant took the things from his arms, and Barney unfastened the cable. "Is there anything else down there that we can get?"

"Yeah, did you see a satellite phone by any chance?" Oz asked. "Those things are very expensive."

Barney shook his head. "This is everything I saw, but there could be other things scattered further down."

By the time Charlie landed the chopper again and walked over to them, the men had righted the snowmobile. The windshield sported a long crack, but the keys were still in the ignition.

Cheryl tried to start it, but the engine wouldn't catch.

"Too bad," Grant said.

"Aw, don't give up so easily." Cheryl grinned at him. "We brought a can of fuel, didn't we?"

"You think it's just out of gas?"

She shrugged. "The engine was running when Michael barreled over the edge, and the key was still in the on position. They must have been getting low anyway at the end of the day. I'm thinking it ran for a little while and then quit. It was upside down, after all."

Barney ran to the chopper for the gas can and poured the contents into the snowmobile's tank.

Cheryl turned the key again. The engine roared.

"Hey, lady! Good job!" Grant high-fived her.

Oz laughed. "I told you she's something!"

Cheryl put it in gear and let it run forward a few feet, then stopped it. She yelled, "The chassis is pretty beat up, but I think I can drive it back to camp."

"I'll come with you." Oz climbed on behind her.

"All right," Grant said. "We'll see you back at camp. I'm going to see if Charlie and his son are willing to make one more try at finding that sat phone."

"If Barney doesn't want to go down again, I'm willing to try," Nick said.

"Okay, you guys sort it out," Oz said. "Oh, wait a sec. I brought the dart rifle. It's in the chopper. I'd better grab it, just in case." He ran to the helicopter and got the gun. Once he was seated again behind Cheryl, he waved to the four men. "See you later."

Cheryl drove the damaged snowmobile slowly. He didn't really need to hold on to her, but he wanted to, so he rode with his arms around her waist all the way back to base camp. There was no sign of the helicopter, so Oz assumed Charlie and Barney had agreed to go fishing again in the ravine.

As they puttered toward the camp, Cheryl suddenly backed off on the throttle and stopped their progress. "Oh, great! Just what we needed."

Oz stared toward the camp. The larger tent lay in a heap. In the middle of it sat a white bear, licking a cardboard box.

"Man! I *told* Nick not to leave those extra doughnuts lying around."

Cheryl looked over her shoulder at him. "Look at it this way—you don't have to chase around all afternoon to find a bear."

"Right you are. Do you want to shoot this one?" He hefted the dart gun.

"Don't mind if I do." She reached for the weapon. "One of those doughnuts was mine."

Chapter 18

While the men put their tent to rights, Cheryl went over the snow machine again. The fiberglass engine cover had taken quite a beating, but the mechanical parts seemed none the worse.

The large tent was up again. She walked over and called to Oz, "So, he didn't tear the tent to shreds?"

"Apparently he swiped the door open and just walked right in. There are a couple of slices in the ceiling. That's probably where he fought his way out. But I think we can fix it. There's an extra awning we haven't been using, and we can use it for patching."

"Sounds like a good day's work."

"Probably so. I don't think he'd been here long when we arrived. Otherwise, he'd have done more damage." He smiled at her. "I'm glad he was happy to leave when we let him wake up."

"I'm sure the roaring monster that chased him away had something to do with that."

"Yeah, helicopters do have their good points, don't they?"

"Yes, I have to admit, we probably wouldn't have found the satellite phone if Charlie and Barney hadn't helped us out with the chopper. I just hope that greedy bear doesn't come back." She spotted the camp stove sitting outside the tent. "So, is the stove workable?"

"Sure. Are you in the cooking mood?"

"I don't know. Those doughnuts are sitting kind of heavy."

Oz pulled her to him. "Sometime I'm going to hug you when we're not both wearing Arctic gear. But you know what? There's no one I'd rather be in a rough spot with than you."

⚜

Five days later they walked together out of security at the Ted Stevens Anchorage Airport and strolled hand in hand toward baggage claim. As they came down the escalator, Cheryl stiffened. "There they are!" She began walking down the steps to get to her family faster.

Steve, Rick, and Robyn clustered about them for hugs and handshakes. Everyone talked at once as they ambled toward the baggage carousels.

"Mom, are you sure you're okay?" Robyn asked.

"Yes. I told you on the phone that we're both fine."

"I know, but we saw pictures on the news the other night of a helicopter pulling that snow machine out of the hole—"

"Honey, Oz and I weren't on it when it crashed. We were miles away."

"I know, but then they showed you doing something to a very lethargic polar bear."

Cheryl laughed. "Oz let me tattoo that sucker's tag number on his lip. He ate my doughnut, and I wanted revenge."

Robyn turned to her husband with a helpless stare. "I've never seen her like this before."

Oz laughed and put his arm around Cheryl. "Your mother is an amazing woman. Wait until you hear all the things she did in the last two weeks."

"Well, I want to see the gun you used to drug those bears," Steve said.

Rick held up his hands. "Hold on, folks. Let's collect the luggage and go get something to eat. I'm sure Cheryl and Ozzy would like to have dinner in a nice restaurant."

"Would we ever," Oz said. "And I don't care if I never see another granola bar again as long as I live."

"He's rather partial to ham sandwiches though," Cheryl said with a smirk.

⊰⊱

Oz drove to the Hollands' house at eleven the next morning. He and Cheryl had been ordered by Rick to take a day off and get some rest before they returned to work. But Oz couldn't relax, knowing he had unfinished business.

Cheryl came to the door wearing corduroy pants and a faded flannel shirt over a black T-shirt. "Ozzy. Come in."

He stepped inside and looked around for Grandpa Steve. "Where's Mr. Holland?"

"He's out back with Robyn, in the dog yard."

"Oh."

"I didn't expect to see you today. Would you like some coffee?"

"Sure, if it's no trouble."

"Not a bit."

He let her hang up his coat and followed her to the kitchen. As she got out mugs, he perched on a high stool beside her work island. "I woke up early this morning and couldn't go back to sleep."

"Not me," she said. "I just got up about an hour ago. That mattress felt *so* good."

"I, uh. . .drove in to Anchorage."

She turned and cocked an eyebrow at him. "You went to Anchorage this morning? We just came from there last night."

"I know, but there was something I wanted to do."

She stamped her foot in mock frustration. "Did you go to Title Wave without me?"

He laughed. "No, if I'm heading for the bookstore, I'll be sure and invite you along."

"Good. So what were you up to?"

He reached into his pocket and drew out a small wooden box and placed it on the counter.

"What's this?"

"Open it."

She eyed him suspiciously. "Ozzy? What did you do?"

She was going to make him work hard, he could see that. He left the stool and walked over to stand beside her. Looking down into her eyes, just the color of coffee the way he liked it, set his pulse pounding. "Cheryl, I. . ."

Something in her expression softened. She was no longer teasing him. Her mouth twitched, and she waited, eyes full of questions, but not in a hurry.

He cleared his throat and went down on one knee, reaching for her hand. "I feel as though God brought us together. Not Rick, not the job. It's meant to be. Cheryl, I love you. And I love Alaska. I want to stay here and share it with you. Please, will you marry me?"

One tear escaped her eyelid and rolled down her cheek. "Of course," she whispered.

He considered making a wisecrack about how glad his achy knees were that she hadn't kept him waiting. Instead, he pushed himself to his feet and hauled her into his embrace. He hadn't kissed her nearly enough when the back door rattled.

The two of them sprang apart. Cheryl's face was red as she turned to face Robyn and Steve. Oz wondered if he looked as guilty.

"Hey, Mom. Hello, Ozzy," Robyn said uncertainly.

"Hi, honey. Come on in. We were just going to have some coffee."

Grandpa Steve chortled. "Oh, so that's what you call it now."

Oz couldn't help grinning.

Robyn stepped over to the work island and picked up the tiny wooden box. "What's this?"

"Uh. . ." Cheryl threw him a panicky glance.

"It's something I bought in Anchorage," Oz said. "Open it and tell me what you think."

Robyn raised her eyebrows and glanced at her mother, but Cheryl turned her back and reached for the coffeepot. Robyn sprang the clasp and gasped. "Oh! That is so. . .gorgeous. Mom?"

"It's Alaska jade and gold, isn't it?" Steve asked.

"Yes," Oz said. "I thought it was pretty myself and should be worn by a beautiful woman."

"Mom?" Robyn walked deliberately around her mother and faced her. "Look at me, Mother."

Slowly Cheryl raised her gaze to Robyn's. Her daughter searched her face eagerly.

Cheryl looked down at the box in Robyn's hand. Another tear rolled down her cheek. She looked over at Oz. "It's beautiful. Thank you."

"Seems to me this calls for a celebration," Steve said.

"Uh, that's what we were doing when you walked in," Oz said.

Robyn laughed. "Then, by all means, carry on. Come on, Grandpa. Let's go in the other room and call Rick. He ought to come over for lunch if he can get away from the office and help us all celebrate. Then we'll run to the store and buy an ice cream cake."

"You don't need to do that," Cheryl said quickly. "I mean, you can stay for lunch if you want, but. . . On second thought, I don't think I have anything to feed you. I need to get some groceries into the house. I can make cheese sandwiches, maybe."

Robyn threw her arms around her mother. "No. Don't cook anything. Grandpa and I will go over to my house. I'll fix lunch for all of us over there. You and Ozzy come over when you're ready. Not too soon though. Take your time." She let go of her mother and propelled Steve toward the back door as she spoke.

"Hey, wait," Steve said. "I want to know if this means they're getting married. I mean, that there is a serious rock."

Robyn stopped, and they both looked at Oz and Cheryl.

Oz waited for her to speak.

A slow smile curved Cheryl's lips. "Yes, it most certainly does."

Epilogue

A month later, Cheryl and Oz took their vows in the church in Wasilla. Oz had already submitted their grant application for a longer research trip to the North Slope the following spring. To his surprise, Cheryl had insisted he ask for the use of a helicopter during the entire expedition.

Several of Oz's former colleagues had flown to Alaska for the wedding. He suspected some of them used it as an excuse to travel on afterward and ogle the state's bears.

Rick stood beside him at the front of the church. When the music began, Robyn came down the aisle first, resplendent in a shimmery green dress, the color of the stone in the ring Oz had given Cheryl. With her hair bound up in a delicate twist sprigged with flowers, Robyn looked more feminine than Oz had ever seen her. Rick's eyes sparkled as he watched her. In the front pew, Aven and Caddie juggled little Axel back and forth between them.

The cadence changed, and Oz looked toward the entrance. Cheryl entered on her father-in-law's arm. Her eyes sought him, and his heart lurched. Absolutely beautiful. No sad memories beleaguered him. When she placed her hand in his, he knew they could conquer any differences that came up.

They drove as far as Anchorage that evening. Oz called the charter airline from their hotel room, to make sure all was well for their flight to Kodiak the next day.

When he hung up, he joined Cheryl at the window, where she stood looking out at the Chugach Mountains. He slid his arms around her. "Last chance to change your mind and take the ferry instead of flying."

She shook her head. "It would take too long. We'll be fine. Flying doesn't—"

"I know. Flying doesn't bother you."

"Right." She bounced up on her toes and kissed him. "I'm just surprised you didn't insist on a honeymoon in the tropics."

"No, Kodiak is perfect. Your son lives there. . ."

"Yes, I've always wanted to see it. Of course, Aven and Caddie will still be in Wasilla. . ."

"I'm told it's one of the most beautiful places on earth."

"I've heard that. And—oh—did you know?" She smiled mischievously. "They have bears, too."

"Seems like someone mentioned that to me."

She nodded and ran her hands through his hair. "All in all, I thought it was the perfect destination."

A Letter to Our Readers

Dear Readers:

In order that we might better contribute to your reading enjoyment, we would appreciate you taking a few minutes to respond to the following questions. When completed, please return to the following: Fiction Editor, Barbour Publishing, Inc., P.O. Box 719, Uhrichsville, OH 44683.

1. Did you enjoy reading *Alaska Weddings* by Susan Page Davis?
   ❑ Very much. I would like to see more books like this.
   ❑ Moderately—I would have enjoyed it more if _____
   _____
   _____

2. What influenced your decision to purchase this book?
   (Check those that apply.)
   ❑ Cover   ❑ Back cover copy   ❑ Title   ❑ Price
   ❑ Friends   ❑ Publicity   ❑ Other

3. Which story was your favorite?
   ❑ *Always Ready*   ❑ *Polar Opposites*
   ❑ *Fire and Ice*

4. Please check your age range:
   ❑ Under 18   ❑ 18–24   ❑ 25–34
   ❑ 35–45   ❑ 46–55   ❑ Over 55

5. How many hours per week do you read? _____

Name _____

Occupation _____

Address _____

City_____ State _____ Zip_____

E-mail _____